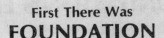

First There Was
FOUNDATION

Next There Was
FOUNDATION AND EMPIRE

Then There Was
SECOND FOUNDATION

Then for 32 long years
there was nothing...

NOW
Del Rey Books brings you,
Bigger and Better than ever,

FOUNDATION'S EDGE

FOUNDATION'S EDGE

FOUNDATION'S EDGE

"Asimov has pulled enough cards out of his sleeves to beat all the odds. Not only does the novel build upon the structures set up in the three earlier volumes, it pulls in themes from the author's whole body of work."
—*Newsday*

"Suspense is high, and there is the usual Asimov clarity of expression. It will be an unusual reader who will put the book down unfinished."
—*Washington Post Book World*

By Isaac Asimov
Published by Ballantine Books:

THE CLASSIC FOUNDATION SERIES:

Foundation
Foundation and Empire
Second Foundation
Foundation's Edge

THE GALACTIC EMPIRE NOVELS:

The Stars, Like Dust
The Currents of Space
Pebble in the Sky

ISAAC ASIMOV
FOUNDATION'S EDGE

A Del Rey Book
Published by Ballantine Books

Copyright © 1982 by Nightfall, Inc.

All rights reserved under International and Pan-American Copyright Conventions. Published in the United States by Ballantine Books, a division of Random House, Inc., New York, and simultaneously in Canada by Random House of Canada Limited, Toronto.

Library of Congress Catalog Card Number: 82-90481

ISBN 0-345-30898-6

This edition published by arrangement with Doubleday & Company, Inc.

A DEL REY BOOK

BALLANTINE BOOKS • **NEW YORK**

A Del Rey Book
Published by Ballantine Books

Copyright © 1982 by Nightfall Inc.

Library of Congress Catalog Card Number: 82-45450

ISBN 0-345-30898-0

This edition published by arrangement with Doubleday & Company, Inc.

Manufactured in the United States of America

First Ballantine Books Edition: November 1983

Cover art by Michael Whelan

Dedicated to Betty Prashker, who insisted,
and to Lester del Rey, who nagged.

CONTENTS

PROLOGUE

The First Galactic Empire was falling. It had been decaying and breaking down for centuries and only one man fully realized that fact.

He was Hari Seldon, the last great scientist of the First Empire, and it was he who perfected psychohistory—the science of human behavior reduced to mathematical equations.

The individual human being is unpredictable, but the reactions of human mobs, Seldon found, could be treated statistically. The larger the mob, the greater the accuracy that could be achieved. And the size of the human masses that Seldon worked with was no less than the population of all the inhabited millions of worlds of the Galaxy.

Seldon's equations told him that, left to itself, the Empire would fall and that thirty thousand years of human misery and agony would elapse before a Second Empire would arise from the ruins. And yet, if one could adjust some of the conditions that existed, that Interregnum could be decreased to a single millennium—just one thousand years.

It was to insure this that Seldon set up two colonies of scientists that he called "Foundations." With deliberate intention, he set them up "at opposite ends of the Galaxy." The First Foundation, which centered on physical science, was set up in the full daylight of publicity. The existence of the other, the Second Foundation, a world of psychohistorical and "mentalic" scientists, was drowned in silence.

In *The Foundation Trilogy*, the story of the first four centuries of the Interregnum is told. The First Foundation (commonly known as simply "The Foundation," since the existence of another was unknown to almost all) began as a small community lost in the emptiness of the Outer Periphery of the Galaxy. Periodically it faced a crisis in which the variables of human intercourse—and of the social and economic currents of the time—constricted about it. Its freedom to move lay along only one certain line and when it moved in that direction, a new horizon of development opened before it. All had been planned by Hari Seldon, long dead now.

The First Foundation, with its superior science, took over the barbarized planets that surrounded it. It faced the anarchic warlords who broke away from the dying Empire and beat them. It faced the remnant of the Empire itself under its last strong Emperor and its last strong general—and beat it.

It seemed as though the "Seldon Plan" was going through smoothly and that nothing would prevent the Second Empire from being established on time—and with a minimum of intermediate devastation.

But psychohistory is a statistical science. Always there is a small chance that something will go wrong, and something did—something which Hari Seldon could not have foreseen. One man, called the Mule, appeared from nowhere. He had mental powers in a Galaxy that lacked them. He could mold men's emotions and shape their minds so that his bitterest opponents were made into his devoted servants. Armies could not, *would* not, fight him. The First Foundation fell and Seldon's Plan seemed to lie in ruins.

There was left the mysterious Second Foundation, which had been caught unprepared by the sudden appearance of the Mule, but which was now slowly working out a counterattack. Its great defense was the fact of its unknown location. The Mule sought it in order to make his conquest of the Galaxy complete. The faithful of what was left of the First Foundation sought it to obtain help.

Neither found it. The Mule was stopped first by the action of a woman, Bayta Darell, and that bought enough time for the Second Foundation to organize the proper action and, with that, to stop the Mule permanently. Slowly they prepared to reinstate the Seldon Plan.

But, in a way, the cover of the Second Foundation was gone. The First Foundation knew of the Second's existence, and the First did not want a future in which they were overseen by the mentalists. The First Foundation was the superior in physical force, while the Second Foundation was hampered not only by that fact, but by being faced by a double task: it had not only to stop the First Foundation but had also to regain its anonymity.

This the Second Foundation, under its greatest "First Speaker," Preem Palver, managed to do. The First Foundation was allowed to seem to win, to seem to defeat the Second Foundation, and it moved on to greater and greater strength in the Galaxy, totally ignorant that the Second Foundation still existed.

It is now four hundred and ninety-eight years after the First Foundation had come into existence. It is at the peak of its strength, but one man does not accept appearances—

FOUNDATION'S EDGE

1. COUNCILMAN

I.

"I don't believe it, of course," said Golan Trevize, standing on the wide steps of Seldon Hall and looking out over the city as it sparkled in the sunlight.

Terminus was a mild planet, with a high water/land ratio. The introduction of weather control had made it all the more comfortable and considerably less interesting, Trevize often thought.

"I don't believe any of it," he repeated and smiled. His white, even teeth gleamed out of his youthful face.

His companion and fellow Councilman, Munn Li Compor, who had adopted a middle name in defiance of Terminus tradition, shook his head uneasily. "What don't you believe? That we saved the city?"

"Oh, I believe that. We did, didn't we? And Seldon said that we *would*, and he said we would be *right* to do so, and that he knew all about it five hundred years ago."

Compor's voice dropped and he said in a half-whisper, "Look, I don't mind your talking like this to me, because I take it as just talk, but if you shout it out in crowds others will hear and, frankly, I don't want to be standing near you when the lightning strikes. I'm not sure how precise the aim will be."

Trevize's smile did not waver. He said, "Is there harm in saying that the city is saved? And that we did it without a war?"

"There was no one to fight," said Compor. He had hair of a buttery yellow, eyes of a sky blue, and he always resisted the impulse to alter those unfashionable hues.

"Have you never heard of civil war, Compor?" said Trevize. He was tall, his hair was black, with a gentle wave to it, and he had a habit of walking with his thumbs hitched into the soft-fibered sash he always wore.

"A civil war over the location of the capital?"

"The question was enough to bring on a Seldon Crisis. It destroyed Hannis's political career. It put you and me into the Council last election and the issue hung——" He twisted one hand slowly, back and forth, like a balance coming to rest on the level.

He paused on the steps, ignoring the other members of the government and the media, as well as the fashionable society types who had finagled an invitation to witness Seldon's return (or the return of his image, at any rate).

All were walking down the stairs, talking, laughing, glorying in the correctness of everything, and basking in Seldon's approval.

Trevize stood still and let the crowd swirl past him. Compor, having walked two steps ahead, paused—an invisible cord stretched between them. He said, "Aren't you coming?"

"There's no hurry. They won't start the Council meeting until Mayor Branno has reviewed the situation in her usual flat-footed, one-syllable-at-a-time way. I'm in no hurry to endure another ponderous speech. —Look at the city!"

"I see it. I saw it yesterday, too."

"Yes, but did you see it five hundred years ago when it was founded?"

"Four hundred ninety-eight," Compor corrected him automatically. "Two years from now, they'll have the hemi-millennial celebration and Mayor Branno will still be in the office at the time, barring events of, we hope, minor probability."

"We hope," said Trevize dryly. "But what was it like five hundred years ago when it was founded? One city! One small city, occupied by a group of men preparing an Encyclopedia that was never finished!"

"Of course it was finished."

"Are you referring to the Encyclopedia Galactica we have

now? What we have isn't what they were working on. What we have is in a computer and it's revised daily. Have you ever looked at the uncompleted original?"

"You mean in the Hardin Museum?"

"The Salvor Hardin Museum of Origins. Let's have the full name, please, since you're so careful about exact dates. Have you looked at it?"

"No. Should I?"

"No, it isn't worth it. But anyway—there they were—a group of Encyclopedists, forming the nucleus of a town—one small town in a world virtually without metals, circling a sun isolated from the rest of the Galaxy, at the edge, the very edge. And now, five hundred years later, we're a suburban world. The whole place is one big park, with all the metal we want. We're at the center of everything now!"

"Not really," said Compor. "We're still circling a sun isolated from the rest of the Galaxy. Still at the very edge of the Galaxy."

"Ah no, you're saying that without thinking. That was the whole point of this little Seldon Crisis. We are more than the single world of Terminus. We are the Foundation, which sends out its tentacles Galaxy-wide and rules that Galaxy from its position at the very edge. We can do it because we're *not* isolated, except in position, and that doesn't count."

"All right. I'll accept that." Compor was clearly uninterested and took another step downward. The invisible cord between them stretched farther.

Trevize reached out a hand as though to haul his companion up the steps again. "Don't you see the significance, Compor? There's this enormous change, but we don't accept it. In our hearts we want the small Foundation, the small one-world operation we had in the old days—the days of iron heroes and noble saints that are gone forever."

"Come on!"

"I mean it. Look at Seldon Hall. To begin with, in the first crises in Salvor Hardin's day, it was just the Time Vault, a small auditorium in which the holographic image of Seldon appeared. That was all. Now it's a colossal mausoleum, but is there a force-field ramp in the place? A slideway? A gravitic lift? —No, just these steps, and we walk down them and we walk up them as Hardin would have had to do. At odd and unpredictable times, we cling in fright to the past."

He flung his arm outward passionately. "Is there any structural component visible that is metal? Not one. It wouldn't do to have any, since in Salvor Hardin's day there was no native metal to speak of and hardly any imported metal. We even installed old plastic, pink with age, when we built this huge pile, so that visitors from other worlds can stop and say, 'Galaxy! What lovely old plastic!' I tell you, Compor, it's a sham."

"Is that what you don't believe, then? Seldon Hall?"

"And all its contents," said Trevize in a fierce whisper. "I don't really believe there's any sense in hiding here at the edge of the Universe, just because our ancestors did. I believe we ought to be out there, in the middle of everything."

"But Seldon says you're wrong. The Seldon Plan is working out as it should."

"I know. I know. And every child on Terminus is brought up to believe that Hari Seldon formulated a Plan, that he foresaw everything five centuries ago, that he set up the Foundation in such a way that he could spot certain crises, and that his image would appear holographically at those crises, and tell us the minimum we had to know to go on to the next crisis, and thus lead us through a thousand years of history until we could safely build a Second and Greater Galactic Empire on the ruins of the old decrepit structure that was falling apart five centuries ago and had disintegrated completely by two centuries ago."

"Why are you telling me all this, Golan?"

"Because I'm telling you it's a sham. It's all a sham. —Or if it was real to begin with, it's a sham now! We are not our own masters. It is not we who are following the Plan."

Compor looked at the other searchingly. "You've said things like this before, Golan, but I've always thought you were just saying ridiculous things to stir me up. By the Galaxy, I actually think you're serious."

"Of course I'm serious!"

"You can't be. Either this is some complicated piece of fun at my expense or you're out of your mind."

"Neither. Neither," said Trevize, quiet now, hitching his thumbs into his sash as though he no longer needed the gestures of hands to punctuate passion. "I speculated on it before, I admit, but that was just intuition. That farce in there this morning, however, has made it suddenly all quite plain to me and I intend, in turn, to make it quite plain to the Council."

Compor said, "You *are* crazy!"

"All right. Come with me and listen."

The two walked down the stairs. They were the only ones left—the last to complete the descent. And as Trevize moved slightly to the fore, Compor's lips moved silently, casting a voiceless word in the direction of the other's back: "Fool!"

2.

Mayor Harla Branno called the session of the Executive Council to order. Her eyes had looked with no visible sign of interest at the gathering; yet no one there doubted that she had noted all who were present and all who had not yet arrived.

Her gray hair was carefully arranged in a style that was neither markedly feminine nor imitation masculine. It was simply *the* way she wore it, no more. Her matter-of-fact face was not notable for beauty, but somehow it was never for beauty that one searched there.

She was the most capable administrator on the planet. No one could, or did, accuse her of the brilliance of the Salvor Hardins and the Hober Mallows whose histories enlivened the first two centuries of the Foundation's existence, but neither would anyone associate her with the follies of the hereditary Indburs who had ruled the Foundation just prior to the time of the Mule.

Her speeches did not stir men's minds, nor did she have a gift for the dramatic gesture, but she had a capacity for making quiet decisions and sticking by them as long as she was convinced she was right. Without any obvious charisma, she had the knack of persuading the voters those quiet decisions would *be* right.

Since by the Seldon doctrine, historical change is to a large degree difficult to swerve (always barring the unpredictable, something most Seldonists forget, despite the wrenching incident of the Mule), the Foundation might have retained its capital on Terminus under any conditions. That is a "might," however. Seldon, in his just-finished appearance as a five-century-old simulacrum, had calmly placed the probability of remaining on Terminus at 87.2 percent.

Nevertheless, even to Seldonists, that meant there was a 12.8 percent chance that the shift to some point closer to the center of the Foundation Federation would have been made, with all the dire consequences that Seldon had outlined. That this one-out-of-eight chance did not take place was surely due to Mayor Branno.

It was certain she would not have allowed it. Through periods of considerable unpopularity, she had held to her decision that Terminus was the traditional seat of the Foundation and there it would remain. Her political enemies had caricatured her strong jaw (with some effectiveness, it had to be admitted) as an underslung granite block.

And now Seldon had backed her point of view and, for the while at least, that would give her an overwhelming political advantage. She had been reported to have said a year earlier that if in the coming appearance Seldon *did* back her, she would consider her task successfully completed. She would then retire and take up the role of elder statesperson, rather than risk the dubious results of further political wars.

No one had really believed her. She was at home in the political wars to an extent few before her had been, and now that Seldon's image had come and gone there was no hint of retirement about her.

She spoke in a perfectly clear voice with an unashamed

Foundation accent (she had once served as Ambassador to Mandress, but had not adopted the old Imperial style of speech that was so fashionable now—and was part of what had been a quasi-Imperial drive to the Inner Provinces).

She said, "The Seldon Crisis is over and it is a tradition, and a wise one, that no reprisals of any kind—either in deed or in speech—be taken against those who supported the wrong side. Many honest people believed they had good reason for wanting that which Seldon did not want. There is no point in humiliating them to the point where they can retrieve their self-respect only by denouncing the Seldon Plan itself. In turn, it is a strong and desirable custom that those who supported the lost side accept the loss cheerfully and without further discussion. The issue is behind us, on both sides, forever."

She paused, gazed levelly at the assembled faces for a moment, then went on, "Half the time has passed, people of the Council—half the thousand-year stretch between Empires. It has been a time of difficulties, but we have come a long way. We are, indeed, almost a Galactic Empire already and there remain no external enemies of consequence.

"The Interregnum would have endured thirty thousand years, were it not for the Seldon Plan. After thirty thousand years of disintegration, it might be there would be no strength left with which to form an Empire again. There might be left only isolated and probably dying worlds.

"What we have today we owe to Hari Seldon, and it is upon his long-dead mind that we must rely for the rest. The danger henceforward, Councillors, is ourselves, and from this point on there must be no official doubt of the value of the Plan. Let us agree now, quietly and firmly, that there are to be no official doubts, criticisms, or condemnations of the Plan. We must support it completely. It has proved itself over five centuries. It is the security of humanity and it must not be tampered with. Is it agreed?"

There was a quiet murmur. The Mayor hardly looked up to seek visual proof of agreement. She knew every member of the Council and how each would react. In the wake of the victory, there would be no objection now. Next year perhaps. Not now. She would tackle the problems of next year next year.

Always except for—

"Thought control, Mayor Branno?" asked Golan Trevize, striding down the aisle and speaking loudly, as though to make up for the silence of the rest. He did not bother to take his seat which, since he was a new member, was in the back row.

Branno still did not look up. She said, "Your views, Councilman Trevize?"

"That the government cannot impose a ban on free speech; that all individuals—most certainly including Councilmen and Councilwomen who have been elected for the purpose—have a right to discuss the political issues of the day; and that no political issue can possibly be divorced from the Seldon Plan."

Branno folded her hands and looked up. Her face was expressionless. She said, "Councilman Trevize, you have entered this debate irregularly and were out of order in doing so. However, I asked you to state your views and I will now answer you.

"There is no limit to free speech within the context of the Seldon Plan. It is only the Plan itself that limits us by its very nature. There can be many ways of interpreting events before the image makes the final decision, but once he makes that decision it can be questioned no further in Council. Nor may it be questioned in advance as though one were to say, 'If Hari Seldon were to state thus-and-so, he would be wrong.'"

"And yet if one honestly felt so, Madam Mayor?"

"Then one could say so, if one were a private individual, discussing the matter in a private context."

"You mean, then, that the limitations on free speech which you propose are to apply entirely and specifically to government officials?"

"Exactly. This is not a new principle of Foundation law. It has been applied before by Mayors of all parties. A private point of view means nothing; an official expression of opinion carries weight and can be dangerous. We have not come this far to risk danger now."

"May I point out, Madam Mayor, that this principle of yours has been applied, sparsely and occasionally, to specific acts of Council. It has never been applied to something as vast and indefinable as the Seldon Plan."

"The Seldon Plan needs the protection most, for it is precisely there that questioning can be most fatal."

"Will you not consider, Mayor Branno—" Trevize turned, addressing now the seated rows of Council members, who seemed one and all to have caught their breath, as though awaiting the outcome of a duel. "Will *you* not consider, Council members, that there is every reason to think that there is no Seldon Plan at all?"

"We have all witnessed its workings today," said Mayor Branno, even more quietly as Trevize became louder and more oratorical.

"It is precisely because we have seen its workings today, Councilmen and Councilwomen, that we can see that the Seldon Plan, as we have been taught to believe it to be, cannot exist."

"Councilman Trevize, you are out of order and must not continue along these lines."

"I have the privilege of office, Mayor."

"That privilege has been withdrawn, Councilman."

"You cannot withdraw the privilege. Your statement limiting free speech cannot, in itself, have the force of law. There has been no formal vote in Council, Mayor, and even if there were I would have the right to question its legality."

"The withdrawal, Councilman, has nothing to do with my statement protecting the Seldon Plan."

"On what, then, does it depend?"

"You are accused of treason, Councilman. I wish to do the Council the courtesy of not arresting you within the Council Chamber, but waiting at the door are members of Security who will take you into custody as you leave. I will ask you now to leave quietly. If you make any ill-considered move, then, of course, that will be considered a present danger and Security will enter the Chamber. I trust you will not make that necessary."

Trevize frowned. There was absolute silence in the hall. (Did everyone expect this—everyone but himself and Compor?) He looked back at the exit. He saw nothing, but he had no doubt that Mayor Branno was not bluffing.

He stammered in rage. "I repre—represent an important constituency, Mayor Branno—"

"No doubt, they will be disappointed in you."

"On what evidence do you bring forth this wild charge?"

"That will appear in due course, but be assured that we have all we need. You are a most indiscreet young man and should realize that someone may be your friend and yet not be willing to accompany you into treason."

Trevize whirled to meet Compor's blue eyes. They met his stonily.

Mayor Branno said calmly, "I call upon all to witness that when I made my last statement, Councilman Trevize turned to look at Councilman Compor. Will you leave now, Councilman, or will you force us to engage in the indignity of an arrest within the Chamber?"

Golan Trevize turned, mounted the steps again, and, at the door, two men in uniform, well armed, fell in on either side.

And Harla Branno, looking after him impassively, whispered through barely parted lips, "Fool!"

3.

Liono Kodell had been Director of Security through all of Mayor Branno's administration. It was not a backbreaking job, as he liked to say, but whether he was lying or not, one could not, of course, tell. He didn't look like a liar, but that did not necessarily mean anything.

He looked comfortable and friendly, and it might well be that this was appropriate for the job. He was rather below the average height, rather above the average weight, had a bushy mustache (most unusual for a citizen of Terminus) that was now more white than gray, bright brown eyes, and a characteristic patch of primary color marking the outer breast pocket of his drab coverall.

He said, "Sit down, Trevize. Let us keep this on a friendly basis if we can."

"Friendly? With a traitor?" Trevize hooked both his thumbs in his sash and remained standing.

"With an *accused* traitor. We have not yet come to the point where accusation—even by the Mayor herself—is the equivalent of conviction. I trust we never do. My job is to clear you, if I can. I would much rather do so now while no harm is done—except, perhaps, to your pride—rather than be forced to make it all a matter of a public trial. I hope you are with me in this."

Trevize didn't soften. He said, "Let's not bother with ingratiation. Your job is to badger me as though I *were* a traitor. I am not one, and I resent the necessity of having to have that point demonstrated to your satisfaction. Why should you not have to prove *your* loyalty to *my* satisfaction?"

"In principle, none. The sad fact, however, is that I have power on my side, and you have none on yours. Because of that, it is my privilege to question, and not yours. If any suspicion of disloyalty or treason fell upon me, by the way, I imagine I would find myself replaced, and I would then be questioned by someone else, who, I earnestly hope, would treat me no worse than I intend to treat you."

"And how do you intend to treat me?"

"Like, I trust, a friend and an equal, if you will so treat me."

"Shall I stand you a drink?" asked Trevize bitterly.

"Later, perhaps, but for now, please sit down. I ask it as a friend."

Trevize hesitated, then sat. Any further defiance suddenly seemed meaningless to him. "What now?" he said.

"Now, may I ask that you will answer my questions truthfully and completely and without evasion?"

"And if not? What is the threat behind it? A Psychic Probe?"

"I trust not."

"I trust not, too. Not on a Councilman. It will reveal no treason, and when I am then acquitted, I will have your political head and the Mayor's too, perhaps. It might almost be worth making you try a Psychic Probe."

Kodell frowned and shook his head slightly. "Oh no. Oh no. Too much danger of brain damage. It's slow healing sometimes, and it would not be worth your while. Definitely. You know, sometimes, when the Probe is used in exasperation—"

"A threat, Kodell?"

"A statement of fact, Trevize. —Don't mistake me, Councilman. If I must use the Probe I will, and even if you are innocent you will have no recourse."

"What do you want to know?"

Kodell closed a switch on the desk before him. He said, "What I ask and what you answer to my questions will be recorded, both sight and sound. I do not want any volunteered statements from you, or anything nonresponsive. Not at this time. You understand that, I am sure."

"I understand that you will record only what you please," said Trevize contemptuously.

"That is right, but again, don't mistake me. I will not distort anything you say. I will use it or not use it, that is all. But you will know what I will not use and you will not waste my time and yours."

"We'll see."

"We have reason to think, Councilman Trevize"—and somehow the touch of added formality in his voice was evidence enough that he was recording—"that you have stated openly, and on a number of occasions, that you do not believe in the existence of the Seldon Plan."

Trevize said slowly, "If I have said so openly, and on a number of occasions, what more do you need?"

"Let us not waste time with quibbles, Councilman. You know that what I want is an open admission in your own voice, characterized by its own voiceprints, under conditions where you are clearly in perfect command of yourself."

"Because, I suppose, the use of any hypno-effect, chemical or otherwise, would alter the voiceprints?"

"Quite noticeably."

"And you are anxious to demonstrate that you have made use of no illegal methods in questioning a Councilman? I don't blame you."

"I'm glad you do not blame me, Councilman. Then let us continue. You have stated openly, and on a number of occasions, that you do not believe in the existence of the Seldon Plan. Do you admit that?"

Trevize said slowly, choosing his words, "I do not believe that what we call Seldon's Plan has the significance we usually apply to it."

"A vague statement. Would you care to elaborate?"

"My view is that the usual concept that Hari Seldon, five hundred years ago, making use of the mathematical science of psychohistory, worked out the course of human events to the last detail and that we are following a course designed to take us from the First Galactic Empire to the Second Galactic Empire along the line of maximum probability, is naïve. It cannot be so."

"Do you mean that, in your opinion, Hari Seldon never existed?"

"Not at all. Of course he existed."

"That he never evolved the science of psychohistory?"

"No, of course I don't mean any such thing. See here, Director, I would have explained this to the Council if I had been allowed to, and I will explain it to you. The truth of what I am going to say is so plain—"

The Director of Security had quietly, and quite obviously, turned off the recording device.

Trevize paused and frowned. "Why did you do that?"

"You are wasting my time, Councilman. I am not asking you for speeches."

"You are asking me to explain my views, aren't you?"

"Not at all. I am asking you to answer questions—simply, directly, and straightforwardly. Answer *only* the questions and offer nothing that I do not ask for. Do that and this won't take long."

Trevize said, "You mean you will elicit statements from me that will reinforce the official version of what I am supposed to have done."

"We ask you only to make truthful statements, and I assure you we will not distort them. Please, let me try again. We were talking about Hari Seldon." The recording device was in action once more and Kodell repeated calmly, "That he never evolved the science of psychohistory?"

"Of course he evolved the science that we call psychohistory," said Trevize, failing to mask his impatience, and gesturing with exasperated passion.

"Which you would define—how?"

"Galaxy! It is usually defined as that branch of mathematics that deals with the overall reactions of large groups of human beings to given stimuli under given conditions. In other words, it is supposed to predict social and historical changes."

"You say 'supposed to.' Do you question that from the standpoint of mathematical expertise?"

"No," said Trevize. "I am not a psychohistorian. Nor is any member of the Foundation government, nor any citizen of Terminus, nor any—"

Kodell's hand raised. He said softly, "Councilman, please!" and Trevize was silent.

Kodell said, "Have you any reason to suppose that Hari Seldon did not make the necessary analysis that would combine, as efficiently as possible, the factors of maximum probability and shortest duration in the path leading from the First to the Second Empire by way of the Foundation?"

"I wasn't there," said Trevize sardonically. "How can I know?"

"Can you know he didn't?"

"No."

"Do you deny, perhaps, that the holographic image of Hari Seldon that has appeared during each of a number of historical crises over the past five hundred years is, in actual fact, a reproduction of Hari Seldon himself, made in the last year of his life, shortly before the establishment of the Foundation?"

"I suppose I can't deny that."

"You 'suppose.' Would you care to say that it is a fraud, a hoax devised by someone in past history for some purpose?"

Trevize sighed. "No. I am not maintaining that."

"Are you prepared to maintain that the messages that Hari Seldon delivers are in any way manipulated by anyone at all?"

"No. I have no reason to think that such manipulation is either possible or useful."

"I see. You witnessed this most recent appearance of Seldon's image. Did you find that his analysis—prepared five hundred years ago—did not match the actual conditions of today quite closely?"

"On the contrary," said Trevize with sudden glee. "It matched very closely."

Kodell seemed indifferent to the other's emotion. "And yet, Councilman, after the appearance of Seldon, you still maintain that the Seldon Plan does not exist."

"Of course I do. I maintain it does not exist precisely *because* the analysis matched so perfectly—"

Kodell had turned off the recorder. "Councilman," he said, shaking his head, "you put me to the trouble of erasing. I ask if you still maintain this odd belief of yours and you start giving me reasons. Let me repeat my question."

He said, "And yet, Councilman, after the appearance of Seldon, you still maintain that the Seldon Plan does not exist."

"How do you know that? No one had a chance to speak to my informer friend, Compor, after the appearance."

"Let us say we guessed, Councilman. And let us say you have already answered, 'Of course I do.' If you will say that once more without volunteering added information, we can get on with it."

"Of course I do," said Trevize ironically.

"Well," said Kodell, "I will choose whichever of the 'Of course I do's' sounds more natural. Thank you, Councilman," and the recording device was turned off again.

Trevize said, "Is that it?"

"For what I need, yes."

"What you need, quite clearly, is a set of questions and answers that you can present to Terminus and to all the Foundation Federation which it rules, in order to show that I accept the legend of the Seldon Plan totally. That will make any denial of it that I later make seem quixotic or outright insane."

"Or even treasonable in the eyes of an excited multitude which sees the plan as essential to the Foundation's safety. It will perhaps not be necessary to publicize this, Councilman Trevize, if we can come to some understanding, but if it should prove necessary we will see to it that the Federation hears."

"Are you fool enough, sir," said Trevize, frowning, "to be entirely uninterested in what I really have to say?"

"As a human being I am very interested, and if an appropriate time comes I will listen to you with interest and a certain amount of skepticism. As Director of Security, however, I have, at the present moment, exactly what I want."

"I hope you know that this will do you, *and* the Mayor, no good."

"Oddly enough, I am not at all of that opinion. You will now leave. Under guard, of course."

"Where am I to be taken?"

Kodell merely smiled. "Good-bye, Councilman. You were not perfectly co-operative, but it would have been unrealistic to have expected you to be."

He held out his hand.

Trevize, standing up, ignored it. He smoothed the creases out of his sash and said, "You only delay the inevitable. Others must think as I do now, or will come to think that way later. To imprison me or to kill me will serve to inspire wonder and, eventually, accelerate such thinking. In the end the truth and I shall win."

Kodell took back his hand and shook his head slowly. "Really, Trevize," he said. "You are a fool."

4.

It was not till midnight that two guards came to remove Trevize from what was, he had to admit, a luxurious room at Security Headquarters. Luxurious but locked. A prison cell by any name.

Trevize had over four hours to second-guess himself bitterly, striding restlessly across the floor for much of the period.

Why did he trust Compor?

Why not? He had seemed so clearly in agreement. —No, not that. He had seemed so ready to be argued into agreement. —No, not that, either. He had seemed so stupid, so easily dominated, so surely lacking a mind and opinions of his own that Trevize enjoyed the chance of using him as a comfortable sounding board. Compor had helped Trevize improve and hone his opinions. He had been useful and Trevize had trusted him for no other reason than that it had been convenient to do so.

But it was useless *now* to try to decide whether he ought to have seen through Compor. He should have followed the simple generalization: Trust nobody.

Yet can one go through life trusting nobody?

Clearly one had to.

And who would have thought that Branno would have had the audacity to pluck a Councilman out of the Council— and that not one of the other Councilmen would move to protect one of their own? Though they had disagreed with Trevize to their very hearts; though they would have been ready to bet their blood, drop by drop, on Branno's rightness; they should still, on principle, have interposed themselves against this violation of their prerogatives. Branno the Bronze she was sometimes called, and she certainly acted with metallic rigor—

Unless she herself was already in the grip—

No! That way led to paranoia!

And yet—

His mind tiptoed in circles, and had not broken out of uselessly repetitive thought when the guards came.

"You will have to come with us, Councilman," the senior of the two said with unemotional gravity. His insignia showed him to be a lieutenant. He had a small scar on his right cheek, and he looked tired, as though he had been at his job too long and had done too little—as might be expected of a soldier whose people had been at peace for over a century.

Trevize did not budge. "Your name, Lieutenant."

"I am Lieutenant Evander Sopellor, Councilman."

"You realize you are breaking the law, Lieutenant Sopellor. You cannot arrest a Councilman."

The lieutenant said, "We have our direct orders, sir."

"That does not matter. You cannot be ordered to arrest a Councilman. You must understand that you will be liable for court-martial as a result."

The lieutenant said, "You are not being arrested, Councilman."

"Then I don't have to go with you, do I?"

"We have been instructed to escort you to your home."

"I know the way."

"And to protect you en route."

"From what? —Or from whom?"

"From any mob that may gather."

"At midnight?"

"It is why we have waited for midnight, sir. —And now, sir, for your protection we must ask you to come with us. May I say—not as a threat but as a matter of information— that we are authorized to use force if necessary."

Trevize was aware of the neuronic whips with which they were armed. He rose with what he hoped was dignity. "To my home, then. —Or will I find out that you are going to take me to prison?"

"We have not been instructed to lie to you, sir," said the lieutenant with a pride of his own. Trevize became aware that he was in the presence of a professional man who would require a direct order before he would lie—and that even then his expression and his tone of voice would give him away.

Trevize said, "I ask your pardon, Lieutenant. I did not mean to imply that I doubted your word."

A ground-car was waiting for them outside. The street was empty and there was no sign of any human being, let alone a mob—but the lieutenant had been truthful. He had not said there was a mob outside or that one would form. He had referred to "any mob that may gather." He had only said "may."

The lieutenant had carefully kept Trevize between himself and the car. Trevize could not have twisted away and made a run for it. The lieutenant entered immediately after him and sat beside him in the back.

The car moved off.

Trevize said, "Once I am home, I presume I may then go about my business freely—that I may leave, for instance, if I choose."

"We have no order to interfere with you, Councilman, in any way, except insofar as we are ordered to protect you."

"Insofar? What does that mean in this case?"

"I am instructed to tell you that once you are home, you may not leave it. The streets are not safe for you and I am responsible for your safety."

"You mean I am under house arrest."

"I am not a lawyer, Councilman. I do not know what that means."

He gazed straight ahead, but his elbow made contact with Trevize's side. Trevize could not have moved, however slightly, without the lieutenant becoming aware of it.

The car stopped before Trevize's small house in the suburb of Flexner. At the moment, he lacked a housemate—Flavella having wearied of the erratic life that Council membership had forced upon him—so he expected no one to be waiting for him.

"Do I get out now?" Trevize asked.

"I will get out first, Councilman. We will escort you in."

"For my safety?"

"Yes, sir."

There were two guards waiting inside his front door. A night-light was gleaming, but the windows had been opacified and it was not visible from outside.

For a moment, he was indignant at the invasion and then he dismissed it with an inward shrug. If the Council could not protect him in the Council Chamber itself, then surely his house could not serve as his castle.

Trevize said, "How many of you do I have in here altogether? A regiment?"

"No, Councilman," came a voice, hard and steady. "Just one person aside from those you see, and I have been waiting for you long enough."

Harla Branno, Mayor of Terminus, stood in the door that led into the living room. "Time enough, don't you think, for us to talk?"

Trevize stared. "All this rigmarole to—"

But Branno said in a low, forceful voice, "Quiet, Councilman. —And you four, outside. Outside!—All will be well in here."

The four guards saluted and turned on their heels. Trevize and Branno were alone.

2. MAYOR

1.

Branno had been waiting for an hour, thinking wearily. Technically speaking, she was guilty of breaking and entering. What's more, she had violated, quite unconstitutionally, the rights of a Councilman. By the strict laws that held Mayors to account—since the days of Indbur III and the Mule, nearly two centuries before—she was impeachable.

On this one day, however, for twenty-four hours she could do no wrong.

But it would pass. She stirred restlessly.

The first two centuries had been the Golden Age of the Foundation, the Heroic Era—at least in retrospect, if not to the unfortunates who had lived in that insecure time. Salvor Hardin and Hober Mallow had been the two great heroes, semideified to the point of rivaling the incomparable Hari Seldon himself. The three were a tripod on which all Foundation legend (and even Foundation history) rested.

In those days, though, the Foundation had been one puny world, with a tenuous hold on the Four Kingdoms and with only a dim awareness of the extent to which the Seldon Plan was holding its protective hand over it, caring for it even against the remnant of the mighty Galactic Empire.

And the more powerful the Foundation grew as a political and commercial entity, the less significant its rulers and fighters had come to seem. Lathan Devers was almost forgotten. If he was remembered at all, it was for his tragic death in the slave mines, rather than for his unnecessary but successful fight against Bel Riose.

As for Bel Riose, the noblest of the Foundation's ad-

21

versaries, he too was nearly forgotten, overshadowed by
the Mule, who alone among enemies had broken the Seldon
Plan and defeated and ruled the Foundation. He alone was
the Great Enemy—indeed, the last of the Greats.

It was little remembered that the Mule had been, in essence, defeated by one person—a woman, Bayta Darell—
and that she had accomplished the victory without the help
of anyone, *without even the support of the Seldon Plan*. So,
too, was it almost forgotten that her son and granddaughter,
Toran and Arkady Darell, had defeated the Second Foundation, leaving the Foundation, the *First* Foundation, supreme.

These latter-day victors were no longer heroic figures.
The times had become too expansive to do anything but
shrink heroes into ordinary mortals. Then, too, Arkady's
biography of her grandmother had reduced her from a her-
oine to a figure of romance.

And since then there had been no heroes—not even
figures of romance. The Kalganian war had been the last
moment of violence engulfing the Foundation and that had
been a minor conflict. Nearly two centuries of virtual peace!
A hundred and twenty years without so much as a ship
scratched.

It had been a good peace—Branno would not deny that—
a profitable peace. The Foundation had not established a
Second Galactic Empire—it was only halfway there by the
Seldon Plan—but, as the Foundation Federation, it held a
strong economic grip on over a third of the scattered political
units of the Galaxy, and influenced what it didn't control.
There were few places where "I am of the Foundation" was
not met with respect. There was no one who ranked higher
in all the millions of inhabited worlds than the Mayor of
Terminus.

That was still the title. It was inherited from the leader
of a single small and almost disregarded city on a lonely
world on the far edge of civilization, some five centuries
before, but no one would dream of changing it or of giving

it one atom more glory-in-sound. As it was, only the all-forgotten title of Imperial Majesty could rival it in awe.

—Except on Terminus itself, where the powers of the Mayor were carefully limited. The memory of the Indburs still remained. It was not their tyranny that people could not forget but the fact that they had lost to the Mule.

And here she was, Harla Branno, the strongest to rule since the Mule's death (she knew that) and only the fifth woman to do so. On this day only had she been able to use her strength openly.

She had fought for her interpretation of what was right and what should be—against the dogged opposition of those who longed for the prestige-filled Interior of the Galaxy and for the aura of Imperial power—and she had won.

Not yet, she had said. Not yet! Jump too soon for the Interior and you will lose for this reason and for that. And Seldon had appeared and had supported her in language almost identical with her own.

It made her, for a time, in the eyes of all the Foundation, as wise as Seldon himself. She knew they could forget that any hour, however.

And this young man dared to challenge her on this day of days.

And he dared to be right!

That was the danger of it. He was right! And by being right, he might destroy the Foundation!

And now she faced him and they were alone.

She said sadly, "Could you not have come to see me privately? Did you have to shout it all out in the Council Chamber in your idiotic desire to make a fool of me? What have you done, you mindless boy?"

2.

Trevize felt himself flushing and fought to control his anger. The Mayor was an aging woman who would be sixty-three on her next birthday. He hesitated to engage in a shouting match with someone nearly twice his age.

Besides, she was well practiced in the political wars and knew that if she could place her opponent off-balance at the start then the battle was half-won. But it took an audience to make such a tactic effective and there was no audience before whom one might be humiliated. There were just the two of them.

So he ignored her words and did his best to survey her dispassionately. She was an old woman wearing the unisex fashions which had prevailed for two generations now. They did not become her. The Mayor, the leader of the Galaxy— if leader there could be—was just a plain old woman who mighty easily have been mistaken for an old man, except that her iron-gray hair was tied tightly back, instead of being worn free in the traditional male style.

Trevize smiled engagingly. However much an aged opponent strove to make the epithet "boy" sound like an insult, this particular "boy" had the advantage of youth and good looks—and the full awareness of both.

He said, "It's true. I'm thirty-two and, therefore, a boy— in a manner of speaking. And I'm a Councilman and, therefore, *ex officio*, mindless. The first condition is unavoidable. For the second, I can only say I'm sorry."

"Do you know what you've done? Don't stand there and strive for wit. Sit down. Put your mind into gear, if you can, and answer me rationally."

"I know what I've done. I've told the truth as I've seen it."

"And on this day you try to defy me with it? On this one day when my prestige is such that I could pluck you out of the Council Chamber and arrest you, with no one daring to protest?"

"The Council will recover its breath and it will protest. They may be protesting now. And they will listen to me all the more for the persecution to which you are subjecting me."

"No one will listen to you, because if I thought you would continue what you have been doing, I would continue to treat you as a traitor to the full extent of the law."

"I would then have to be tried. I'd have my day in court."

"Don't count on that. A Mayor's emergency powers are enormous, even if they are rarely used."

"On what grounds would you declare an emergency?"

"I'll invent the grounds. I have that much ingenuity left, and I do not fear taking the political risk. Don't push me, young man. We are going to come to an agreement here or you will never be free again. You will be imprisoned for the rest of your life. I guarantee it."

They stared at each other: Branno in gray, Trevize in multishade brown.

Trevize said, "What kind of an agreement?"

"Ah. You're curious. That's better. Then we can engage in conversation instead of confrontation. What is your point of view?"

"You know it well. You have been crawling in the mud with Councilman Compor, have you not?"

"I want to hear it from *you*—in the light of the Seldon Crisis just passed."

"Very well, if that's what you want—Madam Mayor!" (He had been on the brink of saying "old woman.") "The image of Seldon was too correct, too impossibly correct after five hundred years. It's the eighth time he has appeared, I believe. On some occasions, no one was there to hear him. On at least one occasion, in the time of Indbur III, what he had to say was utterly out of synchronization with reality—but that was in the time of the Mule, wasn't it? But when, on any of those occasions, was he as correct as he was now?"

Trevize allowed himself a small smile. "Never before, Madam Mayor, as far as our recordings of the past are concerned, has Seldon managed to describe the situation so perfectly, in all its smallest details."

Branno said, "Is it your suggestion that the Seldon appearance, the holographic image, is faked; that the Seldon recordings have been prepared by a contemporary such as myself, perhaps; that an actor was playing the Seldon role?"

"Not impossible, Madam Mayor, but that's not what I

mean. The truth is far worse. I believe that it is Seldon's image we see, and that his description of the present moment in history is the description he prepared five hundred years ago. I have said as much to your man, Kodell, who carefully guided me through a charade in which I seemed to support the superstitions of the unthinking Foundationer."

"Yes. The recording will be used, if necessary, to allow the Foundation to see that you were never really in the opposition."

Trevize spread his arms. "But I am. There is no Seldon Plan in the sense that we believe there is, and there hasn't been for perhaps two centuries. I have suspected that for years now, and what we went through in the Time Vault twelve hours ago proves it."

"Because Seldon was too accurate?"

"Precisely. Don't smile. That is the final proof."

"I'm not smiling, as you can see. Go on."

"How could he have been so accurate? Two centuries ago, Seldon's analysis of what was then the present was completely wrong. Three hundred years had passed since the Foundation was set up and he was wide of the mark. Completely!"

"That, Councilman, you yourself explained a few moments ago. It was because of the Mule. The Mule was a mutant with intense mental power and there had been no way of allowing for him in the Plan."

"But he was there just the same—allowed or not. The Seldon Plan was derailed. The Mule didn't rule for long and he had no successor. The Foundation regained its independence and its domination, but how could the Seldon Plan have gotten back on target after so enormous a tearing of its fabric?"

Branno looked grim and her aging hands clasped together tightly. "You know the answer to that. We were one of two Foundations. You've read the history books."

"I've read Arkady's biography of her grandmother— required reading in school, after all—and I've read her novels, too. I've read the official view of the history of the Mule and afterward. Am I to be allowed to doubt them?"

"In what way?"

"Officially we, the First Foundation, were to retain the knowledge of the physical sciences and to advance them. We were to operate openly, our historical development following—whether we knew it or not—the Seldon Plan. There was, however, also the Second Foundation, which was to preserve and further develop the psychological sciences, including psychohistory, and their existence was to be a secret even from us. The Second Foundation was the fine-tuning agency of the Plan, acting to adjust the currents of Galactic history, when they turned from the paths outlined by the Plan."

"Then you answer yourself," said the Mayor. "Bayta Darell defeated the Mule, perhaps under the inspiration of the Second Foundation, although her granddaughter insists that was not so. It was the Second Foundation without doubt, however, which labored to bring Galactic history back to the Plan after the Mule died and, quite obviously, they succeeded. —What on Terminus, then, are you talking about, Councilman?"

"Madam Mayor, if we follow Arkady Darell's account, it is clear that the Second Foundation, in making the attempt to correct Galactic history, undermined Seldon's entire scheme, since in their attempt to correct they destroyed their own secrecy. We, the First Foundation, realized that our mirror image, the Second Foundation, existed, and we could not live with the knowledge that we were being manipulated. We therefore labored to find the Second Foundation and to destroy it."

Branno nodded. "And we succeeded, according to Arkady Darell's account, but quite obviously, not until the Second Foundation had placed Galactic history firmly on track again after its disruption by the Mule. It is still on track."

"Can you believe that? The Second Foundation, according to the account, was located and its various members dealt with. That was in 378 F.E., a hundred twenty years ago. For five generations, we have supposedly been operating without the Second Foundation, and yet have remained so close to target where the Plan is concerned that you and the image of Seldon spoke almost identically."

"This might be interpreted to mean that I have seen into the significance of developing history with keen insight."

"Forgive me. I do not intend to cast doubt upon your keen insight, but to me it seems that the more obvious explanation is that the Second Foundation was never destroyed. It still rules us. It still manipulates us. —And *that* is why we have returned to the track of the Seldon Plan."

3.

If the Mayor was shocked by the statement, she showed no sign of it.

It was past 1 A.M. and she wanted desperately to bring an end to it, and yet could not hasten. The young man had to be played and she did not want to have him break the fishing line. She did not want to have to dispose of him uselessly, when he might first be made to serve a function.

She said, "Indeed? You say then that Arkady's tale of the Kalganian war and the destruction of the Second Foundation was false? Invented? A game? A lie?"

Trevize shrugged. "It doesn't have to be. That's beside the point. Suppose Arkady's account were completely true, to the best of her knowledge. Suppose all took place exactly as Arkady said it did; that the nest of Second Foundationers was discovered, and that they were disposed of. How can we possibly say, though, that we got every last one of them? The Second Foundation was dealing with the entire Galaxy. They were not manipulating the history of Terminus alone or even of the Foundation alone. Their responsibilities involved more than our capital world or our entire Federation. There were bound to be some Second Foundationers that were a thousand—or more—parsecs away. Is it likely we would have gotten them all?

"And if we failed to get them all, could we say we had won? Could the Mule have said it in his time? He took Terminus, and with it all the worlds it directly controlled—but the Independent Trading Worlds still stood. He took the Trading Worlds—yet three fugitives remained: Ebling Mis, Bayta Darell, and her husband. He kept both men under control and left Bayta—only Bayta—uncontrolled. He did this out of sentiment, if we are to believe Arkady's romance. And that was enough. According to Arkady's account, one person—only Bayta—was left to do as she pleased, and because of her actions the Mule was not able to locate the Second Foundation and was therefore defeated.

"One person left untouched, and all was lost! That's the importance of one person, despite all the legends that surround Seldon's Plan to the effect that the individual is nothing and the mass is all.

"And if we left not just one Second Foundationer behind, but several dozen, as seems perfectly likely, what then? Would they not gather together, rebuild their fortunes, take up their careers again, multiply their numbers by recruitment and training, and once more make us all pawns?"

Branno said gravely, "Do you believe that?"

"I am sure of it."

"But tell me, Councilman? Why should they bother? Why should the pitiful remnant continue to cling desperately to a duty no one welcomes? What drives them to keep the Galaxy along its path to the Second Galactic Empire? And if the small band insists on fulfilling its mission, why should we care? Why not accept the path of the Plan and be thankful that they will see to it that we do not stray or lose our way?"

Trevize put his hand over his eyes and rubbed them. Despite his youth, he seemed the more tired of the two. He stared at the Mayor and said, "I can't believe you. Are you under the impression that the Second Foundation is doing this for *us*? That they are some sort of idealists? Isn't it clear to you from your knowledge of politics—of the practical issues of power and manipulation—that they are doing it for themselves?

"We are the cutting edge. We are the engine, the force. We labor and sweat and bleed and weep. They merely control—adjusting an amplifier here, closing a contact there, and doing it all with ease and without risk to themselves. Then, when it is all done and when, after a thousand years of heaving and straining, we have set up the Second Galactic Empire, the people of the Second Foundation will move in as the ruling elite."

Branno said, "Do you want to eliminate the Second Foundation then? Having moved halfway to the Second Empire, do you want to take the chance of completing the task on our own and serving as our own elite? Is that it?"

"Certainly! Certainly! Shouldn't that be what you want, too? You and I won't live to see it, but you have grandchildren and someday I may, and they will have grandchildren, and so on. I want them to have the fruit of our labors and I want them to look back to us as the source, and to praise us for what we have accomplished. I don't want it all to fall to a hidden conspiracy devised by Seldon—who is no hero of mine. I tell you he is a greater threat than the Mule—if we allow his Plan to go through. By the Galaxy, I wish the Mule *had* disrupted the Plan altogether—and forever. We would have survived him. He was one of a kind and very mortal. The Second Foundation seems to be immortal."

"But you would like to destroy the Second Foundation, is that not so?"

"If I knew how!"

"Since you don't know how, don't you think it quite likely they will destroy you?"

Trevize looked contemptuous. "I have had the thought that even you might be under their control. Your accurate guess as to what Seldon's image would say and your subsequent treatment of me could be all Second Foundation. You could be a hollow shell with a Second Foundation content."

"Then why are you talking to me as you are?"

"Because if you are under Second Foundation control, I am lost in any case and I might as well expel some of the anger within me—and because, in actual fact, I am gambling that you are *not* under their control, that you are merely unaware of what you do."

Branno said, "You win that gamble, at any rate. I am not under anyone's control but my own. Still, can you be sure I am telling the truth? Were I under control of the Second Foundation, would I admit it? Would I even myself know that I was under their control?

"But there is no profit in such questions. I believe I am not under control and you have no choice but to believe it, too. Consider this, however. If the Second Foundation exists, it is certain that their biggest need is to make sure that no one in the Galaxy knows they exist. The Seldon Plan only works well if the pawns—we—are not aware of how the Plan works and of how we are manipulated. It was because the Mule focused the attention of the Foundation on the Second Foundation that the Second Foundation was destroyed in Arkady's time. —Or should I say *nearly* destroyed, Councilman?

"From this we can deduce two corollaries. First, we can reasonably suppose that they interfere grossly as little as they can. We can assume it would be impossible to take us all over. Even the Second Foundation, if it exists, must have limits to its power. To take over some and allow others to guess the fact would introduce distortions to the Plan. Consequently, we come to the conclusion that their interference is as delicate, as indirect, as sparse as is possible—and therefore I am *not* controlled. Nor are you."

Trevize said, "That is one corollary and I tend to accept it—out of wishful thinking, perhaps. What is the other?"

"A simpler and more inevitable one. If the Second Foundation exists and wishes to guard the secret of that existence, then one thing is sure. Anyone who thinks it still exists, and talks about it, and announces it, and shouts it to all the Galaxy must, in some subtle way, be removed by them at once, wiped out, done away with. Wouldn't that be your conclusion, too?"

Trevize said, "Is that why you have taken me into custody, Madam Mayor? To protect me from the Second Foundation?"

"In a way. To an extent. Liono Kodell's careful recording of your beliefs will be publicized not only in order to keep the people of Terminus and the Foundation from being unduly disturbed by your silly talk—but to keep the Second Foundation from being disturbed. If it exists, I do not want to have its attention drawn to you."

"Imagine that," said Trevize with heavy irony. "For my sake? For my lovely brown eyes?"

Branno stirred and then, quite without warning, laughed quietly. She said, "I am not so old, Councilman, that I am not aware that you have lovely brown eyes and, thirty years ago, that might have been motive enough. At this time, however, I wouldn't move a millimeter to save them—or all the rest of you—if only your eyes were involved. But if the Second Foundation exists, and if their attention is drawn to you, they may not stop with you. There's my life to consider, and that of a number of others far more intelligent and valuable than you—and all the plans we have made."

"Oh? Do you believe the Second Foundation exists, then, that you react so carefully to the possibility of their response?"

Branno brought her fist down upon the table before her. "Of course I do, you consummate fool! If I didn't know the Second Foundation exists, and if I weren't fighting them as hard and as effectively as I could, would I care what you say about such a subject? If the Second Foundation did not exist, would it matter that you are announcing they do? I've wanted for months to shut you up before you went public, but lacked the political power to deal roughly with a Councilman. Seldon's appearance made me look good and gave me the power—if only temporarily—and at that moment, you *did* go public. I moved at once, and now I will have you killed without a twinge of conscience or a microsecond of hesitation—if you don't do exactly as you're told.

"Our entire conversation now, at an hour in which I would much rather be in bed and asleep, was designed to bring you to the point of believing me when I tell you this. I want you to know that the problem of the Second Foundation, which I was careful to have *you* outline, gives me reason enough and inclination to have you brainstopped without trial."

Trevize half-rose from his seat.

Branno said, "Oh, don't make any moves. I'm only an old woman, as you're undoubtedly telling yourself, but before you could place a hand on me, you'd be dead. We are under observation, foolish young man, by my people."

Trevize sat down. He said, just a bit shakily, "You make no sense. If you believed the Second Foundation existed, you wouldn't be speaking of it so freely. You wouldn't expose yourself to the dangers to which you say I am exposing myself."

"You recognize, then, that I have a bit more good sense than you do. In other words, you believe the Second Foundation exists, yet you speak freely about it, because you are foolish. I believe it exists, and I speak freely, too—but only because I have taken precautions. Since you seem to have read Arkady's history carefully, you may recall that she speaks of her father having invented what she called a 'Mental Static Device.' It serves as a shield to the kind of mental power the Second Foundation has. It still exists and has been improved on, too, under conditions of the greatest secrecy. This house is, for the moment, reasonably safe against their prying. With that understood, let me tell you what you are to do."

"What's that?"

"You are to find out whether what you and I think is so is indeed so. You are to find out if the Second Foundation still exists and, if so, where. That means you will have to leave Terminus and go I know not where—even though it may in the end turn out, as in Arkady's day, that the Second

Foundation exists among us. It means you will not return till you have something to tell us; and if you have nothing to tell us, you will never return, and the population of Terminus will be less one fool."

Trevize found himself stammering. "How on Terminus can I look for them without giving away the fact? They will simply arrange a death for me, and you will be none the wiser."

"Then *don't* look for them, you naïve child. Look for something else. Look for something else with all your heart and mind, and *if*, in the process, you come across *them* because they have not bothered to pay you any attention, then good! You may, in that case, send us the information by shielded and coded hyperwave, and you may then return as a reward."

"I suppose you have something in mind that I should look for."

"Of course I do. Do you know Janov Pelorat?"

"Never heard of him."

"You will meet him tomorrow. He will tell you what you are looking for and he will leave with you in one of our most advanced ships. There will be just the two of you, for two are quite enough to risk. And if you ever try to return without satisfying us that you have the knowledge we want, then you will be blown out of space before you come within a parsec of Terminus. That's all. This conversation is over."

She arose, looked at her bare hands, then slowly drew on her gloves. She turned toward the door, and through it came two guards, weapons in hand. They stepped apart to let her pass.

At the doorway she turned. "There are other guards outside. Do nothing that disturbs them or you will save us all the trouble of your existence."

"You will also then lose the benefits I might bring you," said Trevize and, with an effort, he managed to say it lightly.

"We'll chance that," said Branno with an unamused smile.

4.

Outside Liono Kodell was waiting for her. He said, "I listened to the whole thing, Mayor. You were extraordinarily patient."

"And I am extraordinarily tired. I think the day has been seventy-two hours long. You take over now."

"I will, but tell me— Was there really a Mental Static Device about the house?"

"Oh, Kodell," said Branno wearily. "You know better than that. What was the chance anyone was watching? Do you imagine the Second Foundation is watching everything, everywhere, always? I'm not the romantic young Trevize is; *he* might think that, but I don't. And even if that were the case, if Second Foundational eyes and ears were everywhere, would not the presence of an MSD have given us away at once? For that matter, would not its use have shown the Second Foundation a shield against its powers existed—once they detected a region that was mentally opaque? Isn't the secret of such a shield's existence—until we are quite ready to use it to the full—something worth not only more than Trevize, but more than you and I together? And yet—"

They were in the ground-car, with Kodell driving. "And yet—" said Kodell.

"And yet what?" said Branno. "—Oh yes. And yet that young man is intelligent. I called him a fool in various ways half a dozen times just to keep him in his place, but he isn't one. He's young and he's read too many of Arkady Darell's novels, and they have made him think that that's the way the Galaxy is—but he has a quick insight about him and it will be a pity to lose him."

"You are sure then that he will be lost?"

"Quite sure," said Branno sadly. "Just the same, it is better that way. We don't need young romantics charging about blindly and smashing in an instant, perhaps, what it has taken us years to build. Besides, he will serve a purpose. He will surely attract the attention of the Second Foundationers—always assuming they exist and are indeed con-

cerning themselves with us. And while they are attracted to
him, they will, perchance, ignore us. Perhaps we can gain
even more than the good fortune of being ignored. They
may, we can hope, unwittingly give themselves away to us
in their concern with Trevize, and let us have an opportunity
and time to devise countermeasures."

"Trevize, then, draws the lightning."

Branno's lips twitched. "Ah, the metaphor I've been
looking for. He is our lightning rod, absorbing the stroke
and protecting us from harm."

"And this Pelorat, who will also be in the path of the
lightning bolt?"

"He may suffer, too. That can't be helped."

Kodell nodded. "Well, you know what Salvor Hardin
used to say— 'Never let your sense of morals keep you
from doing what is right.'"

"At the moment, I haven't got a sense of morals," muttered Branno. "I have a sense of bone-weariness. And yet—
I could name a number of people I would sooner lose than
Golan Trevize. He is a handsome young man. —And, of
course, he knows it." Her last words slurred as she closed
her eyes and fell into a light sleep.

3. HISTORIAN

1.

Janov Pelorat was white-haired and his face, in repose, looked rather empty. It was rarely in anything but repose. He was of average height and weight and tended to move without haste and to speak with deliberation. He seemed considerably older than his fifty-two years.

He had never left Terminus, something that was most unusual, especially for one of his profession. He himself wasn't sure whether his sedentary ways were because of—or in spite of—his obsession with history.

The obsession had come upon him quite suddenly at the age of fifteen when, during some indisposition, he was given a book of early legends. In it, he found the repeated motif of a world that was alone and isolated—a world that was not even aware of its isolation, since it had never known anything else.

His indisposition began to clear up at once. Within two days, he had read the book three times and was out of bed. The day after that he was at his computer terminal, checking for any records that the Terminus University Library might have on similar legends.

It was precisely such legends that had occupied him ever since. The Terminus University Library had by no means been a great resource in this respect but, when he grew older, he discovered the joys of interlibrary loans. He had printouts in his possession which had been taken off hyper-radiational signals from as far away as Ifnia.

He had become a professor of ancient history and was now beginning his first sabbatical—one for which he had applied with the idea of taking a trip through space (his first) to Trantor itself—thirty-seven years later.

Pelorat was quite aware that it was most unusual for a person of Terminus to have never been in space. It had never been his intention to be notable in this particular way. It was just that whenever he might have gone into space, some new book, some new study, some new analysis came his way. He would delay his projected trip until he had wrung the new matter dry and had added, if possible, one more item of fact, or speculation, or imagination to the mountain he had collected. In the end, his only regret was that the particular trip to Trantor had never been made.

Trantor had been the capital of the First Galactic Empire. It had been the seat of Emperors for twelve thousand years and, before that, the capital of one of the most important pre-Imperial kingdoms, which had, little by little, captured or otherwise absorbed the other kingdoms to establish the Empire.

Trantor had been a world-girdling city, a metal-coated city. Pelorat had read of it in the works of Gaal Dornick, who had visited it in the time of Hari Seldon himself. Dornick's volume no longer circulated and the one Pelorat owned might have been sold for half the historian's annual salary. A suggestion that he might part with it would have horrified the historian.

Of course, what Pelorat cared about, as far as Trantor was concerned, was the Galactic Library, which in Imperial times (when it was the Imperial Library) had been the largest in the Galaxy. Trantor was the capital of the largest and most populous Empire humanity had ever seen. It had been a single worldwide city with a population well in excess of forty billion, and its Library had been the gathered record of all the creative (and not-so-creative) work of humanity, the full summary of its knowledge. And it was all computerized in so complex a manner that it took experts to handle the computers.

What was more, the Library had survived. To Pelorat, that was the amazing thing about it. When Trantor had fallen and been sacked, nearly two and a half centuries before, it had undergone appalling destruction, and the tales of human misery and death would not bear repeating—yet the Library had survived, protected (it was said) by the University students, who used ingeniously devised weapons. (Some thought the defense by the students might well have been thoroughly romanticized.)

In any case, the Library had endured through the period of devastation. Ebling Mis had done his work in an intact Library in a ruined world when he had almost located the Second Foundation (according to the story which the people of the Foundation still believed, but which historians have always treated with reserve). The three generations of Darells—Bayta, Toran, and Arkady—had each, at one time or another, been on Trantor. However, Arkady had not visited the Library, and since her time the Library had not impinged on Galactic history.

No Foundationer had been on Trantor in a hundred and twenty years, but there was no reason to believe the Library was not still there. That it had made no impingement was the surest evidence in favor of its being there. Its destruction would surely have made a noise.

The Library was outmoded and archaic—it had been so even in Ebling Mis's time—but that was all to the good. Pelorat always rubbed his hands with excitement when he thought of an *old* and *outmoded* Library. The older and the more outmoded, the more likely it was to have what he needed. In his dreams, he would enter the Library and ask in breathless alarm, "Has the Library been modernized? Have you thrown out the old tapes and computerizations?" And always he imagined the answer from dusty and ancient librarians, "As it has been, Professor, so is it still."

And now his dream would come true. The Mayor herself had assured him of that. How she had known of his work, he wasn't quite sure. He had not succeeded in publishing many papers. Little of what he had done was solid enough to be acceptable for publication and what had appeared had left no mark. Still, they said Branno the Bronze knew all that went on in Terminus and had eyes at the end of every finger and toe. Pelorat could almost believe it, but if she knew of his work, why on Terminus didn't she see its importance and give him a little financial support before this?

Somehow, he thought, with as much bitterness as he could generate, the Foundation had its eyes fixed firmly on the future. It was the Second Empire and their destiny that absorbed them. They had no time, no desire, to peer back into the past—and they were irritated by those who did.

The more fools they, of course, but he could not single-handedly wipe out folly. And it might be better so. He could hug the great pursuit to his own chest and the day would come when he would be remembered as the great Pioneer of the Important.

That meant, of course (and he was too intellectually honest to refuse to perceive it), that he, too, was absorbed in the future—a future in which he would be recognized, and in which he would be a hero on a par with Hari Seldon. In fact, he would be the greater, for how could the working out of a clearly visualized future a millennium long stand comparison with the working out of a lost past at least twenty-five millennia old.

And this was the day; *this* was the day.

The Mayor had said it would be the day after Seldon's image made its appearance. That was the only reason Pelorat had been interested in the Seldon Crisis that for months had occupied every mind on Terminus and indeed almost every mind in the Federation.

It had seemed to him to make the most trifling difference as to whether the capital of the Foundation had remained here at Terminus, or had been shifted somewhere else. And now that the crisis had been resolved, he remained unsure as to which side of the matter Hari Seldon had championed, or if the matter under dispute had been mentioned at all.

It was enough that Seldon had appeared and that now *this* was the day.

It was a little after two in the afternoon that a ground-car slid to a halt in the driveway of his somewhat isolated house just outside Terminus proper.

A rear door slid back. A guard in the uniform of the Mayoralty Security Corps stepped out, then a young man, then two more guards.

Pelorat was impressed despite himself. The Mayor not only knew of his work but clearly considered it of the highest importance. The person who was to be his companion was given an honor guard, and he had been promised a first-class vessel which his companion would be able to pilot. Most flattering! Most—

Pelorat's housekeeper opened the door. The young man entered and the two guards positioned themselves on either side of the entrance. Through the window, Pelorat saw that the third guard remained outside and that a second ground-car now pulled up. Additional guards!

Confusing!

He turned to find the young man in his room and was surprised to find that he recognized him. He had seen him on holocasts. He said, "You're that Councilman. You're Trevize!"

"Golan Trevize. That's right. You are Professor Janov Pelorat?"

"Yes, yes," said Pelorat. "Are you he who will—"

"We are going to be fellow travelers," said Trevize woodenly. "Or so I have been told."

"But you're not a historian."

"No, I'm not. As you said, I'm a Councilman, a politician."

"Yes— Yes— But what am I thinking about? *I* am a historian, therefore what need for another? *You* can pilot a spaceship."

"Yes, I'm pretty good at that."

"Well, *that's* what we need, then. Excellent! I'm afraid I'm not one of your practical thinkers, young man, so if it should happen that you are, we'll make a good team."

Trevize said, "I am not, at the moment, overwhelmed

with the excellence of my thinking, but it seems we have no choice but to try to make it a good team."

"Let's hope, then, that I can overcome my uncertainty about space. I've never been in space, you know, Councilman. I am a groundhog, if that's the term. Would you like a glass of tea, by the way? I'll have Kloda prepare us something. It is my understanding that it will be some hours before we leave, after all. I am prepared right now, however. I have what is necessary for both of us. The Mayor has been *most* co-operative. Astonishing—her interest in the project."

Trevize said, "You've known about this, then? How long?"

"The Mayor approached me" (here Pelorat frowned slightly and seemed to be making certain calculations) "two, or maybe three, weeks ago. I was *delighted*. And now that I have got it clear in my head that I need a pilot and not a second historian, I am also delighted that my companion will be you, my dear fellow."

"Two, maybe three, weeks ago," repeated Trevize, sounding a little dazed. "She was prepared all this time, then. And I—" He faded out.

"Pardon me?"

"Nothing, Professor. I have a bad habit of muttering to myself. It is something you will have to grow accustomed to, if our trip extends itself."

"It will. It will," said Pelorat, bustling the other to the dining room table, where an elaborate tea was being prepared by his housekeeper. "Quite open-ended. The Mayor said we were to take as long as we liked and that the Galaxy lay all before us and, indeed, that wherever we went we could call upon Foundation funds. She said, of course, that we would have to be reasonable. I promised that much." He chuckled and rubbed his hands. "Sit down, my good fellow, sit down. This may be our last meal on Terminus for a very long time."

Trevize sat down. He said, "Do you have a family, Professor?"

"I have a son. He's on the faculty at Santanni University. A chemist, I believe, or something like that. He took after his mother's side. She hasn't been with me for a long time, so you see I have no responsibilities, no active hostages to fortune. I trust you have none—help yourself to the sandwiches, my boy."

"No hostages at the moment. A few women. They come and go."

"Yes. Yes. Delightful when it works out. Even more delightful when you find it need not be taken seriously. —No children, I take it."

"None."

"Good! You know, I'm in the most remarkable good humor. I was taken aback when you first came in. I admit it. But I find you quite exhilarating now. What I need is youth and enthusiasm and someone who can find his way about the Galaxy. We're on a search, you know. A remarkable search." Pelorat's quiet face and quiet voice achieved an unusual animation without any particular change in either expression or intonation. "I wonder if you have been told about this."

Trevize's eyes narrowed. "A remarkable search?"

"Yes indeed. A pearl of great price is hidden among the tens of millions of inhabited worlds in the Galaxy and we have nothing but the faintest clues to guide us. Just the same, it will be an incredible prize if we can find it. If you and I can carry it off, my boy—Trevize, I should say, for I don't mean to patronize—our names will ring down the ages to the end of time."

"The prize you speak of—this pearl of great price—"

"I sound like Arkady Darell—the writer, you know— speaking of the Second Foundation, don't I? No wonder you look astonished." Pelorat leaned his head back as though he were going to break into loud laughter but he merely smiled. "Nothing so silly and unimportant, I assure you."

Trevize said, "If you are not speaking of the Second Foundation, Professor, what *are* you speaking of?"

Pelorat was suddenly grave, even apologetic. "Ah, then

the Mayor has not told you? —It is odd, you know. I've
spent decades resenting the government and its inability to
understand what I'm doing, and now Mayor Branno is being
remarkably generous."

"Yes," said Trevize, not trying to conceal an intonation
of irony, "she is a woman of remarkable hidden philan-
thropy, but she has not told me what this is all about."

"You are not aware of my research, then?"

"No. I'm sorry."

"No need to excuse yourself. Perfectly all right. I have
not exactly made a splash. Then let me tell you. You and
I are going to search for—and find, for I have an excellent
possibility in mind—Earth."

2.

Trevize did not sleep well that night.

Over and over, he thrashed about the prison that the old
woman had built around him. Nowhere could he find a way
out.

He was being driven into exile and he could do nothing
about it. She had been calmly inexorable and did not even
take the trouble to mask the unconstitutionality of it all. He
had relied on his rights as a Councilman and as a citizen of
the Federation, and she hadn't even paid them lip service.

And now this Pelorat, this odd academic who seemed to
be located in the world without being part of it, told him
that the fearsome old woman had been making arrangements
for this for weeks.

He felt like the "boy" that she had called him.

He was to be exiled with a historian who kept "dear
fellowing" him and who seemed to be in a noiseless fit of
joy over beginning a Galactic search for—Earth?

What in the name of the Mule's grandmother was Earth?

He had asked. Of course! He had asked upon the moment
of its mention.

He had said, "Pardon me, Professor. I am ignorant of

your specialty and I trust you won't be annoyed if I ask for an explanation in simple terms. What is Earth?"

Pelorat stared at him gravely while twenty seconds moved slowly past. He said, "It is a planet. The original planet. The one on which human beings first appeared, my dear fellow."

Trevize stared. "First appeared? From where?"

"From nowhere. It's the planet on which humanity developed through evolutionary processes from lower animals."

Trevize thought about it, then shook his head. "I don't know what you mean."

An annoyed expression crossed Pelorat's face briefly. He cleared his throat and said, "There was a time when Terminus had no human beings upon it. It was settled by human beings from other worlds. You know that, I suppose?"

"Yes, of course," said Trevize impatiently. He was irritated at the other's sudden assumption of pedagogy.

"Very well. This is true of all the other worlds. Anacreon, Santanni, Kalgan—all of them. They were all, at some time in the past, *founded*. People arrived there from other worlds. It's true even of Trantor. It may have been a great metropolis for twenty thousand years, but before that it wasn't."

"Why, what was it before that?"

"Empty! At least of human beings."

"That's hard to believe."

"It's true. The old records show it."

"Where did the people come from who first settled Trantor?"

"No one is certain. There are hundreds of planets which claim to have been populated in the dim mists of antiquity and whose people present fanciful tales about the nature of the first arrival of humanity. Historians tend to dismiss such things and to brood over the 'Origin Question.'"

"What is that? I've never heard of it."

"That doesn't surprise me. It's not a popular historical problem now, I admit, but there was a time during the decay of the Empire when it roused a certain interest among intellectuals. Salvor Hardin mentions it briefly in his memoirs. It's the question of the identity and location of the one planet from which it all started. If we look backward in time, humanity flows inward from the most recently established worlds to older ones, to still older ones, until all concentrates on one—the original."

Trevize thought at once of the obvious flaw in the argument. "Might there not have been a large number of originals?"

"Of course not. All human beings all over the Galaxy are of a single species. A single species *cannot* originate on more than one planet. Quite impossible."

"How do you know?"

"In the first place—" Pelorat ticked off the first finger of his left hand with the first finger of his right, and then seemed to think better of what would undoubtedly have been a long and intricate exposition. He put both hands at his side and said with great earnestness, "My dear fellow, I give you my word of honor."

Trevize bowed formally and said, "I would not dream of doubting it, Professor Pelorat. Let us say, then, that there is one planet of origin, but might there not be hundreds who lay claim to the honor?"

"There not only might be, there *are*. Yet every claim is without merit. Not one of those hundreds that aspire to the credit of priority shows any trace of a prehyperspatial society, let alone any trace of human evolution from prehuman organisms."

"Then are you saying that there *is* a planet of origin, but that, for some reason, it is not making the claim?"

"You have hit it precisely."

"And you are going to search for it?"

"We are. That is our mission. Mayor Branno has arranged it all. You will pilot our ship to Trantor."

"To Trantor? It's not the planet of origin. You said that much a while ago."

"Of course Trantor isn't. Earth is."

"Then why aren't you telling me to pilot the ship to Earth?"

"I am not making myself clear. Earth is a legendary name. It is enshrined in ancient myths. It has no meaning we can be certain of, but it is convenient to use the word as a one-syllable synonym for 'the planet of origin of the human species.' Just which planet in real space is the one we are defining as 'Earth' is not known."

"Will they know on Trantor?"

"I hope to find information there, certainly. Trantor possesses the Galactic Library, the greatest in the system."

"Surely that Library has been searched by those people you said were interested in the 'Origin Question' in the time of the First Empire."

Pelorat nodded thoughtfully, "Yes, but perhaps not well enough. I have learned a great deal about the 'Origin Question' that perhaps the Imperials of five centuries back did not know. I might search the old records with greater understanding, you see. I have been thinking about this for a long time and I have an excellent possibility in mind."

"You have told Mayor Branno all this, I imagine, and she approves?"

"Approves? My dear fellow, she was ecstatic. She told me that Trantor was surely the place to find out all I needed to know."

"No doubt," muttered Trevize.

That was part of what occupied him that night. Mayor Branno was sending him out to find out what he could about the Second Foundation. She was sending him with Pelorat so that he might mask his real aim with the pretended search for Earth—a search that could carry him anywhere in the Galaxy. It was a perfect cover, in fact, and he admired the Mayor's ingenuity.

But Trantor? Where was the sense in that? Once they were on Trantor, Pelorat would find his way into the Galactic Library and would never emerge. With endless stacks of books, films, and recordings, with innumerable com-

puterizations and symbolic representations, he would surely
never want to leave.

Besides that—

Ebling Mis had once gone to Trantor, in the Mule's time.
The story was that he had found the location of the Second
Foundation there and had died before he could reveal it.
But then, so had Arkady Darell, and she had succeeded in
locating the Second Foundation. But the location she had
found was on Terminus itself, and there the nest of Second
Foundationers was wiped out. Wherever the Second Foun-
dation was *now* would be elsewhere, so what more had
Trantor to tell? If he were looking for the Second Foun-
dation, it was best to go anywhere *but* Trantor.

Besides that—

What further plans Branno had, he did not know, but he
was not in the mood to oblige her. Branno had been ecstatic,
had she, about a trip to Trantor? Well, if Branno wanted
Trantor, they were not going to Trantor! —Anywhere else.
—But not Trantor!

And worn out, with the night verging toward dawn, Trevize fell at last into a fitful slumber.

3.

Mayor Branno had had a good day on the one following
the arrest of Trevize. She had been extolled far beyond her
deserts and the incident was never mentioned.

Nevertheless, she knew well that the Council would soon
emerge from its paralysis and that questions would be raised.
She would have to act quickly. So, putting a great many
matters to one side, she pursued the matter of Trevize.

At the time when Trevize and Pelorat were discussing
Earth, Branno was facing Councilman Munn Li Compor in
the Mayoralty Office. As he sat across the desk from her,
perfectly at ease, she appraised him once again.

He was smaller and slighter than Trevize and only two
years older. Both were freshmen Councilmen, young and

brash, and that must have been the only thing that held them together, for they were different in all other respects.

Where Trevize seemed to radiate a glowering intensity, Compor shone with an almost serene self-confidence. Perhaps it was his blond hair and blue eyes, not at all common among Foundationers. They lent him an almost feminine delicacy that (Branno judged) made him less attractive to women than Trevize was. He was clearly vain of his looks, though, and made the most of them, wearing his hair rather long and making sure that it was carefully waved. He wore a faint blue shadowing under his eyebrows to accentuate the eye color. (Shadowing of various tints had become common among men these last ten years.)

He was no womanizer. He lived sedately with his wife, but had not yet registered parental intent and was not known to have a clandestine second companion. That, too, was different from Trevize, who changed housemates as often as he changed the loudly colored sashes for which he was notorious.

There was little about either young Councilman that Kodell's department had not uncovered, and Kodell himself sat quietly in one corner of the room, exuding a comfortable good cheer as always.

Branno said, "Councilman Compor, you have done the Foundation good service, but unfortunately for yourself, it is not of the sort that can be praised in public or repaid in ordinary fashion."

Compor smiled. He had white and even teeth, and Branno idly wondered for one flashing moment if all the inhabitants of the Sirius Sector looked like that. Compor's tale of stemming from that particular, rather peripheral, region went back to his maternal grandmother, who had also been blond-haired and blue-eyed and who had maintained that *her* mother was from the Sirius Sector. According to Kodell, however, there was no hard evidence in favor of that.

Women being what they were, Kodell had said, she might well have claimed distant and exotic ancestry to add to her glamour and her already formidable attractiveness.

"Is that how women are?" Branno had asked drily, and Kodell had smiled and muttered that he was referring to ordinary women, of course.

Compor said, "It is not necessary that the people of the Foundation know of my service—only that *you* do."

"I know and I will not forget. What I also will not do is to let you assume that your obligations are not over. You have embarked on a complicated course and you must continue. We want more about Trevize."

"I have told you all I know concerning him."

"That may be what you would have me believe. That may even be what you truly believe yourself. Nevertheless, answer my questions. Do you know a gentleman named Janov Pelorat?"

For just a moment Compor's forehead creased, then smoothed itself almost at once. He said carefully, "I might know him if I were to see him, but the name does not seem to cause any association within me."

"He is a scholar."

Compor's mouth rounded into a rather contemptuous but unsounded "Oh?" as though he were surprised that the Mayor would expect him to know scholars.

Branno said, "Pelorat is an interesting person who, for reasons of his own, has the ambition of visiting Trantor. Councilman Trevize will accompany him. Now, since you have been a good friend of Trevize and perhaps know his system of thinking, tell me— Do you think Trevize will consent to go to Trantor?"

Compor said, "If you see to it that Trevize gets on the ship, and if the ship is piloted to Trantor, what can he do but go there? Surely you don't suggest he will mutiny and take over the ship."

"You don't understand. He and Pelorat will be alone on the ship and it will be Trevize at the controls."

"You are asking whether he would go voluntarily to Trantor?"

"Yes, that is what I am asking."

"Madam Mayor, how can I possibly know what he will do?"

"Councilman Compor, you have been close to Trevize. You know his belief in the existence of the Second Foundation. Has he never spoken to you of his theories as to where it might exist, where it might be found?"

"Never, Madam Mayor."

"Do you think he will find it?"

Compor chuckled. "I think the Second Foundation, whatever it was and however important it might have been, was wiped out in the time of Arkady Darell. I believe her story."

"Indeed? In that case, why did you betray your friend? If he were searching for something that does not exist, what harm could he have done by propounding his quaint theories?"

Compor said, "It is not the truth alone that can harm. His theories may have been merely quaint, but they might have succeeded in unsettling the people of Terminus and, by introducing doubts and fears as to the Foundation's role in the great drama of Galactic history, have weakened its leadership of the Federation and its dreams of a Second Galactic Empire. Clearly you thought this yourself, or you would not have seized him on the floor of the Council, and you would not now be forcing him into exile without trial. Why have you done so, if I may ask, Mayor?"

"Shall we say that I was cautious enough to wonder if there were some faint chance that he might be right, and that the expression of his views might be actively and directly dangerous?"

Compor said nothing.

Branno said, "I agree with you, but I am forced by the responsibilities of my position to consider the possibility. Let me ask you again if you have any indication as to where he might think the Second Foundation exists, and where he might go."

"I have none."

"He has never given you any hints in that direction?"

"No, of course not."

"Never? Don't dismiss the thought easily. Think! Never?"

"Never," said Compor firmly.

"No hints? No joking remarks? No doodles? No thoughtful abstractions at moments that achieve significance as you look back on them?"

"None. I tell you, Madam Mayor, his dreams of the Second Foundation are the most nebulous starshine. You know it, and you but waste your time and your emotions in your concern over it."

"You are not by some chance suddenly changing sides again and protecting the friend you delivered into my hands?"

"No," said Compor. "I turned him over to you for what seemed to me to be good and patriotic reasons. I have no reason to regret the action, or to change my attitude."

"Then you can give me no hint as to where he might go once he has a ship at his disposal?"

"As I have already said—"

"And yet, Councilman," and here the lines of the Mayor's face so folded as to make her seem wistful, "I would like to know where he goes."

"In that case, I think you ought to place a hyper-relay on his ship."

"I have thought of that, Councilman. He is, however, a suspicious man and I suspect he will find it—however cleverly it might be placed. Of course, it might be placed in such a way that he cannot remove it without crippling the ship, and he might therefore be forced to leave it in place—"

"An excellent notion."

"Except that," said Branno, "he would then be inhibited. He might not go where he would go if he felt himself free and untrammeled. The knowledge I would gain would be useless to me."

"In that case, it appears you cannot find out where he will go."

"I might, for I intend to be very primitive. A person who expects the completely sophisticated and who guards against it is quite apt never to think of the primitive. —I'm thinking of having Trevize followed."

"Followed?"

"Exactly. By another pilot in another spaceship. See how astonished you are at the thought? He would be equally astonished. He might not think of scouring space for an accompanying mass and, in any case, we will see to it that his ship is not equipped with our latest mass-detection devices."

Compor said, "Madam Mayor, I speak with all possible respect, but I must point out that you lack experience in space flight. To have one ship followed by another is never done—because it won't work. Trevize will escape with the first hyperspatial Jump. Even if he doesn't know he is being followed, that first Jump will be his path to freedom. If he doesn't have a hyper-relay on board ship, he can't be traced."

"I admit my lack of experience. Unlike you and Trevize, I have had no naval training. Nevertheless, I am told by my advisers—who *have* had such training—that if a ship is observed immediately prior to a Jump, its direction, speed, and acceleration make it possible to guess what the Jump might be—in a general way. Given a good computer and an excellent sense of judgment, a follower might duplicate the Jump closely enough to pick up the trail at the other end—especially if the follower has a good mass-detector."

"That might happen once," said Compor energetically, "even twice if the follower is very lucky, but that's it. You can't rely on such things."

"Perhaps we can. —Councilman Compor, you have hyper-raced in your time. You see, I know a great deal about you. You are an excellent pilot and have done amazing things when it comes to following a competitor through a Jump."

Compor's eyes widened. He almost squirmed in his chair. "I was in college then. I am older now."

"Not too old. Not yet thirty-five. Consequently *you* are going to follow Trevize, Councilman. Where he goes, you will follow, and you will report back to me. You will leave soon after Trevize does, and he will be leaving in a few hours. If you refuse the task, Councilman, you will be imprisoned for treason. If you take the ship that we will provide for you, and if you fail to follow, you need not bother coming back. You will be shot out of space if you try."

Compor rose sharply to his feet. "I have a life to live. I have work to do. I have a wife. I cannot leave it all."

"You will have to. Those of us who choose to serve the Foundation must be prepared at all times to serve it in a prolonged and uncomfortable fashion, if that should become necessary."

"My wife must go with me, of course."

"Do you take me for an idiot? She stays here, *of course*."

"As a hostage?"

"If you like the word. I prefer to say that you will be taking yourself into danger and my kind heart wants her to stay here where she will not be in danger. —There is no room for discussion. You are as much under arrest as Trevize is, and I am sure you understand I must act quickly—before the euphoria enveloping Terminus wears off. I fear my star will soon be in the descendant."

4.

Kodell said, "You were not easy on him, Madam Mayor."

The Mayor said with a sniff, "Why should I have been? He betrayed a friend."

"That was useful to us."

"Yes, as it happened. His next betrayal, however, might not be."

"Why should there be another?"

"Come, Liono," said Branno impatiently, "don't play games with me. Anyone who displays a capacity for double-dealing must forever be suspected of being capable of displaying it again."

"He may use the capability to combine with Trevize once again. Together, they may—"

"You don't believe that. With all his folly and naïveté,

Trevize goes straight for his goal. He does not understand betrayal and he will never, under any circumstances, trust Compor a second time."

Kodell said, "Pardon me, Mayor, but let me make sure I follow your thinking. How far, then, can *you* trust Compor? How do you know he will follow Trevize and report honestly? Do you count on his fears for the welfare of his wife as a restraint? His longing to return to her?"

"Both are factors, but I don't entirely rely on that. On Compor's ship there will be a hyper-relay. Trevize would suspect pursuit and would search for one. However Compor—being the pursuer—will, I assume, not suspect pursuit and will not search for one. —Of course, if he does, and if he finds it, then we must depend on the attractions of his wife."

Kodell laughed. "To think I once had to give you lessons. And the purpose of the pursuit?"

"A double layer of protection. If Trevize is caught, it may be that Compor will carry on and give us the information that Trevize will not be able to."

"One more question. What if, by some chance, Trevize finds the Second Foundation, and we learn of it through him, or through Compor, or if we gain reason to suspect its existence—despite the deaths of both?"

"I'm hoping the Second Foundation *does* exist, Liono," she said. "In any case, the Seldon Plan is not going to serve us much longer. The great Hari Seldon devised it in the dying days of the Empire, when technological advance had virtually stopped. Seldon was a product of his times, too, and however brilliant this semimythical science of psychohistory must have been, it could not rise out of its roots. It surely would not allow for *rapid* technological advance. The Foundation has been achieving that, especially in this last century. We have mass-detection devices of a kind undreamed of earlier, computers that can respond to thought, and—most of all—mental shielding. The Second Foundation cannot control us for much longer, if they can do so now. I want, in my final years in power, to be the one to start Terminus on a new path."

"And if there is, in fact, no Second Foundation?"

"Then we start on a new path at once."

5.

The troubled sleep that had finally come to Trevize did not last long. A touch on his shoulder was repeated a second time.

Trevize started up, bleary and utterly failing to understand why he should be in a strange bed. "What— What—?"

Pelorat said to him apologetically, "I'm sorry, Councilman Trevize. You are my guest and I owe you rest, but the Mayor is here." He was standing at the side of the bed in flannel pajamas and shivering slightly. Trevize's senses leaped to a weary wakefulness and he remembered.

The Mayor was in Pelorat's living room, looking as composed as always. Kodell was with her, rubbing lightly at his white mustache.

Trevize adjusted his sash to the proper snugness and wondered how long the two of them—Branno and Kodel—were ever apart.

Trevize said mockingly, "Has the Council recovered yet? Are its members concerned over the absence of one of them?"

The Mayor said, "There are signs of life, yes, but not enough to do you any good. There is no question but that I still have the power to force you to leave. You will be taken to Ultimate Spaceport—"

"Not Terminus Spaceport, Madam Mayor? Am I to be deprived of a proper farewell from weeping thousands?"

"I see you have recovered your penchant for teenage silliness, Councilman, and I am pleased. It stills what might otherwise be a certain rising twinge of conscience. At Ultimate Spaceport, you and Professor Pelorat will leave quietly."

"And never return?"

"And perhaps never return. Of course," and here she smiled briefly, "if you discover something of so great an importance and usefulness that even I will be glad to have you back with your information, you will return. You may even be treated with honor."

Trevize nodded casually, "That may happen."

"Almost anything *may* happen. —In any case, you will be comfortable. You are being assigned a recently completed pocket-cruiser, the *Far Star*, named for Hober Mallow's cruiser. One person can handle it, though it will hold as many as three with reasonable comfort."

Trevize was jolted out of his carefully assumed mood of light irony. "Fully armed?"

"Unarmed but otherwise fully equipped. Wherever you go, you will be citizens of the Foundation and there will always be a consul to whom you can turn, so you will not require arms. You will be able to draw on funds at need. —Not unlimited funds, I might add."

"You are generous."

"I know that, Councilman. But, Councilman, understand me. You are helping Professor Pelorat search for Earth. Whatever you *think* you are searching for, you are searching for *Earth*. All whom you meet must understand that. And always remember that the *Far Star* is *not* armed."

"I am searching for Earth," said Trevize. "I understand that perfectly."

"Then you will go now."

"Pardon me, but surely there is more to all of this than we have discussed. I have piloted ships in my time, but I have had no experience with a late-model pocket-cruiser. What if I cannot pilot it?"

"I am told that the *Far Star* is thoroughly computerized. —And before you ask, you don't have to know how to handle a late-model ship's computer. It will itself tell you anything you need to know. Is there anything else you need?"

Trevize looked down at himself ruefully. "A change of clothing."

"You will find them on board ship. Including those girdles you wear, or sashes, whichever they are called. The professor is also supplied with what he needs. Everything reasonable is already aboard, although I hasten to add that this does *not* include female companions."

"Too bad," said Trevize. "It would be pleasant, but then, I have no likely candidate at the moment, as it happens. Still, I presume the Galaxy is populous and that once away from here I may do as I please."

"With regard to companions? Suit yourself."

She rose heavily. "I will not take you to the spaceport," she said, "but there are those who will, and you must make no effort to do anything you are not told to do. I believe they will kill you if you make an effort to escape. The fact that I will not be with them will remove any inhibition."

Trevize said, "I will make no unauthorized effort, Madam Mayor, but one thing—"

"Yes?"

Trevize searched his mind rapidly and finally said with a smile that he very much hoped looked unforced, "The time may come, Madam Mayor, when you will *ask* me for an effort. I will then do as I choose, but I will remember the past two days."

Mayor Branno sighed. "Spare me the melodrama. If the time comes, it will come, but for now—I am *asking* for nothing."

4. SPACE

I.

The ship looked even more impressive than Trevize—with his memories of the time when the new cruiser-class had been glowingly publicized—had expected.

It was not the size that was impressive—for it was rather small. It was designed for maneuverability and speed, for totally gravitic engines, and most of all for advanced computerization. It didn't need size—size would have defeated its purpose.

It was a one-man device that could replace, with advantage, the older ships that required a crew of a dozen or more. With a second or even a third person to establish shifts of duty, one such ship could fight off a flotilla of much larger non-Foundation ships. In addition, it could outspeed and escape from any other ship in existence.

There was a sleekness about it—not a wasted line, not a superfluous curve inside or out. Every cubic meter of volume was used to its maximum, so as to leave a paradoxical aura of spaciousness within. Nothing the Mayor might have said about the importance of his mission could have impressed Trevize more than the ship with which he was asked to perform it.

Branno the Bronze, he thought with chagrin, had maneuvered him into a dangerous mission of the greatest significance. He might not have accepted with such determination had she not so arranged matters that he *wanted* to show her what he could do.

As for Pelorat, he was transported with wonder. "Would you believe," he said, placing a gentle finger on the hull before he had climbed inside, "that I've never been close to a spaceship?"

"I'll believe it, of course, if you say so, Professor, but how did you manage it?"

"I scarcely know, to be honest with you, dear fel—, I mean, my dear Trevize. I presume I was overly concerned with my research. When one's home has a really excellent computer capable of reaching other computers anywhere in the Galaxy, one scarcely needs to budge, you know. —Somehow I expected spaceships to be larger than this."

"This is a small model, but even so, it's much larger inside than any other ship of this size."

"How can that be? You are making fun of my ignorance."

"No, no. I'm serious. This is one of the first ships to be completely graviticized."

"What does that mean? —But please don't explain if it requires extensive physics. I will take your word, as you took mine yesterday in connection with the single species of humanity and the single world of origin."

"Let's try, Professor Pelorat. Through all the thousands of years of space flight, we've had chemical motors and ionic motors and hyperatomic motors, and all these things have been bulky. The old Imperial Navy had ships five hundred meters long with no more living space in them than would fit into a small apartment. Fortunately the Foundation has specialized in miniaturization through all the centuries of its existence, thanks to its lack of material resources. This ship is the culmination. It makes use of antigravity and the device that makes that possible takes up virtually no space and is actually included in the hull. If it weren't that we still need the hyperatomic—"

A Security guard approached. "You will have to get on, gentlemen!"

The sky was growing light, though sunrise was still half an hour off.

Trevize looked about. "Is my baggage loaded?"

"Yes, Councilman, you will find the ship fully equipped."

"With clothing, I suppose, that is not my size or to my taste."

The guard smiled, quite suddenly and almost boyishly. "I think it is," he said. "The Mayor had us working overtime these last thirty or forty hours and we've matched what you had closely. Money no object. Listen," he looked about, as though to make sure no one noticed his sudden fraternization, "you two are lucky. Best ship in the world. Fully equipped, except for armament. You're swimming in cream."

"Sour cream, possibly," said Trevize. "Well, Professor, are you ready?"

"With this I am," Pelorat said and held up a square wafer about twenty centimeters to the side and encased in a jacket of silvery plastic. Trevize was suddenly aware that Pelorat had been holding it since they had left his home, shifting it from hand to hand and never putting it down, even when they had stopped for a quick breakfast.

"What's that, Professor?"

"My library. It's indexed by subject matter and origin and I've gotten it all into *one* wafer. If you think this ship is a marvel, how about this wafer? A whole library! Everything I have collected! Wonderful! Wonderful!"

"Well," said Trevize, "we *are* swimming in cream."

2.

Trevize marveled at the inside of the ship. The utilization of space was ingenious. There was a storeroom, with supplies of food, clothing, films, and games. There was a gym, a parlor, and two nearly identical bedrooms.

"This one," said Trevize, "must be yours, Professor. At least, it contains an FX Reader."

"Good," said Pelorat with satisfaction. "What an ass I have been to avoid space flight as I have. I could live here, my dear Trevize, in utter satisfaction."

"Roomier than I expected," said Trevize with pleasure.

"And the engines are really in the hull, as you said?"

"The controlling devices are, at any rate. We don't have to store fuel or make use of it on the spot. We're making use of the fundamental energy store of the Universe, so that the fuel and the engines are all—out there." He gestured vaguely.

"Well, now that I think of it—what if something goes wrong?"

Trevize shrugged. "I've been trained in space navigation, but not on *these* ships. If something goes wrong with the gravitics, I'm afraid there's nothing I can do about it."

"But can you run this ship? Pilot it?"

"I'm wondering that myself."

Pelorat said, "Do you suppose this is an automated ship? Might we not merely be passengers? We might simply be expected to sit here."

"They have such things in the case of ferries between planets and space stations within a stellar system, but I never heard of automated hyperspace travel. At least, not so far. —Not so far."

He looked about again and there was a trickle of apprehension within him. Had that harridan Mayor managed to maneuver that far ahead of him? Had the Foundation automated interstellar travel, too, and was he going to be deposited on Trantor quite against his will, and with no more to say about it than any of the rest of the furniture aboard ship?

He said with a cheerful animation he didn't feel, "Professor, you sit down. The Mayor said this ship was completely computerized. If your room has the FX Reader, mine ought to have a computer in it. Make yourself comfortable and let me look around a bit on my own."

Pelorat looked instantly anxious. "Trevize, my dear chap— You're not getting off the ship, are you?"

"Not my plan at all, Professor. And if I tried, you can count on my being stopped. It is not the Mayor's intention to allow me off. All I'm planning to do is to learn what operates the *Far Star*." He smiled, "I won't desert you, Professor."

He was still smiling as he entered what he felt to be his own bedroom, but his face grew sober as he closed the door softly behind him. Surely there must be some means of communicating with a planet in the neighborhood of the ship. It was impossible to imagine a ship deliberately sealed off from its surroundings and, therefore, somewhere—perhaps in a wall recess—there would have to be a Reacher. He could use it to call the Mayor's office to ask about controls.

Carefully he inspected the walls, the headboard of the bed, and the neat, smooth furniture. If nothing turned up here, he would go through the rest of the ship.

He was about to turn away when his eye caught a glint of light on the smooth, light brown surface of the desk. A round circle of light, with neat lettering that read: COMPUTER INSTRUCTIONS.

Ah!

Nevertheless his heart beat rapidly. There were computers and computers, and there were programs that took a long time to master. Trevize had never made the mistake of underestimating his own intelligence, but, on the other hand, he was not a Grand Master. There were those who had a knack for using a computer, and those who had not—and Trevize knew very well into which class he fell.

In his hitch in the Foundation Navy, he had reached the rank of lieutenant and had, on occasion, been officer of the day and had had occasion to use the ship's computer. He had never been in sole charge of it, however, and he had never been expected to know anything more than the routine maneuvers being officer of the day required.

He remembered, with a sinking feeling, the volumes taken up by a fully described program in printout, and he could recall the behavior of Technical Sergeant Krasnet at the console of the ship's computer. He played it as though it were the most complex musical instrument in the Galaxy, and did it all with an air of nonchalance, as though he were bored at its simplicity—yet even he had had to consult the volumes at times, swearing at himself in embarrassment.

Hesitantly Trevize placed a finger on the circle of light and at once the light spread out to cover the desk top. On it were the outline of two hands: a right and a left. With a sudden, smooth movement, the desk top tilted to an angle of forty-five degrees.

Trevize took the seat before the desk. No words were necessary. It was clear what he was expected to do.

He placed his hands on the outlines on the desk, which were positioned for him to do so without strain. The desk top seemed soft, nearly velvety, where he touched it—and his hands sank in.

He stared at his hands with astonishment, for they had not sunk in at all. They were on the surface, his eyes told him. Yet to his sense of touch it was as though the desk surface had given way, and as though something were holding his hands softly and warmly.

Was that all?

Now what?

He looked about and then closed his eyes in response to a suggestion.

He had heard nothing. He had heard *nothing*!

But inside his brain, as though it were a vagrant thought of his own, there was the sentence, "Please close your eyes. Relax. We will make connection."

Through the hands?

Somehow Trevize had always assumed that if one were going to communicate by thought with a computer, it would be through a hood placed over the head and with electrodes against the eyes and skull.

The hands?

But why not the hands? Trevize found himself floating away, almost drowsy, but with no loss of mental acuity. Why not the hands?

The eyes were no more than sense organs. The brain was no more than a central switchboard, encased in bone and removed from the working surface of the body. It was the hands that were the working surface, the hands that felt and manipulated the Universe.

Human beings thought with their hands. It was their hands that were the answer of curiosity, that felt and pinched and turned and lifted and hefted. There were animals that had brains of respectable size, but they had no hands and that made all the difference.

And as he and the computer held hands, their thinking merged and it no longer mattered whether his eyes were open or closed. Opening them did not improve his vision nor did closing them dim it.

Either way, he saw the room with complete clarity—not just in the direction in which he was looking, but all around and above and below.

He saw every room in the spaceship and he saw outside as well. The sun had risen and its brightness was dimmed in the morning mist, but he could look at it directly without being dazzled, for the computer automatically filtered the light waves.

He felt the gentle wind and its temperature, and the sounds of the world about him. He detected the planet's magnetic field and the tiny electrical charges on the wall of the ship.

He became aware of the controls of the ship, without even knowing what they were in detail. He knew only that if he wanted to lift the ship, or turn it, or accelerate it, or make use of any of its abilities, the process was the same as that of performing the analogous process to his body. He had but to use his will.

Yet his will was not unalloyed. The computer itself could override. At the present moment, there was a formed sentence in his head and he knew exactly when and how the ship would take off. There was no flexibility where *that* was concerned. Thereafter, he knew just as surely, he would himself be able to decide.

He found—as he cast the net of his computer-enhanced consciousness outward—that he could sense the condition of the upper atmosphere; that he could see the weather patterns; that he could detect the other ships that were swarming upward and the others that were settling downward. All of this had to be taken into account and the computer *was* taking it into account. If the computer had not been doing so, Trevize realized, he need only desire the computer to do so—and it would be done.

So much for the volumes of programming; there were none. Trevize thought of Technical Sergeant Krasnet and smiled. He had read often enough of the immense revolution that gravitics would make in the world, but the fusion of computer and mind was still a state secret. It would surely produce a still greater revolution.

He was aware of time passing. He knew exactly what time it was by Terminus Local and by Galactic Standard.

How did he let go?

And even as the thought entered his mind, his hands were released and the desk top moved back to its original position—and Trevize was left with his own unaided senses.

He felt blind and helpless as though, for a time, he had been held and protected by a superbeing and now was abandoned. Had he not known that he could make contact again at any time, the feeling might have reduced him to tears.

As it was he merely struggled for re-orientation, for adjustment to limits, then rose uncertainly to his feet and walked out of the room.

Pelorat looked up. He had adjusted his Reader, obviously, and he said, "It works very well. It has an excellent Search Program. —Did you find the controls, my boy?"

"Yes, Professor. All is well."

"In that case, shouldn't we do something about takeoff? I mean, self-protection? Aren't we supposed to strap ourselves in or something? I looked about for instructions, but I didn't find anything and that made me nervous. I had to turn to my library. Somehow when I am at my work—"

Trevize had been pushing his hands at the professor as though to dam and stop the flood of words. Now he had to speak loudly in order to override him. "None of that is necessary, Professor. Antigravity is the equivalent of non-inertia. There is no feeling of acceleration when velocity changes, since everything on the ship undergoes the change simultaneously."

"You mean, we won't know when we are off the planet and out in space?"

"It's exactly what I mean, because even as I speak to you, we have taken off. We will be cutting through the upper atmosphere in a very few minutes and within half an hour we will be in outer space."

3.

Pelorat seemed to shrink a little as he stared at Trevize. His long rectangle of a face grew so blank that, without showing any emotion at all, it radiated a vast uneasiness.

Then his eyes shifted right—left.

Trevize remembered how he had felt on his own first trip beyond the atmosphere.

He said, in as matter-of-fact a manner as he could, "Janov," (it was the first time he had addressed the professor familiarly, but in this case experience was addressing inexperience and it was necessary to seem the older of the two) "we are perfectly safe here. We are in the metal womb of a warship of the Foundation Navy. We are not fully armed, but there is no place in the Galaxy where the name of the Foundation will not protect us. Even if some ship went mad and attacked, we could move out of its reach in a moment. And I assure you I have discovered that I can handle the ship perfectly."

Pelorat said, "It is the thought, Go—Golan, of nothingness—"

"Why, there's nothingness all about Terminus. There's just a thin layer of very tenuous air between ourselves on the surface and the nothingness just above. All we're doing is to go past that inconsequential layer."

"It may be inconsequential, but we breathe it."

"We breathe here, too. The air on this ship is cleaner

and purer, and will indefinitely remain cleaner and purer
than the natural atmosphere of Terminus."

"And the meteorites?"

"What about meteorites?"

"The atmosphere protects us from meteorites. Radiation,
too, for that matter."

Trevize said, "Humanity has been traveling through space
for twenty millennia, I believe—"

"Twenty-two. If we go by the Hallblockian chronology,
it is quite plain that, counting the—"

"Enough! Have you heard of meteorite accidents or of
radiation deaths? —I mean, recently? —I mean, in the case
of Foundation ships?"

"I have not really followed the news in such matters, but
I am a historian, my boy, and—"

"Historically, yes, there have been such things, but technology improves. There isn't a meteorite large enough to
damage us that can possibly approach us before we take the
necessary evasive action. Four meteorites—coming at us
simultaneously from the four directions drawn from the
vertices of a tetrahedron—might conceivably pin us down,
but calculate the chances of that and you'll find that you'll
die of old age a trillion trillion times over before you will
have a fifty-fifty chance of observing so interesting a phenomenon."

"You mean, if you were at the computer?"

"No," said Trevize in scorn. "If I were running the computer on the basis of my own senses and responses, we
would be hit before I ever knew what was happening. It is
the computer itself that is at work, responding millions of
times faster than you or I could." He held out his hand
abruptly. "Janov, come let me show you what the computer
can do, and let me show you what space is like."

Pelorat stared, goggling a bit. Then he laughed briefly.
"I'm not sure I wish to know, Golan."

"Of course you're not sure, Janov, because you don't
know what it is that is waiting there to be known. Chance
it! Come! Into my room!"

Trevize held the other's hand, half leading him, half drawing him. He said, as he sat down at the computer, "Have you ever seen the Galaxy, Janov? Have you ever looked at it?"

Pelorat said, "You mean in the sky?"

"Yes, certainly. Where else?"

"I've seen it. Everyone has seen it. If one looks up, one sees it."

"Have you ever stared at it on a dark, clear night, when the Diamonds are below the horizon?"

The "Diamonds" referred to those few stars that were luminous enough and close enough to shine with moderate brightness in the night sky of Terminus. They were a small group that spanned a width of no more than twenty degrees, and for large parts of the night they were all below the horizon. Aside from the group, there was a scattering of dim stars just barely visible to the unaided eye. There was nothing more but the faint milkiness of the Galaxy—the view one might expect when one dwelt on a world like Terminus which was at the extreme edge of the outermost spiral of the Galaxy.

"I suppose so, but why stare? It's a common sight."

"Of course it's a common sight," said Trevize. "That's why no one sees it. Why see it if you can always see it? But now you'll *see* it, and not from Terminus, where the mist and the clouds are forever interfering. You'll see it as you'd never see it from Terminus—no matter how you stared, and no matter how clear and dark the night. How I wish *I* had never been in space before, so that—like you— I could see the Galaxy in its bare beauty for the first time."

He pushed a chair in Pelorat's direction. "Sit there, Janov. This may take a little time. I have to continue to grow accustomed to the computer. From what I've already felt, I know the viewing is holographic, so we won't need a screen of any sort. It makes direct contact with my brain, but I think I can have it produce an objective image that you will see, too. —Put out the light, will you? —No, that's foolish of me. I'll have the computer do it. Stay where you are."

Trevize made contact with the computer, holding hands warmly and intimately.

The light dimmed, then went out completely, and in the darkness, Pelorat stirred.

Trevize said, "Don't get nervous, Janov. I may have a little trouble trying to control the computer, but I'll start easy and you'll have to be patient with me. Do you see it? The crescent?"

It hung in the darkness before them. A little dim and wavering at first, but getting sharper and brighter.

Pelorat's voice sounded awed. "Is that Terminus? Are we that far from it?"

"Yes, the ship's moving quickly."

The ship was curving into the night shadow of Terminus, which appeared as a thick crescent of bright light. Trevize had a momentary urge to send the ship in a wide arc that would carry them over the daylit side of the planet to show it in all its beauty, but he held back.

Pelorat might find novelty in this, but the beauty would be tame. There were too many photographs, too many maps, too many globes. Every child knew what Terminus looked like. A water planet—more so than most—rich in water and poor in minerals, good in agriculture and poor in heavy industry, but the best in the Galaxy in high technology and in miniaturization.

If he could have the computer use microwaves and translate it into a visible model, they would see every one of Terminus's ten thousand inhabited islands, together with the only one of them large enough to be considered a continent, the one that bore Terminus City and—

Turn away!

It was just a thought, an exercise of the will, but the view shifted at once. The lighted crescent moved off toward the borders of vision and rolled off the edge. The darkness of starless space filled his eyes.

Pelorat cleared his throat. "I wish you would bring back

Terminus, my boy. I feel as though I've been blinded."
There was a tightness in his voice.

"You're not blind. Look!"

Into the field of vision came a filmy fog of pale trans-
lucence. It spread and became brighter, until the whole room
seemed to glow.

Shrink!

Another exercise of will and the Galaxy drew off, as
though seen through a diminishing telescope that was steadily growing more powerful in its ability to diminish. The
Galaxy contracted and became a structure of varying luminosity.

Brighten!

It grew more luminous without changing size, and because the stellar system to which Terminus belonged was
above the Galactic plane, the Galaxy was not seen exactly
edge-on. It was a strongly foreshortened double spiral, with
curving dark-nebula rifts streaking the glowing edge of the
Terminus side. The creamy haze of the nucleus—far off
and shrunken by the distance—looked unimportant.

Pelorat said in an awed whisper, "You are right. I have
never seen it like this. I never dreamed it had so much
detail."

"How could you? You can't see the outer half when
Terminus's atmosphere is between you and it. You can
hardly see the nucleus from Terminus's surface."

"What a pity we're seeing it so nearly head-on."

"We don't have to. The computer can show it in any
orientation. I just have to express the wish—and not even
aloud."

Shift co-ordinates!

This exercise of will was by no means a precise command. Yet as the image of Galaxy began to undergo a slow
change, his mind guided the computer and had it do what
he wished.

Slowly the Galaxy was turning so that it could be seen
at right angles to the Galactic plane. It spread out like a

gigantic, glowing whirlpool, with curves of darkness, and knots of brightness, and a central all-but-featureless blaze.

Pelorat asked, "How can the computer see it from a position in space that must be more than fifty thousand parsecs from this place?" Then he added, in a choked whisper, "Please forgive me that I ask. I know nothing about all this."

Trevize said, "I know almost as little about this computer as you do. Even a simple computer, however, can adjust co-ordinates and show the Galaxy in any position, starting with what it can sense in the natural position, the one, that is, that would appear from the computer's local position in space. Of course, it makes use only of the information it can sense to begin with, so when it changes to the broadside view we would find gaps and blurs in what it would show. In this case, though—"

"Yes?"

"We have an excellent view. I suspect that the computer is outfitted with a complete map of the Galaxy and can therefore view it from any angle with equal ease."

"How do you mean, a complete map?"

"The spatial co-ordinates of every star in it must be in the computer's memory banks."

"*Every* star?" Pelorat seemed awed.

"Well, perhaps not all three hundred billion. It would include the stars shining down on populated planets, certainly, and probably every star of spectral class K and brighter. That means about seventy-five billion, at least."

"*Every* star of a populated system?"

"I wouldn't want to be pinned down; perhaps not all. There were, after all, twenty-five million inhabited systems in the time of Hari Seldon—which sounds like a lot but is only one star out of every twelve thousand. And then, in the five centuries since Seldon, the general breakup of the Empire didn't prevent further colonization. I should think it would have encouraged it. There are still plenty of habitable planets to expand into, so there may be thirty million now. It's possible that not all the new ones are in the Foundation's records."

"But the old ones? Surely they must all be there without exception."

"I imagine so. I can't guarantee it, of course, but I would be surprised if any long-established inhabited system were missing from the records. Let me show you something— if my ability to control the computer will go far enough."

Trevize's hands stiffened a bit with the effort and they seemed to sink further into the clasp of the computer. That might not have been necessary; he might only have had to think quietly and casually: Terminus!

He did think that and there was, in response, a sparkling red diamond at the very edge of the whirlpool.

"There's our sun," he said with excitement. "That's the star that Terminus circles."

"Ah," said Pelorat with a low, tremulous sigh.

A bright yellow dot of light sprang into life in a rich cluster of stars deep in the heart of the Galaxy but well to one side of the central haze. It was rather closer to the Terminus edge of the Galaxy than to the other side.

"And that," said Trevize, "is Trantor's sun."

Another sigh, then Pelorat said, "Are you sure? They always speak of Trantor as being located in the center of the Galaxy."

"It is, in a way. It's as close to the center as a planet can get and still be habitable. It's closer than any other major populated system. The actual center of the Galaxy consists of a black hole with a mass of nearly a million stars, so that the center is a violent place. As far as we know, there is no life in the actual center and maybe there just can't be any life there. Trantor is in the innermost subring of the spiral arms and, believe me, if you could see its night sky, you would think it was in the center of the Galaxy. It's surrounded by an extremely rich clustering of stars."

"Have you been on Trantor, Golan?" asked Pelorat in clear envy.

"Actually no, but I've seen holographic representations of its sky."

Trevize stared at the Galaxy somberly. In the great search for the Second Foundation during the time of the Mule, how everyone had played with Galactic maps—and how many volumes had been written and filmed on the subject.

And all because Hari Seldon had said, at the beginning, that the Second Foundation would be established "at the other end of the Galaxy," calling the place "Star's End."

At the other end of the Galaxy! Even as Trevize thought it, a thin blue line sprang into view, stretching from Terminus, through the Galaxy's central black hole, to the other end. Trevize nearly jumped. He had not directly ordered the line, but he had thought of it quite clearly and that had been enough for the computer.

But, of course, the straight-line route to the opposite side of the Galaxy was not necessarily an indication of the "other end" that Seldon had spoken of. It was Arkady Darell (if one could believe her autobiography) who had made use of the phrase "a circle has no end" to indicate what everyone now accepted as truth—

And though Trevize suddenly tried to suppress the thought, the computer was too quick for him. The blue line vanished and was replaced with a circle that neatly rimmed the Galaxy in blue and that passed through the deep red dot of Terminus's sun.

A circle has no end, and if the circle began at Terminus, then if we searched for the other end, it would merely return to Terminus, and there the Second Foundation had indeed been found, inhabiting the same world as the First.

But if, in reality, it had not been found—if the so-called finding of the Second Foundation had been an illusion— what then? What beside a straight line and a circle would make sense in this connection?

Pelorat said, "Are you creating illusions? Why is there a blue circle?"

"I was just testing my controls. —Would you like to locate Earth?"

There was silence for a moment or two, then Pelorat said, "Are you joking?"

"No. I'll try."

He did. Nothing happened.

"Sorry," said Trevize.

"It's not there? No Earth?"

"I suppose I might have misthought my command, but that doesn't seem likely. I suppose it's more likely that Earth isn't listed in the computer's vitals."

Pelorat said, "It may be listed under another name."

Trevize jumped at that quickly, "What other name, Janov?"

Pelorat said nothing and, in the darkness, Trevize smiled. It occurred to him that things might just possibly be falling into place. Let it go for a while. Let it ripen. He deliberately changed the subject and said, "I wonder if we can manipulate time."

"Time! How can we do that?"

"The Galaxy is rotating. It takes nearly half a billion years for Terminus to move about the grand circumference of the Galaxy once. Stars that are closer to the center complete the journey much more quickly, of course. The motion of each star, relative to the central black hole, might be recorded in the computer and, if so, it may be possible to have the computer multiply each motion by millions of times and make the rotational effect visible. I can try to have it done."

He did and he could not help his muscles tightening with the effort of will he was exerting—as though he were taking hold of the Galaxy and accelerating it, twisting it, forcing it to spin against terrible resistance.

The Galaxy was moving. Slowly, mightily, it was twisting in the direction that should be working to tighten the spiral arms.

Time was passing incredibly rapidly as they watched—a false, artificial time—and, as it did so, stars became evanescent things.

Some of the larger ones—here and there—reddened and

grew brighter as they expanded into red giants. And then a star in the central clusters blew up soundlessly in a blinding blaze that, for a tiny fraction of a second, dimmed the Galaxy and then was gone. Then another in one of the spiral arms, then still another not very far away from it.

"Supernovas," said Trevize a little shakily.

Was it possible that the computer could predict exactly which stars would explode and when? Or was it just using a simplified model that served to show the starry future in general terms, rather than precisely?

Pelorat said in a husky whisper, "The Galaxy looks like a living thing, crawling through space."

"It does," said Trevize, "but I'm growing tired. Unless I learn to do this less tensely, I'm not going to be able to play this kind of game for long."

He let go. The Galaxy slowed, then halted, then tilted, until it was in the view-from-the-side from which they had seen it at the start.

Trevize closed his eyes and breathed deeply. He was aware of Terminus shrinking behind them, with the last perceptible wisps of atmosphere gone from their surroundings. He was aware of all the ships filling Terminus's near-space.

It did not occur to him to check whether there was anything special about any one of those ships. Was there one that was gravitic like his own and matched his trajectory more closely than chance would allow?

5. SPEAKER

I.

Trantor!

For eight thousand years, it was the capital of a large and mighty political entity that spanned an ever-growing union of planetary systems. For twelve thousand years after that, it was the capital of a political entity that spanned the entire Galaxy. It was the center, the heart, the *epitome* of the Galactic Empire.

It was impossible to think of the Empire without thinking of Trantor.

Trantor did not reach its physical peak until the Empire was far gone in decay. In fact, no one noticed that the Empire had lost its drive, its forward look, because Trantor gleamed in shining metal.

Its growth had peaked at the point where it was a planet-girdling city. Its population was stabilized (by law) at forty-five billion and the only surface greenery was at the Imperial Palace and the Galactic University/Library complex.

Trantor's land surface was metal-coated. Its deserts and its fertile areas were alike engulfed and made into warrens of humanity, administrative jungles, computerized elaborations, vast storehouses of food and replacement parts. Its mountain ranges were beaten down; its chasms filled in. The city's endless corridors burrowed under the continental shelves and the oceans were turned into huge underground aquacultural cisterns—the only (and insufficient) native source of food and minerals.

The connections with the Outer Worlds, from which Trantor obtained the resources it required, depended upon its thousand spaceports, its ten thousand warships, its hundred thousand merchant ships, its million space freighters.

No city so vast was ever recycled so tightly. No planet in the Galaxy had ever made so much use of solar power or went to such extremes to rid itself of waste heat. Glittering radiators stretched up into the thin upper atmosphere upon the nightside and were withdrawn into the metal city on the dayside. As the planet turned, the radiators rose as night progressively fell around the world and sank as day progressively broke. So Trantor always had an artificial asymmetry that was almost its symbol.

At this peak, Trantor ran the Empire!

It ran it poorly, but nothing could have run the Empire well. The Empire was too large to be run from a single world—even under the most dynamic of Emperors. How could Trantor have helped but run it poorly when, in the ages of decay, the Imperial crown was traded back and forth by sly politicians and foolish incompetents and the bureaucracy had become a subculture of corruptibles?

But even at its worst, there was some self-propelled worth to the machinery. The Galactic Empire could not have been run without Trantor.

The Empire crumbled steadily, but as long as Trantor remained Trantor, a core of the Empire remained and it retained an air of pride, of millennia, of tradition and power and—exaltation.

Only when the unthinkable happened—when Trantor finally fell and was sacked; when its citizens were killed by the millions and left to starve by the billions; when its mighty metal coating was scarred and punctured and fused by the attack of the "barbarian" fleet—only then was the Empire *considered* to have fallen. The surviving remnants on the once-great world undid further what had been left and, in a generation, Trantor was transformed from the greatest planet the human race had ever seen to an inconceivable tangle of ruins.

That had been nearly two and a half centuries ago. In the rest of the Galaxy, Trantor-as-it-had-been still was not forgotten. It would live forever as the favored site of historical novels, the favored symbol and memory of the past, the favored word for sayings such as "All starships land on Trantor," "Like looking for a person in Trantor," and "No more alike than this and Trantor."

In all the rest of the Galaxy—

But that was not true on Trantor itself! Here the old Trantor was forgotten. The surface metal was gone, almost everywhere. Trantor was now a sparsely settled world of self-sufficient farmers, a place where trading ships rarely came and were not particularly welcome when they did come. The very word "Trantor," though still in official use, had dropped out of popular speech. By present-day Trantorians, it was called "Hame," which in their dialect was what would be called "Home" in Galactic Standard.

Quindor Shandess thought of all this and much more as he sat quietly in a welcome state of half-drowse, in which he could allow his mind to run along a self-propelled and unorganized stream of thought.

He had been First Speaker of the Second Foundation for eighteen years, and he might well hold on for ten or twelve years more if his mind remained reasonably vigorous and if he could continue to fight the political wars.

He was the analog, the mirror image, of the Mayor of Terminus, who ruled over the First Foundation, but how different they were in every respect. The Mayor of Terminus was known to all the Galaxy and the First Foundation was therefore simply "the Foundation" to all the worlds. The First Speaker of the Second Foundation was known only to his associates.

And yet it was the Second Foundation, under himself and his predecessors, who held the real power. The First Foundation was supreme in the realm of physical power, of technology, of war weapons. The Second Foundation was supreme in the realm of mental power, of the mind, of the ability to control. In any conflict between the two, what would it matter how many ships and weapons the First Foundation disposed of, if the Second Foundation could control the minds of those who controlled the ships and weapons?

But how long could he revel in this realization of secret power?

He was the twenty-fifth First Speaker and his incumbency was already a shade longer than average. Ought he, perhaps, not be too keen on holding on and keeping out the younger aspirants? There was Speaker Gendibal, the keenest and newest at the Table. Tonight they would spend time together and Shandess looked forward to it. Ought he look forward also to Gendibal's possible accession some day?

The answer to the question was that Shandess had no real thought of leaving his post. He enjoyed it too much.

He sat there, in his old age, still perfectly capable of performing his duties. His hair was gray, but it had always been light in color and he wore it cut an inch long so that the color scarcely mattered. His eyes were a faded blue and his clothing conformed to the drab styling of the Trantorian farmers.

The First Speaker could, if he wished, pass among the Hamish people as one of them, but his hidden power nevertheless existed. He could choose to focus his eyes and mind at any time and they would then act according to his will and recall nothing about it afterward.

It rarely happened. Almost never. The Golden Rule of the Second Foundation was, "Do nothing unless you must, and when you must act—hesitate."

The First Speaker sighed softly. Living in the old University, with the brooding grandeur of the ruins of the Imperial Palace not too far distant, made one wonder on occasion how Golden the Rule might be.

In the days of the Great Sack, the Golden Rule had been strained to the breaking point. There was no way of saving Trantor without sacrificing the Seldon Plan for establishing a Second Empire. It would have been humane to spare the forty-five billion, but they could not have been spared without retention of the core of the First Empire and that would have only delayed the reckoning. It would have led to a greater destruction some centuries later and perhaps no Second Empire ever—

The early First Speakers had worked over the clearly

foreseen Sack for decades but had found no solution—no way of assuring both the salvation of Trantor and the eventual establishment of the Second Empire. The lesser evil had to be chosen and Trantor had died!

The Second Foundationers of the time had managed—by the narrowest of margins—to save the University/Library complex and there had been guilt forever after because of that, too. Though no one had ever demonstrated that saving the complex had led to the meteoric rise of the Mule, there was always the intuition that there was a connection.

How nearly that had wrecked everything!

Yet following the decades of the Sack and the Mule came the Golden Age of the Second Foundation.

Prior to that, for over two and a half centuries after Seldon's death, the Second Foundation had burrowed like moles into the Library, intent only on staying out of the way of the Imperials. They served as librarians in a decaying society that cared less and less for the ever-more-misnamed Galactic Library, which fell into the desuetude that best suited the purpose of the Second Foundation.

It was an ignoble life. They merely conserved the Plan, while out at the end of the Galaxy, the First Foundation fought for its life against always greater enemies with neither help from the Second Foundation nor any real knowledge of it.

It was the Great Sack that liberated the Second Foundation—another reason (young Gendibal—who had courage—had recently said that it was the chief reason) why the Sack was allowed to proceed.

After the Great Sack, the Empire was gone and, in all the later times, the Trantorian survivors never trespassed on Second Foundation territory uninvited. The Second Foundationers saw to it that the University/Library complex which had survived the Sack also survived the Great Renewal. The ruins of the Palace were preserved, too. The metal was gone over almost all the rest of the world. The great and endless corridors were covered up, filled in, twisted, destroyed, ignored; all under rock and soil—all except here, where metal still surrounded the ancient open places.

It might be viewed as a grand memorial of greatness, the sepulcher of Empire, but to the Trantorians—the Hamish people—these were haunted places, filled with ghosts, not to be stirred. Only the Second Foundationers ever set foot in the ancient corridors or touched the titanium gleam.

And even so, all had nearly come to nothing because of the Mule.

The Mule had actually been on Trantor. What if he had found out the nature of the world he had been standing on? His physical weapons were far greater than those at the disposal of the Second Foundation, his mental weapons almost as great. The Second Foundation would have been hampered always by the necessity of doing nothing but what they must, and by the knowledge that almost any hope of winning the immediate fight might portend a greater eventual loss.

Had it not been for Bayta Darell and her swift moment of action— And that, too, had been without the help of the Second Foundation!

And then—the Golden Age, when somehow the First Speakers of the time found ways of becoming active, stopping the Mule in his career of conquest, controlling his mind at last; and then stopping the First Foundation itself when *it* grew wary and overcurious concerning the nature and identity of the Second Foundation. There was Preem Palver, nineteenth First Speaker and greatest of them all, who had managed to put an end to all danger—not without terrible sacrifice—and who had rescued the Seldon Plan.

Now, for a hundred and twenty years, the Second Foundation was again as it once had been, hiding in a haunted portion of Trantor. They were hiding no longer from the Imperials, but from the First Foundation still—a First Foundation almost as large as the Galactic Empire had been and even greater in technological expertise.

The First Speaker's eyes closed in the pleasant warmth and he passed into that never-never state of relaxing hallucinatory experiences that were not quite dreams and not quite conscious thought.

Enough of gloom. All would be well. Trantor was *still* capital of the Galaxy, for the Second Foundation was here and it was mightier and more in control than ever the Emperor had been.

The First Foundation would be contained and guided and would move correctly. However formidable their ships and weapons, they could do nothing as long as key leaders could be, at need, mentally controlled.

And the Second Empire would come, but it would not be like the first. It would be a Federated Empire, with its parts possessing considerable self-rule, so that there would be none of the apparent strength and actual weakness of a unitary, centralized government. The new Empire would be looser, more pliant, more flexible, more capable of withstanding strain, and it would be guided always—always— by the hidden men and women of the Second Foundation. Trantor would then be still the capital, more powerful with its forty thousand psychohistorians than ever it had been with its forty-five billion—

The First Speaker snapped awake. The sun was lower in the sky. Had he been mumbling? Had he said anything aloud?

If the Second Foundation had to know much and say little, the ruling Speakers had to know more and say less, and the First Speaker had to know most and say least.

He smiled wryly. It was always so tempting to become a Trantorian patriot—to see the whole purpose of the Second Empire as that of bringing about Trantorian hegemony. Seldon had warned of it; he had foreseen even that, five centuries before it could come to pass.

The First Speaker had not slept too long, however. It was not yet time for Gendibal's audience.

Shandess was looking forward to that private meeting. Gendibal was young enough to look at the Plan with new eyes, and keen enough to see what others might not. And it was not beyond possibility that Shandess would learn from what the youngest had to say.

No one would ever be certain how much Preem Palver—

the great Palver himself—had profited from that day when the young Kol Benjoam, not yet thirty, came to talk to him about possible ways of handling the First Foundation. Benjoam, who was later recognized as the greatest theorist since Seldon, never spoke of that audience in later years, but eventually he became the twenty-first First Speaker. There were some who credited Benjoam, rather than Palver, for the great accomplishments of Palver's administration.

Shandess amused himself with the thought of what Gendibal might say. It was traditional that keen youngsters, confronting the First Speaker alone for the first time, would place their entire thesis in the first sentence. And surely they would not ask for that precious first audience for something trivial—something that might ruin their entire subsequent career by convincing the First Speaker they were lightweights.

Four hours later, Gendibal faced him. The young man showed no sign of nervousness. He waited calmly for Shandess to speak first.

Shandess said, "You have asked for a private audience, Speaker, on a matter of importance. Could you please summarize the matter for me?"

And Gendibal, speaking quietly, almost as though he were describing what he had just eaten at dinner, said, "First Speaker, the Seldon Plan is meaningless!"

2.

Stor Gendibal did not require the evidence of others to give him a sense of worth. He could not recall a time when he did not know himself to be unusual. He had been recruited for the Second Foundation when he was only a ten-year-old boy by an agent who had recognized the potentiality of his mind.

He had then done remarkably well at his studies and had taken to psychohistory as a spaceship responds to a gravitational field. Psychohistory had pulled at him and he had curved toward it, reading Seldon's text on the fundamentals when others his age were merely trying to handle differential equations.

When he was fifteen, he entered Trantor's Galactic University (as the University of Trantor had been officially renamed), after an interview during which, when asked what his ambitions were, he had answered firmly, "To be First Speaker before I am forty."

He had not bothered to aim for the First Speaker's chair without qualification. To gain it, one way or another, seemed to him to be a certainty. It was to do it in youth that seemed to him to be the goal. Even Preem Palver had been forty-two on his accession.

The interviewer's expression had flickered when Gendibal had said that, but the young man already had the feel of psycholanguage and could interpret that flicker. He knew, as certainly as though the interviewer had announced it, that a small notation would go on his records to the effect that he would be difficult to handle.

Well, of course!

Gendibal intended to be difficult to handle.

He was thirty now. He would be thirty-one in a matter of two months and he was already a member of the Council of Speakers. He had nine years, at most, to become First Speaker and he knew he would make it. This audience with the present First Speaker was crucial to his plans and, laboring to present precisely the proper impression, he had spared no effort to polish his command of psycholanguage.

When two Speakers of the Second Foundation communicate with each other, the language is like no other in the Galaxy. It is as much a language of fleeting gestures as of words, as much a matter of detected mental-change patterns as anything else.

An outsider would hear little or nothing, but in a short time, much in the way of thought would be exchanged and the communication would be unreportable in its literal form to anyone but still another Speaker.

The language of Speakers had its advantage in speed and

in infinite delicacy, but it had the disadvantage of making it almost impossible to mask true opinion.

Gendibal knew his own opinion of the First Speaker. He felt the First Speaker to be a man past his mental prime. The First Speaker—in Gendibal's assessment—expected no crisis, was not trained to meet one, and lacked the sharpness to deal with one if it appeared. With all Shandess's goodwill and amiability, he was the stuff of which disaster was made.

All of this Gendibal had to hide not merely from words, gestures, and facial expressions, but even from his thoughts. He knew no way of doing so efficiently enough to keep the First Speaker from catching a whiff of it.

Nor could Gendibal avoid knowing something of the First Speaker's feeling toward him. Through bonhomie and goodwill—quite apparent and reasonably sincere—Gendibal could feel the distant edge of condescension and amusement, and tightened his own mental grip to avoid revealing any resentment in return—or as little as possible.

The First Speaker smiled and leaned back in his chair. He did not actually lift his feet to the desk top, but he got across just the right mixture of self-assured ease and informal friendship—just enough of each to leave Gendibal uncertain as to the effect of his statement.

Since Gendibal had not been invited to sit down, the actions and attitudes available to him that might be designed to minimize the uncertainty were limited. It was impossible that the First Speaker did not understand this.

Shandess said, "The Seldon Plan is meaningless? What a remarkable statement! Have you looked at the Prime Radiant lately, Speaker Gendibal?"

"I study it frequently, First Speaker. It is my duty to do so and my pleasure as well."

"Do you, by any chance, study only those portions of it that fall under your purview, now and then? Do you observe it in microfashion—an equation system here, an adjustment rivulet there? Highly important, of course, but I have always thought it an excellent occasional exercise to observe the whole course. Studying the Prime Radiant, acre by acre, has its uses—but observing it as a continent is inspirational. To tell you the truth, Speaker, I have not done it for a long time myself. Would you join me?"

Gendibal dared not pause too long. It had to be done, and it must be done easily and pleasantly or it might as well not be done. "It would be an honor and a pleasure, First Speaker."

The First Speaker depressed a lever on the side of his desk. There was one such in the office of every Speaker and the one in Gendibal's office was in no way inferior to that of the First Speaker. The Second Foundation was an equalitarian society in all its surface manifestations—the unimportant ones. In fact, the only *official* prerogative of the First Speaker was that which was explicit in his title—he always spoke first.

The room grew dark with the depression of the lever but, almost at once, the darkness lifted into a pearly dimness. Both long walls turned faintly creamy, then brighter and whiter, and finally there appeared neatly printed equations—so small that they could not be easily read.

"If you have no objections," said the First Speaker, making it quite clear that there would be none allowed, "we will reduce the magnification in order to see as much at one time as we can."

The neat printing shrank down into fine hairlines, faint black meanderings over the pearly background.

The First Speaker touched the keys of the small console built into the arm of his chair. "We'll bring it back to the start—to the lifetime of Hari Seldon—and we'll adjust it to a small forward movement. We'll shutter it so that we can only see a decade of development at a time. It gives one a wonderful feeling of the flow of history, with no distractions by the details. I wonder if you have ever done this."

"Never exactly this way, First Speaker."

"You should. It's a marvelous feeling. Observe the sparseness of the black tracery at the start. There was not much chance for alternatives in the first few decades. The branch points, however, increase exponentially with time.

Were it not for the fact that, as soon as a particular branch is taken, there is an extinction of a vast array of others in its future, all would soon become unmanageable. Of course, in dealing with the future, we must be careful what extinctions we rely upon."

"I know, First Speaker." There was a touch of dryness in Gendibal's response that he could not quite remove.

The First Speaker did not respond to it. "Notice the winding lines of symbols in red. There is a pattern to them. To all appearances, they should exist randomly, as every Speaker earns his place by adding refinements to Seldon's original Plan. It would seem there is no way, after all, of predicting where a refinement can be added easily or where a particular Speaker will find his interests or his ability tending, and yet I have long suspected that the admixture of Seldon Black and Speaker Red follows a strict law that is strongly dependent on time and on very little else."

Gendibal watched as the years passed and as the black and red hairlines made an almost hypnotic interlacing pattern. The pattern meant nothing in itself, of course. What counted were the symbols of which it was composed.

Here and there a bright-blue rivulet made its appearance, bellying out, branching, and becoming prominent, then falling in upon itself and fading into the black or red.

The First Speaker said, "Deviation Blue," and the feeling of distaste, originating in each, filled the space between them. "We catch it over and over, and we'll be coming to the Century of Deviations eventually."

They did. One could tell precisely when the shattering phenomenon of the Mule momentarily filled the Galaxy, as the Prime Radiant suddenly grew thick with branching rivulets of blue——more starting than could be closed down —until the room itself seemed to turn blue as the lines thickened and marked the wall with brighter and brighter pollution. (It was the only word.)

It reached its peak and then faded, thinned, and came together for a long century before it trickled to its end at last. When it was gone, and when the Plan had returned to black and red, it was clear that Preem Palver's hand had been there.

Onward, onward—

"That's the present," said the First Speaker comfortably.

Onward, onward—

Then a narrowing into a veritable knot of close-knit black with little red in it.

"That's the establishment of the Second Empire," said the First Speaker.

He shut off the Prime Radiant and the room was bathed in ordinary light.

Gendibal said, "That was an emotional experience."

"Yes," smiled the First Speaker, "and you are careful not to identify the emotion, as far as you can manage to fail to identify it. It doesn't matter. Let me make the points I wish to make.

"You will notice, first, the all-but-complete absence of Deviation Blue after the time of Preem Palver—over the last twelve decades, in other words. You will notice that there are no reasonable probabilities of Deviations above the fifth-class over the next five centuries. You will notice, too, that we have begun extending the refinements of psychohistory beyond the establishment of the Second Empire. As you undoubtedly know, Hari Seldon—although a transcendent genius—is not, and could not, be all-knowing. We have improved on him. We know more about psychohistory than he could possibly have known.

"Seldon ended his calculations with the Second Empire and we have continued beyond it. Indeed, if I may say so without offense, the new Hyper-Plan that goes past the establishment of the Second Empire is very largely my doing and has earned me my present post.

"I tell you all this so that you can spare me unnecessary talk. With all this, how do you manage to conclude that the Seldon Plan is meaningless? It is without flaw. The mere fact that it survived the Century of Deviations—with all due respect to Palver's genius—is the best evidence we have that it is without flaw. Where is its weakness, young man, that you should brand the Plan as meaningless?"

Gendibal stood stiffly upright. "You are right, First Speaker. The Seldon Plan has no flaw."

"You withdraw your remark, then?"

"No, First Speaker. Its lack of flaw is its flaw. Its flawlessness is fatal!"

3.

The First Speaker regarded Gendibal with equanimity. He had learned to control his expressions and it amused him to watch Gendibal's ineptness in this respect. At every exchange, the young man did his best to hide his feelings, but each time, he exposed them completely.

Shandess studied him dispassionately. He was a thin young man, not much above the middle height, with thin lips and bony, restless hands. He had dark, humorless eyes that tended to smolder.

He would be, the First Speaker knew, a hard person to talk out of his convictions.

"You speak in paradoxes, Speaker," he said.

"It *sounds* like a paradox, First Speaker, because there is so much about Seldon's Plan that we take for granted and accept in so unquestioning a manner."

"And what is it you question, then?"

"The Plan's very basis. We all know that the Plan will not work if its nature—or even its existence—is known to too many of those whose behavior it is designed to predict."

"I believe Hari Seldon understood that. I even believe he made it one of his two fundamental axioms of psychohistory."

"He did not anticipate the Mule, First Speaker, and therefore he could not anticipate the extent to which the Second Foundation would become an obsession with the people of the First Foundation, once they had been shown its importance by the Mule."

"Hari Seldon—" and for one moment, the First Speaker shuddered and fell silent.

Hari Seldon's physical appearance was known to all the members of the Second Foundation. Reproductions of him in two and in three dimensions, photographic and holographic, in bas-relief and in the round, sitting and standing, were ubiquitous. They all represented him in the last few years of his life. All were of an old and benign man, face wrinkled with the wisdom of the aged, symbolizing the quintessence of well-ripened genius.

But the First Speaker now recalled seeing a photograph reputed to be Seldon as a young man. The photograph was neglected, since the thought of a young Seldon was almost a contradiction in terms. Yet Shandess had seen it, and the thought had suddenly come to him that Stor Gendibal looked remarkably like the young Seldon.

Ridiculous! It was the sort of superstition that afflicted everyone, now and then, however rational they might be. He was deceived by a fugitive similarity. If he had the photograph before him, he would see at once that the similarity was an illusion. Yet why should that silly thought have occurred to him *now*?

He recovered. It had been a momentary quaver—a transient derailment of thought—too brief to be noticed by anyone but a Speaker. Gendibal might interpret it as he pleased.

"Hari Seldon," he said very firmly the second time, "knew well that there were an infinite number of possibilities he could not foresee, and it was for that reason that he set up the Second Foundation. We did not foresee the Mule either, but we recognized him once he was upon us and we stopped him. We did not foresee the subsequent obsession of the First Foundation with ourselves, but we saw it when it came and we stopped it. What is it about this that you can possibly find fault with?"

"For one thing," said Gendibal, "the obsession of the First Foundation with us is not yet over."

There was a distinct ebb in the deference with which

Gendibal had been speaking. He had noted the quaver in the First Speaker's voice (Shandess decided) and had interpreted it as uncertainty. That had to be countered.

The First Speaker said briskly, "Let me anticipate. There would be people on the First Foundation, who—comparing the hectic difficulties of the first nearly four centuries of existence with the placidity of the last twelve decades—will come to the conclusion that this cannot be unless the Second Foundation is taking good care of the Plan—and, of course, they will be right in so concluding. They will decide that the Second Foundation may not have been destroyed after all—and, of course, they will be right in so deciding. In fact, we've received reports that there is a young man on the First Foundation's capital world of Terminus, an official of their government, who is quite convinced of all this. —I forget his name—"

"Golan Trevize," said Gendibal softly. "It was I who first noted the matter in the reports, and it was I who directed the matter to your office."

"Oh?" said the First Speaker with exaggerated politeness. "And how did your attention come to be focused on him?"

"One of our agents on Terminus sent in a tedious report on the newly elected members of their Council—a perfectly routine matter usually sent to and ignored by all Speakers. This one caught my eye because of the nature of the description of one new Councilman, Golan Trevize. From the description, he seemed unusually self-assured and combative."

"You recognized a kindred spirit, did you?"

"Not at all," said Gendibal, stiffly. "He seemed a reckless person who enjoyed doing ridiculous things, a description which does not apply to me. In any case, I directed an in-depth study. It did not take long for me to decide that he would have made good material for us if he had been recruited at an early age."

"Perhaps," said the First Speaker, "but you know that we do not recruit on Terminus."

"I know that well. In any case, even without our training,

he has an unusual intuition. It is, of course, thoroughly
undisciplined. I was, therefore, not particularly surprised
that he had grasped the fact that the Second Foundation still
exists. I felt it important enough, however, to direct a memo
on the matter to your office."

"And I take it from your manner that there is a new
development?"

"Having grasped the fact that we still exist, thanks to his
highly developed intuitive abilities, he then used it in a
characteristically undisciplined fashion and has, as a result,
been exiled from Terminus."

The First Speaker lifted his eyebrows. "You stop suddenly. You want me to interpret the significance. Without
using my computer, let me mentally apply a rough approx-
imation of Seldon's equations and guess that a shrewd Mayor,
capable of suspecting that the Second Foundation exists,
prefers not to have an undisciplined individual shout it to
the Galaxy and thus alert said Second Foundation to the
danger. I take it Branno the Bronze decided that Terminus
is safer with Trevize off the planet."

"She might have imprisoned Trevize or had him quietly
assassinated."

"The equations are not reliable when applied to individuals, as you well know. They deal only with humanity in mass.
Individual behavior is therefore unpredictable and it is possible to assume that the Mayor is a humane individual who
feels imprisonment, let alone assassination, is unmerciful."

Gendibal said nothing for a while. It was an eloquent
nothing, and he maintained it just long enough for the First
Speaker to grow uncertain of himself but not so long as to
induce a defensive anger.

He timed it to the second and then he said, "That is not
my interpretation. I believe that Trevize, at this moment,
represents the cutting edge of the greatest threat to the Second Foundation in its history—a greater danger even than
the Mule!"

4.

Gendibal was satisfied. The force of the statement had worked well. The First Speaker had not expected it and was caught off-balance. From this moment, the whip hand was Gendibal's. If he had any doubt of that at all, it vanished with Shandess's next remark.

"Does this have anything to do with your contention that Seldon's Plan is meaningless?"

Gendibal gambled on complete certainty, driving in with a didacticism that would not allow the First Speaker to recover. He said, "First Speaker, it is an article of faith that it was Preem Palver who restored the Plan to its course after the wild aberrance of the Century of Deviations. Study the Prime Radiant and you will see that the Deviations did not disappear till two decades after Palver's death and that not one Deviation has appeared since. The credit might rest with the First Speakers since Palver, but that is improbable."

"Improbable? Granted none of us have been Palvers, but—why improbable?"

"Will you allow me to demonstrate, First Speaker? Using the mathematics of psychohistory, I can clearly show that the chances of total disappearance of Deviation are too microscopically small to have taken place through anything the Second Foundation can do. You need not allow me if you lack the time or the desire for the demonstration, which will take half an hour of close attention. I can, as an alternative, call for a full meeting of the Speaker's Table and demonstrate it there. But that would mean a loss of time for me and unnecessary controversy."

"Yes, and a possible loss of face for me. —Demonstrate the matter to me now. But a word of warning." The First Speaker was making a heroic effort to recover. "If what you show me is worthless, I will not forget that."

"If it proves worthless," said Gendibal with an effortless pride that overrode the other, "you will have my resignation on the spot."

It took, actually, considerably more than half an hour,

for the First Speaker questioned the mathematics with near-savage intensity.

Gendibal made up some of the time by his smooth use of his Micro-Radiant. The device—which could locate any portion of the vast Plan holographically and which required neither wall nor desk-sized console—had come into use only a decade ago and the First Speaker had never learned the knack of handling it. Gendibal was aware of that. The First Speaker knew that he was.

Gendibal hooked it over his right thumb and manipulated its controls with his four fingers, using his hand deliberately as though it were a musical instrument. (Indeed, he had written a small paper on the analogies.)

The equations Gendibal produced (and found with sure ease) moved back and forth snakily to accompany his commentary. He could obtain definitions, if necessary; set up axioms; and produce graphics, both two-dimensional and three-dimensional (to say nothing of projections of multi-dimensional relationships).

Gendibal's commentary was clear and incisive and the First Speaker abandoned the game. He was won over and said, "I do not recall having seen an analysis of this nature. Whose work is it?"

"First Speaker, it is my own. I have published the basic mathematics involved."

"Very clever, Speaker Gendibal. Something like this will put you in line for the First Speakership, should I die—or retire."

"I have given that matter no thought, First Speaker—but since there's no chance of your believing that, I withdraw the comment. I *have* given it thought and I hope I *will* be First Speaker, since whoever succeeds to the post *must* follow a procedure that only I see clearly."

"Yes," said the First Speaker, "inappropriate modesty can be very dangerous. What procedure? Perhaps the present First Speaker may follow it, too. If I am too old to have made the creative leap you have, I am not so old that I cannot follow your direction."

It was a graceful surrender and Gendibal's heart warmed, rather unexpectedly, toward the older man, even as he realized that this was precisely the First Speaker's intention.

"Thank you, First Speaker, for I will need your help badly. I cannot expect to sway the Table without your enlightened leadership." (Grace for grace.) "I assume, then, that you have already seen from what I have demonstrated that it is impossible for the Century of Deviations to have been corrected under our policies or for all Deviations to have ceased since then."

"This is clear to me," said the First Speaker. "If your mathematics is correct, then in order for the Plan to have recovered as it did and to work as perfectly as it seems to be working, it would be necessary for us to be able to predict the reactions of small groups of people—even of individuals—with some degree of assurance."

"Quite so. Since the mathematics of psychohistory does not allow this, the Deviations should not have vanished and, even more so, should not have remained absent. You see, then, what I meant when I said earlier that the flaw in the Seldon Plan was its flawlessness."

The First Speaker said, "Either the Seldon Plan does possess Deviations, then, or there is something wrong in your mathematics. Since I must admit that the Seldon Plan has *not* shown Deviations in a century and more, it follows that there *is* something wrong with your mathematics— except that I detected no fallacies or missteps."

"You do wrong," said Gendibal, "to exclude a third alternative. It is quite possible for the Seldon Plan to possess no Deviations and yet for there to be nothing wrong in my mathematics when it predicts that to be impossible."

"I fail to see the third alternative."

"Suppose the Seldon Plan is being controlled by means of a psychohistorical method so advanced that the reactions of small groups of people—even perhaps of individual persons—*can* be predicted, a method that we of the Second Foundation do not possess. Then, and *only* then, my mathematics would predict that the Seldon Plan should indeed experience no Deviations!"

For a while (by Second Foundation standards) the First Speaker made no response. He said, "There is no such advanced psychohistorical method that is known to me or, I am certain from your manner, to you. If you and I know of none, the chance that any other Speaker, or any group of Speakers, has developed such a micropsychohistory—if I may call it that—and has kept it secret from the rest of the Table is infinitesimally small. Don't you agree?"

"I agree."

"Then either your analysis is wrong or else micropsychohistory is in the hands of some group outside the Second Foundation."

"Exactly, First Speaker, the latter alternative must be correct."

"Can you demonstrate the truth of such a statement?"

"I cannot, in any formal way; but consider— Has there not already been a person who could affect the Seldon Plan by dealing with individual people?"

"I presume you are referring to the Mule."

"Yes, certainly."

"The Mule could only disrupt. The problem here is that the Seldon Plan is working too well, considerably closer to perfection than your mathematics would allow. You would need an Anti-Mule—someone who is as capable of overriding the Plan as the Mule was, but who acts for the opposite motive—overriding not to disrupt but to perfect."

"Exactly, First Speaker. I wish I had thought of that expression. What was the Mule? A mutant. But where did he come from? How did he come to be? No one really knows. Might there not be more?"

"Apparently not. The one thing that is best known about the Mule is that he was sterile. Hence his name. Or do you think that is a myth?"

"I am not referring to descendants of the Mule. Might it not be that the Mule was an aberrant member of what is— or has now become—a sizable group of people with Mulish powers who—for some reason of their own—are not disrupting the Seldon Plan but supporting it?"

"Why in the Galaxy should they support it?"

"Why do *we* support it? We plan a Second Empire in which we—or, rather, our intellectual descendants—will be the decision-makers. If some other group is supporting the Plan even more efficiently than we are, they cannot be planning to leave the decision-making to us. *They* will make the decisions—but to what end? Ought we not try to find out what kind of a Second Empire they are sweeping us into?"

"And how do you propose to find out?"

"Well, why has the Mayor of Terminus exiled Golan Trevize? By doing so, she allows a possibly dangerous person to move freely about the Galaxy. That she does it out of motives of humanity, I cannot believe. Historically the rulers of the First Foundation have always acted realistically, which means, usually, without regard for 'morality.' One of their heroes—Salvor Hardin—counseled *against* morality, in fact. No, I think the Mayor acted under compulsion from agents of the Anti-Mules, to use your phrase. I think Trevize has been recruited by them and I think he is the spearhead of danger to us. Deadly danger."

And the First Speaker said, "By Seldon, you may be right. But how will we ever convince the Table of this?"

"First Speaker, you underestimate your eminence."

6. EARTH

I.

Trevize was hot and annoyed. He and Pelorat were sitting in the small dining area, having just completed their midday meal.

Pelorat said, "We've only been in space two days and I find myself quite comfortable, although I miss fresh air, nature, and all that. Strange! Never seemed to notice all that sort of thing when it was all round me. Still between my wafer and that remarkable computer of yours, I have my entire library with me—or all that matters, at any rate. And I don't feel the least bit frightened of being out in space now. Astonishing!"

Trevize made a noncommittal sound. His eyes were inwardly focused.

Pelorat said gently, "I don't mean to intrude, Golan, but I don't really think you're listening. Not that I'm a particularly interesting person—always been a bit of a bore, you know. Still, you seem preoccupied in another way. —Are we in trouble? Needn't be afraid to tell me, you know. Not much I could do, I suppose, but I won't go into panic, dear fellow."

"In trouble?" Trevize seemed to come to his senses, frowning slightly.

"I mean the ship. It's a new model, so I suppose there could be something wrong." Pelorat allowed himself a small, uncertain smile.

Trevize shook his head vigorously. "Stupid of me to leave you in such uncertainty, Janov. There's nothing wrong at all with the ship. It's working perfectly. It's just that I've been looking for a hyper-relay."

"Ah, I see. —Except that I don't. What is a hyper-relay?"

"Well, let me explain, Janov. I am in communication with Terminus. At least, I can be anytime I wish and Terminus can, in reverse, be in communication with us. They know the ship's location, having observed its trajectory. Even if they had not, they could locate us by scanning near-space for mass, which would warn them of the presence of a ship or, possibly, a meteoroid. But they could further detect an energy pattern, which would not only distinguish a ship from a meteoroid but would identify a particular ship, for no two ships make use of energy in quite the same way. In some way, our pattern remains characteristic, no matter what appliances or instruments we turn on and off. The ship may be unknown, of course, but if it is a ship whose energy pattern is on record in Terminus—as ours is—it can be identified as soon as detected."

Pelorat said, "It seems to me, Golan, that the advance of civilization is nothing but an exercise in the limiting of privacy."

"You may be right. Sooner or later, however, we must move through hyperspace or we will be condemned to remain within a parsec or two of Terminus for the rest of our lives. We will then be unable to engage in interstellar travel to any but the slightest degree. In passing through hyperspace, on the other hand, we undergo a discontinuity in ordinary space. We pass from here to there—and I mean across a gap of hundreds of parsecs sometimes—in an instant of experienced time. We are suddenly enormously far away in a direction that is very difficult to predict and, in a practical sense, we can no longer be detected."

"I see that. Yes."

"Unless, of course, they have planted a hyper-relay on board. A hyper-relay sends out a signal through hyperspace—a signal characteristic of this ship—and the authorities on Terminus would know where we are at all times. That answers your question, you see. There would be nowhere in the Galaxy we could hide and no combination of

Jumps through hyperspace would make it possible for us to evade their instruments."

"But, Golan," said Pelorat softly, "don't we want Foundation protection?"

"Yes, Janov, but only when we ask for it. You said the advance of civilization meant the continuing restriction of privacy. —Well, I don't want to be that advanced. I want freedom to move undetected as I wish—unless and until I want protection. So I would feel better, a great deal better, if there *weren't* a hyper-relay on board."

"Have you found one, Golan?"

"No, I have not. If I had, I might be able to render it inoperative somehow."

"Would you know one if you saw it?"

"That's one of the difficulties. I might not be able to recognize it. I know what a hyper-relay looks like generally and I know ways of testing a suspicious object—but this is a late-model ship, designed for special tasks. A hyper-relay may have been incorporated into its design in such a way as to show no signs of its presence."

"On the other hand, maybe there is no hyper-relay present and that's why you haven't found it."

"I don't dare assume that and I don't like the thought of making a Jump until I know."

Pelorat looked enlightened. "That's why we've just been drifting through space. I've been wondering why we haven't Jumped. I've heard about Jumps, you know. Been a little nervous about it, actually—been wondering when you'd order me to strap myself in or take a pill or something like that."

Trevize managed a smile. "No need for apprehension. These aren't ancient times. On a ship like this, you just leave it all to the computer. You give it your instructions and it does the rest. You won't know that anything has happened at all, except that the view of space will suddenly change. If you've ever seen a slide show, you'll know what happens when one slide is suddenly projected in place of another. Well, that's what the Jump will seem like."

"Dear me. One won't feel anything? Odd! I find that somewhat disappointing."

"*I've* never felt anything and the ships I've been in haven't been as advanced as this baby of ours. —But it's not because of the hyper-relay that we haven't Jumped. We have to get a bit further away from Terminus—and from the sun, too. The farther we are from any massive object, the easier to control the Jump, to make re-emergence into space at exactly desired co-ordinates. In an emergency, you might risk a Jump when you're only two hundred kilometers off the surface of a planet and just trust to luck that you'll end up safely. Since there is much more safe than unsafe volume in the Galaxy, you can reasonably count on safety. Still, there's always the possibility that random factors will cause you to re-emerge within a few million kilometers of a large star or in the Galactic core—and you will find yourself fried before you can blink. The further away you are from mass, the smaller those factors and the less likely it is that anything untoward will happen."

"In that case, I commend your caution. We're not in a tearing hurry."

"Exactly. —Especially since I would dearly love to find the hyper-relay before I make a move. —Or find a way of convincing myself there is no hyper-relay."

Trevize seemed to drift off again into his private concentration and Pelorat said, raising his voice a little to surmount the preoccupation barrier, "How much longer do we have?"

"What?"

"I mean, when would you make the Jump if you had no concerns over the hyper-relay, my dear chap?"

"At our present speed and trajectory, I should say on our fourth day out. I'll work out the proper time on the computer."

"Well, then, you still have two days for your search. May I make a suggestion?"

"Go ahead."

"I have always found in my own work—quite different

from yours, of course, but possibly we may generalize—that zeroing in tightly on a particular problem is self-defeating. Why not relax and talk about something else, and your unconscious mind—not laboring under the weight of concentrated thought—may solve the problem for you."

Trevize looked momentarily annoyed and then laughed. "Well, why not? —Tell me, Professor, what got you interested in Earth? What brought up this odd notion of a particular planet from which we all started?"

"Ah!" Pelorat nodded his head reminiscently. "That's going back a while. Over thirty years. I planned to be a biologist when I was going to college. I was particularly interested in the variation of species on different worlds. The variation, as you know—well, maybe you don't know, so you won't mind if I tell you—is very small. All forms of life throughout the Galaxy—at least all that we have yet encountered—share a water-based protein/nucleic acid chemistry."

Trevize said, "I went to military college, which emphasized nucleonics and gravitics, but I'm not exactly a narrow specialist. I know a bit about the chemical basis of life. We were taught that water, proteins, and nucleic acids are the only possible basis for life."

"That, I think, is an unwarranted conclusion. It is safer to say that no other form of life has yet been found—or, at any rate, been recognized—and let it go at that. What is more surprising is that indigenous species—that is, species found on only a single planet and no other—are few in number. Most of the species that exist, including *Homo sapiens* in particular, are distributed through all or most of the inhabited worlds of the Galaxy and are closely related biochemically, physiologically, and morphologically. The indigenous species, on the other hand, are widely separated in characteristics from both the widespread forms and from each other."

"Well, what of that?"

"The conclusion is that one world in the Galaxy—*one* world—is different from the rest. Tens of millions of worlds in the Galaxy—no one knows exactly how many—have developed life. It was simple life, sparse life, feeble life— not very variegated, not easily maintained, and not easily spread. One world, *one* world alone, developed life in millions of species—easily millions—some of it very specialized, highly developed, very prone to multiplication and to spreading, and including *us*. We were intelligent enough to form a civilization, to develop hyperspatial flight, and to colonize the Galaxy—and, in spreading through the Galaxy, we took many other forms of life—forms related to each other and to ourselves—along with us."

"If you stop to think of it," said Trevize rather indifferently, "I suppose that stands to reason. I mean, here we are in a human Galaxy. If we assume that it all started on some one world, then that one world would have to be different. But why not? The chances of life developing in that riotous fashion must be very slim indeed—perhaps one in a hundred million—so the chances are that it happened in one life-bearing world out of a hundred million. It had to be one."

"But what is it that made that particular one world so different from the others?" said Pelorat excitedly. "What were the conditions that made it unique?"

"Merely chance, perhaps. After all, human beings and the life-forms they brought with them now exist on tens of millions of planets, all of which can support life, so all those worlds must be good enough."

"No! Once the human species had evolved, once it had developed a technology, once it had toughened itself in the hard struggle for survival, it could then adapt to life on any world that is in the least hospitable—on Terminus, for instance. But can you imagine intelligent life having *developed* on Terminus? When Terminus was first occupied by human beings in the days of the Encyclopedists, the highest form of plant life it produced was a mosslike growth on rocks; the highest forms of animal life were small coral-like growths in the ocean and insectlike flying organisms on land. We just about wiped them out and stocked sea and land with fish and rabbits and goats and grass and grain and trees and so on. We have nothing left of the indigenous life, except for what exists in zoos and aquaria."

"Hmm," said Trevize.

Pelorat stared at him for a full minute, then sighed and said, "You don't really care, do you? Remarkable! I find no one who does, somehow. My fault, I think. I cannot make it interesting, even though it interests *me* so much."

Trevize said, "It's interesting. It is. But—but—so what?"

"It doesn't strike you that it might be interesting scientifically to study a world that gave rise to the only really flourishing indigenous ecological balance the Galaxy has ever seen?"

"Maybe, if you're a biologist. —I'm not, you see. You must forgive me."

"Of course, dear fellow. It's just that I never found any biologists who were interested, either. I told you I was a biology major. I took it up with my professor and *he* wasn't interested. He told me to turn to some practical problem. That so disgusted me I took up history instead—which had been rather a hobby of mine from my teenage years, in any case—and tackled the 'Origin Question' from that angle."

Trevize said, "But at least it has given you a lifework, so you must be pleased that your professor was so unenlightened."

"Yes, I suppose one might look at it that way. And the lifework is an interesting one, of which I have never tired. —But I do wish it interested *you*. I hate this feeling of forever talking to myself."

Trevize leaned his head back and laughed heartily.

Pelorat's quiet face took on a trace of hurt. "Why are you laughing at me?"

"Not you, Janov," said Trevize. "I was laughing at my own stupidity. Where you're concerned, I am completely grateful. You were perfectly right, you know."

"To take up the importance of human origins?"

"No, no. —Well, yes, that too. —But I meant you were right to tell me to stop consciously thinking of my problem and to turn my mind elsewhere. It worked. When you were talking about the manner in which life evolved, it finally occurred to me that I knew how to find that hyper-relay— if it existed."

"Oh, that!"

"Yes, that! That's *my* monomania at the moment. I've been looking for that hyper-relay as though I were on my old scow of a training ship, studying every part of the ship by eye, looking for something that stood out from the rest. I had forgotten that this ship is a developed product of thousands of years of technological evolution. Don't you see?"

"No, Golan."

"We have a computer aboard. How could I have forgotten?"

He waved his hand and passed into his own room, urging Pelorat along with him.

"I need only try to communicate," he said, placing his hands onto the computer contact.

It was a matter of trying to reach Terminus, which was now some thousands of kilometers behind.

Reach! Speak! It was as though nerve endings sprouted and extended, reaching outward with bewildering speed— the speed of light, of course—to make contact.

Trevize felt himself touching—well, not quite touching, but sensing—well, not quite sensing, but—it didn't matter, for there wasn't a word for it.

He was *aware* of Terminus within reach and, although the distance between himself and it was lengthening by some twenty kilometers per second, contact persisted as though planet and ship were motionless and separated by a few meters.

He said nothing. He clamped shut. He was merely testing the *principle* of communication; he was not actively communicating.

Out beyond, eight parsecs away, was Anacreon, the nearest large planet—in their backyard, by Galactic standards. To send a message by the same light-speed system that had just worked for Terminus—and to receive an answer as well—would take fifty-two years.

Reach for Anacreon! Think Anacreon! Think it as clearly as you can. You know its position relative to Terminus and the Galactic core; you've studied its planetography and history; you've solved military problems where it was necessary to recapture Anacreon (in the impossible case—these days—that it was taken by an enemy).

Space! You've been *on* Anacreon.

Picture it! Picture it! You will sense being *on* it via hyper-relay.

Nothing! His nerve endings quivered and came to rest nowhere.

Trevize pulled loose. "There's no hyper-relay on board the *Far Star*, Janov. I'm positive. —And if I hadn't followed your suggestion, I wonder how long it would have taken me to reach this point."

Pelorat, without moving a facial muscle, positively glowed. "I'm so pleased to have been of help. Does this mean we Jump?"

"No, we still wait two more days, to be safe. We have to get away from mass, remember? —Ordinarily, considering that I have a new and untried ship with which I am thoroughly unacquainted, it would probably take me two days to calculate the exact procedure—the proper hyper-thrust for the first Jump, in particular. I have a feeling, though, the computer will do it all."

"Dear me! That leaves us facing a rather boring stretch of time, it seems to me."

"Boring?" Trevize smiled broadly. "Anything but! You and I, Janov, are going to talk about Earth."

Pelorat said, "Indeed? You are trying to please an old man? That is kind of you. Really it is."

"Nonsense! I'm trying to please myself. Janov, you have made a convert. As a result of what you have told me, I realize that Earth is the most important and the most devouringly interesting object in the Universe."

2.

It must surely have struck Trevize at the moment that Pelorat had presented his view of Earth. It was only because his mind was reverberating with the problem of the hyper-relay that he hadn't responded at once. And the instant the problem had gone, he *had* responded.

Perhaps the one statement of Hari Seldon's that was most often repeated was his remark concerning the Second Foundation being "at the other end of the Galaxy" from Terminus. Seldon had even named the spot. It was to be "at Star's End."

This had been included in Gaal Dornick's account of the day of the trial before the Imperial court. "The other end of the Galaxy"—those were the words Seldon had used to Dornick and ever since that day their significance had been debated.

What was it that connected one end of the Galaxy with "the other end"? Was it a straight line, a spiral, a circle, or what?

And now, luminously, it was suddenly clear to Trevize that it was no line and no curve that should—or could— be drawn on the map of the Galaxy. It was more subtle than that.

It was perfectly clear that the one end of the Galaxy was Terminus. It was at the edge of the Galaxy, yes—*our* Foundation's edge—which gave the word "end" a literal meaning. It was, however, also the *newest* world of the Galaxy at the time Seldon was speaking, a world that was about to be founded, that had not as yet been in existence for a single moment.

What would be the other end of the Galaxy, in that light? The *other* Foundation's edge? Why, the *oldest* world of the Galaxy? And according to the argument Pelorat had presented—without knowing what he was presenting—that could only be Earth. The Second Foundation might well be on Earth.

Yet Seldon had said the other end of the Galaxy was "at

Star's End." Who could say he was not speaking metaphorically? Trace the history of humanity backward as Pelorat did and the line would stretch back from each planetary
system, each star that shone down on an inhabited planet,
to some other planetary system, some other star from which
the first migrants had come, then back to a star before that—
until finally, all the lines stretched back to the planet on
which humanity had originated. It was the star that shone
upon Earth that was "Star's End."

Trevize smiled and said almost lovingly, "Tell me more
about Earth, Janov."

Pelorat shook his head. "I have told you all there is,
really. We will find out more on Trantor."

Trevize said, "No, we won't, Janov. We'll find out nothing there. Why? Because we're not going to Trantor. I
control this ship and I assure you we're not."

Pelorat's mouth fell open. He struggled for breath for a
moment and then said, woebegone, "Oh, my *dear* fellow!"

Trevize said, "Come on, Janov. Don't look like that.
We're going to find *Earth*."

"But it's only on Trantor that—"

"No, it's not. Trantor is just someplace you can study
brittle films and dusty documents and turn brittle and dusty
yourself."

"For decades, I've dreamed—"

"You've dreamed of finding Earth."

"But it's only—"

Trevize stood up, leaned over, caught the slack of Pelorat's tunic, and said, "Don't repeat that, Professor. Don't
repeat it. When you first told me we were going to look for
Earth, before ever we got onto this ship, you said we were
sure to find it because, and I quote your own words, 'I have
an excellent possibility in mind.' Now I don't ever want to
hear you say 'Trantor' again. I just want you to tell me
about this excellent possibility."

"But it must be *confirmed*. So far, it's only a thought,
a hope, a vague possibility."

"Good! Tell me about it!"

"You don't understand. You simply don't understand. It is not a field in which anyone but myself has done research. There is nothing historical, nothing firm, nothing real. People talk about Earth as though it's a fact, and also as though it's a myth. There are a million contradictory tales—"

"Well then, what has *your* research consisted of?"

"I've been forced to collect every tale, every bit of supposed history, every legend, every misty myth. Even *fiction*. Anything that includes the name of Earth or the idea of a planet of origin. For over thirty years, I've been collecting everything I could find from every planet of the Galaxy. Now if I could only get something more reliable than all of these from the Galactic Library at— But you don't want me to say the word."

"That's right. Don't say it. Tell me instead that one of these items has caught your attention, and tell me your reasons for thinking why it, of them all, should be legitimate."

Pelorat shook his head. "There, Golan, if you will excuse my saying so, you talk like a soldier or a politician. That is not the way history works."

Trevize took a deep breath and kept his temper. "Tell me how it works, Janov. We've got two days. Educate me."

"You can't rely on any one myth or even on any one group. I've had to gather them all, analyze them, organize them, set up symbols to represent different aspects of their content—tales of impossible weather, astronomic details of planetary systems at variance with what actually exists, place of origin of culture heroes specifically stated not to be native, quite literally hundreds of other items. No use going through the entire list. Even two days wouldn't be enough. I spent over thirty years, I tell you.

"I then worked up a computer program that searched through all these myths for common components and sought a transformation that would eliminate the true impossibilities. Gradually I worked up a model of what Earth must have been like. After all, if human beings all originated on a single planet, that single planet must represent the one fact that all origin myths, all culture-hero tales, have in common. —Well, do you want me to go into mathematical detail?"

Trevize said, "Not at the moment, thank you, but how do you know you won't be misled by your mathematics? We know for a fact that Terminus was founded only five centuries ago and that the first human beings arrived as a colony from Trantor but had been assembled from dozens— if not hundreds—of other worlds. Yet someone who did not know this could assume that Hari Seldon and Salvor Hardin, neither of whom were born on Terminus, came from Earth and that Trantor was really a name that stood for Earth. Certainly, if the Trantor as described in Seldon's time were searched for—a world with all its land surface coated with metal—it would not be found and it might be considered an impossible myth."

Pelorat looked pleased. "I withdraw my earlier remark about soldiers and politicians, my dear fellow. You have a remarkable intuitive sense. Of course, I had to set up controls. I invented a hundred falsities based on distortions of actual history and imitating myths of the type I had collected. I then attempted to incorporate my inventions into the model. One of my inventions was even based on Terminus's early history. The computer rejected them all. Every one. To be sure, that might have meant I simply lacked the fictional talents to make up something reasonable, but I did my best."

"I'm sure you did, Janov. And what did your model tell you about Earth?"

"A number of things of varying degrees of likelihood. A kind of profile. For instance, about 90 percent of the inhabited planets in the Galaxy have rotation periods of between twenty-two and twenty-six Galactic Standard Hours. Well—"

Trevize cut in. "I hope you didn't pay any attention to that, Janov. There's no mystery there. For a planet to be habitable, you don't want it to rotate so quickly that air circulation patterns produce impossibly stormy conditions or so slowly that temperature variation patterns are extreme. It's a property that's self-selective. Human beings prefer to live on planets with suitable characteristics, and then when all habitable planets resemble each other in these characteristics, some say, 'What an amazing coincidence,' when it's not amazing at all and not even a coincidence."

"As a matter of fact," said Pelorat calmly, "that's a well-known phenomenon in social science. In physics, too, I believe—but I'm not a physicist and I'm not certain about that. In any case, it is called the 'anthropic principle.' The observer influences the events he observes by the mere act of observing them or by being there to observe them. But the question is: Where is the planet that served as a model? Which planet rotates in precisely one Galactic Standard Day of twenty-four Galactic Standard Hours?"

Trevize looked thoughtful and thrust out his lower lip. "You think that might be Earth? Surely Galactic Standard could have been based on the local characteristics of *any* world, might it not?"

"Not likely. It's not the human way. Trantor was the capital world of the Galaxy for twelve thousand years—the most populous world for twenty thousand years—yet it did not impose its rotation period of 1.08 Galactic Standard Days on all the Galaxy. And Terminus's rotation period is 0.91 GSD, and we don't enforce ours on the planets dominated by us. Every planet makes use of its own private calculations in its own Local Planetary Day system, and for matters of interplanetary importance converts—with the help of computers—back and forth between LPD and GSD. The Galactic Standard Day *must* come from Earth!"

"Why is it a must?"

"For one thing, Earth was once the *only* inhabited world, so naturally its day and year would be standard and would very likely remain standard out of a social inertia as other worlds were populated. Then, too, the model I produced was that of an Earth that rotated on its axis in just twenty-four Galactic Standard Hours and that revolved about its sun in just one Galactic Standard Year."

"Might that not be coincidence?"

Pelorat laughed. "Now it is you who are talking coincidence. Would you care to lay a wager on such a thing happening by coincidence?"

"Well well," muttered Trevize.

"In fact, there's more to it. There's an archaic measure of time that's called the month—"

"I've heard of it."

"It, apparently, about fits the period of revolution of Earth's satellite about Earth. However—"

"Yes?"

"Well, one rather astonishing factor of the model is that the satellite I just mentioned is huge—over one quarter the diameter of the Earth itself."

"Never heard of such a thing, Janov. There isn't a populated planet in the Galaxy with a satellite like that."

"But that's *good*," said Pelorat with animation. "If Earth is a unique world in its production of variegated species and the evolution of intelligence, then we want some physical uniqueness."

"But what could a large satellite have to do with variegated species, intelligence, and all that?"

"Well now, there you hit a difficulty. I don't really know. But it's worth examination, don't you think?"

Trevize rose to his feet and folded his arms across his chest. "But what's the problem, then? Look up the statistics on inhabited planets and find one that has a period of rotation and of revolution that are exactly one Galactic Standard Day and one Galactic Standard Year in length, respectively. And if it also has a gigantic satellite, you'd have what you want. I presume, from your statement that you 'have an excellent possibility in mind,' that you've done just this, and that you have your world."

Pelorat looked disconcerted. "Well, now, that's not exactly what happened. I did look through the statistics, or at least I had it done by the astronomy department and—well, to put it bluntly, there's no such world."

Trevize sat down again abruptly. "But that means your whole argument falls to the ground."

"Not quite, it seems to me."

"What do you mean, not quite? You produce a model with all sorts of detailed descriptions and you can't find anything that fits. Your model is useless, then. You must start from the beginning."

"No. It just means that the statistics on populated planets are incomplete. After all, there are tens of millions of them and some are very obscure worlds. For instance, there is no good data on the population of nearly half. And concerning six hundred and forty thousand populated worlds there is almost no information other than their names and sometimes the location. Some galactographers have estimated that there may be up to ten thousand inhabited planets that aren't listed at all. The worlds prefer it that way, presumably. During the Imperial Era, it might have helped them avoid taxation."

"And in the centuries that followed," said Trevize cynically. "It might have helped them serve as home bases for pirates, and that might have, on occasion, proved more enriching than ordinary trade."

"I wouldn't know about that," said Pelorat doubtfully.

Trevize said, "Just the same, it seems to me that Earth would have to be on the list of inhabited planets, whatever its own desires. It would be the oldest of them all, by definition, and it could not have been overlooked in the early centuries of Galactic civilization. And once on the list, it would stay on. Surely we could count on social inertia there."

Pelorat hesitated and looked anguished. "Actually, there —there *is* a planet named Earth on the list of inhabited planets."

Trevize stared. "I'm under the impression that you told me a while ago that Earth was not on the list?"

"As Earth, it is not. There is, however, a planet named Gaia."

"What has that got to do with it? Gahyah?"

"It's spelled G-A-I-A. It means 'Earth.'"

"Why should it mean Earth, Janov, any more than anything else? The name is meaningless to me."

Pelorat's ordinarily expressionless face came close to a grimace. "I'm not sure you'll believe this— If I go by my analysis of the myths, there were several different, mutually unintelligible, languages on Earth."

"What?"

"Yes. After all, we have a thousand different ways of speaking across the Galaxy—"

"Across the Galaxy, there are certainly dialectical variations, but these are not mutually unintelligible. And even if understanding some of them is a matter of difficulty, we all share Galactic Standard."

"Certainly, but there is constant interstellar travel. What if some world was in isolation for a prolonged period?"

"But you're talking of Earth. A single planet. Where's the isolation?"

"Earth is the planet of origin, don't forget, where humanity must at one time have been primitive beyond imagining. Without interstellar travel, without computers, without technology at all, struggling up from nonhuman ancestors."

"This is so ridiculous."

Pelorat hung his head in embarrassment at that. "There is perhaps no use discussing this, old chap. I never have managed to make it convincing to anyone. My own fault, I'm sure."

Trevize was at once contrite. "Janov, I apologize. I spoke without thinking. These are views, after all, to which I am not accustomed. You have been developing your theories for over thirty years, while I've been introduced to them all at once. You must make allowances. —Look, I'll imagine that we have primitive people on Earth who speak two completely different, mutually unintelligible, languages—"

"Half a dozen, perhaps," said Pelorat diffidently. "Earth may have been divided into several large land masses and it may be that there were, at first, no communications among them. The inhabitants of each land mass might have developed an individual language."

Trevize said with careful gravity, "And on each of these land masses, once they grew cognizant of one another, they might have argued an 'Origin Question' and wondered on which one human beings had first arisen from other animals."

"They might very well, Golan. It would be a very natural attitude for them to have."

"And in one of those languages, Gaia means Earth. And the word 'Earth' itself is derived from another one of those languages."

"Yes, yes."

"And while Galactic Standard is the language that descended from the particular language in which 'Earth' means 'Earth,' the people of Earth for some reason call their planet 'Gaia' from another of their languages."

"Exactly! You are indeed quick, Golan."

"But it seems to me that there's no need to make a mystery of this. If Gaia is really Earth, despite the difference in names, then Gaia, by your previous argument, ought to have a period of rotation of just one Galactic Day, a period of revolution of just one Galactic Year, and a giant satellite that revolves about it in just one month."

"Yes, it would have to be so."

"Well then, does it or doesn't it fulfill these requirements?"

"Actually I can't say. The information isn't given in the tables."

"Indeed? Well, then, Janov, shall we go to Gaia and time its periods and stare at its satellite?"

"I would like to, Golan," Pelorat hesitated. "The trouble is that the location isn't given exactly, either."

"You mean, all you have is the name and nothing more, and *that* is your excellent possibility?"

"But that is just why I want to visit the Galactic Library!"

"Well, wait. You say the table doesn't give the location exactly. Does it give any information at all?"

"It lists it in the Sayshell Sector—and adds a question mark."

"Well, then— Janov, don't be downcast. We will go to the Sayshell Sector and somehow we will find Gaia!"

7. FARMER

1.

Stor Gendibal jogged along the country road outside the University. It was not common practice for Second Foundationers to venture into the farming world of Trantor. They could do so, certainly, but when they did, they did not venture either far or for long.

Gendibal was an exception and he had, in times past, wondered why. Wondering meant exploring his own mind, something that Speakers, in particular, were encouraged to do. Their minds were at once their weapons and their targets, and they had to keep both offense and defense well honed.

Gendibal had decided, to his own satisfaction, that one reason he was different was because he had come from a planet that was both colder and more massive than the average inhabited planet. When he was brought to Trantor as a boy (through the net that was quietly cast throughout the Galaxy by agents of the Second Foundation on the lookout for talent), he found himself, therefore, in a lighter gravitational field and a delightfully mild climate. Naturally he enjoyed being in the open more than some of the others might.

In his early years on Trantor, he grew conscious of his puny, undersized frame, and he was afraid that settling back into the comfort of a benign world would turn him flabby indeed. He therefore undertook a series of self-developing exercises that had left him still puny in appearance but kept him wiry and with a good wind. Part of his regimen were these long walks and joggings — about which some at the Speaker's Table muttered. Gendibal disregarded their chattering.

He kept his own ways, despite the fact that he was first-generation. All the others at the Table were second- and third-generation, with parents and grandparents who had been Second Foundationers. And they were all older than he, too. What, then, was to be expected but muttering?

By long custom, all minds at the Speaker's Table were open (supposedly altogether, though it was a rare Speaker who didn't maintain a corner of privacy somewhere—in the long run, ineffectively, of course) and Gendibal knew that what they felt was envy. So did they; just as Gendibal knew his own attitude was defensive, overcompensating ambition. And so did they.

Besides (Gendibal's mind reverted to the reasons for his ventures into the hinterland) he had spent his childhood in a whole world—a large and expansive one, with grand and var-iegated scenery—and in a fertile valley of that world, sur-rounded by what he believed to be the most beautiful mountain ranges in the Galaxy. They were unbelievably spectacular in the grim winter of that world. He remembered his former world and the glories of a now-distant childhood. He dreamed about it often. How could he bring himself to be confined to a few dozen square miles of ancient architecture?

He looked about disparagingly as he jogged. Trantor was a mild and pleasant world, but it was not a rugged and beautiful one. Though it was a farming world, it was not a fertile planet.

It never had been. Perhaps that, as much as any other factor, had led to its becoming the administrative center of, first, an extensive union of planets and then of a Galactic Empire. There was no strong push to have it be anything else. It wasn't extraordinarily good for anything else.

After the Great Sack, one thing that kept Trantor going was its enormous supply of metal. It was a great mine, supplying half a hundred worlds with cheap alloy steel, aluminum, titanium, copper, magnesium—returning, in this way, what it had collected over thousands of years; depleting its supplies at a rate hundreds of times faster than the original rate of accumulation.

There were still enormous metal supplies available, but they were underground and harder to obtain. The Hamish farmers (who never called themselves "Trantorians," a term they considered ill-omened and which the Second Foundationers therefore reserved for themselves) had grown reluctant to deal with the metal any further. Superstition, undoubtedly.

Foolish of them. The metal that remained underground might well be poisoning the soil and further lowering its fertility. And yet, on the other hand, the population was thinly spread and the land supported them. And there were *some* sales of metal, always.

Gendibal's eyes roved over the flat horizon. Trantor was alive geologically, as almost all inhabited planets were, but it had been a hundred million years, at least, since the last major geological mountain-building period had occurred. What uplands existed had been eroded into gentle hills. Indeed, many of them had been leveled during the great metal-coating period of Trantor's history.

Off to the south, well out of sight, was the shore of Capital Bay, and beyond that, the Eastern Ocean, both of which had been re-established after the disruption of the underground cisterns.

To the north were the towers of Galactic University, obscuring the comparatively squat-but-wide Library (most of which was underground), and the remains of the Imperial Palace still farther north.

Immediately on either side were farms, on which there was an occasional building. He passed groups of cattle, goats, chickens—the wide variety of domesticated animals found on any Trantorian farm. None of them paid him any mind.

Gendibal thought casually that anywhere in the Galaxy, on any of the vast number of inhabited worlds, he would see these animals and that on no two worlds would they be exactly alike. He remembered the goats of home and his own tame nanny whom he had once milked. They were much larger and more resolute than the small and philosophical specimens that had been brought to Trantor and established there since the Great Sack. Over the inhabited worlds of the Galaxy, there were varieties of each of these animals, in numbers almost beyond counting, and there was no sophisticate on any world who didn't swear by his favorite variety, whether for meat, milk, eggs, wool, or anything else they could produce.

As usual, there were no Hamish in view. Gendibal had the feeling that the farmers avoided being seen by those whom they referred to as "scowlers" (a mispronunciation—perhaps deliberately—of the word "scholars" in their dialect). —Superstition, again.

Gendibal glanced up briefly at Trantor's sun. It was quite high in the sky, but its heat was not oppressive. In this location, at this latitude, the warmth stayed mild and the cold never bit. (Gendibal even missed the biting cold sometimes or so he imagined. He had never revisited his native world. Perhaps, he admitted to himself, because he didn't want to be disillusioned.)

He had the pleasant feel of muscles that were sharpened and tightened to keenness and he decided he had jogged just long enough. He settled down to a walk, breathing deeply.

He would be ready for the upcoming Table meeting and for one last push to force a change in policy, a new attitude that would reorganize the growing danger from the First Foundation and elsewhere and that would put an end to the fatal reliance on the "perfect" working of the Plan. When would they realize that the very perfection was the surest sign of danger?

Had anyone but himself proposed it, he knew, it would have gone through without trouble. As things stood now, there would be trouble, but it would go through, just the same, for old Shandess was supporting him and would undoubtedly continue to do so. He would not wish to enter the history books as the particular First Speaker under whom the Second Foundation had withered.

Hamish!

Gendibal was startled. He became aware of the distant tendril of mind well before he saw the person. It was Hamish mind—a farmer—coarse and unsubtle. Carefully Gendibal withdrew, leaving a touch so light as to be undetectable. Second Foundation policy was very firm in this respect.

The farmers were the unwitting shields of the Second Foundation. They must be left as untouched as possible.

No one who came to Trantor for trade or tourism ever saw anything other than the farmers, plus perhaps a few unimportant scholars living in the past. Remove the farmers or merely tamper with their innocence and the scholars would become more noticeable—with catastrophic results. (That was one of the classic demonstrations which neophytes at the University were expected to work out for themselves. The tremendous Deviations displayed on the Prime Radiant when the farmer minds were even slightly tampered with were astonishing.)

Gendibal saw him. It was a farmer, certainly, Hamish to the core. He was almost a caricature of what a Trantorian farmer should be—tall and wide, brown-skinned, roughly dressed, arms bare, dark-haired, dark-eyed, a long ungainly stride. Gendibal felt as though he could smell the barnyard about him. (Not too much scorn, he thought. Preem Palver had not minded playing the role of farmer, when that was necessary to his plans. Some farmer he was—short and plump and soft. It was his mind that had fooled the teenaged Arkady, never his body.)

The farmer was approaching him, clumping down the road, staring at him openly—something that made Gendibal frown. No Hamish man or woman had ever looked at him in this manner. Even the children ran away and peered from a distance.

Gendibal did not slow his own stride. There would be room enough to pass the other with neither comment nor glance and that would be best. He determined to stay away from the farmer's mind.

Gendibal drifted to one side, but the farmer was not going to have that. He stopped, spread his legs wide, stretched out his large arms as though to block passage, and said, "Ho! Be you scowler?"

Try as he might, Gendibal could not refrain from sensing the wash of pugnacity in the approaching mind. He stopped. It would be impossible to attempt to pass by without conversation and that would be, in itself, a weary task. Used as one was to the swift and subtle interplay of sound and expression and thought and mentality that combined to make up the communication between Second Foundationers, it was wearisome to resort to word combination alone. It was like prying up a boulder by arm and shoulder, with a crowbar lying nearby.

Gendibal said, quietly and with careful lack of emotion, "I am a scholar. Yes."

"Ho! You *am* a scowler. Don't we speak outlandish now? And cannot I see that you be one or *am* one?" He ducked his head in a mocking bow. "Being, as you be, small and weazen and pale and up-nosed."

"What is it you want of me, Hamishman?" asked Gendibal, unmoved.

"I be titled Rufirant. And Karoll be my previous." His accent became noticeably more Hamish. His *r*'s rolled throatily.

Gendibal said, "What is it you want with me, Karoll Rufirant?"

"And how be you titled, scowler?"

"Does it matter? You may continue to call me 'scholar.'"

"If I ask, it matters that I be answered, little up-nosed scowler."

"Well then, I am titled Stor Gendibal and I will now go about my business."

"What be your business?"

Gendibal felt the hair prickling on the back of his neck. There were other minds present. He did not have to turn to know there were three more Hamishmen behind him. Off in the distance, there were others. The farmer smell was strong.

"My business, Karoll Rufirant, is certainly none of yours."

"Say you so?" Rufirant's voice rose. "Mates, he says his business be not ours."

There was a laugh from behind him and a voice sounded. "Right he be, for his business be book-mucking and 'puter-rubbing, and that be naught for true men."

"Whatever my business is," said Gendibal firmly, "I will be about it now."

"And how will you do that, wee scowler?" said Rufirant.

"By passing you."

"You would try? You would not fear arm-stopping?"

"By you and all your mates? Or by you alone?" Gendibal suddenly dropped into thick Hamish dialect. "Art not feared alane?"

Strictly speaking, it was not proper to prod him in this manner, but it would stop a mass attack and that *had* to be stopped, lest it force a still greater indiscretion on his part.

It worked. Rufirant's expression grew lowering. "If fear there be, book-boy, th'art the one to be full of it. Mates, make room. Stand back and let him pass that he may see if I be feared alane."

Rufirant lifted his great arms and moved them about. Gendibal did not fear the farmer's pugilistic science; but there was always a chance that a goodly blow might land.

Gendibal approached cautiously, working with delicate speed within Rufirant's mind. Not much—just a touch, unfelt—but enough to slow reflexes that crucial notch. Then out, and into all the others, who were now gathering in greater numbers. Gendibal's Speaker mind darted back and forth with virtuosity, never resting in one mind long enough to leave a mark, but just long enough for the detection of something that might be useful.

He approached the farmer catlike, watchful, aware and relieved that no one was making a move to interfere.

Rufirant struck suddenly, but Gendibal saw it in his mind before any muscle had begun to tighten and he stepped to one side. The blow whistled past, with little room to spare. Yet Gendibal still stood there, unshaken. There was a collective sigh from the others.

Gendibal made no attempt to either parry or return a blow. It would be difficult to parry without paralyzing his own arm and to return a blow would be of no use, for the farmer would withstand it without trouble.

He could only maneuver the man as though he were a bull, forcing him to miss. That would serve to break his morale as direct opposition would not.

Bull-like and roaring, Rufirant charged. Gendibal was ready and drifted to one side just sufficiently to allow the farmer to miss his clutch. Again the charge. Again the miss.

Gendibal felt his own breath begin to whistle through his nose. The physical effort was small, but the mental effort of trying to control without controlling was enormously difficult. He could not keep it up long.

He said—as calmly as he could while batting lightly at Rufirant's fear-depressant mechanism, trying to rouse in a minimalist manner what must surely be the farmer's superstitious dread of scholars—"I will now go about my business."

Rufirant's face distorted with rage, but for a moment he did not move. Gendibal could sense his thinking. The little scholar had melted away—like magic. Gendibal could feel the other's fear rise and for a moment—

But then the Hamish rage surged higher and drowned the fear.

Rufirant shouted, "Mates! Scowler be dancer. He do duck on nimble toes and scorns the rules of honest Hamish blow-for-blow. Seize him. Hold him. We will trade blow for blow, then. He may be first-striker, gift of me, and I—I will be last-striker."

Gendibal found the gaps among those who now surrounded him. His only chance was to maintain a gap long enough to get through, then to run, trusting to his own wind and to his ability to dull the farmers' will.

Back and forth he dodged, with his mind cramping in effort.

It would not work. There were too many of them and the necessity of abiding within the rules of Trantorian behavior was too constricting.

He felt hands on his arms. He was held.

He would have to interfere with at least a few of the minds. It would be unacceptable and his career would be destroyed. But his life—his very life—was at hazard.

How had this happened?

2.

The meeting of the Table was not complete.

It was not the custom to wait if any Speaker were late. Nor, thought Shandess, was the Table in a mood to wait, in any case. Stor Gendibal was the youngest and far from sufficiently aware of the fact. He acted as though youth were in itself a virtue and age a matter of negligence on the part of those who should know better. Gendibal was not popular with the other Speakers. He was not, in point of fact, entirely popular with Shandess himself. But popularity was not at issue here.

Delora Delarmi broke in on his reverie. She was looking at him out of wide blue eyes, her round face—with its accustomed air of innocence and friendliness—masking an acute mind (to all but other Second Foundationers of her own rank) and ferocity of concentration.

She said, smiling, "First Speaker, do we wait longer?" (The meeting had not yet been formally called to order so that, strictly speaking, she could open the conversation, though another might have waited for Shandess to speak first by right of his title.)

Shandess looked at her disarmingly, despite the slight breach in courtesy. "Ordinarily we would not, Speaker Delarmi, but since the Table meets precisely to hear Speaker Gendibal, it is suitable to stretch the rules."

"Where is he, First Speaker?"

"That, Speaker Delarmi, I do not know."

Delarmi looked about the rectangle of faces. There was the First Speaker and what should have been eleven other Speakers. —Only twelve. Through five centuries, the Second Foundation had expanded its powers and its duties, but all attempts to expand the Table beyond twelve had failed.

Twelve it had been after Seldon's death, when the second First Speaker (Seldon himself had always been considered as having been the first of the line) had established it, and twelve it still was.

Why twelve? That number divided itself easily into groups

of identical size. It was small enough to consult as a whole and large enough to do work in subgroups. More would have been too unwieldy; fewer, too inflexible.

So went the explanations. In fact, no one knew why the number had been chosen—or why it should be immutable. But then, even the Second Foundation could find itself a slave to tradition.

It took Delarmi only a flashing moment to have her mind twiddle the matter as she looked from face to face, and mind to mind, and then, sardonically, at the empty seat—the junior seat.

She was satisfied that there was no sympathy at all with Gendibal. The young man, she had always felt, had all the charm of a centipede and was best treated as one. So far, only his unquestioned ability and talent had kept anyone from openly proposing trial for expulsion. (Only two Speakers had been impeached—but not convicted—in the hemi-millennial history of the Second Foundation.)

The obvious contempt, however, of missing a meeting of the Table was worse than many an offense and Delarmi was pleased to sense that the mood for trial had moved forward rather more than a notch.

She said, "First Speaker, if you do not know the where-abouts of Speaker Gendibal, I would be pleased to tell you."

"Yes, Speaker?"

"Who among us does not know that this young man" (she used no honorific in speaking of him, and it was some-thing that everyone noted, of course) "finds business among the Hamish continually? What that business might be, I do not ask, but he is among them now and his concern with them is clearly important enough to take precedence over this Table."

"I believe," said another of the Speakers, "that he merely walks or jogs as a form of physical exercise."

Delarmi smiled again. She enjoyed smiling. It cost her nothing. "The University, the Library, the Palace, and the entire region surrounding these are ours. It is small in com-parison with the planet itself, but it contains room enough,

I think, for physical exercise. —First Speaker, might we not begin?"

The First Speaker sighed inwardly. He had the full power to keep the Table waiting—or, indeed, to adjourn the meeting until a time when Gendibal was present.

No First Speaker could long function smoothly, however, without at least the passive support of the other Speakers and it was never wise to irritate them. Even Preem Palver had occasionally been forced into cajolery to get his way. —Besides, Gendibal's absence was annoying, even to the First Speaker. The young Speaker might as well learn he was not a law unto himself.

And now, as First Speaker, he did speak first, saying, "We will begin. Speaker Gendibal has presented some startling deductions from Prime Radiant data. He believes that there is some organization that is working to maintain the Seldon Plan more efficiently than we can and that it does so for its own purpose. We must, in his view therefore, learn more about it out of self-defense. You all have been informed of this, and this meeting is to allow you all a chance to question Speaker Gendibal, in order that we may come to some conclusion as to future policy."

It was, in fact, even unnecessary to say this much. Shandess held his mind open, so they all knew. Speaking was a matter of courtesy.

Delarmi looked about swiftly. The other ten seemed content to allow her to take on the role of anti-Gendibal spokesperson. She said, "Yet Gendibal" (again the omission of the honorific) "does not know and cannot say what or who this other organization is."

She phrased it unmistakably as a statement, which skirted the edge of rudeness. It was as much as to say: I can analyze your mind; you need not bother to explain.

The First Speaker recognized the rudeness and made the swift decision to ignore it. "The fact that Speaker Gendibal" (he punctiliously avoided the omission of the honorific and did not even point up the fact by stressing it) "does not know and cannot say what the other organization is, does not mean it does not exist. The people of the First Foundation, through most of their history, knew virtually nothing about us and, in fact, know next to nothing about us now. Do you question our existence?"

"It does not follow," said Delarmi, "that because we are unknown and yet exist, that anything, in order to exist, need only be unknown." And she laughed lightly.

"True enough. That is why Speaker Gendibal's assertion must be examined most carefully. It is based on rigorous mathematical deduction, which I have gone over myself and which I urge you all to consider. It is" (he searched for a cast of mind that best expressed his views) "not unconvincing."

"And this First Foundationer, Golan Trevize, who hovers in your mind but whom you do not mention?" (Another rudeness and this time the First Speaker flushed a bit.) "What of him?"

The First Speaker said, "It is Speaker Gendibal's thought that this man, Trevize, is the tool—perhaps an unwitting one—of this organization and that we must not ignore him."

"If," said Delarmi, sitting back in her chair and pushing her graying hair backward and out of her eyes, "this organization—whatever it is—exists and if it is dangerously powerful in its mental capabilities and is so hidden, is it likely to be maneuvering so openly by way of someone as noticeable as an exiled Councilman of the First Foundation?"

The First Speaker said gravely, "One would think not. And yet I have noticed something that is most disquieting. I do not understand it." Almost involuntarily he buried the thought in his mind, ashamed that others might see it.

Each of the Speakers noted the mental action and, as was rigorously required, respected the shame. Delarmi did, too, but she did so impatiently. She said, in accordance with the required formula, "May we request that you let us know your thoughts, since we understand and forgive any shame you may feel?"

The First Speaker said, "Like you, I do not see on what grounds one should suppose Councilman Trevize to be a tool of the other organization, or what purpose he could possibly serve if he were. Yet Speaker Gendibal seems sure of it, and one cannot ignore the possible value of intuition in anyone who has qualified for Speaker. I therefore attempted to apply the Plan to Trevize."

"To a single person?" said one of the Speakers in low-voiced surprise, and then indicated his contrition at once for having accompanied the question with a thought that was clearly the equivalent of: What a fool!

"To a single person," said the First Speaker, "and you are right. What a fool I am! I know very well that the Plan cannot possibly apply to individuals, not even to small groups of individuals. Nevertheless, I was curious. I extrapolated the Interpersonal Intersections far past the reasonable limits, but I did it in sixteen different ways and chose a region rather than a point. I then made use of all the details we know about Trevize—a Councilman of the First Foundation does not go completely unnoticed—and of the Foundation's Mayor. I then threw it all together, rather higgledy-piggledy, I'm afraid." He paused.

"Well?" said Delarmi. "I gather you— Were the results surprising?"

"There weren't any results, as you might all expect," said the First Speaker. "Nothing can be done with a single individual, and yet—and yet—"

"And yet?"

"I have spent forty years analyzing results and I have grown used to obtaining a clear feeling of what the results would be *before* they were analyzed—and I have rarely been mistaken. In this case, even though there were no results, I developed the strong feeling that Gendibal was right and that Trevize should not be left to himself."

"Why not, First Speaker?" asked Delarmi, clearly taken aback at the strong feeling in the First Speaker's mind.

"I am ashamed," said the First Speaker, "that I have let myself be tempted into using the Plan for a purpose for which it is not fit. I am further ashamed now that I am allowing myself to be influenced by something that is purely intuitive. —Yet I must, for I feel this very strongly. If

Speaker Gendibal is right—if we are in danger from an unknown direction—then I feel that when the time comes that our affairs are at a crisis, it will be Trevize who will hold and play the deciding card."

"On what basis do you feel this?" said Delarmi, shocked.

First Speaker Shandess looked about the table miserably, "I have no basis. The psychohistorical mathematics produces nothing, but as I watched the interplay of relationships, it seemed to me that Trevize is the key to everything. Attention must be paid to this young man."

3.

Gendibal knew that he would not get back in time to join the meeting of the Table. It might be that he would not get back at all.

He was held firmly and he tested desperately about him to see how he could best manage to force them to release him.

Rufirant stood before him now, exultant. "Be you ready now, scowler? Blow for blow, strike for strike, Hamish-fashion. Come then, art the smaller; strike then first."

Gendibal said, "Will someone hold thee, then, as I be held?"

Rufirant said, "Let him go. Nah nah. His arms alane. Leave arms free, but hold legs strong. We want no dancing."

Gendibal felt himself pinned to the ground. His arms were free.

"Strike, scowler," said Rufirant. "Give us a blow."

And then Gendibal's probing mind found something that answered—indignation, a sense of injustice and pity. He had no choice; he would have to run the risk of outright strengthening and then improvising on the basis of—

There was no need! He had not touched this new mind, yet it reacted as he would have wished. Precisely.

He suddenly became aware of a small figure—stocky, with long, tangled black hair and arms thrust outward—

careening madly into his field of view and pushing madly at the Hamish farmer.

The figure was that of a woman. Gendibal thought grimly that it was a measure of his tension and preoccupation that he had not noted this till his eyes told him so.

"Karoll Rufirant!" She shrieked at the farmer. "Art bully and coward! Strike for strike, Hamish-fashion? You be two times yon scowler's size. You'll be in more sore danger attacking me. Be there renown in pashing yon poor spalp? There be shame, I'm thinking. It will be a fair heap of finger-pointing and there'll be full saying, 'Yon be Rufirant, renowned baby-smasher.' It'll be laughter, I'm thinking, and no decent Hamishman will be drinking with you—and no decent Hamishwoman will be ought with you."

Rufirant was trying to stem the torrent, warding off the blows she was aiming at him, attempting weakly to answer with a placating, "Now, Sura. Now, Sura."

Gendibal was aware that hands no longer grasped him, that Rufirant no longer glared at him, that the minds of all were no longer concerned with him.

Sura was not concerned with him, either; her fury was concentrated solely on Rufirant. Gendibal, recovering, now looked to take measures to keep that fury alive and to strengthen the uneasy shame flooding Rufirant's mind, and to do both so lightly and skillfully as to leave no mark. Again, there was no need.

The woman said, "All of you back-step. Look here. If it be not sufficient that this Karoll-heap be like giant to this starveling, there must be five or six more of you ally-friends to share in shame and go back to farm with glorious tale of derring-do in baby-smashing. 'I held the spalp's arm,' you'll say, 'and giant Rufirant-block pashed him in face when he was not to back-strike.' And you'll say, 'But I held his foot, so give me also-glory.' And Rufirant-chunk will say, 'I could not have him on his lane, so my furrow-mates pinned him and, with help of all six, I gloried on him.'"

"But Sura," said Rufirant, almost whining, "I told scowler he might have first-strike."

"And fearful you were of the mighty blows of his thin arms, not so, Rufirant-thickhead. Come. Let him go where he be going, and the rest of you to your homes back-crawl, if so be those homes will still find a welcome-making for you. You had all best hope the grand deeds of this day be forgotten. And they will *not* be, for I be spreading them far-wide, if you do make me any the more fiercely raging than I be raging now."

They trooped off quietly, heads hanging, not looking back.

Gendibal stared after them, then back at the woman. She was dressed in blouse and trousers, with roughmade shoes on her feet. Her face was wet with perspiration and she breathed heavily. Her nose was rather large, her breasts heavy (as best Gendibal could tell through the looseness of her blouse), and her bare arms muscular. —But then, the Hamishwomen worked in the fields beside their men.

She was looking at him sternly, arms akimbo. "Well, scowler, why be lagging? Go on to Place of Scowlers. Be you feared? Shall I company you?"

Gendibal could smell the perspiration on clothes that were clearly not freshly laundered, but under the circumstances it would be most discourteous to show any repulsion.

"I thank you, Miss Sura—"

"The name be Novi," she said gruffly. "Sura Novi. You may say Novi. It be unneeded to moresay."

"I thank you, Novi. You have been very helpful. You be welcome to company me, not for fear of mine but for company-pleasure in you." And he bowed gracefully, as he might have bowed to one of the young women at the University.

Novi flushed, seemed uncertain, and then tried to imitate his gesture. "Pleasure—be mine," she said, as though searching for words that would adequately express her pleasure and lend an air of culture.

They walked together. Gendibal knew well that each leisurely step made him the more unforgivably late for the Table meeting, but by now he had had a chance to think on the significance of what had taken place and he was icily content to let the lateness grow.

The University buildings were looming ahead of them when Sura Novi stopped and said hesitantly, "Master Scowler?"

Apparently, Gendibal thought, as she approached what she called the "Place of Scowlers," she grew more polite. He had a momentary urge to say, "Address you not yon poor spalp?" —But that would embarrass her beyond reason.

"Yes, Novi?"

"Be it very fine-like and rich in Place of Scowlers?"

"It's nice," said Gendibal.

"I once dreamed I be in Place. And—and I be scowler."

"Someday," said Gendibal politely, "I'll show it thee."

Her look at him showed plainly she didn't take it for mere politeness. She said, "I can write. I be taught by schoolmaster. If I write letter to thee," she tried to make it casual, "how do I mark it so it come to thee?"

"Just say, 'Speaker's House, Apartment 27,' and it will come to me. But I must go, Novi."

He bowed again, and again she tried to imitate the action. They moved off in opposite directions and Gendibal promptly put her out of his mind. He thought instead of the Table meeting and, in particular, of Speaker Delora Delarmi. His thoughts were not gentle.

8. FARMWOMAN

1.

The Speakers sat about the Table, frozen in their mental shielding. It was as though all—with one accord—had hidden their minds to avoid irrevocable insult to the First Speaker after his statement concerning Trevize. Surreptitiously they glanced toward Delarmi and even that gave away much. Of them all, she was best-known for her irreverence. —Even Gendibal paid more lip service to convention.

Delarmi was aware of the glances and she knew that she had no choice but to face up to this impossible situation. In fact, she did not want to duck the issue. In all the history of the Second Foundation, no First Speaker had ever been impeached for misanalysis (and behind the term, which she had invented as coverup, was the unacknowledged *incompetence*). Such impeachment now became possible. She would not hang back.

"First Speaker!" she said softly, her thin, colorless lips more nearly invisible than usual in the general whiteness of her face. "You yourself say you have no basis for your opinion, that the psychohistorical mathematics show nothing. Do you ask us to base a crucial decision on a mystical feeling?"

The First Speaker looked up, his forehead corrugated. He was aware of the universal shielding at the Table. He knew what it meant. He said coldly, "I do not hide the lack of evidence. I present you with nothing falsely. What I offer is the strongly intuitive feeling of a First Speaker, one with decades of experience who has spent nearly a lifetime in the close analysis of the Seldon Plan." He looked about him with a proud rigidity he rarely displayed, and one by one the mental shields softened and dropped. Delarmi's (when he turned to stare at her) was the last.

She said, with a disarming frankness that filled her mind as though nothing else had ever been there, "I accept your statement, of course, First Speaker. Nevertheless, I think you might perhaps want to reconsider. As you think about it now, having already expressed shame at having to fall back on intuition, would you wish your remarks to be stricken from the record—if, in your judgment they should be—"

And Gendibal's voice cut in. "What are these remarks that should be stricken from the record?"

Every pair of eyes turned in unison. Had their shields not been up during the crucial moments before, they would have been aware of his approach long before he was at the door.

"All shields up a moment ago? All unaware of my entrance?" said Gendibal sardonically. "What a commonplace meeting of the Table we have here. Was no one on their guard for my coming? Or did you all fully expect that I would not arrive?"

This outburst was a flagrant violation of all standards. For Gendibal to arrive late was bad enough. For him to then enter unannounced was worse. For him to speak before the First Speaker had acknowledged his attendance was worst of all.

The First Speaker turned to him. All else was superceded. The question of discipline came first.

"Speaker Gendibal," he said, "you are late. You arrive unannounced. You speak. Is there any reason why you should not be suspended from your seat for thirty days?"

"Of course. The move for suspension should not be considered until first we consider who it was that made it certain I *would* be late—and why." Gendibal's words were cool and measured, but his mind clothed his thoughts with anger and he did not care who sensed it.

Certainly Delarmi sensed it. She said forcefully, "This man is mad."

"Mad? This woman is mad to say so. Or aware of guilt.
—First Speaker, I address myself to you and move a point
of personal privilege," said Gendibal.

"Personal privilege of what nature, Speaker?"

"First Speaker, I accuse someone here of attempted
murder."

The room exploded as every Speaker rose to his or her
feet in a simultaneous babble of words, expression, and
mentality.

The First Speaker raised his arms. He cried, "The Speaker
must have his chance to express his point of personal privilege." He found himself forced to intensify his authority,
mentally, in a manner most inappropriate to the place—yet
there was no choice.

The babble quieted.

Gendibal waited unmoved until the silence was both au-
dibly and mentally profound. He said, "On my way here,
moving along a Hamish road at a distance and approaching
at a speed that would have easily assured my arrival in good
time for the meeting, I was stopped by several farmers and
narrowly escaped being beaten, perhaps being killed. As it
was, I was delayed and have but just arrived. May I point
out, to begin with, that I know of no instance since the
Great Sack that a Second Foundationer has been spoken to
disrespectfully—let alone manhandled—by one of these
Hamish people."

"Nor do I," said the First Speaker.

Delarmi cried out, "Second Foundationers do not habitually walk alone in Hamish territory! You *invite* this by
doing so!"

"It is true," said Gendibal, "that I habitually walk alone
in Hamish territory. I have walked there hundreds of times
in every direction. Yet I have never been accosted before.
Others do not walk with the freedom that I do, but no one
exiles himself from the world or imprisons himself in the
University and no one has ever been accosted. I recall occasions when Delarmi—" and then, as though remembering
the honorific too late, he deliberately converted it into a

deadly insult. "I mean to say, I recall when *Speakeress* Delarmi was in Hamish territory, at one time or another, and yet *she* was not accosted."

"Perhaps," said Delarmi, with eyes widened into a glare, "because I did not speak to them first and because I maintained my distance. Because I behaved as though I deserved respect, I was accorded it."

"Strange," said Gendibal, "and I was about to say that it was because you presented a more formidable appearance than I did. After all, few dare approach you even here. —But tell me, why should it be that of all times for interference, the Hamish would choose this day to face me, when I am to attend an important meeting of the Table?"

"If it were not because of your behavior, then it must have been chance," said Delarmi. "I have not heard that even all of Seldon's mathematics has removed the role of chance from the Galaxy—certainly not in the case of individual events. Or are you, too, speaking from intuitional inspiration?" (There was a soft mental sigh from one or two Speakers at this sideways thrust at the First Speaker.)

"It was not my behavior. It was not chance. It was deliberate interference," said Gendibal.

"How can we know that?" asked the First Speaker gently. He could not help but soften toward Gendibal as a result of Delarmi's last remark.

"My mind is open to you, First Speaker. I give you— and all the Table—my memory of events."

The transfer took but a few moments. The First Speaker said, "Shocking! You behaved very well, Speaker, under circumstances of considerable pressure. I agree that the Hamish behavior is anomalous and warrants investigation. In the meantime, please join our meeting—"

"A moment!" cut in Delarmi. "How certain are we that the Speaker's account is accurate?"

Gendibal's nostrils flared at the insult, but he retained his level composure. "My mind is open."

"I have known open minds that were not open."

"I have no doubt of that, Speaker," said Gendibal, "since

you, like the rest of us, must keep your own mind under inspection at all times. My mind, when open, however, is open."

The First Speaker said, "Let us have no further—"

"A point of personal privilege, First Speaker, with apologies for the interruption," said Delarmi.

"Personal privilege of what nature, Speaker?"

"Speaker Gendibal has accused one of us of attempted murder, presumably by instigating the farmer to attack him. As long as the accusation is not withdrawn, I must be viewed as a possible murderer, as would every person in this room—including you, First Speaker."

The First Speaker said, "Would you withdraw the accusation, Speaker Gendibal?"

Gendibal took his seat and put his hands down upon its arms, gripping them tightly, as though taking ownership of it, and said, "I will do so, as soon as someone explains why a Hamish farmer, rallying several others, should deliberately set out to delay me on my way to this meeting."

"A thousand reasons, perhaps," said the First Speaker. "I repeat that this event will be investigated. Will you, for now, Speaker Gendibal, and in the interest of continuing the present discussion, withdraw your accusation?"

"I cannot, First Speaker. I spent long minutes trying, as delicately as I might, to search his mind for ways to alter his behavior without damage and failed. His mind lacked the give it should have had. His emotions were fixed, as though by an outside mind."

Delarmi said with a sudden little smile, "And you think one of us was the outside mind? Might it not have been your mysterious organization that is competing with us, that is more powerful than we are?"

"It might," said Gendibal.

"In that case, we—who are not members of this organization that only you know of—are not guilty and you should withdraw your accusation. Or can it be that you are accusing someone here of being under the control of this strange organization? Perhaps one of us here is not quite what he or she seems?"

"Perhaps," said Gendibal stolidly, quite aware that Delarmi was feeding him rope with a noose at the end of it.

"It might seem," said Delarmi, reaching the noose and preparing to tighten it, "that your dream of a secret, unknown, hidden, mysterious organization is a nightmare of paranoia. It would fit in with your paranoid fantasy that Hamish farmers are being influenced, that Speakers are under hidden control. I am willing, however, to follow this peculiar thought line of yours for a while longer. Which of us here, Speaker, do you think is under control? Might it be me?"

Gendibal said, "I would not think so, Speaker. If you were attempting to rid yourself of me in so indirect a manner, you would not so openly advertise your dislike for me."

"A double-double-cross, perhaps?" said Delarmi. She was virtually purring. "That would be a common conclusion in a paranoid fantasy."

"So it might be. You are more experienced in such matters than I."

Speaker Lestim Gianni interrupted hotly. "See here, Speaker Gendibal, if you are exonerating Speaker Delarmi, you are directing your accusations the more tightly at the rest of us. What grounds would *any* of us have to delay your presence at this meeting, let alone wish you dead?"

Gendibal answered quickly, as though he had been waiting for the question. "When I entered, the point under discussion was the striking of remarks from the record, remarks made by the First Speaker. I was the only Speaker not in a position to hear those remarks. Let me know what they were and I rather think I will tell you the motive for delaying me."

The First Speaker said, "I had stated—and it was something to which Speaker Delarmi and others took serious exception—that I had decided, on the basis of intuition and of a most inappropriate use of psychohistorical mathematics, that the entire future of the Plan may rest on the exile of First Foundationer Golan Trevize."

Gendibal said, "What other Speakers may think is up to them. For my part, I agree with this hypothesis. Trevize is the key. I find his sudden ejection by the First Foundation too curious to be innocent."

Delarmi said, "Would you care to say, Speaker Gendibal, that Trevize is in the grip of this mystery organization—or that the people who exiled him are? Is perhaps everyone and everything in their control except you and the First Speaker—and me, whom you have declared to be uncontrolled?"

Gendibal said, "These ravings require no answer. Instead let me ask if there is any Speaker here who would like to express agreement on this matter with the First Speaker and myself? You have read, I presume, the mathematical treatment that I have, with the First Speaker's approval, circulated among you."

There was silence.

"I repeat my request," said Gendibal. "Anyone?"

There was silence.

Gendibal said, "First Speaker, you now have the motive for delaying me."

The First Speaker said, "State it explicitly."

"You have expressed the need to deal with Trevize, with this First Foundationer. It represents an important initiative in policy and if the Speakers had read my treatment, they would have known in a general way what was in the wind. If, nevertheless, they had unanimously disagreed with you—unanimously—then, by traditional self-limitation, you would have been unable to go forward. If even one Speaker backed you, then you would be able to implement this new policy. I was the *one* Speaker who would back you, as anyone who had read my treatment would know, and it was necessary that I must, at all costs, be kept from the Table. That trick proved nearly successful, but I am now here and I back the First Speaker. I agree with him and he can, in accordance with tradition, disregard the disagreement of the ten other Speakers."

Delarmi struck the table with her fist. "The implication is that someone knew in advance what the First Speaker would advise, knew in advance that Speaker Gendibal would support it and that all the rest would not—that someone knew what he could not have known. There is the further implication that this initiative is not to the liking of Speaker Gendibal's paranoia-inspired organization and that they are fighting to prevent it and that, therefore, one or more of us is under the control of that organization."

"The implication is there," agreed Gendibal. "Your analysis is masterly."

"Whom do you accuse?" cried out Delarmi.

"No one. I call upon the First Speaker to take up the matter. It is clear that there is someone in our organization who is working against us. I suggest that everyone working for the Second Foundation should undergo a thorough mental analysis. Everyone, including the Speakers themselves. Even including myself—and the First Speaker."

The meeting of the Table broke up in greater confusion and greater excitement than any on record.

And when the First Speaker finally spoke the phrase of adjournment, Gendibal—without speaking to anyone—made his way back to his room. He knew well that he had not one friend among the Speakers, that even whatever support the First Speaker could give him would be half-hearted at best.

He could not tell whether he feared for himself or for the entire Second Foundation. The taste of doom was sour in his mouth.

2.

Gendibal did not sleep well. His waking thoughts and his sleeping dreams were alike engaged in quarreling with Delora Delarmi. In one passage of one dream, there was even a confusion between her and the Hamish farmer, Rufirant, so that Gendibal found himself facing an out-of-proportion Delarmi advancing upon him with enormous fists and a sweet smile that revealed needlelike teeth.

He finally woke, later than usual, with no sensation of having rested and with the buzzer on his night table in muted action. He turned over to bring his hand down upon the contact.

"Yes? What is it?"

"Speaker!" The voice was that of the floor proctor, rather less than suitably respectful. "A visitor wishes to speak to you."

"A visitor?" Gendibal punched his appointment schedule and the screen showed nothing before noon. He pushed the time button; it was 8:32 A.M. He said peevishly, "Who in space and time is it?"

"Will not give a name, Speaker." Then, with clear disapproval, "One of these Hamishers, Speaker. Arrived at your invitation." The last sentence was said with even clearer disapproval.

"Let him wait in the reception room till I come down. It will take time."

Gendibal did not hurry. Throughout the morning ablutions, he remained lost in thought. That someone was using the Hamish to hamper his movements made sense—but he would like to know who that someone was. And what was this new intrusion of the Hamish into his very quarters? A complicated trap of some sort?

How in the name of Seldon would a Hamish farmer get into the University? What reason could he advance? What reason could he really have?

For one fleeting moment, Gendibal wondered if he ought to arm himself. He decided against it almost at once, since he felt contemptuously certain of being able to control any single farmer on the University grounds without any danger to himself—and without any unacceptable marking of a Hamish mind.

Gendibal decided he had been too strongly affected by

the incident with Karoll Rufirant the day before. —Was it the very farmer, by the way? No longer under the influence, perhaps—of whatever or whoever it was—he might well have come to Gendibal to apologize for what he had done and with apprehension of punishment. —But how would Rufirant know where to go? Whom to approach?

Gendibal swung down the corridor resolutely and entered the waiting room. He stopped in astonishment, then turned to the proctor, who was pretending to be busy in his glass-walled cubicle.

"Proctor, you did not say the visitor was a woman."

The proctor said quietly, "Speaker, I said a Hamisher. You did not ask further."

"Minimal information, Proctor? I must remember that as one of your characteristics." (And he must check to see if the proctor was a Delarmi appointee. And he must remember, from now on, to note the functionaries who surrounded him, "Lowlies" whom it was too easy to ignore from the height of his still-new Speakership.) "Are any of the conference rooms available?"

The proctor said, "Number 4 is the only one available, Speaker. It will be free for three hours." He glanced briefly at the Hamish-woman, then at Gendibal, with blank innocence.

"We will use Number 4, Proctor, and I would advise you to mind your thoughts." Gendibal struck, not gently, and the proctor's shield closed far too slowly. Gendibal knew well it was beneath his dignity to manhandle a lesser mind, but a person who was incapable of shielding an unpleasant conjecture against a superior ought to learn not to indulge in one. The proctor would have a mild headache for a few hours. It was well deserved.

3.

Her name did not spring immediately to mind and Gendibal was in no mood to delve deeper. She could scarcely expect him to remember, in any case.

He said peevishly, "You are—"

"I be Novi, Master Scowler," she said in what was almost a gasp. "My previous be Sura, but I be called Novi plain."

"Yes. Novi. We met yesterday; I remember now. I have not forgotten that you came to my defense." He could not bring himself to use the Hamish accent on the very University grounds. "Now how did you get here?"

"Master, you said I might write letter. You said, it should say, 'Speaker's House, Apartment 27.' I self-bring it and I show the writing—my own writing, Master." She said it with a kind of bashful pride. "They ask, 'For whom be this writing?' I heared your calling when you said it to that oafish bane-top, Rufirant. I say it be for Stor Gendibal, Master Scowler."

"And they let you pass, Novi? Didn't they ask to see the letter?"

"I be very frightened. I think maybe they feel gentle-sorry. I said, 'Scowler Gendibal promise to show me Place of Scowlers,' and they smile. One of them at gate-door say to other, 'And that not all he be show her.' And they show me where to go, and say not to go elseplace at all or I be thrown out moment-wise."

Gendibal reddened faintly. By Seldon, if he felt the need for Hamish amusement, it would not be in so open a fashion and his choice would have been made more selectively. He looked at the Trantorian woman with an inward shake of his head.

She seemed quite young, younger perhaps than hard work had made her appear. She could not be more than twenty-five, at which age Hamishwomen were usually already married. She wore her dark hair in the braids that signified her to be unmarried—virginal, in fact—and he was not surprised. Her performance yesterday showed her to have enormous talent as a shrew and he doubted that a Hamishman could easily be found who would dare be yoked to her tongue and her ready fist. Nor was her appearance much of an attraction. Though she had gone to pains to make herself look presentable, her face was angular and plain, her hands red and knobby. What he could see of her figure seemed built for endurance rather than for grace.

Her lower lip began to tremble under his scrutiny. He could sense her embarrassment and fright quite plainly and felt pity. She had, indeed, been of use to him yesterday and that was what counted.

He said, in an attempt to be genial and soothing, "So you have come to see the—uh—Place of Scholars?"

She opened her dark eyes wide (they were rather fine) and said, "Master, be not ired with me, but I come to be scowler own-self."

"You want to be a *scholar*?" Gendibal was thunderstruck. "My good woman—"

He paused. How on Trantor could one explain to a completely unsophisticated farmwoman the level of intelligence, training, and mental stamina required to be what Trantorians called a "scowler"?

But Sura Novi drove on fiercely. "I be a writer *and* a reader. I have read whole books to end and from beginning, too. And I have *wish* to be scowler. I do not wish to be farmer's wife. I be no person for farm. I will not wed farmer or have farmer children." She lifted her head and said proudly, "I be asked. Many times. I always say, 'Nay.' Politely, but 'Nay.'"

Gendibal could see plainly enough that she was lying. She had not been asked, but he kept his face straight. He said, "What will you do with your life if you do not marry?"

Novi brought her hand down on the table, palm flat. "I will be scowler. I *not* be farmwoman."

"What if I cannot make you a scholar?"

"Then I be nothing and I wait to die. I be nothing in life if I be not a scowler."

For a moment there was the impulse to search her mind and find out the extent of her motivation. But it would be wrong to do so. A Speaker did not amuse one's self by rummaging through the helpless minds of others. There was a code to the science and technique of mental control—

mentalics—as to other professions. Or there should be. (He was suddenly regretful he had struck out at the proctor.)

He said, "Why *not* be a farmwoman, Novi?" With a little manipulation, he could make her content with that and manipulate some Hamish lout into being happy to marry·her— and she to marry him. It would do no harm. It would be a kindness. —But it was against the law and thus unthinkable.

She said, "I *not* be. A farmer is a clod. He works with earth-lumps, and he becomes earth-lump. If I be farmwoman, I be earth-lump, too. I will be timeless to read and write, and I will forget. My head," she put her hand to her temple, "will grow sour and stale. No! A scowler be different. Thoughtful!" (She meant by the word, Gendibal noted, "intelligent" rather than "considerate.")

"A scowler," she said, "live with books and with—with— I forget what they be name-said." She made a gesture as though she were making some sort of vague manipulations that would have meant nothing to Gendibal—if he did not have her mind radiations to guide him.

"Microfilms," he said. "How do you know about microfilms?"

"In books, I read of many things," she said proudly.

Gendibal could no longer fight off the desire to know more. This was an unusual Hamisher; he had never heard of one like this. The Hamish were never recruited, but if Novi were younger, say ten years old—

What a waste! He would not disturb her; he would not disturb her in the least, but of what use was it to be a Speaker if one could not observe unusual minds and learn from them?

He said, "Novi, I want you to sit there for a moment. Be very quiet. Do not say anything. Do not think of saying anything. Just think of falling asleep. Do you understand?"

Her fright returned at once, "Why must I do this, Master?"

"Because I wish to think how you might become a scholar."

After all, no matter what she had read, there was no possible way in which she could know what being a "scholar" truly meant. It was therefore necessary to find out what she *thought* a scholar was.

Very carefully and with infinite delicacy he probed her mind; sensing without actually touching—like placing one's hand on a polished metal surface without leaving fingerprints. To her a scholar was someone who always read books. She had not the slightest idea of why one read books. For herself to be a scholar—the picture in her mind was that of doing the labor she knew—fetching, carrying, cooking, cleaning, following orders—but on the University grounds where books were available and where she would have time to read them and, very vaguely, "to become learned." What it amounted to was that she wanted to be a servant—*his* servant.

Gendibal frowned. A Hamishwoman servant—and one who was plain, graceless, uneducated, barely literate. Unthinkable.

He would simply have to divert her. There would have to be some way of adjusting her desires to make her content to be a farmwoman, some way that would leave no mark, some way about which even Delarmi could not complain.

—Or had she been sent by Delarmi? Was all this a complicated plan to lure him into tampering with a Hamish mind, so that he might be caught and impeached?

Ridiculous. He *was* in danger of growing paranoid. Somewhere in the simple tendrils of her uncomplicated mind, a trickle of mental current needed to be diverted. It would only take a tiny push.

It was against the letter of the law, but it would do no harm and no one would ever notice.

He paused.

Back. Back. Back.

Space! He had almost missed it!

Was he the victim of an illusion?

No! Now that his attention was drawn to it, he could make it out clearly. There was the tiniest tendril disarrayed—an abnormal disarray. Yet it was so delicate, so ramification-free.

Gendibal emerged from her mind. He said gently, "Novi."

Her eyes focused. She said, "Yes, Master?"

Gendibal said, "You may work with me. I will make you a scholar—"

Joyfully, eyes blazing, she said, "Master—"

He detected it at once. She was going to throw herself at his feet. He put his hands on her shoulders and held her tightly. "Don't move, Novi. Stay where you are. —Stay!"

He might have been talking to a half-trained animal. When he could see the order had penetrated, he let her go. He was conscious of the hard muscles along her upper arms.

He said, "If you are to be a scholar, you must behave like one. That means you will have to be always quiet, always soft-spoken, always doing what I tell you to do. And you must try to learn to talk as I do. You will also have to meet other scholars. Will you be afraid?"

"I be not afeared—afraid, Master, if you be with me."

"I will be with you. But now, first— I must find you a room, arrange to have you assigned a lavatory, a place in the dining room, and clothes, too. You will have to wear clothes more suitable to a scholar, Novi."

"These be all I—" she began miserably.

"We will supply others."

Clearly he would have to get a woman to arrange for a new supply of clothing for Novi. He would also need someone to teach the Hamisher the rudiments of personal hygiene. After all, though the clothes she wore were probably her best and though she had obviously spruced herself up, she still had a distinct odor that was faintly unpleasant.

And he would have to make sure that the relationship between them was understood. It was always an open secret that the men (and women, too) of the Second Foundation made occasional forays among the Hamish for their pleasure. If there was no interference with Hamish minds in the process, no one dreamed of making a fuss about it. Gendibal himself had never indulged in this, and he liked to think it was because he felt no need for sex that might be coarser and more highly spiced than was available at the University. The women of the Second Foundation might be pallid in comparison to the Hamish, but they were clean and their skins were smooth.

But even if the matter were misunderstood and there were sniggers at a Speaker who not only turned to the Hamish but brought one into his quarters, he would have to endure the embarrassment. As it stood, this farmwoman, Sura Novi, was his key to victory in the inevitable forthcoming duel with Speaker Delarmi and the rest of the Table.

4.

Gendibal did not see Novi again till after dinnertime, at which time she was brought to him by the woman to whom he had endlessly explained the situation—at least, the non-sexual character of the situation. She had understood—or, at least, did not dare show any indication of failure to understand, which was perhaps just as good.

Novi stood before him now, bashful, proud, embarrassed, triumphant—all at once, in an incongruous mixture.

He said, "You look very nice, Novi."

The clothes they had given her fit surprisingly well and there was no question that she did not look at all ludicrous. Had they pinched in her waist? Lifted her breasts? Or had that just been not particularly noticeable in her farmwoman clothing?

Her buttocks were prominent, but not displeasingly so. Her face, of course, remained plain, but when the tan of outdoor life faded and she learned how to care for her complexion, it would not look downright ugly.

By the Old Empire, that woman *did* think Novi was to be his mistress. She had tried to make her beautiful for him.

And then he thought: Well, why not?

Novi would have to face the Speaker's Table—and the more attractive she seemed, the more easily he would be able to get his point across.

It was with this thought that the message from the First Speaker reached him. It had the kind of appropriateness that was common in a mentalic society. It was called, more or less informally, the "Coincidence Effect." If you think vaguely of someone when someone is thinking vaguely of you, there is a mutual, escalating stimulation which in a matter of seconds makes the two thoughts sharp, decisive, and, to all appearances, simultaneous.

It can be startling even to those who understand it intellectually, particularly if the preliminary vague thoughts were so dim—on one side or the other (or both)—as to have gone consciously unnoticed.

"I can't be with you this evening, Novi," said Gendibal. "I have scholar work to do. I will take you to your room. There will be some books there and you can practice your reading. I will show you how to use the signal if you need help with anything—and I will see you tomorrow."

5.

Gendibal said politely, "First Speaker?"

Shandess merely nodded. He looked dour and fully his age. He looked as though he were a man who did not drink, but who could use a stiff one. He said finally, "I 'called' you—"

"No messenger. I presumed from the direct 'call' that it was important."

"It is. Your quarry—the First Foundationer—Trevize—"

"Yes?"

"He is *not* coming to Trantor."

Gendibal did not look surprised. "Why should he? The information we received was that he was leaving with a professor of ancient history who was seeking Earth."

"Yes, the legendary Primal Planet. And that is why he should be coming to Trantor. After all, does the professor know where Earth is? Do you? Do I? Can we be sure it exists at all, or ever existed? Surely they would have to

come to this Library to obtain the necessary information—
if it were to be obtained anywhere. I have until this hour
felt that the situation was not at crisis level—that the First
Foundationer would come here and that we would, through
him, learn what we need to know."

"Which would certainly be the reason he is not allowed
to come here."

"But where *is* he going, then?"

"We have not yet found out, I see."

The First Speaker said pettishly, "You seem calm about
it."

Gendibal said, "I wonder if it is not better so. You want
him to come to Trantor to keep him safe and use him as a
source of information. Will he not, however, prove a source
of more important information, involving others still more
important than himself, if he goes where he wants to go
and does what he wants to do—provided we do not lose
sight of him?"

"Not enough!" said the First Speaker. "You have persuaded me of the existence of this new enemy of ours and
now I cannot rest. Worse, I have persuaded myself that we
must secure Trevize or we have lost everything. I cannot
rid myself of the feeling that he—and nothing else—is the
key."

Gendibal said intensely, "Whatever happens, we will not
lose, First Speaker. That would only have been possible, if
these Anti-Mules, to use your phrase again, had continued
to burrow beneath us unnoticed. But we know they are there
now. We no longer work blind. At the next meeting of the
Table, if we can work together, we shall begin the counterattack."

The First Speaker said, "It was not the matter of Trevize
that had me send out the call to you. The subject came up
first only because it seemed to me a personal defeat. I had
misanalyzed that aspect of the situation. I was wrong to
place personal pique above general policy and I apologize.
There is something else."

"More serious, First Speaker?"

"More serious, Speaker Gendibal." The First Speaker sighed and drummed his fingers on the desk while Gendibal stood patiently before it and waited.

The First Speaker finally said, in a mild way, as though that would ease the blow, "At an emergency meeting of the Table, initiated by Speaker Delarmi—"

"Without your consent, First Speaker?"

"For what she wanted, she needed the consent of only three other Speakers, not including myself. At the emergency meeting that was then called, you were impeached, Speaker Gendibal. You have been accused as being unworthy of the post of Speaker and you must be tried. This is the first time in over three centuries that a bill of impeachment has been carried out against a Speaker—"

Gendibal said, fighting to keep down any sign of anger, "Surely you did not vote for my impeachment yourself."

"I did not, but I was alone. The rest of the Table was unanimous and the vote was ten to one for impeachment. The requirement for impeachment, as you know, is eight votes including the First Speaker—or ten without him."

"But I was not present."

"You would not have been able to vote."

"I might have spoken in my defense."

"Not at that stage. The precedents are few, but clear. Your defense will be at the trial, which will come as soon as possible, naturally."

Gendibal bowed his head in thought. Then he said, "This does not concern me overmuch, First Speaker. Your initial instinct, I think, was right. The matter of Trevize takes precedence. May I suggest you delay the trial on that ground?"

The First Speaker held up his hand. "I don't blame you for not understanding the situation, Speaker. Impeachment is so rare an event that I myself have been forced to look up the legal procedures involved. Nothing takes precedence. We are forced to move directly to the trial, postponing everything else."

Gendibal placed his fists on the desk and leaned toward the First Speaker. "You are not serious?"

"It is the law."

"The law can't be allowed to stand in the way of a clear and present danger."

"To the Table, Speaker Gendibal, *you* are the clear and present danger. —No, listen to me! The law that is involved is based on the conviction that nothing can be more important than the possibility of corruption or the misuse of power on the part of a Speaker."

"But I am guilty of neither, First Speaker, and you knew it. This is a matter of a personal vendetta on the part of Speaker Delarmi. If there is misuse of power, it is on her part. My crime is that I have never labored to make myself popular—I admit that much—and I have paid too little attention to fools who are old enough to be senile but young enough to have power."

"Like myself, Speaker?"

Gendibal sighed. "You see, I've done it again. I don't refer to you, First Speaker. —Very well, then, let us have an *instant* trial, then. Let us have it tomorrow. Better yet, tonight. Let us get it over with and then pass on to the matter of Trevize. We dare not wait."

The First Speaker said, "Speaker Gendibal. I don't think you understand the situation. We have had impeachments before—not many, just two. Neither of those resulted in a conviction. You, however, will be convicted! You will then no longer be a member of the Table and you will no longer have a say in public policy. You will not, in fact, even have a vote at the annual meeting of the Assembly."

"And you will not act to prevent that?"

"I cannot. I will be voted down unanimously. I will then be forced to resign, which I think is what the Speakers would like to see."

"And Delarmi will become First Speaker?"

"That is certainly a strong possibility."

"But that must not be allowed to happen!"

"Exactly! Which is why I will have to vote for your conviction."

Gendibal drew a deep breath. "I shall demand an instant trial."

"You must have time to prepare your defense."

"What defense? They will listen to no defense. Instant trial!"

"The Table must have time to prepare *their* case."

"They have no case and will want none. They have me convicted in their minds and will require nothing more. In fact, they would rather convict me tomorrow than the day after—and tonight rather than tomorrow. Put it to them."

The First Speaker rose to his feet. They faced each other across the desk. The First Speaker said, "Why are you in such a hurry?"

"The matter of Trevize will not wait."

"Once you are convicted and I am rendered feeble in the face of a Table united against me, what will have been accomplished?"

Gendibal said in an intense whisper, "Have no fears! Despite everything, I will not be convicted."

9. HYPERSPACE

I.

Trevize said, "Are you ready, Janov?"

Pelorat looked up from the book he was viewing and said, "You mean, for the Jump, old fellow?"

"For the hyperspatial Jump. Yes."

Pelorat swallowed. "Now, you're sure that it will be in no way uncomfortable. I know it is a silly thing to fear, but the thought of having myself reduced to incorporeal tachyons, which no one has ever seen or detected—"

"Come, Janov, it's a perfected thing. Upon my honor! The Jump has been in use for twenty-two thousand years, as you explained, and I've never heard of a single fatality in hyperspace. We might come out of hyperspace in an uncomfortable place, but then the accident would happen in space—not while we are composed of tachyons."

"Small consolation, it seems to me."

"We won't come out in error, either. To tell you the truth, I was thinking of carrying it through without telling you, so that you would never know it had happened. On the whole, though, I felt it would be better if you experienced it consciously, saw that it was no problem of any kind, and could forget it totally henceforward."

"Well—" said Pelorat dubiously. "I suppose you're right, but honestly I'm in no hurry."

"I assure you—"

"No no, old fellow, I accept your assurances unequivocally. It's just that— Did you ever read *Santerestil Matt*?"

"Of course. I'm not illiterate."

"Certainly. Certainly. I should not have asked. Do you remember it?"

"Neither am I an amnesiac."

"I seem to have a talent for offending. All I mean is that I keep thinking of the scenes where Santerestil and his friend, Ban, have gotten away from Planet 17 and are lost in space. I think of those perfectly hypnotic scenes among the stars, lazily moving along in deep silence, in changelessness, in— Never believed it, you know. I loved it and I was moved by it, but I never really believed it. But now— after I got used to just the notion of being in space, I'm *experiencing* it and—it's silly, I know—but I don't want to give it up. It's as though I'm Santerestil—"

"And I'm Ban," said Trevize with just an edge of impatience.

"In a way. The small scattering of dim stars out there are motionless, except our sun, of course, which must be shrinking but which we don't see. The Galaxy retains its dim majesty, unchanging. Space is silent and I have no distractions—"

"Except me."

"Except you. —But then, Golan, dear chap, talking to you about Earth and trying to teach you a bit of prehistory has its pleasures, too. I don't want that to come to an end, either."

"It won't. Not immediately, at any rate. You don't suppose we'll take the Jump and come through on the surface of a planet, do you? We'll still be in space and the Jump will have taken no measurable time at all. It may well be a week before we make surface of any kind, so do relax."

"By surface, you surely don't mean Gaia. We may be nowhere near Gaia when we come out of the Jump."

"I know that, Janov, but we'll be in the right sector, if your information is correct. If it isn't—well—"

Pelorat shook his head glumly. "How will being in the right sector help if we don't know Gaia's co-ordinates?"

Trevize said, "Janov, suppose you were on Terminus, heading for the town of Argyropol, and you didn't know where that town was except that it was somewhere on the isthmus. Once you were on the isthmus, what would you do?"

Pelorat waited cautiously, as though feeling there must be a terribly sophisticated answer expected of him. Finally giving up, he said, "I suppose I'd ask somebody."

"*Exactly!* What else *is* there to do? —Now, are you ready?"

"You mean, *now*?" Pelorat scrambled to his feet, his pleasantly unemotional face coming as near as it might to a look of concern. "What am I supposed to do? Sit? Stand? What?"

"Time and Space, Pelorat, you don't do anything. Just come with me to my room so I can use the computer, then sit or stand or turn cartwheels—whatever will make you most comfortable. My suggestion is that you sit before the viewscreen and watch it. It's sure to be interesting. Come!"

They stepped along the short corridor to Trevize's room and he seated himself at the computer. "Would you like to do this, Janov?" he asked suddenly. "I'll give you the figures and all you do is think them. The computer will do the rest."

Pelorat said, "No thank you. The computer doesn't work well with me, somehow. I know you say I just need practice, but I don't believe that. There's something about your mind, Golan—"

"Don't be foolish."

"No no. That computer just seems to fit you. You and it seem to be a single organism when you're hooked up. When I'm hooked up, there are two objects involved— Janov Pelorat and a computer. It's just not the same."

"Ridiculous," said Trevize, but he was vaguely pleased at the thought and stroked the hand-rests of the computer with loving fingertips.

"So I'd rather watch," said Pelorat. "I mean, I'd rather it didn't happen at all, but as long as it will, I'd rather watch." He fixed his eyes anxiously on the viewscreen and on the foggy Galaxy with the thin powdering of dim stars

in the foreground. "Let me know when it's about to happen."
Slowly he backed against the wall and braced himself.

Trevize smiled. He placed his hands on the rests and felt
the mental union. It came more easily day by day, and more
intimately, too, and however he might scoff at what Pelorat
said—he actually *felt* it. It seemed to him he scarcely needed
to think of the co-ordinates in any conscious way. It almost
seemed the computer knew what he wanted, without the
conscious process of "telling." It lifted the information out
of his brain for itself.

But Trevize "told" it and then asked for a two-minute
interval before the Jump.

"All right, Janov. We have two minutes: 120 — 115 —
110 — Just watch the viewscreen."

Pelorat did, with a slight tightness about the corners of
his mouth and with a holding of his breath.

Trevize said softly, "15 — 10 — 5 — 4 — 3 — 2 —
1 — 0."

With no perceptible motion, no perceptible sensation,
the view on the screen changed. There was a distinct thickening of the starfield and the Galaxy vanished.

Pelorat started and said, "Was that it?"

"Was *what* it? You flinched. But that was your fault.
You felt nothing. Admit it."

"I admit it."

"Then that's it. Way back when hyperspatial travel was
relatively new—according to the books, anyway—there
would be a queer internal sensation and some people felt
dizziness or nausea. It was perhaps psychogenic, perhaps
not. In any case, with more and more experience with hy-
perspatiality and with better equipment, that decreased. With
a computer like the one on board this vessel, any effect is
well below the threshold of sensation. At least, I find it so."

"And I do, too, I must admit. Where are we, Golan?"

"Just a step forward. In the Kalganian region. There's a
long way to go yet and before we make another move, we'll
have to check the accuracy of the Jump."

"What bothers me is—where's the Galaxy?"

"All around us, Janov. We're well inside it, now. If we focus the viewscreen properly, we can see the more distant parts of it as a luminous band across the sky."

"The Milky Way!" Pelorat cried out joyfully. "Almost every world describes it in their sky, but it's something we don't see on Terminus. Show it to me, old fellow!"

The viewscreen tilted, giving the effect of a swimming of the starfield across it, and then there was a thick, pearly luminosity nearly filling the field. The screen followed it around, as it thinned, then swelled again.

Trevize said, "It's thicker in the direction of the center of the Galaxy. Not as thick or as bright as it might be, however, because of the dark clouds in the spiral arms. You see something like this from most inhabited worlds."

"And from Earth, too."

"That's no distinction. That would not be an identifying characteristic."

"Of course not. But you know— You haven't studied the history of science, have you?"

"Not really, though I've picked up some of it, naturally. Still, if you have questions to ask, don't expect me to be an expert."

"It's just that making this Jump has put me in mind of something that has always puzzled me. It's possible to work out a description of the Universe in which hyperspatial travel is impossible and in which the speed of light traveling through a vacuum is the absolute maximum where speed is concerned."

"Certainly."

"Under those conditions, the geometry of the Universe is such that it is impossible to make the trip we have just undertaken in less time than a ray of light would make it. And if we did it at the speed of light, our experience of duration would not match that of the Universe generally. If this spot is, say, forty parsecs from Terminus, then if we had gotten here at the speed of light, we would have felt no time lapse—but on Terminus and in the entire Galaxy, about a hundred and thirty years would have passed. Now we have made a trip, not at the speed of light but at thousands of times the speed of light actually, and there has been no time advance anywhere. At least, I hope not."

Trevize said, "Don't expect me to give you the mathematics of the Olanjen Hyperspatial Theory to you. All I can say is that if you had traveled at the speed of light within normal space, time would indeed have advanced at the rate of 3.26 years per parsec, as you described. The so-called relativistic Universe, which humanity has understood as far back as we can probe into prehistory—though that's your department, I think—remains, and its laws have not been repealed. In our hyperspatial Jumps, however, we do something outside the conditions under which relativity operates and the rules are different. Hyperspatially the Galaxy is a tiny object—ideally a nondimensional dot—and there are no relativistic effects at all.

"In fact, in the mathematical formulations of cosmology, there are two symbols for the Galaxy: G^r for the 'relativistic Galaxy,' where the speed of light is a maximum, and G^h for the 'hyperspatial Galaxy,' where speed does not really have a meaning. Hyperspatially the value of all speed is zero and we do not move; with reference to space itself, speed is infinite. I can't explain things a bit more than that.

"Oh, except that one of the beautiful catches in theoretical physics is to place a symbol or a value that has meaning in G^r into an equation dealing with G^h—or vice versa—and leave it there for a student to deal with. The chances are enormous that the student falls into the trap and generally remains there, sweating and panting, with nothing seeming to work, till some kindly elder helps him out. I was neatly caught that way, once."

Pelorat considered that gravely for a while, then said in a perplexed sort of way, "But which is the true Galaxy?"

"Either, depending on what you're doing. If you're back on Terminus, you can use a car to cover distance on land and a ship to cover distance across the sea. Conditions are different in every way, so which is the *true* Terminus, the land or the sea?"

Pelorat nodded. "Analogies are always risky," he said, "but I'd rather accept that one than risk my sanity by thinking about hyperspace any further. I'll concentrate on what we're doing now."

"Look upon what we just did," said Trevize, "as our first stop toward Earth."

And, he thought to himself, toward what else, I wonder.

2.

"Well," said Trevize. "I've wasted a day."

"Oh?" Pelorat looked up from his careful indexing. "In what way?"

Trevize spread his arms. "I didn't trust the computer. I didn't dare to, so I checked our present position with the position we had aimed at in the Jump. The difference was not measurable. There was no detectable error."

"That's good, isn't it?"

"It's more than good. It's unbelievable. I've never heard of such a thing. I've gone through Jumps and I've directed them, in all kinds of ways and with all kinds of devices. In school, I had to work one out with a hand computer and then I sent off a hyper-relay to check results. Naturally I couldn't send a real ship, since—aside from the expense— I could easily have placed it in the middle of a star at the other end.

"I never did anything that bad, of course," Trevize went on, "but there would always be a sizable error. There's always some error, even with experts. There's got to be, since there are so many variables. Put it this way—the geometry of space is too complicated to handle and hyper-space compounds all those complications with a complexity of its own that we can't even pretend to understand. That's why we have to go by steps, instead of making one big Jump from here to Sayshell. The errors would grow worse with distance."

Pelorat said, "But you said *this* computer didn't make an error."

"*It* said it didn't make an error. I directed it to check our actual position with our precalculated position—'what is' against 'what was asked for.' *It* said that the two were identical within its limits of measurement and I thought: What if it's lying?"

Until that moment, Pelorat had held his printer in his hand. He now put it down and looked shaken. "Are you joking? A computer can't lie. Unless you mean you thought it might be out of order."

"No, that's not what I thought. Space! I thought it was *lying*. This computer is so advanced I can't think of it as anything but human—superhuman, maybe. Human enough to have pride—and to lie, perhaps. I gave it directions— to work out a course through hyperspace to a position near Sayshell Planet, the capital of the Sayshell Union. It did, and charted a course in twenty-nine steps, which is arrogance of the worst sort."

"Why arrogance?"

"The error in the first Jump makes the second Jump that much less certain, and the added error then makes the third Jump pretty wobbly and untrustworthy, and so on. How do you calculate twenty-nine steps all at once? The twenty-ninth could end up anywhere in the Galaxy, anywhere at all. So I directed it to make the first step only. Then we could check that before proceeding."

"The cautious approach," said Pelorat warmly. "I approve!"

"Yes, but having made the first step, might the computer not feel wounded at my having mistrusted it? Would it then be forced to salve its pride by telling me there was no error at all when I asked it? Would it find it impossible to admit a mistake, to own up to imperfection? If that were so, we might as well not have a computer."

Pelorat's long and gentle face saddened. "What can we do in that case, Golan?"

"We can do what I did—waste a day. I checked the

position of several of the surrounding stars by the most
primitive possible methods: telescopic observation, photog-
raphy, and manual measurement. I compared each actual
position with the position expected if there had been no
error. The work of it took me all day and wore me down
to nothing."

"Yes, but what happened?"

"I found two whopping errors and checked them over
and found them in my calculations. I had made the mistakes
myself. I corrected the calculations, then ran them through
the computer from scratch—just to see if it would come
up with the same answers independently. Except that it
worked them out to several more decimal places, it turned
out that my figures were right and *they* showed that the
computer had made no errors. The computer may be an
arrogant son-of-the-Mule, but it's got something to be arrogant *about*."

Pelorat exhaled a long breath. "Well, that's good."

"Yes indeed! So I'm going to let it take the other twenty-
eight steps."

"All at once? But—"

"Not all at once. Don't worry. I haven't become a dare-
devil just yet. It will do them one after the other—but after
each step it will check the surroundings and, if that is where
it is supposed to be within tolerable limits, it can take the
next one. Any time it finds the error too great—and, believe
me, I didn't set the limits generously at all—it will have
to stop and recalculate the remaining steps."

"When are you going to do this?"

"When? Right now. —Look, you're working on indexing
your Library—"

"Oh, but this is the chance to do it, Golan. I've been
meaning to do it for years, but something always seemed
to get in the way."

"I have no objections. You go on and do it and don't
worry. Concentrate on the indexing. I'll take care of everything else."

, Pelorat shook his head. "Don't be foolish. I can't relax till this is over. I'm scared stiff."

"I shouldn't have told you, then—but I had to tell *someone* and you're the only one here. Let me explain frankly. There's always the chance that we'll come to rest in a perfect position in interstellar space and that that will happen to be the precise position which a speeding meteoroid is occupying, or a mini-black hole, and the ship is wrecked, and we're dead. Such things could—in theory—happen.

"The chances are very small, however. After all, you could be at home, Janov—in your study and working on your films or in your bed sleeping—and a meteoroid could be streaking toward you through Terminus's atmosphere and hit you right in the head and you'd be dead. But the chances are small.

"In fact, the chance of intersecting the path of something fatal, but too small for the computer to know about, in the course of a hyperspatial Jump is far, far smaller than that of being hit by a meteor in your home. I've never heard of a ship being lost that way in all the history of hyperspatial travel. Any other type of risk—like ending in the middle of a star—is even smaller."

Pelorat said, "Then why do you tell me all this, Golan?"

Trevize paused, then bent his head in thought, and finally said, "I don't know. —Yes, I do. What I suppose it is, is that however small the chance of catastrophe might be, if enough people take enough chances, the catastrophe must happen eventually. No matter how sure I am that nothing will go wrong, there's a small nagging voice inside me that says, 'Maybe it will happen *this* time.' And it makes me feel guilty. —I guess that's it. Janov, if something goes wrong, forgive me!"

"But, Golan, my *dear* chap, if something goes wrong, we will both be dead instantly. I will not be able to forgive, nor you to receive forgiveness."

"I understand that, so forgive me *now*, will you?"

Pelorat smiled. "I don't know why, but this cheers me up. There's something pleasantly humorous about it. Of course, Golan, I'll forgive you. There are plenty of myths about some form of afterlife in world literature and if there should happen to be such a place—about the same chance as landing on a mini-black hole, I suppose, or less—and we both turn up in the same one, then I will bear witness that you did your honest best and that my death should not be laid at your door."

"Thank you! Now I'm relieved. I'm willing to take my chance, but I did not enjoy the thought of you taking my chance as well."

Pelorat wrung the other's hand. "You know, Golan, I've only known you less than a week and I suppose I shouldn't make hasty judgments in these matters, but I think you're an excellent chap. —And now let's do it and get it over with."

"Absolutely! All I have to do is touch that little contact. The computer has its instructions and it's just waiting for me to say: 'Start!' —Would *you* like to—"

"Never! It's all yours! It's your computer."

"Very well. And it's my responsibility. I'm still trying to duck it you see. Keep your eye on the screen!"

With a remarkably steady hand and with his smile looking utterly genuine, Trevize made contact.

There was a momentary pause and then the starfield changed—and again—and again. The stars spread steadily thicker and brighter over the viewscreen.

Pelorat was counting under his breath. At "15" there was a halt, as though some piece of apparatus had jammed.

Pelorat whispered, clearly afraid that any noise might jar the mechanism fatally. "What's wrong? What's happened?"

Trevize shrugged. "I imagine it's recalculating. Some object in space is adding a perceptible bump to the general shape of the overall gravitational field—some object not taken into account—some uncharted dwarf star or rogue planet—"

"Dangerous?"

"Since we're still alive, it's almost certainly not dangerous. A planet could be a hundred million kilometers away and still introduce a large enough gravitational modification to require recalculation. A dwarf star could be ten billion kilometers away and—"

The screen shifted again and Trevize fell silent. It shifted again—and again— Finally, when Pelorat said, "28," there was no further motion.

Trevize consulted the computer. "We're here," he said.

"I counted the first Jump as '1' and in this series I started with '2.' That's twenty-eight Jumps altogether. You said twenty-nine."

"The recalculation at Jump 15 probably saved us one Jump. I can check with the computer if you wish, but there's really no need. We're in the vicinity of Sayshell Planet. The computer says so and I don't doubt it. If I were to orient the screen properly, we'd see a nice, bright sun, but there's no point in placing a needless strain on its screening capacity. Sayshell Planet is the fourth one out and it's about 3.2 million kilometers away from our present position, which is about as close as we want to be at a Jump conclusion. We can get there in three days—two, if we hurry."

Trevize drew a deep breath and tried to let the tension drain.

"Do you realize what this means, Janov?" he said. "Every ship I've ever been in—or heard of—would have made those Jumps with at least a day in between for painstaking calculation and re-checking, even *with* a computer. The trip would have taken nearly a month. Or perhaps two or three weeks, if they were willing to be reckless about it. *We* did it in half an hour. When every ship is equipped with a computer like this one—"

Pelorat said, "I wonder why the Mayor let us have a ship this advanced. It must be incredibly expensive."

"It's experimental," said Trevize dryly. "Maybe the good woman was perfectly willing to have us try it out and see what deficiencies might develop."

"Are you serious?"

"Don't get nervous. After all, there's nothing to worry about. We haven't found any deficiencies. I wouldn't put it past her, though. Such a thing would put no great strain on her sense of humanity. Besides, she hasn't trusted us with offensive weapons and that cuts the expense considerably."

Pelorat said thoughtfully, "It's the computer I'm thinking about. It seems to be adjusted so well for you—and it can't be adjusted that well for everyone. It just barely works with *me*."

"So much the better for us, that it works so well with one of us."

"Yes, but is that merely chance?"

"What else, Janov?"

"Surely the Mayor knows you pretty well."

"I think she does, the old battlecraft."

"Might she not have had a computer designed particularly for you?"

"Why?"

"I just wonder if we're not going where the computer wants to take us."

Trevize stared. "You mean that while I'm connected to the computer, it is the computer—and not me—who's in real charge?"

"I just wonder."

"That is ridiculous. Paranoid. Come *on*, Janov."

Trevize turned back to the computer to focus Sayshell Planet on the screen and to plot a normal-space course to it.

Ridiculous!

But why had Pelorat put the notion into his head?

10. TABLE

1.

Two days had passed and Gendibal found himself not so much heavy-hearted as enraged. There was no reason why there could not have been an immediate hearing. Had he been unprepared—had he needed time—they would have forced an immediate hearing on him, he was sure.

But since there was nothing more facing the Second Foundation than the greatest crisis since the Mule, they wasted time—and to no purpose but to irritate him.

They *did* irritate him and, by Seldon, that would make his counterstroke the heavier. He was determined on that.

He looked about him. The anteroom was empty. It had been like that for two days now. He was a marked man, a Speaker whom all knew would—by means of an action unprecedented in the five-century history of the Second Foundation—soon lose his position. He would be demoted to the ranks, demoted to the position of a Second Foundationer, plain and simple.

It was one thing, however—and a very honored thing—to be a Second Foundationer of the ranks, particularly if one held a respectable title, as Gendibal might even after the impeachment. It would be quite another thing to have once been a Speaker and to have been demoted.

It won't happen though, thought Gendibal savagely, even though for days he had been avoided. Only Sura Novi treated him as before, but she was too naïve to understand the situation. To her, Gendibal was still "Master."

It irritated Gendibal that he found a certain comfort in this. He felt ashamed when he began to notice that his spirits rose when he noticed her gazing at him worshipfully. Was he becoming grateful for gifts *that* small?

A clerk emerged from the Chamber to tell him that the Table was ready for him and Gendibal stalked in. The clerk was one Gendibal knew well; he was one who knew—to the tiniest fraction—the precise gradation of civility that each Speaker deserved. At the moment, that accorded Gendibal was appallingly low. Even the clerk thought him as good as convicted.

They were all sitting about the Table gravely, wearing the black robes of judgment. First Speaker Shandess looked a bit uncomfortable, but he did not allow his face to crease into the smallest touch of friendliness. Delarmi—one of the three Speakers who were women—did not even look at him.

The First Speaker said, "Speaker Stor Gendibal, you have been impeached for behaving in a manner unbecoming a Speaker. You have, before us all, accused the Table— vaguely and without evidence—of treason and attempted murder. You have implied that all Second Foundationers— including the Speakers and the First Speaker—require a thorough mental analysis to ascertain who among them are no longer to be trusted. Such behavior breaks the bonds of community, without which the Second Foundation cannot control an intricate and potentially hostile Galaxy and without which they cannot build, with surety, a viable Second Empire.

"Since we have all witnessed those offenses, we will forego the presentation of a formal case for the prosecution. We will therefore move directly to the next stage. Speaker Stor Gendibal, do you have a defense?"

Now Delarmi—still not looking at him—allowed herself a small catlike smile.

Gendibal said, "If truth be considered a defense, I have one. There *are* grounds for suspecting a breach of security. That breach may involve the mental control of one or more Second Foundationers—not excluding members here present—and this has created a deadly crisis for the Second

Foundation. If, indeed, you hasten this trial because you cannot waste time, you may all perhaps dimly recognize the seriousness of the crisis, but in that case, why have you wasted two days after I had formally requested an immediate trial? I submit that it is this deadly crisis that has forced me to say what I have said. I would have behaved in a manner unbecoming a Speaker—had I *not* done so."

"He but repeats the offense, First Speaker," said Delarmi softly.

Gendibal's seat was further removed from the Table than that of the others—a clear demotion already. He pushed it farther back, as though he cared nothing for that, and rose.

He said, "Will you convict me now, out of hand, in defiance of law—or may I present my defense in detail?"

The First Speaker said, "This is not a lawless assemblage, Speaker. Without much in the way of precedent to guide us, we will lean in your direction, recognizing that if our too-human abilities should cause us to deviate from absolute justice, it is better to allow the guilty to go free than to convict the innocent. Therefore, although the case before us is so grave that we may not lightly allow the guilty to go free, we will permit you to present your case in such manner as you wish and for as long as you require, until it is decided by unanimous vote, *including my own*" (and he raised his voice at that phrase) "that enough has been heard."

Gendibal said, "Let me begin, then, by saying that Golan Trevize—the First Foundationer who has been driven from Terminus and whom the First Speaker and I believe to be the knife-edge of the gathering crisis—has moved off in an unexpected direction."

"Point of information," said Delarmi softly. "How does the speaker" (the intonation clearly indicated that the word was not capitalized) "know this?"

"I was informed of this by the First Speaker," said Gendibal, "but I confirm it of my own knowledge. Under the circumstances, however, considering my suspicions concerning the level of the security of the Chamber, I must be allowed to keep my sources of information secret."

The First Speaker said, "I will suspend judgment on that. Let us proceed without that item of information but if, in the judgment of the Table, the information must be obtained, Speaker Gendibal will have to yield it."

Delarmi said, "If the speaker does not yield the information now, it is only fair to say that I assume he has an agent serving him—an agent who is privately employed by him and who is not responsible to the Table generally. We cannot be sure that such an agent is obeying the rules of behavior governing Second Foundation personnel."

The First Speaker said with some displeasure, "I see all the implications, Speaker Delarmi. There is no need to spell them out for me."

"I merely mention it for the record, First Speaker, since this aggravates the offense and it is not an item mentioned in the bill of impeachment, which, I would like to say, has not been read in full and to which I move this item be added."

"The clerk is directed to add the item," said the First Speaker, "and the precise wording will be adjusted at the appropriate time. —Speaker Gendibal" (*he*, at least, capitalized) "your defense is indeed a step backward. Continue."

Gendibal said, "Not only has this Trevize moved in an unexpected direction, but at an unprecedented speed. My information, which the First Speaker does not yet have, is that he has traveled nearly ten thousand parsecs in well under an hour."

"In a single Jump?" said one of the Speakers incredulously.

"In over two dozen Jumps, one after the other, with virtually no time intervening," said Gendibal, "something that is even more difficult to imagine than a single Jump. Even if he is now located, it will take time to follow him and, if he detects us and really means to flee us, we will not be able to overtake him. —And you spend your time in games of impeachment and allow two days to pass so that you might savor them the more."

The First Speaker managed to mask his anguish. "Please tell us, Speaker Gendibal, what you think the significance of this might be."

"It is an indication, First Speaker, of the technological advances that are being made by the First Foundation, who are far more powerful now than they were in the time of Preem Palver. We could not stand up against them if they found us and were free to act."

Speaker Delarmi rose to her feet. She said, "First Speaker, our time is being wasted with irrelevancies. We are not children to be frightened with tales by Grandmother Spacewarp. It does not matter how impressive the machinery of the First Foundation is when, in any crisis, their minds will be in our control."

"What do you have to say to that, Speaker Gendibal?" asked the First Speaker.

"Merely that we will come to the matter of minds in due course. For the moment, I merely wish to stress the superior—and increasing—technological might of the First Foundation."

The First Speaker said, "Pass on to the next point, Speaker Gendibal. Your first point, I must tell you, does not impress me as very pertinent to the matter contained in the bill of impeachment."

There was a clear gesture of agreement from the Table generally.

Gendibal said, "I pass on. Trevize has a companion in his present journey" (he paused momentarily to consider pronunciation) "one Janov Pelorat, a rather ineffectual scholar who has devoted his life to tracking down myths and legends concerning Earth."

"You know all this about him? Your hidden source, I presume?" said Delarmi, who had settled into her role of prosecutor with a clear feeling of comfort.

"Yes, I know all this about him," said Gendibal stolidly. "A few months ago, the Mayor of Terminus, an energetic and capable woman, grew interested in this scholar for no clear reason, and so I grew interested, too, as a matter of course. Nor have I kept this to myself. All the information I have gained has been made available to the First Speaker."

"I bear witness to that," said the First Speaker in a low voice.

An elderly Speaker said, "What is this Earth? Is it the world of origin we keep coming across in fables? The one they made a fuss about in old Imperial times?"

Gendibal nodded. "In the tales of Grandmother Spacewarp, as Speaker Delarmi would say. —I suspect it was Pelorat's dream to come to Trantor to consult the Galactic Library, in order to find information concerning Earth that he could not obtain in the interstellar library service available on Terminus.

"When he left Terminus with Trevize, he must have been under the impression that that dream was to be fulfilled. Certainly we were expecting the two and counted on having the opportunity to examine them—to our own profit. As it turns out—and as you all know by now—they are not coming. They have turned off to some destination that is not yet clear and for some reason that is not yet known."

Delarmi's round face looked positively cherubic as she said, "And why is this disturbing? We are no worse off for their absence, surely. Indeed, since they dismiss us so easily, we can deduce that the First Foundation does not know the true nature of Trantor and we can applaud the handiwork of Preem Palver."

Gendibal said, "If we thought no further, we might indeed come to such a comforting solution. Could it be, though, that the turnoff was not the result of any failure to see the importance of Trantor? Could it be that the turnoff resulted from anxiety lest Trantor, by examining these two men, see the importance of Earth?"

There was a stir about the Table.

"Anyone," said Delarmi coldly, "can invent formidable-sounding propositions and couch them in balanced sentences. But do they make sense when you do invent them? Why should anyone care what we of the Second Foundation think of Earth? Whether it is the true planet of origin, or whether it is a myth, or whether there is no one place of origin to begin with, is surely something that should interest only historians, anthropologists, and folk-tale collectors, such as this Pelorat of yours. Why us?"

"Why indeed?" said Gendibal. "How is it, then, that there are no references to Earth in the Library?"

For the first time, something in the atmosphere that was other than hostility made itself felt about the Table.

Delarmi said, "Aren't there?"

Gendibal said quite calmly, "When word first reached me that Trevize and Pelorat might be coming here in search of information concerning Earth, I, as a matter of course, had our Library computer make a listing of documents containing such information. I was mildly interested when it turned up nothing. Not minor quantities. Not very little. —Nothing!

"But then you insisted I wait for two days before this hearing could take place, and at the same time, my curiosity was further piqued by the news that the First Foundationers were not coming here after all. I had to amuse myself somehow. While the rest of you therefore were, as the saying goes, sipping wine while the house was falling, I went through some history books in my own possession. I came across passages that specifically mentioned some of the investigations on the 'Origin Question' in late-Imperial times. Particular documents—both printed and filmed—were referred to and quoted from. I returned to the Library and made a personal check for those documents. I assure you there was nothing."

Delarmi said, "Even if this is so, it need not be surprising. If Earth is indeed a myth—"

"Then I would find it in mythological references. If it were a story of Grandmother Spacewarp, I would find it in the collected tales of Grandmother Spacewarp. If it were a

figment of the diseased mind, I would find it under psycho-
pathology. The fact is that something about Earth exists or
you would not all have heard of it and, indeed, immediately
recognized it as the name of the putative planet of origin
of the human species. Why, then, is there no reference to
it in the Library, *anywhere*?"

Delarmi was silent for a moment and another Speaker
interposed. He was Leonis Cheng, a rather small man with
an encyclopedic knowledge of the minutiae of the Seldon
Plan and a rather myopic attitude toward the actual Galaxy.
His eyes tended to blink rapidly when he spoke.

He said, "It is well known that the Empire in its final
days attempted to create an Imperial mystique by soft-ped-
aling all interest in pre-Imperial times."

Gendibal nodded. "Soft-pedaled is the precise term,
Speaker Cheng. That is not equivalent to destroying evidence. As you should know better than anyone, another
characteristic of Imperial decay was a sudden interest in
earlier—and presumably better—times. I have just referred
to the interest in the 'Origin Question' in Hari Seldon's
time."

Cheng interrupted with a formidable clearing of the throat.
"I know this very well, young man, and know far more of
these social problems of Imperial decay than you seem to
think I do. The process of 'Imperialization' overtook these
dilettantish games concerning Earth. Under Cleon II, during
the Empire's last resurgence, two centuries *after* Seldon,
Imperialization reached its peak and all speculation on the
question of Earth came to an end. There was even a directive
in Cleon's time concerning this, referring to the interest in
such things as (and I think I quote it correctly) 'stale and
unproductive speculation that tends to undermine the people's love of the Imperial throne.'"

Gendibal smiled. "Then it was in the time of Cleon II,
Speaker Cheng, that you would place the destruction of all
reference to Earth?"

"I draw no conclusions. I have simply stated what I have
stated."

"It is shrewd of you to draw no conclusions. By Cleon's time, the Empire may have been resurgent, but the University and Library, at least, were in our hands or, at any rate, in those of our predecessors. It would have been impossible for any material to be removed from the Library without the Speakers of the Second Foundation knowing it. In fact, it would have been the Speakers to whom the task would have had to be entrusted, though the dying Empire would not have known that."

Gendibal paused, but Cheng, saying nothing, looked over the other's head.

Gendibal said, "It follows that the Library could not have been emptied of material on Earth during Seldon's time, since the 'Origin Question' was then an active preoccupation. It could not have been emptied afterward because the Second Foundation was in charge. Yet the Library is empty of it now. How can this be?"

Delarmi broke in impatiently, "You may stop weaving the dilemma, Gendibal. We see it. What is it that you suggest as a solution? That you have removed the documents yourself?"

"As usual, Delarmi, you penetrate to the heart." And Gendibal bent his head to her in sardonic respect (at which she allowed herself a slight lifting of the lip). "One solution is that the cleansing was done by a Speaker of the Second Foundation, someone who would know how to use curators without leaving a memory behind—and computers without leaving a record behind."

First Speaker Shandess turned red. "Ridiculous, Speaker Gendibal. I cannot imagine a Speaker doing this. What would the motivation be? Even if, for some reason, the material on Earth were removed, why keep it from the rest of the Table? Why risk a complete destruction of one's career by tampering with the Library when the chances of its being discovered are so great? Besides, I don't think that even the most skillful Speaker could perform the task without leaving a trace."

"Then it must be, First Speaker, that you disagree with Speaker Delarmi in her suggestion that I did it."

"I certainly do," said the First Speaker. "Sometimes I doubt your judgment, but I have yet to consider you downright insane."

"Then it must never have happened, First Speaker. The material on Earth must still be in the Library, for we now seem to have eliminated all the possible ways in which it could have been removed—and yet the material is not there."

Delarmi said with an affectation of weariness, "Well well, let us finish. Again, what is it you suggest as a solution? I am sure you think you have one."

"If you are sure, Speaker, we may all be sure as well. My suggestion is that the Library was cleansed by someone of the Second Foundation who was under the control of a subtle force from outside the Second Foundation. The cleansing went unnoticed because that same force saw to it that it was not noticed."

Delarmi laughed. "Until you found out. You—the uncontrolled and uncontrollable. If this mysterious force existed, how did *you* find out about the absence of material from the Library? Why weren't you controlled?"

Gendibal said gravely, "It's not a laughing matter, Speaker. They may feel, as we feel, that all tampering should be held to a minimum. When my life was in danger a few days ago, I was more concerned with refraining from fiddling with a Hamish mind than with protecting myself. So it might be with these others—as soon as they felt it was safe they ceased tampering. That is the danger, the deadly danger. The fact that I could find out what has happened may mean they no longer care that I do. The fact that they no longer care may mean that they feel they have already won. And *we* continue to play our games here!"

"But what aim do they have in all this? What conceivable aim?" demanded Delarmi, shuffling her feet and biting her lips. She felt her power fading as the Table grew more interested—concerned—

Gendibal said, "Consider— The First Foundation, with its enormous arsenal of physical power, is searching for Earth. They pretend to send out two exiles, hoping we will think that is all they are, but would they equip them with ships of unbelievable power—ships that can move ten thousand parsecs in less than an hour—if that was all they were?

"As for the Second Foundation, we have *not* been searching for Earth and, clearly, steps have been taken *without our knowledge* to keep any information of Earth away from us. The First Foundation is now so close to finding Earth and we are so far from doing so, that—"

Gendibal paused and Delarmi said, "That what? Finish your childish tale. Do you know anything or don't you?"

"I don't know *everything*, Speaker. I have not penetrated the total depth of the web that is encircling us, but I know the web is there. I don't know what the significance of finding Earth might be, but I am certain the Second Foundation is in enormous danger and, with it, the Seldon Plan and the future of all humanity."

Delarmi rose to her feet. She was not smiling and she spoke in a tense but tightly controlled voice. "Trash! First Speaker, put an end to this! What is at issue is the accused's behavior. What he tells us is not only childish but irrelevant. He cannot extenuate his behavior by building a cobwebbery of theories that makes sense only in his own mind. I call for a vote on the matter now—a unanimous vote for conviction."

"Wait," said Gendibal sharply. "I have been told I would have an opportunity to defend myself, and there remains one more item—one more. Let me present that, and you may proceed to a vote with no further objection from me."

The First Speaker rubbed his eyes wearily. "You may continue, Speaker Gendibal. Let me point out to the Table that the conviction of an impeached Speaker is so weighty and, indeed, unprecedented an action that we dare not give the appearance of not allowing a full defense. Remember, too, that even if the verdict satisfies us, it may not satisfy

those who come after us, and I cannot believe that a Second
Foundationer of any level—let alone the Speakers of the
Table—would not have a full appreciation of the importance
of historical perspective. Let us so act that we can be certain
of the approval of the Speakers who will follow us in the
coming centuries."

Delarmi said bitterly, "We run the risk, First Speaker,
of having posterity laugh at us for belaboring the obvious.
To continue the defense is *your* decision."

Gendibal drew a deep breath. "In line with *your* decision,
then, First Speaker, I wish to call a witness—a young
woman I met three days ago and without whom I might not
have reached the Table meeting at all, instead of merely
being late."

"Is the woman you speak of known to the Table?" asked
the First Speaker.

"No, First Speaker. She is native to this planet."

Delarmi's eyes opened wide. "A *Hamishwoman*?"

"Indeed! Just so!"

Delarmi said, "What have we to do with one of those?
Nothing they say can be of any importance. They don't
exist!"

Gendibal's lips drew back tightly over his teeth in something that could not possibly have been mistaken for a smile.
He said sharply, "Physically all the Hamish exist. They are
human beings and play their part in Seldon's Plan. In their
indirect protection of the Second Foundation, they play a
crucial part. I wish to dissociate myself from Speaker Delarmi's inhumanity and hope that her remark will be retained
in the record and be considered hereafter as evidence for
her possible unfitness for the position of Speaker. —Will
the rest of the Table agree with the Speaker's incredible
remark and deprive me of my witness?"

The First Speaker said, "Call your witness, Speaker."

Gendibal's lips relaxed into the normal expressionless
features of a Speaker under pressure. His mind was guarded
and fenced in, but behind this protective barrier, he felt that
the danger point had passed and that he had won.

2.

Sura Novi looked strained. Her eyes were wide and her lower lip was faintly trembling. Her hands were slowly clenching and unclenching and her chest was heaving slightly. Her hair had been pulled back and braided into a bun; her sun-darkened face twitched now and then. Her hands fumbled at the pleats of her long skirt. She looked hastily around the Table—from Speaker to Speaker—her wide eyes filled with awe.

They glanced back at her with varying degrees of contempt and discomfort. Delarmi kept her eyes well above the top of Novi's head, oblivious to her presence.

Carefully Gendibal touched the skin of her mind, soothing and relaxing it. He might have done the same by patting her hand or stroking her cheek, but here, under these circumstances, that was impossible, of course.

He said, "First Speaker, I am numbing this woman's conscious awareness so that her testimony will not be distorted by fear. Will you please observe—will the rest of you, if you wish, join me and observe that I will, in no way, modify her mind?"

Novi had started back in terror at Gendibal's voice, and Gendibal was not surprised at that. He realized that she had never heard Second Foundationers of high rank speak among themselves. She had never experienced that odd swift combination of sound, tone, expression and thought. The terror, however, faded as quickly as it came, as he gentled her mind.

A look of placidity crossed her face.

"There is a chair behind you, Novi," Gendibal said. "Please sit down."

Novi curtsied in a small and clumsy manner and sat down, holding herself stiffly.

She talked quite clearly, but Gendibal made her repeat when her Hamish accent became too thick. And because he kept his own speech formal in deference to the Table, he occasionally had to repeat his own questions to her.

The tale of the fight between himself and Rufirant was described quietly and well.

Gendibal said, "Did you see all this yourself, Novi?"

"Nay, Master, or I would have sooner-stopped it. Rufirant be good fellow, but not quick in head."

"But you described it all. How is that possible if you did not see it all?"

"Rufirant be telling me thereof, on questioning. He be ashamed."

"Ashamed? Have you ever known him to behave in this manner in earlier times?"

"Rufirant? Nay, Master. He be gentle, though he be large. He be no fighter and he be afeared of scowlers. He say often they are mighty and possessed of power."

"Why didn't he feel this way when he met me?"

"It be strange. It be not understood." She shook her head. "He be not his ain self. I said to him, 'Thou blubber-head. Be it your place to assault scowler?' And he said, 'I know not how it happened. It be like I am to one side, standing and watching not-I.'"

Speaker Cheng interrupted. "First Speaker, of what value is it to have this woman report what a man has told her? Is not the man available for questioning?"

Gendibal said, "He is. If, on completion of this woman's testimony, the Table wishes to hear more evidence, I will be ready to call Karoll Rufirant—my recent antagonist— to the stand. If not, the Table can move directly to judgment when I am done with this witness."

"Very well," said the First Speaker. "Proceed with your witness."

Gendibal said, "And you, Novi? Was it like you to interfere in a fight in this manner?"

Novi did not say anything for a moment. A small frown appeared between her thick eyebrows and then disappeared. She said, "I know not. I wish no harm to scowlers. I be *driven*, and without thought I in-middled myself." A pause, then, "I be do it over if need arise."

Gendibal said, "Novi, you will sleep now. You will think of nothing. You will rest and you will not even dream."

Novi mumbled for a moment. Her eyes closed and her head fell back against the headrest of her chair.

Gendibal waited a moment, then said, "First Speaker, with respect, follow me into this woman's mind. You will find it remarkably simple and symmetrical, which is fortunate, for what you will see might not have been visible otherwise. —Here—here! Do you observe? —If the rest of you will enter—it will be easier if it is done one at a time."

There was a rising buzz about the Table.

Gendibal said, "Is there any doubt among you?"

Delarmi said, "*I* doubt it, for—" She paused on the brink of what was—even for her—unsayable.

Gendibal said it for her. "You think I deliberately tampered with this mind in order to present false evidence? You think, therefore, that I am capable of bringing about so delicate an adjustment—one mental fiber clearly out of shape with nothing about it or its surroundings that is in the least disturbed? If I could do that, what need would I have to deal with any of you in this manner? Why subject myself to the indignity of a trial? Why labor to convince you? If I could do what is visible in this woman's mind, you would all be helpless before me unless you were well prepared. —The blunt fact is that none of you could manipulate a mind as this woman's has been manipulated. Neither can I. Yet it has been done."

He paused, looking at all the Speakers in turn, then fixing his gaze on Delarmi. He spoke slowly. "Now, if anything more is required, I will call in the Hamish farmer, Karoll Rufirant, whom I have examined and whose mind has also been tampered with in this manner."

"That will not be necessary," said the First Speaker, who was wearing an appalled expression. "What we have seen is mindshaking."

"In that case," said Gendibal, "may I rouse this Hamishwoman and dismiss her? I have arranged for there to be those outside who will see to her recovery."

When Novi had left, directed by Gendibal's gentle hold on her elbow, he said, "Let me quickly summarize. Minds can be—and have been—altered in ways that are beyond our power. In this way, the curators themselves could have been influenced to remove Earth material from the Library—without our knowledge or their own. We see how it was arranged that I should be delayed in arriving at a meeting of the Table. I was threatened; I was rescued. The result was that I was impeached. The result of this apparently natural concatenation of events is that I may be removed from a position of power—and the course of action which I champion and which threatens these people, whoever they are, may be negated."

Delarmi leaned forward. She was clearly shaken. "If this secret organization is so clever, how were you able to discover all this?"

Gendibal felt free to smile, now. "No credit to me," he said. "I lay no claim to expertise superior to that of other Speakers; certainly not to the First Speaker. However, neither are these Anti-Mules—as the First Speaker has rather engagingly called them—infinitely wise or infinitely immune to circumstance. Perhaps they chose this particular Hamishwoman as their instrument precisely because she needed very little adjustment. She was, of her own character, sympathetic to what she calls 'scholars,' and admired them intensely.

"But then, once this was over, her momentary contact with me strengthened her fantasy of becoming a 'scholar' herself. She came to me the next day with that purpose in mind. Curious at this peculiar ambition of hers, I studied her mind—which I certainly would not otherwise have done—and, more by accident than anything else, stumbled upon the adjustment and noted its significance. Had another woman been chosen—one with a less natural pro-scholar bias—the Anti-Mules might have had to labor more at the adjustment, but the consequences might well not have followed and I would have remained ignorant of all this. The

Anti-Mules miscalculated—or could not sufficiently allow for the unforeseen. That they can stumble so is heartening."

Delarmi said, "The First Speaker and you call this—organization—the 'Anti-Mules,' I presume, because they seem to labor to keep the Galaxy in the path of the Seldon Plan, rather than to disrupt it as the Mule himself did. If the Anti-Mules do this, why are they dangerous?"

"Why should they labor, if not for some purpose? We don't know what that purpose is. A cynic might say that they intend to step in at some future time and turn the current in another direction, one that may please them far more than it would please us. That is my own feeling, even though I do not major in cynicism. Is Speaker Delarmi prepared to maintain, out of the love and trust that we all know form so great a part of her character, that these are cosmic altruists, doing our work for us, without dream of reward?"

There was a gentle susurration of laughter about the Table at this and Gendibal knew that he had won. And Delarmi knew that she had lost, for there was a wash of rage that showed through her harsh mentalic control like a momentary ray of ruddy sunlight through a thick canopy of leaves.

Gendibal said, "When I first experienced the incident with the Hamish farmer, I leaped to the conclusion that another Speaker was behind it. When I noted the adjustment of the Hamishwoman's mind, I knew that I was right as to the plot but wrong as to the plotter. I apologize for the misinterpretation and I plead the circumstances as an extenuation."

The First Speaker said, "I believe this may be construed as an apology—"

Delarmi interrupted. She was quite placid again—her face was friendly, her voice downright saccharine. "With total respect, First Speaker, if I may interrupt— Let us drop this matter of impeachment. At this moment, I would not vote for conviction and I imagine no one will. I would even suggest the impeachment be stricken from the Speaker's unblemished record. Speaker Gendibal has exonerated himself ably. I congratulate him on that—and for uncovering a crisis that the rest of us might well have allowed to smolder on indefinitely, with incalculable results. I offer the Speaker *my* wholehearted apologies for my earlier hostility."

She virtually beamed at Gendibal, who felt a reluctant admiration for the manner in which she shifted direction instantly in order to cut her losses. He also felt that all this was but preliminary to an attack from a new direction.

He was certain that what was coming would not be pleasant.

3.

When she exerted herself to be charming, Speaker Delora Delarmi had a way of dominating the Speaker's Table. Her voice grew soft, her smile indulgent, her eyes sparkling, all of her sweet. No one cared to interrupt her and everyone waited for the blow to fall.

She said, "Thanks to Speaker Gendibal, I think we all now understand what we must do. We do not see the Anti-Mules; we know nothing about them, except for their fugitive touches on the minds of people right here in the stronghold of the Second Foundation itself. We do not know what the power center of the First Foundation is planning. We may face an alliance of the Anti-Mules and the First Foundation. We don't know.

"We do know that this Golan Trevize and his companion, whose name escapes me at the moment, are going we know not where—and that the First Speaker and Gendibal feel that Trevize holds the key to the outcome of this great crisis. What, then, are we to do? Clearly we must find out everything we can about Trevize; where he is going, what he is thinking, what his purpose may be; or, indeed, whether he has any destination, any thought, any purpose; whether he might not, in fact, be a mere tool of a force greater than he."

Gendibal said, "He is under observation."

Delarmi pursed her lips in an indulgent smile. "By whom?

By one of our outworld agents? Are such agents to be expected to stand against those with the powers we have seen demonstrated here? Surely not. In the Mule's time, and later on, too, the Second Foundation did not hesitate to send out—and even to sacrifice—volunteers from among the best we had, since nothing less would do. When it was necessary to restore the Seldon Plan, Preem Palver himself scoured the Galaxy as a Trantorian trader in order to bring back that girl, Arkady. We cannot sit here and wait, now, when the crisis may be greater than in either previous case. We cannot rely on minor functionaries—watchers and messenger boys."

Gendibal said, "Surely you are not suggesting that the First Speaker leave Trantor at this time?"

Delarmi said, "Certainly not. We need him badly here. On the other hand, there is you, Speaker Gendibal. It is you who have correctly sensed and weighed the crisis. It is you who detected the subtle outside interference with the Library and with Hamish minds. It is you who have maintained your views against the united opposition of the Table—and won. No one here has seen as clearly as you have and no one can be trusted, as you can, to continue to see clearly. It is *you* who must, in my opinion, go out to confront the enemy. May I have the sense of the Table?"

There was no formal vote needed to reveal that sense. Each Speaker felt the minds of the others and it was clear to a suddenly appalled Gendibal that, at the moment of his victory and Delarmi's defeat, this formidable woman was managing to send him irrevocably into exile on a task that might occupy him for some indefinite period, while she remained behind to control the Table and, therefore, the Second Foundation and, therefore, the Galaxy—sending all alike, perhaps, to their doom.

And if Gendibal-in-exile should, somehow, manage to gather the information that would enable the Second Foundation to avert the gathering crisis, it would be Delarmi who would have the credit for having arranged it, and *his* success would but confirm *her* power. The quicker Gendibal would be, the more efficiently he succeeded, the more surely he would confirm her power.

It was a beautiful maneuver, an unbelievable recovery.

And so clearly was she dominating the Table even now that she was virtually usurping the First Speaker's role. Gendibal's thought to that effect was overtaken by the rage he sensed from the First Speaker.

He turned. The First Speaker was making no effort to hide his anger—and it soon was clear that another internal crisis was building to replace the one that had been resolved.

4.

Quindor Shandess, the twenty-fifth First Speaker, had no extraordinary illusions about himself.

He knew he was not one of those few dynamic First Speakers who had illuminated the five-century-long history of the Second Foundation—but then, he didn't have to be. He controlled the Table in a quiet period of Galactic prosperity and it was not a time for dynamism. It had seemed to be a time to play a holding game and he had been the man for this role. His predecessor had chosen him for that reason.

"You are not an adventurer, you are a scholar," the twenty-fourth First Speaker had said. "You will preserve the Plan, where an adventurer might ruin it. Preserve! Let that be the key word for your Table."

He had tried, but it had meant a passive First Speakership and this had been, on occasion, interpreted as weakness. There had been recurrent rumors that he meant to resign and there had been open intrigue to assure the succession in one direction or another.

There was no doubt in Shandess's mind that Delarmi had been a leader in the fight. She was the strongest personality at the Table and even Gendibal, with all the fire and folly of youth, retreated before her as he was doing right now.

But, by Seldon, passive he might be, or even weak, but

there was one prerogative of the First Speaker that not one in the line had ever given up, and neither would he do so.

He rose to speak and at once there was a hush about the Table. When the First Speaker rose to speak, there could be no interruptions. Even Delarmi or Gendibal would not dare to interrupt.

He said, "Speakers! I agree that we face a dangerous crisis and that we must take strong measures. It is I who should go out to meet the enemy. Speaker Delarmi, with the gentleness that characterizes her, excuses me from the task by stating that I am needed here. The truth, however, is that I am needed neither here nor there. I grow old; I grow weary. There has long been expectation I would some-day resign and perhaps I ought to. When this crisis is successfully surmounted, I *shall* resign.

"But, of course, it is the privilege of the First Speaker to choose his successor. I am going to do so now. There is one Speaker who has long dominated the proceedings of the Table; one Speaker who, by force of personality, has often supplied the leadership that I could not. You all know I am speaking of Speaker Delarmi."

He paused, then said, "You alone, Speaker Gendibal, are registering disapproval. May I ask why?" He sat down, so that Gendibal might have the right to answer.

"I do not disapprove, First Speaker," said Gendibal in a low voice. "It is your prerogative to choose your successor."

"And so I will. When you return—having succeeded in initiating the process that will put an end to this crisis—it will be time for my resignation. My successor will then be directly in charge of conducting whatever policies may be required to carry on and complete that process. —Do you have anything to say, Speaker Gendibal?"

Gendibal said quietly, "When you make Speaker Delarmi your successor, First Speaker, I hope you will see fit to advise her to—"

The First Speaker interrupted him roughly. "I have spoken of Speaker Delarmi, but I have not named her as my successor. Now what do you have to say?"

"My apologies, First Speaker. I should have said, *assuming* you make Speaker Delarmi your successor upon my return from this mission, would you see fit to advise her to—"

"Nor will I make her my successor in the future, under any conditions. *Now* what do you have to say?" The First Speaker was unable to make this announcement without a stab of satisfaction at the blow he was delivering to Delarmi. He could not have done it in a more humiliating fashion.

"Well, Speaker Gendibal," he said, "what do you have to say?"

"That I am confused."

The First Speaker rose again. He said, "Speaker Delarmi has dominated and led, but that is not all that is needed for the post of First Speaker. Speaker Gendibal has seen what we have not seen. He has faced the united hostility of the Table, and forced it to rethink matters, and has dragged it into agreement with him. I have my suspicions as to the motivation of Speaker Delarmi in placing the responsibility of the pursuit of Golan Trevize on the shoulders of Speaker Gendibal, but that is where the burden belongs. I *know* he will succeed—I trust my intuition in this—and when he returns, Speaker Gendibal will become the twenty-sixth First Speaker."

He sat down abruptly and each Speaker began to make clear his opinion in a bedlam of sound, tone, thought, and expression. The First Speaker paid no attention to the cacophony, but stared indifferently before him. Now that it was done, he realized—with some surprise—the great comfort there was in laying down the mantle of responsibility. He should have done it before this—but he couldn't have.

It was not till now that he had found his obvious successor.

And then, somehow, his mind caught that of Delarmi and he looked up at her.

By Seldon! She was calm and smiling. Her desperate disappointment did not show—she had not given up. He wondered if he had played into her hands. What was there left for her to do?

5.

Delora Delarmi would freely have shown her desperation and disappointment, if that would have proven of any use whatever.

It would have given her a great deal of satisfaction to strike out at that senile fool who controlled the Table or at that juvenile idiot with whom Fortune had conspired—but satisfaction wasn't what she wanted. She wanted something more.

She wanted to be First Speaker.

And while there was a card left to play, she would play it.

She smiled gently, and managed to lift her hand as though she were about to speak, and then held the pose just long enough to insure that when she did speak, all would be not merely normal, but radiantly quiet.

She said, "First Speaker, as Speaker Gendibal said earlier, I do not disapprove. It is your prerogative to choose your successor. If I speak now, it is in order that I may contribute—I hope—to the success of what has now become Speaker Gendibal's mission. May I explain my thoughts, First Speaker?"

"Do so," said the First Speaker curtly. She was entirely too smooth, too pliant, it seemed to him.

Delarmi bent her head gravely. She no longer smiled. She said, "We have ships. They are not as technologically magnificent as those of the First Foundation, but they will carry Speaker Gendibal. He knows how to pilot one, I believe, as do we all. We have our representatives on every major planet in the Galaxy, and he will be welcomed everywhere. Moreover, he can defend himself against even these Anti-Mules, now that he is thoroughly aware of the danger. Even when we were unaware, I suspect they have preferred to work through the lower classes and even the Hamish farmers. We will, of course, thoroughly inspect the minds of all the Second Foundationers, including the Speakers, but I am sure they have remained inviolate. The Anti-Mules did not dare interfere with us.

"Nevertheless, there is no reason why Speaker Gendibal should risk more than he must. He is not intending to engage in derring-do and it will be best if his mission is to some extent disguised—if he takes *them* unaware. It will be useful if he goes in the role of a Hamish trader. Preem Palver, we all know, went off into the Galaxy as a supposed trader."

The First Speaker said, "Preem Palver had a specific purpose in doing so; Speaker Gendibal has not. If it appears a disguise of some sort is necessary, I am sure he will be ingenious enough to adopt one."

"With respect, First Speaker, I wish to point out a subtle disguise. Preem Palver, you will remember, took with him his wife and companion of many years. Nothing so thoroughly established the rustic nature of his character as the fact that he was traveling with his wife. It allayed all suspicion."

Gendibal said, "I have no wife. I have had companions, but none who would now volunteer to assume the marital role."

"This is well known, Speaker Gendibal," said Delarmi, "but then people will take the role for granted if *any* woman is with you. Surely some volunteer can be found. And if you feel the need to be able to present documentary evidence, that can be provided. I think a woman should come with you."

For a moment, Gendibal was breathless. Surely she did not mean—

Could it be a ploy to achieve a share in the success? Could she be playing for a joint—or rotating—occupation of the First Speakership?

Gendibal said grimly, "I am flattered that Speaker Delarmi should feel that she—"

And Delarmi broke into an open laugh and looked at

Gendibal with what was almost true affection. He had fallen into the trap and looked foolish for having done so. The Table would not forget that.

She said, "Speaker Gendibal, I would not have the impertinence to attempt to share in this task. It is yours and yours alone, as the post of First Speaker will be yours and yours alone. I would not have thought you wanted me with you. Really, Speaker, at my age, I no longer think of myself as a charmer—"

There were smiles around the Table and even the First Speaker tried to hide one.

Gendibal felt the stroke and labored not to compound the loss by failing to match her lightness. It was labor lost.

He said, as unsavagely as he could, "Then what is it you would suggest? It was not in my thoughts, I assure you, that you would wish to accompany me. You are at your best at the Table and not in the hurly-burly of Galactic affairs, I know."

"I agree, Speaker Gendibal, I agree," said Delarmi. "My suggestion, however, refers back to your role as Hamish trader. To make it indisputably authentic, what better companion need you ask but a Hamishwoman?"

"A Hamishwoman?" For a second time in rapid succession, Gendibal was caught by surprise and the Table enjoyed it.

"*The* Hamishwoman," Delarmi went on. "The one who saved you from a beating. The one who gazes at you worshipfully. The one whose mind you probed and who then, quite unwittingly, saved you a second time from considerably more than a beating. I suggest you take her."

Gendibal's impulse was to refuse, but he knew that she expected that. It would mean more enjoyment for the Table. It was clear now that the First Speaker, anxious to strike out at Delarmi, had made a mistake by naming Gendibal his successor—or, at the very least, that Delarmi had quickly converted it into one.

Gendibal was the youngest of the Speakers. He had angered the Table and had then avoided conviction by them.

In a very real way, he had humiliated them. None could see him as the heir apparent without resentment.

That would have been hard enough to overcome, but now they would remember how easily Delarmi had twitched him into ridicule and how much they had enjoyed it. She would use that to convince them, all too easily, that he lacked the age and experience for the role of First Speaker. Their united pressure would force the First Speaker into changing his decision while Gendibal was off on his mission. Or, if the First Speaker held fast, Gendibal would eventually find himself with an office that would be forever helpless in the face of united opposition.

He saw it all in an instant and was able to answer as though without hesitation.

He said, "Speaker Delarmi, I admire your insight. I had thought to surprise you all. It was indeed my intention to take the Hamishwoman, though not quite for the very good reason you suggest. It was for her mind that I wished to take her with me. You have all examined that mind. You saw it for what it was: surprisingly intelligent but, more than that, clear, simple, utterly without guile. No touch upon it by others would go unnoticed, as I'm sure you all concluded.

"I wonder if it occurred to you, then, Speaker Delarmi, that she would serve as an excellent early-warning system. I would detect the first symptomatic presence of mentalism by way of her mind, earlier, I think, than by way of mine."

There was a kind of astonished silence at that, and he said, lightly, "Ah, none of you saw that. Well well, not important! And I will take my leave now. There's no time to lose."

"Wait," said Delarmi, her initiative lost a third time. "What do you intend to do?"

Gendibal said with a small shrug, "Why go into details? The less the Table knows, the less the Anti-Mules are likely to attempt to disturb it."

He said it as though the safety of the Table was his prime concern. He filled his mind with that, and let it show.

It would flatter them. More than that, the satisfaction it would bring might keep them from wondering whether, in fact, Gendibal knew exactly what it was he intended to do.

6.

The First Speaker spoke to Gendibal alone that evening.

"You were right," he said. "I could not help brushing below the surface of your mind. I saw you considered the announcement a mistake and it was. It was my eagerness to wipe that eternal smile off her face and to strike back at the casual way in which she so frequently usurps my role."

Gendibal said gently, "It might have been better if you had told me privately and had then waited for my return to go further."

"That would not have allowed me to strike out at her. —Poor motivation for a First Speaker, I know."

"This won't stop her, First Speaker. She will still intrigue for the post and perhaps with good reason. I'm sure there are some who would argue that I should have refused your nomination. It would not be hard to argue that Speaker Delarmi has the best mind at the Table and would make the best First Speaker."

"The best mind *at* the Table, not away from it," grumbled Shandess. "She recognizes no real enemies, except for other Speakers. She ought never to have been made a Speaker in the first place. —See here, shall I forbid you to take the Hamishwoman? She maneuvered you into that, I know."

"No no, the reason I advanced for taking her is a true one. She *will* be an early-warning system and I am grateful to Speaker Delarmi for pushing me into realizing that. The woman will prove very useful, I'm convinced."

"Good, then. By the way, I wasn't lying, either. I am truly certain that you will accomplish whatever is needed to end this crisis—if you can trust my intuition."

"I think I can trust it, for I agree with you. I promise you that whatever happens, I will return better than I receive.

I will come back to be First Speaker, whatever the Anti-Mules—or Speaker Delarmi—can do."

Gendibal studied his own satisfaction even as he spoke. Why was he so pleased, so insistent, on this one-ship venture into space? Ambition, of course. Preem Palver had once done just this sort of thing—and he was going to show that Stor Gendibal could do it, too. No one could withhold the First Speakership from him after that. And yet was there more than ambition? The lure of combat? The generalized desire for excitement in one who had been confined to a hidden patch on a backward planet all his adult life? —He didn't entirely know, but he knew he was desperately intent on going.

11. SAYSHELL

1.

Janov Pelorat watched, for the first time in his life, as the bright star graduated into an orb after what Trevize had called a "micro-Jump." The fourth planet—the habitable one and their immediate destination, Sayshell—then grew in size and prominence more slowly—over a period of days.

A map of the planet had been produced by the computer and was displayed on a portable screening device, which Pelorat held in his lap.

Trevize—with the aplomb of someone who had, in his time, touched down upon several dozen worlds—said, "Don't start watching too hard too soon, Janov. We have to go through the entry station first and that can be tedious."

Pelorat looked up. "Surely that's just a formality."

"It is. But it can still be tedious."

"But it's peacetime."

"Of course. That means we'll be passed through. First, though, there's a little matter of the ecological balance. Every planet has its own and they don't want it upset. So they make a natural point of checking the ship for undesirable organisms, or infections. It's a reasonable precaution."

"We don't have such things, it seems to me."

"No, we don't and they'll find that out. Remember, too, that Sayshell is not a member of the Foundation Federation, so there's certain to be some leaning over backward to demonstrate their independence."

A small ship came out to inspect them and a Sayshellian Customs official boarded. Trevize was brisk, not having forgotten his military days.

"The *Far Star*, out of Terminus," he said. "Ship's papers.

197

Unarmed. Private vessel. My passport. There is one passenger. His passport. We are tourists."

The Customs official wore a garish uniform in which crimson was the dominating color. Cheeks and upper lip were smooth-shaven, but he wore a short beard parted in such a way that tufts thrust out to both sides of his chin. He said, "Foundation ship?"

He pronounced it "Foundaysun sip," but Trevize was careful neither to correct him nor to smile. There were as many varieties of dialects to Galactic Standard as there were planets, and you just spoke your own. As long as there was cross-comprehension, it didn't matter.

"Yes, sir," said Trevize. "Foundation ship. Privately owned."

"Very nice. —Your lading, if you please."

"My what?"

"Your lading. What are you carrying?"

"Ah, my cargo. Here is the itemized list. Personal property only. We are not here to trade. As I told you, we are simply tourists."

The Customs official looked about curiously. "This is rather an elaborate vessel for tourists."

"Not by Foundation standards," said Trevize with a display of good humor. "And I'm well off and can afford this."

"Are you suggesting that I might be richified?" The official looked at him briefly, then looked away.

Trevize hesitated a moment in order to interpret the meaning of the word, then another moment to decide his course of action. He said, "No, it is not my intention to bribe you. I have no reason to bribe you—and you don't look like the kind of person who could be bribed, if that were my intention. You can look over the ship, if you wish."

"No need," said the official, putting away his pocket recorder. "You have already been examined for specific contraband infection and have passed. The ship has been assigned a radio wavelength that will serve as an approach beam."

He left. The whole procedure had taken fifteen minutes.

Pelorat said in a low voice. "Could he have made trouble? Did he really expect a bribe?"

Trevize shrugged. "Tipping the Customs man is as old as the Galaxy and I would have done it readily if he had made a second try for it. As it is—well, I presume he prefers not to take a chance with a Foundation ship, and a fancy one, at that. The old Mayor, bless her cross-grained hide, said the name of the Foundation would protect us wherever we went and she wasn't wrong. —It could have taken a great deal longer."

"Why? He seemed to find out what he wanted to know."

"Yes, but he was courteous enough to check us by remote radio-scanning. If he had wished, he could have gone over the ship with a hand-machine and taken hours. He could have put us both in a field hospital and kept us days."

"What? My *dear* fellow!"

"Don't get excited. He didn't do it. I thought he might, but he didn't. Which means we're free to land. I'd like to go down gravitically—which could take us fifteen minutes—but I don't know where the permitted landing sites might be and I don't want to cause trouble. That means we'll have to follow the radio beam—which will take hours—as we spiral down through the atmosphere."

Pelorat looked cheerful. "But that's excellent, Golan. Will we be going slowly enough to watch the terrain?" He held up his portable viewscreen with the map spread out on it at low magnification.

"After a fashion. We'd have to get beneath the cloud deck, and we'll be moving at a few kilometers per second. It won't be ballooning through the atmosphere, but you'll spot the planetography."

"Excellent! Excellent!"

Trevize said thoughtfully, "I'm wondering, though, if we'll be on Sayshell Planet long enough to make it worth our while to adjust the ship's clock to local time."

"It depends on what we plan to do, I suppose. What do you think we'll be doing, Golan?"

"Our job is to find Gaia and I don't know how long that will take."

Pelorat said, "We can adjust our wrist-strips and leave the ship's clock as is."

"Good enough," said Trevize. He looked down at the planet spreading broadly beneath them. "No use waiting any longer. I'll adjust the computer to our assigned radio beam and it can use the gravitics to mimic conventional flight. So! —Let's go down, Janov, and see what we can find."

He stared at the planet thoughtfully as the ship began to move on its smoothly adjusted gravitational potential-curve.

Trevize had never been in the Sayshell Union, but he knew that over the last century it had been steadfastly unfriendly to the Foundation. He was surprised—and a little dismayed—they had gotten through Customs so quickly.

It didn't seem reasonable.

2.

The Customs official's name was Jogoroth Sobhaddartha and he had been serving on the station on and off for half his life.

He didn't mind the life, for it gave him a chance—one month out of three—to view his books, to listen to his music, and to be away from his wife and growing son.

Of course, during the last two years the current Head of Customs had been a Dreamer, which was irritating. There is no one so insufferable as a person who gives no other excuse for a peculiar action than saying he had been directed to it in a dream.

Personally Sobhaddartha decided he believed none of it, though he was careful not to say so aloud, since most people on Sayshell rather disapproved of antipsychic doubts. To become known as a materialist might put his forthcoming pension at risk.

He stroked the two tufts of hair at his chin, one with his right hand and the other with his left, cleared his throat rather loudly, and then, with inappropriate casualness, said, "Was that the ship, Head?"

The Head, who bore the equally Sayshellian name of Namarath Godhisavatta, was concerned with a matter involving some computer-born data and did not look up. "What ship?" he said.

"The *Far Star*. The Foundation ship. The one I just sent past. The one that was holographed from every angle. Was that the one you dreamed of?"

Godhisavatta looked up now. He was a small man, with eyes that were almost black and that were surrounded by fine wrinkles that had not been produced by any penchant for smiling. He said, "Why do you ask?"

Sobhaddartha straightened up and allowed his dark and luxuriant eyebrows to approach each other. "They said they were tourists, but I've never seen a ship like that before and my own opinion is they're Foundation agents."

Godhisavatta sat back in his chair. "See here, my man, try as I might I cannot recall asking for your opinion."

"But Head, I consider it my patriotic duty to point out that—"

Godhisavatta crossed his arms over his chest and stared hard at the underling, who (though much the more impressive in physical stature and bearing) allowed himself to droop and take on a somehow bedraggled appearance under the gaze of his superior.

Godhisavatta said, "My man, *if* you know what is good for you, you will do your job *without* comment—or I'll see to it that there will be no pension when you retire, which will be soon if I hear any more on a subject that does not concern you."

In a low voice, Sobhaddartha said, "Yes, sir." Then, with a suspicious degree of subservience in his voice, he added, "Is it within the range of my duties, sir, to report that a second ship is in range of our screens?"

"Consider it reported," Godhisavatta said irritably, returning to his work.

"With," said Sobhaddartha even more humbly, "characteristics very similar to the one I just sent through."

Godhisavatta placed his hands on the desk and lifted himself to his feet. "A *second* one?"

Sobhaddartha smiled inwardly. That sanguinary person born of an irregular union (he was referring to the Head) had clearly not dreamed of *two* ships. He said, "Apparently, sir! I will now return to my post and await orders and I hope, sir—"

"Yes?"

Sobhaddartha could not resist, pension-risk notwithstanding. "And I hope, sir, we didn't send the wrong one through."

3.

The *Far Star* moved rapidly across the face of Sayshell Planet and Pelorat watched with fascination. The cloud layer was thinner and more scattered than upon Terminus and, precisely as the map showed, the land surfaces were more compact and extensive—including broader desert areas, to judge by the rusty color of much of the continental expanse.

There were no signs of anything living. It seemed a world of sterile desert, gray plain, of endless wrinkles that might have represented mountainous areas, and, of course, of ocean.

"It looks lifeless," muttered Pelorat.

"You don't expect to see any life-signs at this height," said Trevize. "As we get lower, you'll see the land turn green in patches. Before that, in fact, you'll see the twinkling landscape on the nightside. Human beings have a penchant for lighting their worlds when darkness falls; I've never heard of a world that's an exception to that rule. In other words, the first sign of life you'll see will not only be human but technological."

Pelorat said thoughtfully, "Human beings are diurnal in nature, after all. It seems to me that among the very first tasks of a developing technology would be the conversion of night to day. In fact, if a world lacked technology and developed one, you ought to be able to follow the progress of technological development by the increase in light upon the darkened surface. How long would it take, do you suppose, to go from uniform darkness to uniform light?"

Trevize laughed. "You have odd thoughts, but I suppose that comes from being a mythologist. I don't think a world would ever achieve a uniform glow. Night light would follow the pattern of population density, so that the continents would spark in knots and strings. Even Trantor at its height, when it was one huge structure, let light escape that structure only at scattered points."

The land turned green as Trevize had predicted and, on the last circling of the globe, he pointed out markings that he said were cities. "It's not a very urban world. I've never been in the Sayshell Union before, but according to the information the computer gives me, they tend to cling to the past. Technology, in the eyes of all the Galaxy, has been associated with the Foundation, and wherever the Foundation is unpopular, there is a tendency to cling to the past—except, of course, as far as weapons of war are concerned. I assure you Sayshell is quite modern in that respect."

"Dear me, Golan, this is not going to be unpleasant, is it? We are Foundationers, after all, and being in enemy territory—"

"It's not enemy territory, Janov. They'll be perfectly polite, never fear. The Foundation just isn't popular, that's all. Sayshell is not part of the Foundation Federation. Therefore, because they're proud of their independence and because they don't like to remember that they are much weaker than the Foundation and remain independent only because we're willing to let them remain so, they indulge in the luxury of disliking us."

"I fear it will still be unpleasant, then," said Pelorat despondently.

"Not at all," said Trevize. "Come on, Janov. I'm talking

about the official attitude of the Sayshellian government. The individual people on the planet are just people, and if we're pleasant and don't act as though we're Lords of the Galaxy, they'll be pleasant, too. We're not coming to Sayshell in order to establish Foundation mastery. We're just tourists, asking the kind of questions about Sayshell that any tourist would ask.

"And we can have a little legitimate relaxation, too, if the situation permits. There's nothing wrong with staying here a few days and experiencing what they have to offer. They may have an interesting culture, interesting scenery, interesting food, and—if all else fails—interesting women. We have money to spend."

Pelorat frowned, "Oh, my *dear* chap."

"Come on," said Trevize. "You're not *that* old. Wouldn't you be interested?"

"I don't say there wasn't a time when I played that role properly, but surely this isn't the time for it. We have a mission. We want to reach Gaia. I have nothing against a good time—I really don't—but if we start involving ourselves, it might be difficult to pull free." He shook his head and said mildly, "I think you feared that I might have too good a time at the Galactic Library on Trantor and would be unable to pull free. Surely, what the Library is to me, an attractive dark-eyed damsel—or five or six—might be to you."

Trevize said, "I'm not a rakehell, Janov, but I have no intention of being ascetic, either, Very well, I promise you we'll get on with this business of Gaia, but if something pleasant comes my way, there's no reason in the Galaxy I ought not to respond normally."

"If you'll just put Gaia first—"

"I will. Just remember, though, don't tell anyone we're from the Foundation. They'll know we are, because we've got Foundation credits and we speak with strong Terminus accents, but if we say nothing about it, they can pretend we are placeless strangers and be friendly. If we make a *point* of being Foundationers, they will speak politely enough, but they will tell us nothing, show us nothing, take us nowhere, and leave us strictly alone."

Pelorat sighed. "I will never understand people."

"There's nothing to it. All you have to do is take a close look at yourself and you will understand everyone else. We're in no way different ourselves. How would Seldon have worked out his Plan—and I don't care how subtle his mathematics was—if he didn't understand people; and how could he have done that if people weren't easy to understand? You show me someone who can't understand people and I'll show you someone who has built up a false image of himself—no offense intended."

"None taken. I'm willing to admit I'm inexperienced and that I've spent a rather self-centered and constricted life. It may be that I've never really taken a good look at myself, so I'll let you be my guide and adviser where people are concerned."

"Good. Then take my advice now and just watch the scenery. We'll be landing soon and I assure you you'll feel nothing. The computer and I will take care of everything."

"Golan, don't be annoyed. If a young woman should—"

"Forget it! Just let me take care of the landing."

Pelorat turned to look at the world at the end of the ship's contracting spiral. It would be the first foreign world upon which he would ever stand. This thought somehow filled him with foreboding, despite the fact that all the millions of inhabited planets in the Galaxy had been colonized by people who had not been born upon them.

All but one, he thought with a shudder of trepidation/delight.

4.

The spaceport was not large by Foundation standards, but it was well kept. Trevize watched the *Far Star* moved into a berth and locked in place. They were given an elaborate coded receipt.

Pelorat said in a low voice, "Do we just leave it here?"

Trevize nodded and placed his hand on the other's shoulder in reassurance. "Don't worry," he said in an equally low voice.

They stepped into the ground-car they had rented and Trevize plugged in the map of the city, whose towers he could see on the horizon.

"Sayshell City," he said, "the capital of the planet. City—planet—star—all named Sayshell."

"I'm worried about the ship," insisted Pelorat.

"Nothing to worry about," said Trevize. "We'll be back tonight, because it will be our sleeping quarters if we have to stay here more than a few hours. You have to understand, too, that there's an interstellar code of spaceport ethics that—as far as I know—has never been broken, even in wartime, Spaceships that come in peace are inviolate. If that were not so, no one would be safe and trade would be impossible. Any world on which that code was broken would be boycotted by the space pilots of the Galaxy. I assure you, no world would risk that. Besides—"

"Besides?"

"Well, besides, I've arranged with the computer that anyone who doesn't look and sound like one of us will be killed if he—or she—tries to board the ship. I've taken the liberty of explaining that to the Port Commander. I told him very politely that I would love to turn off that particular facility out of deference to the reputation that the Sayshell City Spaceport holds for absolute integrity and security—throughout the Galaxy, I said—but the ship is a new model and I didn't know *how* to turn it off."

"He didn't believe *that*, surely."

"Of course not! But he had to pretend he did, as otherwise he would have no choice but to be insulted. And since there would be nothing he could do about that, being insulted would only lead to humiliation. And since he didn't want *that*, the simplest path to follow was to believe what I said."

"And that's another example of how people are?"

"Yes. You'll get used to this."

"How do you know this ground-car isn't bugged?"

"I thought it might be. So when they offered me one, I took another one at random. If they're all bugged—well, what have we been saying that's so terrible?"

Pelorat looked unhappy. "I don't know how to say this. It seems rather impolite to complain, but I don't like the way it smells. There's an—odor."

"In the ground-car?"

"Well, in the spaceport, to begin with. I suppose that's the way spaceports smell, but the ground-car carries the odor with it. Could we open the window?"

Trevize laughed. "I suppose I could figure out which portion of the control panel will do that trick, but it won't help. This planet stinks. Is it very bad?"

"It's not very strong, but it's noticeable—and somewhat repulsive. Does the whole world smell this way?"

"I keep forgetting you've never been on another world. Every inhabited world has its own odor. It's the general vegetation, mostly, though I suppose the animals and even the human beings contribute. And as far as I know, *nobody* ever likes the smell of any world when he first lands on it. But you'll get used to it, Janov. In a few hours, I promise you won't notice."

"Surely you don't mean that all worlds smell like this."

"No. As I said, each has its own. If we really paid attention or if our noses were a little keener—like those of Anacreonian dogs—we could probably tell which world we were on with one sniff. When I first entered the Navy I could never eat the first day on a new world; then I learned the old spacer trick of sniffing a handkerchief with the world-scent on it during the landing. By the time you get out into the open world, you don't smell it. And after a while, you get hardened to the whole thing; you just learn to disregard it. —The worst of it is returning home, in fact."

"Why?"

"Do you think Terminus doesn't smell?"

"Are you telling me it does?"

"Of course it does. Once you get acclimated to the smell

of another world, such as Sayshell, you'll be surprised at the stench of Terminus. In the old days, whenever the locks opened on Terminus after a sizable tour of duty, all the crew would call out, 'Back home to the crap.'"

Pelorat looked revolted.

The towers of the city were perceptibly closer, but Pelorat kept his eyes fixed on their immediate surroundings. There were other ground-cars moving in both directions and an occasional air-car above, but Pelorat was studying the trees.

He said, "The plant life seems strange. Do you suppose any of it is indigenous?"

"I doubt it," said Trevize absently. He was studying the map and attempting to adjust the programming of the car's computer. "There's not much in the way of indigenous life on any human planet. Settlers always imported their own plants and animals—either at the time of settling or not too long afterward."

"It seems strange, though."

"You don't expect the same varieties from world to world, Janov. I was once told that the Encyclopedia Galactica people put out an atlas of varieties which ran to eighty-seven fat computer-discs and was incomplete even so—and outdated anyway, by the time it was finished."

The ground-car moved on and the outskirts of the city gaped and engulfed them. Pelorat shivered slightly, "I don't think much of their city architecture."

"To each his own," said Trevize with the indifference of the seasoned space traveler.

"Where are we going, by the way?"

"Well," said Trevize with a certain exasperation, "I'm trying to get the computer to guide this thing to the tourist center. I hope the computer knows the one-way streets and the traffic regulations, because I don't."

"What do we do there, Golan?"

"To begin with, we're tourists, so that's the place where we'd naturally go, and we want to be as inconspicuous and natural as we can. And secondly, where would *you* go to get information on Gaia?"

Pelorat said, "To a university—or an anthropological society—or a museum— Certainly not to a tourist center."

"Well, you're wrong. At the tourist center, we will be intellectual types who are eager to have a listing of the universities in the city and the museums and so on. We'll decide where to go to first and *there* we may find the proper people to consult concerning ancient history, galactography, mythology, anthropology, or anything else you can think of. —But the whole thing starts at the tourist center."

Pelorat was silent and the ground-car moved on in a tortuous manner as it joined and became part of the traffic pattern. They plunged into a sub-road and drove past signs that might have represented directions and traffic instructions but were in a style of lettering that made them all-but-unreadable.

Fortunately the ground-car behaved as though it knew the way, and when it stopped and drew itself into a parking spot, there was a sign that said: SAYSHELL OUT-WORLD MILIEU in the same difficult printing, and under it: SAYSHELL TOURIST CENTER in straightforward, easy-to-read Galactic Standard lettering.

They walked into the building, which was not as large as the façade had led them to believe. It was certainly not busy inside.

There were a series of waiting booths, one of which was occupied by a man reading the news-strips emerging from a small ejector; another contained two women who seemed to be playing some intricate game with cards and tiles. Behind a counter too large for him, with winking computer controls that seemed far too complex for him, was a bored-looking Sayshellian functionary wearing what looked like a multicolored checkerboard.

Pelorat stared and whispered, "This is certainly a world of extroverted garb."

"Yes," said Trevize, "I noticed. Still, fashions change from world to world and even from region to region within a world sometimes. And they change with time. Fifty years ago, everyone on Sayshell might have worn black, for all we know. Take it as it comes, Janov."

"I suppose I'll have to," said Pelorat, "but I prefer our own fashions. At least, they're not an assault upon the optic nerve."

"Because so many of us are gray on gray? That offends some people. I've heard it referred to as 'dressing in dirt.' Then too, it's Foundation colorlessness that probably keeps these people in their rainbows—just to emphasize their independence. It's all what you're accustomed to, anyway. —Come on, Janov."

The two headed toward the counter and, as they did so, the man in the booth forsook his news items, rose, and came to meet them, smiling as he did so. *His* clothing was in shades of gray.

Trevize didn't look in his direction at first, but when he did he stopped dead.

He took a deep breath, "By the Galaxy— My friend, the traitor!"

12. AGENT

I.

Munn Li Compor, Councilman of Terminus, looked uncertain as he extended his right hand to Trevize.

Trevize looked at the hand sternly and did not take it. He said, apparently to open air, "I am in no position to create a situation in which I may find myself arrested for disturbing the peace on a foreign planet, but I will do so anyway if this individual comes a step closer."

Compor stopped abruptly, hesitated, and finally said in a low voice after glancing uncertainly at Pelorat, "Am I to have a chance to talk? To explain? Will you listen?"

Pelorat looked from one to the other with a slight frown on his long face. He said, "What's all this, Golan? Have we come to this far world and at once met someone you know?"

Trevize's eyes remained firmly fixed on Compor, but he twisted his body slightly to make it clear that he was talking to Pelorat. Trevize said, "This—human being—we would judge that much from his shape—was once a friend of mine on Terminus. As is my habit with my friends, I trusted him. I told him my views, which were perhaps not the kind that should have received a general airing. He told them to the authorities in great detail, apparently, and did not take the trouble to tell me he had done so. For that reason, I walked neatly into a trap and now I find myself in exile. And now this—human being—wishes to be recognized as a friend."

He turned to Compor full on and brushed his fingers through his hair, succeeding only in disarranging the curls further. "See here, you. I *do* have a question for you. What are you doing here? Of all the worlds in the Galaxy on which you could be, why are you on *this* one? And why *now*?"

Compor's hand, which had remained outstretched throughout Trevize's speech, now fell to his side and the smile left his face. The air of self-confidence, which was ordinarily so much a part of him, was gone and in its absence he looked younger than his thirty-four years and a bit woebegone. "I'll explain," he said, "but only from the start!"

Trevize looked about briefly. "Here? You really want to talk about it here? In a public place? You want me to knock you down *here* after I've listened to enough of your lies?"

Compor lifted both hands now, palms facing each other. "It's the safest place, believe me." And then, checking himself and realizing what the other was about to say, added hurriedly, "Or don't believe me, it doesn't matter. I'm telling the truth. I've been on the planet several hours longer than you and I've checked it out. This is some particular day they have here on Sayshell. It's a day for meditation, for some reason. Almost everyone is at home—or should be. —You see how empty this place is. You don't suppose it's like this every day."

Pelorat nodded and said, "I was wondering why it was so empty, at that." He leaned toward Trevize's ear and whispered, "Why not let him talk, Golan? He looks miserable, poor chap, and he *may* be trying to apologize. It seems unfair not to give him the chance to do so."

Trevize said, "Dr. Pelorat seems anxious to hear you. I'm willing to oblige him, but you'll oblige *me* if you're brief about it. This may be a good day on which to lose my temper. If everyone is meditating, any disturbance I cause may not produce the guardians of the law. I may not be so lucky tomorrow. Why waste an opportunity?"

Compor said in a strained voice, "Look, if you want to take a poke at me, do so. I won't even defend myself, see? Go ahead, hit me—but *listen*!"

"Go ahead and talk, then. I'll listen for a while."

"In the first place, Golan—"

"Address me as Trevize, please. I am not on first-name terms with you."

"In the first place, *Trevize*, you did too good a job convincing me of your views—"

"You hid that well. I could have sworn you were amused by me."

"I tried to be amused to hide from myself the fact that you were being extremely disturbing. —Look, let us sit down up against the wall. Even if the place is empty, some few *may* come in and I don't think we ought to be needlessly conspicuous."

Slowly the three men walked most of the length of the large room. Compor was smiling tentatively again, but remained carefully at more than arm's length from Trevize.

They sat each on a seat that gave as their weight was placed upon it and molded itself into the shape of their hips and buttocks. Pelorat looked surprised and made as though to stand up.

"Relax, Professor," said Compor. "I've been through this already. They're in advance of us in some ways. It's a world that believes in small comforts."

He turned to Trevize, placing one arm over the back of his chair and speaking easily now. "You disturbed me. You made me feel the Second Foundation *did* exist, and that was deeply upsetting. Consider the consequences if they did. Wasn't it likely that they might take care of you somehow? Remove you as a menace? And if I behaved as though I believed you, I might be removed as well. Do you see my point?"

"I see a coward."

"What good would it do to be storybook brave?" said Compor warmly, his blue eyes widening in indignation. "Can you or I stand up to an organization capable of molding our minds and emotions? The only way we could fight effectively would be to hide our knowledge to begin with."

"So you hid it and were safe? —Yet you didn't hide it from Mayor Branno, did you? Quite a risk there."

"Yes! But I thought that was worth it. Just talking between ourselves might do nothing more than get ourselves mentally controlled—or our memories erased altogether. If I told the Mayor, on the other hand— She knew my father well, you know. My father and I were immigrants from Smyrno and the Mayor had a grandmother who—"

"Yes, yes," said Trevize impatiently, "and several generations farther back you can trace ancestry to the Sirius Sector. You've told all that to everyone you know. Get on with it, Compor!"

"Well, I had her ear. If I could convince the Mayor that there was danger, using your arguments, the Federation might take some action. We're not as helpless as we were in the days of the Mule and—at the worst—this dangerous knowledge would be spread more widely and we ourselves would not be in as much *specific* danger."

Trevize said sardonically, "Endanger the Foundation, but keep ourselves safe. That's good patriotic stuff."

"That would be at the worst. I was counting on the best." His forehead had become a little damp. He seemed to be straining against Trevize's immovable contempt.

"And you didn't tell me of this clever plan of yours, did you?"

"No, I didn't and I'm sorry about that, Trevize. The Mayor ordered me not to. She said she wanted to know everything you knew but that you were the sort of person who would freeze if you knew that your remarks were being passed on."

"How right she was!"

"I didn't know—I couldn't guess—I had no way of *conceiving* that she was planning to arrest you and throw you off the planet."

"She was waiting for the right political moment, when my status as Councilman would not protect me. You didn't foresee that?"

"How could I? You yourself did not."

"Had I known that she knew my views, I would have."

Compor said with a sudden trace of insolence, "That's easy enough to say—in hindsight."

"And what is it you want of me here? Now that you have a bit of hindsight, too."

"To make up for all this. To make up for the harm I unwittingly—*unwittingly*—did you."

"Goodness," said Trevize dryly. "How kind of you! But you haven't answered my original question. How did you come to be *here*? How do you happen to be on the very planet I am on?"

Compor said, "There's no complicated answer necessary for that. I followed you!"

"Through hyperspace? With my ship making Jumps in series?"

Compor shook his head. "No mystery. I have the same kind of a ship you do, with the same kind of computer. You know I've always had this trick of being able to guess in which direction through hyperspace a ship would go. It's not usually a very good guess and I'm wrong two times out of three, but with the computer I'm much better. And you hesitated quite a bit at the start and gave me a chance to evaluate the direction and speed in which you were going before entering hyperspace. I fed the data—together with my own intuitive extrapolations—into the computer and it did the rest."

"And you actually got to the city ahead of me?"

"Yes. You didn't use gravitics and I did. I guessed you would come to the capital city, so I went straight down, while you—" Compor made a short spiral motion with his finger as though it were a ship riding a directional beam.

"You took a chance on a run-in with Sayshellian officialdom."

"Well—" Compor's face broke into a smile that lent it an undeniable charm and Trevize felt himself almost warming to him. Compor said, "I'm not a coward at all times and in all things."

Trevize steeled himself. "How did you happen to get a ship like mine?"

"In precisely the same way *you* got a ship like yours. The old lady—Mayor Branno—assigned it to me."

"Why?"

"I'm being entirely frank with you. My assignment was to follow you. The Mayor wanted to know where you were going and what you would be doing."

"And you've been reporting faithfully to her, I suppose. —Or have you been faithless to the Mayor also?"

"I reported to her. I had no choice, actually. She placed a hyper-relay on board ship, which I wasn't supposed to find, but which I did find."

"Well?"

"Unfortunately it's hooked up so that I can't remove it without immobilizing the vessel. At least, there's no way *I* can remove it. Consequently she knows where I am—and she knows where you are."

"Suppose you hadn't been able to follow me. Then she wouldn't have known where I was. Had you thought of that?"

"Of course I did. I thought of just reporting I had lost you—but she wouldn't have believed me, would she? And I wouldn't have been able to get back to Terminus for who knows how long. And I'm not like you, Trevize. I'm not a carefree person without attachments. I have a wife on Terminus—a pregnant wife—and I want to get back to her. You can afford to think only of yourself. I can't. —Besides, I've come to warn you. By Seldon, I'm trying to do that and you won't listen. You keep talking about other things."

"I'm not impressed by your sudden concern for me. What can you warn me against? It seems to me that *you* are the only thing I need to be warned about. You betray me, and now you follow me in order to betray me again. No one else is doing me any harm."

Compor said earnestly, "Forget the dramatics, man. Trevize, you're a lightning rod! You've been sent out to draw Second Foundation response—if there is such a thing as the Second Foundation. I have an intuitive sense for things other than hyperspatial pursuit and I'm sure that's what she's planning. If you try to find the Second Foundation, they'll become aware of it and they'll act against you. If they do, they are very likely to tip their hand. And when they do, Mayor Branno will go for them."

"A pity your famous intuition wasn't working when Branno was planning my arrest."

Compor flushed and muttered, "You know it doesn't always work."

"And now it tells you she's planning to attack the Second Foundation. She wouldn't dare."

"I think she would. But that's not the point. The point is that right now she is throwing you out as bait."

"So?"

"So by all the black holes in space, don't search for the Second Foundation. She won't care if you're killed in the search, but *I* care. I feel responsible for this and I care."

"I'm touched," said Trevize coldly, "but as it happens I have another task on hand at the moment."

"You have?"

"Pelorat and I are on the track of Earth, the planet that some think was the original home of the human race. Aren't we, Janov?"

Pelorat nodded his head. "Yes, it's a purely scientific matter and a long-standing interest of mine."

Compor looked blank for a moment. Then, "Looking for *Earth*? But why?"

"To study it," said Pelorat. "As the one world on which human beings developed—presumably from lower forms of life, instead of, as on all others, merely arriving ready-made—it should be a fascinating study in uniqueness."

"And," said Trevize, "as a world where, just possibly, I may learn more of the Second Foundation. —Just possibly."

Compor said, "But there isn't any Earth. Didn't you know that?"

"No Earth?" Pelorat looked utterly blank, as he always

did when he was preparing to be stubborn. "Are you saying there was no planet on which the human species originated?"

"Oh no. Of course, there was an Earth. There's no question of that! But there isn't any Earth *now*. No inhabited Earth. It's gone!"

Pelorat said, unmoved, "There are tales—"

"Hold on, Janov," said Trevize. "Tell me, Compor, how do you know this?"

"What do you mean, how? It's my heritage. I trace my ancestry from the Sirius Sector, if I may repeat that fact without boring you. We know all about Earth out there. It exists in that sector, which means it's not part of the Foundation Federation, so apparently no one on Terminus bothers with it. But that's where Earth is, just the same."

"That *is* one suggestion, yes," said Pelorat. "There was considerable enthusiasm for that 'Sirius Alternative,' as they called it, in the days of the Empire."

Compor said vehemently, "It's not an alternative. It's a fact."

Pelorat said, "What would you say if I told you I know of many different places in the Galaxy that are called Earth—or were called Earth—by the people who lived in its stellar neighborhood?"

"But this is the real thing," said Compor. "The Sirius Sector is the longest-inhabited portion of the Galaxy. Everyone knows that."

"The Sirians claim it, certainly," said Pelorat, unmoved.

Compor looked frustrated. "I tell you—"

But Trevize said, "Tell us what happened to Earth. You say it's not inhabited any longer. Why not?"

"Radioactivity. The whole planetary surface is radioactive because of nuclear reactions that went out of control, or nuclear explosions—I'm not sure—and now no life is possible there."

The three stared at each other for a while and then Compor felt it necessary to repeat. He said, "I tell you, there's no Earth. There's no use looking for it."

2.

Janov Pelorat's face was, for once, not expressionless. It was not that there was passion in it—or any of the more unstable emotions. It was that his eyes had narrowed—and that a kind of fierce intensity had filled every plane of his face.

He said, and his voice lacked any trace of its usual tentative quality, "How did you say you know all this?"

"I told you," said Compor. "It's my heritage."

"Don't be silly, young man. You are a Councilman. That means you must be born on one of the Federation worlds—Smyrno, I think you said earlier."

"That's right."

"Well then, what heritage are you talking about? Are you telling me that you possess Sirian genes that fill you with inborn knowledge of the Sirian myths concerning Earth?"

Compor looked taken aback. "No, of course not."

"Then what are you talking about?"

Compor paused and seemed to gather his thoughts. He said quietly, "My family has old books of Sirian history. An external heritage, not an internal one. It's not something we talk about outside, especially if one is intent on political advancement. Trevize seems to think I am, but, believe me, I mention it only to good friends."

There was a trace of bitterness in his voice. "Theoretically all Foundation citizens are alike, but those from the old worlds of the Federation are more alike than those from the newer ones—and those that trace from worlds outside the Federation are least alike of all. But, never mind that. Aside from the books, I once visited the old worlds. Trevize—hey, there—"

Trevize had wandered off toward one end of the room, looking out a triangular window. It served to let in a view of the sky and to diminish the view of the city—more light *and* more privacy. Trevize stretched upward to look down.

He returned through the empty room. "Interesting window design," he said. "You called me, Councilman?"

"Yes. Remember the postcollegiate tour I took?"

"After graduation? I remember very well. We were pals. Pals forever. Foundation of trust. Two against the world. You went off on your tour. I joined the Navy, full of patriotism. Somehow I didn't think I wanted to tour with you—some instinct told me not to. I wish the instinct had stayed with me."

Compor did not rise to the bait. He said, "I visited Comporellon. Family tradition said that my ancestors had come from there—at least on my father's side. We were of the ruling family in ancient times before the Empire absorbed us, and my name is derived from the world—or so the family tradition has it. We had an old, poetic name for the star Comporellon circled—Epsilon Eridani."

"What does that mean?" asked Pelorat.

Compor shook his head. "I don't know that it has any meaning. Just tradition. They live with a great deal of tradition. It's an old world. They have long, detailed records of Earth's history, but no one talks about it much. They're superstitious about it. Every time they mention the word, they lift up both hands with first and second fingers crossed to ward off misfortune."

"Did you tell this to anyone when you came back?"

"Of course not. Who would be interested? And I wasn't going to force the tale on anyone. No, thank you! I had a political career to develop and the last thing I want is to stress my foreign origin."

"What about the satellite? Describe Earth's satellite," said Pelorat sharply.

Compor looked astonished. "I don't know anything about that."

"Does it have one?"

"I don't recall reading or hearing about it. But I'm sure if you'll consult the Comporellonian records, you can find out."

"But you know nothing?"

"Not about the satellite. Not that I recall."

"Huh! How did Earth come to be radioactive?"

Compor shook his head and said nothing.

Pelorat said, "Think! You must have heard something."

"It was seven years ago, Professor. I didn't know then you'd be questioning me about it now. There was some sort of legend—they considered it history—"

"What was the legend?"

"Earth was radioactive—ostracized and mistreated by the Empire, its population dwindling—and it was going to destroy the Empire somehow."

"One dying world was going to destroy the whole Empire?" interposed Trevize.

Compor said defensively, "I said it was a legend. I don't know the details. Bel Arvardan was involved in the tale, I know."

"Who was he?" asked Trevize.

"A historical character. I looked him up. He was an honest-to-Galaxy archaeologist back in the early days of the Empire and he maintained that Earth was in the Sirius Sector."

"I've heard the name," said Pelorat.

"He's a folk hero in Comporellon. Look, if you want to know these things—go to Comporellon. It's no use hanging around here."

Pelorat said, "Just how did they say Earth planned to destroy the Empire?"

"Don't know." A certain sullenness was entering Compor's voice.

"Did the radiation have anything to do with it?"

"Don't know. There were tales of some mind-expander developed on Earth—a Synapsifier or something."

"Did it create superminds?" said Pelorat in deepest tones of incredulity.

"I don't think so. What I chiefly remember is that it didn't work. People became bright and died young."

Trevize said, "It was probably a morality myth. If you ask for too much, you lose even that which you have."

Pelorat turned on Trevize in annoyance. "What do *you* know of morality myths?"

Trevize raised his eyebrows. "Your field may not be my field, Janov, but that doesn't mean I'm totally ignorant."

"What else do you remember about what you call the Synapsifier, Councilman Compor?" asked Pelorat.

"Nothing, and I won't submit to any further cross-examination. Look, I followed you on orders from the Mayor. I was *not* ordered to make personal contact with you. I have done so only to warn you that you were followed and to tell you that you had been sent out to serve the Mayor's purposes, whatever those might be. There was nothing else I should have discussed with you, but you surprised me by suddenly bringing up the matter of Earth. Well, let me repeat: Whatever there has existed there in the past—Bel Arvardan, the Synapsifier, whatever—that has nothing to do with what exists now. I'll tell you again: Earth is a dead world. I strongly advise you to go to Comporellon, where you'll find out everything you want to know. Just get away from here."

"And, of course, you will dutifully tell the Mayor that we're going to Comporellon—and you'll follow us to make sure. Or maybe the Mayor knows already. I imagine she has carefully instructed and rehearsed you in every word you have spoken to us here because, for her own purposes, it's in Comporellon that she wants us. Right?"

Compor's face paled. He rose to his feet and almost stuttered in his effort to control his voice. "I've tried to explain. I've tried to be helpful. I shouldn't have tried. You can drop yourself into a black hole, Trevize."

He turned on his heel and walked away briskly without looking back.

Pelorat seemed a bit stunned. "That was rather tactless of you, Golan, old fellow. I could have gotten more out of him."

"No, you couldn't," said Trevize gravely. "You could not have gotten one thing out of him that he was not ready

to let you have. Janov, you don't know what he is —Until
today, I didn't know what he is."

3.

Pelorat hesitated to disturb Trevize. Trevize sat motionless
in his chair, deep in thought.

Finally Pelorat said, "Are we just sitting here all night,
Golan?"

Trevize started. "No, you're quite right. We'll be better
off with people around us. Come!"

Pelorat rose. He said, "There won't be people around
us. Compor said this was some sort of meditation day."

"Is that what he said? Was there traffic when we came
along the road in our ground-car?"

"Yes, some."

"Quite a bit, I thought. And then, when we entered the
city, was it empty?"

"Not particularly. —Still, you've got to admit that this
place has been empty."

"Yes, it has. I noticed that particularly. —But come,
Janov, I'm hungry. There's got to be someplace to eat and
we can afford to find something good. At any rate, we can
find a place in which we can try some interesting Sayshellian
novelty or, if we lose our nerve, good standard Galactic
fare. —Come, once we're safely surrounded, I'll tell you
what I think really happened here."

4.

Trevize leaned back with a pleasant feeling of renewal. The
restaurant was not expensive by Terminus standards, but it
was certainly novel. It was heated, in part, by an open fire
over which food was prepared. Meat tended to be served
in bite-sized portions—in a variety of pungent sauces—
which were picked up by fingers that were protected from

grease and heat by smooth, green leaves that were cold, damp, and had a vaguely minty taste.

It was one leaf to each meat-bit and the whole was taken into the mouth. The waiter had carefully explained how it had to be done. Apparently accustomed to off-planet guests, he had smiled paternally as Trevize and Pelorat gingerly scooped at the steaming bits of meat, and was clearly delighted at the foreigners' relief at finding that the leaves kept the fingers cool and cooled the meat, too, as one chewed.

Trevize said, "Delicious!" and eventually ordered a second helping. So did Pelorat.

They sat over a spongy, vaguely sweet dessert and a cup of coffee that had a caramelized flavor at which they shook dubious heads. They added syrup, at which the waiter shook *his* head.

Pelorat said, "Well, what happened back there at the tourist center?"

"You mean with Compor?"

"Was there anything else there we might discuss?"

Trevize looked about. They were in a deep alcove and had a certain limited privacy, but the restaurant was crowded and the natural hum of noise was a perfect cover.

He said in a low voice, "Isn't it strange that he followed us to Sayshell?"

"He said he had this intuitive ability."

"Yes, he was all-collegiate champion at hypertracking. I never questioned that till today. I quite see that you might be able to judge where someone was going to Jump by how he prepared for it if you had a certain developed skill at it, certain reflexes—but I *don't* see how a tracker can judge a Jump *series*. You prepare only for the first one; the computer does all the others. The tracker can judge that first one, but by what magic can he guess what's in the computer's vitals?"

"But he did it, Golan."

"He certainly did," said Trevize, "and the only possible way I can imagine him doing so is by knowing in advance where we were going to go. By *knowing*, not judging."

Pelorat considered that. "Quite impossible, my boy. How could he know? We didn't decide on our destination till after we were on board the *Far Star*."

"I know that. —And what about this day of meditation?"

"Compor didn't lie to us. The waiter said it was a day of meditation when we came in here and asked him."

"Yes, he did, but he said the restaurant wasn't closed. In fact, what he said was: 'Sayshell City isn't the backwoods. It doesn't close down.' People meditate, in other words, but not in the *big* town, where everyone is sophisticated and there's no place for small-town piety. So there's traffic and it's busy—perhaps not quite as busy as on ordinary days—but busy."

"But, Golan, no one came into the tourist center while we were there. I was aware of that. Not one person entered."

"I noticed that, too. I even went to the window at one point and looked out and saw clearly that the streets around the center had a good scattering of people on foot and in vehicles—and yet not one person entered. The day of meditation made a good cover. We would not have questioned the fortunate privacy we had if I simply hadn't made up my mind not to trust that son of two strangers."

Pelorat said, "What is the significance of all this, then?"

"I think it's simple, Janov. We have here someone who knows where we're going as soon as we do, even though he and we are in separate spaceships, and we also have here someone who can keep a public building empty when it is surrounded by people in order that we might talk in convenient privacy."

"Would you have me believe he can perform miracles?"

"Certainly. If it so happens that Compor is an agent of the Second Foundation and can control minds; if he can read yours and mine in a distant spaceship; if he can influence his way through a customs station at once; if he can land gravitically, with no border patrol outraged at his defiance of the radio beams; and if he can influence minds in such a way as to keep people from entering a building he doesn't want entered.

"By all the stars," Trevize went on with a marked air of grievance, "I can even follow this back to graduation. I *didn't* go on the tour with him. I remember not wanting to. Wasn't that a matter of his influence? He had to be alone. Where was he really going?"

Pelorat pushed away the dishes before him, as though he wanted to clear a space about himself in order to have room to think. It seemed to be a gesture that signaled the busboy-robot, a self-moving table that stopped near them and waited while they placed their dishes and cutlery upon it.

When they were alone, Pelorat said, "But that's mad. Nothing has happened that could not have happened naturally. Once you get it into your head that somebody is controlling events, you can interpret everything in that light and find no reasonable certainty anywhere. Come on, old fellow, it's all circumstantial and a matter of interpretation. Don't yield to paranoia."

"I'm not going to yield to complacency, either."

"Well, let us look at this logically. Suppose he *was* an agent of the Second Foundation. Why would he run the risk of rousing our suspicions by keeping the tourist center empty? What did he say that was so important that a few people at a distance—who would have been wrapped in their own concerns anyway—would have made a difference?"

"There's an easy answer to that, Janov. He would have to keep our minds under close observation and he wanted no interference from other minds. No static. No chance of confusion."

"Again, just your interpretation. What was so important about his conversation with us? It would make sense to suppose, as he himself insisted, that he met us only in order to explain what he had done, to apologize for it, and to warn us of the trouble that might await us. Why would we have to look further than that?"

The small card-receptacle at the farther rim of the table glittered unobtrusively and the figures representing the cost of the meal flashed briefly. Trevize groped beneath his sash for his credit card which, with its Foundation imprint, was good anywhere in the Galaxy—or anywhere a Foundation citizen was likely to go. He inserted it in the appropriate slot. It took a moment to complete the transaction and Trevize (with native caution) checked on the remaining balance before returning it to its pocket.

He looked about casually to make sure there was no undesirable interest in him on the faces of any of the few who still sat in the restaurant and then said, "Why look further than that? Why look further? That was not all he talked about. He talked about Earth. He told us it was dead and urged us very strongly to go to Comporellon. Shall we go?"

"It's something I've been considering, Golan," admitted Pelorat.

"Just leave here?"

"We can come back after we check out the Sirius Sector."

"It doesn't occur to you that his whole purpose in seeing us was to deflect us from Sayshell and get us out of here? Get us anywhere but here?"

"Why?"

"I don't know. See here, they expected us to go to Trantor. That was what *you* wanted to do and maybe that's what they counted on us doing. I messed things up by insisting we go to Sayshell, which is the last thing they wanted, and so now they have to get us out of here."

Pelorat looked distinctly unhappy. "But Golan, you are just making statements. *Why* don't they want us on Sayshell?"

"I don't know, Janov. But it's enough for me that they want us out. I'm staying here. I'm not going to leave."

"But—but— Look, Golan, if the Second Foundation wanted us to leave, wouldn't they just influence our minds to make us want to leave? Why bother reasoning with us?"

"Now that you bring up the point, haven't they done that in your case, Professor?" and Trevize's eyes narrowed in sudden suspicion. "Don't you want to leave?"

Pelorat looked at Trevize in surprise. "I just think there's some sense to it."

"Of course you would, if you've been influenced."

"But I haven't been—"

"Of course you would swear you hadn't been if you had been."

Pelorat said, "If you box me in this way, there is no way of disproving your bare assertion. What are you going to do?"

"I will remain in Sayshell. And you'll stay here, too. You can't navigate the ship without me, so if Compor has influenced you, he has influenced the wrong one."

"Very well, Golan. We'll stay in Sayshell until we have independent reasons to leave. The worst thing we can do, after all—worse than either staying or going—is to fall out with each other. Come, old chap, if I had been influenced, would I be able to change my mind and go along with you cheerfully, as I plan to do now?"

Trevize thought for a moment and then, as though with an inner shake, smiled and held out his hand. "Agreed, Janov. Now let's get back to the ship and make another start tomorrow. —If we can think of one."

5.

Munn Li Compor did not remember when he had been recruited. For one thing, he had been a child at the time; for another, the agents of the Second Foundation were meticulous in removing their traces as far as that was possible.

Compor was an "Observer" and, to a Second Foundationer, he was instantly recognizable as such.

It meant that Compor was acquainted with mentalics and could converse with Second Foundationers in their own fashion to a degree, but he was in the lowest rank of the hierarchy. He could catch glimpses of minds, but he could not adjust them. The education he had received had never gone that far. He was an Observer, not a Doer.

It made him second-class at best, but he did not mind—much. He knew his importance in the scheme of things.

During the early centuries of the Second Foundation, it had underestimated the task before it. It had imagined that its handful of members could monitor the entire Galaxy and that Seldon's Plan, to be maintained, would require only the most occasional, the lightest touch, here and there.

The Mule had stripped them of these delusions. Coming from nowhere, he had caught the Second Foundation (and, of course, the First—though that didn't matter) utterly by surprise and had left them helpless. It took five years before a counterattack could be organized, and then only at the cost of a number of lives.

With Palver a full recovery was made, again at a distressing cost, and he finally took the appropriate measures. The operations of the Second Foundation, he decided, must be enormously expanded without at the same time increasing the chances of detection unduly, so he instituted the corps of Observers.

Compor did not know how many Observers were in the Galaxy or even how many there were on Terminus. It was not his business to know. Ideally there should be no detectable connection between any two Observers, so that the loss of one would not entail the loss of any other. All connections were with the upper echelons on Trantor.

It was Compor's ambition to go to Trantor someday. Though he thought it extremely unlikely, he knew that occasionally an Observer might be brought to Trantor and promoted, but that was rare. The qualities that made for a good Observer were not those that pointed toward the Table.

There was Gendibal, for instance, who was four years younger than Compor. He must have been recruited as a boy, just as Compor was, but *he* had been taken directly to Trantor and was now a Speaker. Compor had no illusions as to why that should be. He had been much in contact with Gendibal of late and he had experienced the power of that young man's mind. He could not have stood up against it for a second.

Compor was not often conscious of a lowly status. There was almost never occasion to consider it. After all (as in the case of other Observers, he imagined) it was only lowly by the standards of Trantor. On their own non-Trantorian worlds, in their own non-mentalic societies, it was easy for Observers to obtain high status.

Compor, for instance, had never had trouble getting into good schools or finding good company. He had been able to use his mentalics in a simple way to enhance his natural intuitive ability (that natural ability had been why he had been recruited in the first place, he was sure) and, in this way, to prove himself a star at hyperspatial pursuit. He became a hero at college and this set his foot on the first rung of a political career. Once this present crisis was over, there was no telling how much farther he might advance.

If the crisis resolved itself successfully, as surely it would, would it not be recalled that it was Compor who had first noted Trevize—not as a human being (anyone could have done that) but as a mind?

He had encountered Trevize in college and had seen him, at first, only as a jovial and quick-witted companion. One morning, however, he had stirred sluggishly out of slumber and, in the stream of consciousness that accompanied the never-never land of half-sleep, he felt what a pity it was that Trevize had never been recruited.

Trevize couldn't have been recruited, of course, since he was Terminus-born and not, like Compor, a native of another world. And even with that aside, it was too late. Only the quite young are plastic enough to receive an education into mentalics; the painful introduction of that art—it was more than a science—into adult brains, set rustily in their mold, was a thing of the first two generations after Seldon only.

But then, if Trevize had been ineligible for recruiting in the first place and had outlived the possibility in the second, what had roused Compor's concern over the matter?

On their next meeting, Compor had penetrated Trevize's mind deeply and discovered what it was that must have initially disturbed him. Trevize's mind had characteristics that did not fit the rules he had been taught. Over and over, it eluded him. As he followed its workings, he found gaps —No, they couldn't be actual gaps—actual leaps of non-existence. They were places where Trevize's manner of mind dove too deeply to be followed.

Compor had no way of determining what this meant, but he watched Trevize's behavior in the light of what he had discovered and he began to suspect that Trevize had an uncanny ability to reach right conclusions from what would seem to be insufficient data.

Did this have something to do with the gaps? Surely this was a matter for mentalism beyond his own powers—for the Table itself, perhaps. He had the uneasy feeling that Trevize's powers of decision were unknown, in their full, to the man himself, and that he might be able to—

To do what? Compor's knowledge did not suffice. He could almost see the meaning of what Trevize possessed— but not quite. There was only the intuitive conclusion—or perhaps just a guess—that Trevize might be, potentially, a person of the utmost importance.

He had to take the chance that this might be so and to risk seeming to be less than qualified for his post. After all, if he were correct—

He was not sure, looking back on it, how he had managed to find the courage to continue his efforts. He could not penetrate the administrative barriers that ringed the Table. He had all but reconciled himself to a broken reputation. He had worked himself down (despairingly) to the most junior member of the Table and, finally, Stor Gendibal had responded to his call.

Gendibal had listened patiently and from that time on there had been a special relationship between them. It was on Gendibal's behalf that Compor had maintained his relationship with Trevize and on Gendibal's direction that he had carefully set up the situation that had resulted in Trevize's exile. And it was through Gendibal that Compor

might yet (he was beginning to hope) achieve his dream of
promotion to Trantor.

All preparations, however, had been designed to send
Trevize to Trantor. Trevize's refusal to do this had taken
Compor entirely by surprise and (Compor thought) had been
unforeseen by Gendibal as well.

At any rate, Gendibal was hurrying to the spot, and to
Compor, that deepened the sense of crisis.

Compor sent out his hypersignal.

6.

Gendibal was roused from his sleep by the touch on his
mind. It was effective and not in the least disturbing. Since
it affected the arousal center directly, he simply awoke.

He sat up in bed, the sheet falling from his well-shaped
and smoothly muscular torso. He had recognized the touch;
the differences were as distinctive to mentalists as were
voices to those who communicated primarily by sound.

Gendibal sent out the standard signal, asking if a small
delay were possible, and the "no emergency" call returned.

Without undue haste, then, Gendibal attended to the
morning routine. He was still in the ship's shower—with
the used water draining into the recycling mechanisms—
when he made contact again.

"Compor?"

"Yes, Speaker."

"Have you spoken with Trevize and the other one."

"Pelorat. Janov Pelorat. Yes, Speaker."

"Good. Give me another five minutes and I'll arrange
visuals."

He passed Sura Novi on his way to the controls. She
looked at him questioningly and made as though to speak,
but he placed a finger on his lips and she subsided at once.
Gendibal still felt a bit uncomfortable at the intensity of
adoration/respect in her mind, but it was coming to be a
comfortingly normal part of his environment somehow.

He had hooked a small tendril of his mind to hers and there would now be no way to affect his mind without affecting hers. The simplicity of her mind (and there was an enormous aesthetic pleasure to be found in contemplating its unadorned symmetry, Gendibal couldn't help thinking) made it impossible for any extraneous mind field to exist in their neighborhood without detection. He felt a surge of gratitude for the courteous impulse that had moved him that moment they had stood together outside the University, and that had led her to come to him precisely when she could be most useful.

He said, "Compor?"

"Yes, Speaker."

"Relax, please. I must study your mind. No offense is intended."

"As you wish, Speaker. May I ask the purpose?"

"To make certain you are untouched."

Compor said, "I know you have political adversaries at the Table, Speaker, but surely none of them—"

"Do not speculate, Compor. Relax. —Yes, you are untouched. Now, if you will co-operate with me, we will establish visual contact."

What followed was, in the ordinary sense of the word, an illusion, since no one but someone who was aided by the mentalic power of a well-trained Second Foundationer would have been able to detect anything at all, either by the senses or by any physical detecting device.

It was the building up of a face and its appearance from the contours of a mind, and even the best mentalist could succeed in producing only a shadowy and somewhat uncertain figure. Compor's face was there in mid-space, as though it were seen through a thin but shifting curtain of gauze, and Gendibal knew that his own face appeared in an identical manner in front of Compor.

By physical hyperwave, communication could have been established through images so clear that speakers who were a thousand parsecs apart might judge themselves to be face-to-face. Gendibal's ship was equipped for the purpose.

There were, however, advantages to the mentalist-vision. The chief was that it could not be tapped by any device known to the First Foundation. Nor, for that matter, could one Second Foundationer tap the mentalist-vision of another. The play of mind might be followed, but not the delicate change of facial expression that gave the communication its finer points.

As for the Anti-Mules— Well, the purity of Novi's mind was sufficient to assure him that none were about.

He said, "Tell me precisely, Compor, the talk you had with Trevize and with this Pelorat. Precisely, to the level of mind."

"Of course, Speaker," said Compor.

It didn't take long. The combination of sound, expression, and mentalism compressed matters considerably, despite the fact that there was far more to tell at the level of mind than if there had been a mere parroting of speech.

Gendibal watched intently. There was little redundancy, if any, in mentalist-vision. In true vision, or even in physical hypervision across the parsecs, one saw enormously more in the way of information bits than was absolutely necessary for comprehension and one could miss a great deal without losing anything significant.

Through the gauze of mentalist-vision, however, one bought absolute security at the price of losing the luxury of being able to miss bits. Every bit was significant.

There were always horror tales that passed from instructor to student on Trantor, tales that were designed to impress on the young the importance of concentration. The most often repeated was certainly the least reliable. It told of the first report on the progress of the Mule before he had taken over Kalgan—of the minor official who received the report and who had no more than the impression of a horselike animal because he did not see or understand the small flick that signified "personal name." The official therefore decided that the whole thing was too unimportant to pass on to Trantor. By the time the next message came, it was too

late to take immediate action and five more bitter years had
to pass.

The event had almost certainly never happened, but that
didn't matter. It was a dramatic story and it served to mo-
tivate every student into the habit of intent concentration.
Gendibal remembered his own student days when he made
an error in reception that seemed, in his own mind, to be
both insignificant and understandable. His teacher—old
Kendast, a tyrant to the roots of his cerebellum—had simply
sneered and said, "A horselike animal, Cub Gendibal?" and
that had been enough to make him collapse in shame.

Compor finished.

Gendibal said, "Your estimate, please, of Trevize's reaction. You know him better than I do, better than anyone
does."

Compor said, "It was clear enough. The mentalic indications were unmistakable. He thinks my words and actions
represent my extreme anxiety to have him go to Trantor or
to the Sirius Sector or to any place but where, in fact, he
is actually going. It meant, in my opinion, that he would
remain firmly where he was. The fact that I attached great
importance to his shifting his position, in short, forced him
to give it the same importance, and since he feels his own
interests to be diametrically opposed to mine, he will deliberately act against what he interprets to be my wish."

"You are certain of that?"

"*Quite* certain."

Gendibal considered this and decided that Compor was
correct. He said, "I am satisfied. You have done well. Your
tale of Earth's radioactive destruction was cleverly chosen
to help produce the proper reaction without the need for
direct manipulation of the mind. Commendable!"

Compor seemed to struggle with himself a short moment.
"Speaker," he said, "I cannot accept your praise. I did not
invent the tale. It is true. There really is a planet called
Earth in the Sirius Sector and it really is considered to be
the original home of humanity. It was radioactive, either to
begin with or eventually, and this grew worse till the planet

died. There was indeed a mind-enhancing invention that came to nothing. All this is considered history on the home planet of my ancestors."

"So? Interesting!" said Gendibal with no obvious conviction. "And better yet. To know when a truth will do is admirable, since no nontruth can be presented with the same sincerity. Palver once said, "'The closer to the truth, the better the lie, and the truth itself, when it can be used, is the best lie.'"

Compor said, "There is one thing more to say. In following instructions to keep Trevize in the Sayshell Sector until you arrived—and to do so at all costs—I had to go so far in my efforts that it is clear that he suspects me of being under the influence of the Second Foundation."

Gendibal nodded. "That, I think, is unavoidable under the circumstances. His monomania on the subject would be sufficient to have him see Second Foundation even where it was not. We must simply take that into account."

"Speaker, if it is absolutely necessary that Trevize stay where he is until you can reach him, it would simplify matters if I came to meet you, took you aboard my ship, and brought you back. It would take less than a day—"

"No, Observer," said Gendibal sharply. "You will not do this. The people on Terminus know where you are. You have a hyper-relay on your ship which you cannot remove, have you not?"

"Yes, Speaker."

"And if Terminus knows you have landed on Sayshell, their ambassador on Sayshell knows of it—and the ambassador knows also that Trevize has landed. Your hyper-relay will tell Terminus that you have left for a specific point hundreds of parsecs away and returned; and the ambassador will inform them that Trevize has, however, remained in the sector. From this, how much will the people at Terminus guess? The Mayor of Terminus is, by all accounts, a shrewd woman and the last thing we want to do is to alarm her by presenting her with an obscure puzzle.

We don't want her to lead a section of her fleet here. The chances of that are, in any case, uncomfortably high."

Compor said, "With respect, Speaker— What reason do we have to fear a fleet if we can control a commander?"

"However little reason there might be, there is still less reason to fear if the fleet is not here. You stay where you are, Observer. When I reach you, I will join you on your ship and then—"

"And then, Speaker?"

"Why, and then I will take over."

7.

Gendibal sat in place after he dismantled the mentalist-vision—and stayed there for long minutes—considering.

During this long trip to Sayshell, unavoidably long in this ship of his which could in no way match the technological advancement of the products of the First Foundation, he had gone over every single report on Trevize. The reports had stretched over nearly a decade.

Seen as a whole and in the light of recent events, there was no longer any doubt Trevize would have been a marvelous recruit for the Second Foundation, if the policy of never touching the Terminus-born had not been in place since Palver's time.

There was no telling how many recruits of highest quality had been lost to the Second Foundation over the centuries. There was no way of evaluating every one of the quadrillions of human beings populating the Galaxy. None of them was likely to have had more promise than Trevize, however, and *certainly* none could have been in a more sensitive spot.

Gendibal shook his head slightly. Trevize should never have been overlooked, Terminus-born or not. —And credit to Observer Compor for seeing it, even after the years had distorted him.

Trevize was of no use to them now, of course. He was too old for the molding, but he still had that inborn intuition, that ability to guess a solution on the basis of totally inadequate information, and something—something—

Old Shandess—who, despite being past his prime, was First Speaker and had, on the whole, been a good one—saw something there, even without the correlated data and the reasoning that Gendibal had worked out in the course of this trip. Trevize, Shandess had thought, was the key to the crisis.

Why was Trevize here at Sayshell? What was he planning? What was he doing?

And he couldn't be touched! Of that Gendibal was sure. Until it was known precisely what Trevize's role was, it would be totally wrong to try to modify him in any way. With the Anti-Mules—whoever they were—whatever they might be—in the field, a wrong move with respect to Trevize (Trevize, above all) might explode a wholly unexpected micro-sun in their faces.

He felt a mind hovering about his own and absently brushed at it as he might at one of the more annoying Trantorian insects—though with mind rather than hand. He felt the instant wash of other-pain and looked up.

Sura Novi had her palm to her furrowed brow. "Your pardon, Master, I be struck with sudden head-anguish."

Gendibal was instantly contrite. "I'm sorry, Novi. I wasn't thinking—or I was thinking too intently." Instantly—and gently—he smoothed the ruffled mind tendrils.

Novi smiled with sudden brightness. "It passed with sudden vanishing. The kind sound of your words, Master, works well upon me."

Gendibal said, "Good! Is something wrong? Why are you here?" He forbore to enter her mind in greater detail in order to find out for himself. More and more, he felt a reluctance to invade her privacy.

Novi hesitated. She leaned toward him slightly. "I be concerned. You were looking at nothing and making sounds and your face was twitching. I stayed there, stick-frozen, afeared you were declining—ill—and unknowing what to do."

"It was nothing, Novi. You are not to fear." He patted her nearer hand. "There is nothing to fear. Do you understand?"

Fear—or any strong emotion—twisted and spoiled the symmetry of her mind somewhat. He preferred it calm and peaceful and happy, but he hesitated at the thought of adjusting it into that position by outer influence. She had felt the previous adjustment to be the effect of his words and it seemed to him that he preferred it that way.

He said, "Novi, why don't I call you Sura?"

She looked up at him in sudden woe. "Oh, Master, do not do so."

"But Rufirant did so on that day that we met. I know you well enough now—"

"I know well he did so, Master. It be how a man speak to girl who have no man, no betrothed, who is—not complete. You say her previous. It is more honorable for me if you say 'Novi' and I be proud that you say so. And if I have not man now, I have master and I be pleased. I hope it be not offensive to you to say 'Novi.'"

"It certainly isn't, Novi."

And her mind was beautifully smooth at that and Gendibal was pleased. Too pleased. Ought he to be *so* pleased?

A little shamefacedly, he remembered that the Mule was supposed to have been affected in this manner by that woman of the First Foundation, Bayta Darell, to his own undoing.

This, of course, was different. This Hamishwoman was his defense against alien minds and he wanted her to serve that purpose most efficiently.

No, that was not true— His function as a Speaker would be compromised if he ceased to understand his own mind or, worse, if he deliberately misconstrued it to avoid the truth. The truth was that it pleased him when she was calm and peaceful and happy endogenously—without his interference—and that it pleased him simply because *she* pleased him; and (he thought defiantly) there was nothing wrong with that.

He said, "Sit down, Novi."

She did so, balancing herself precariously at the edge of the chair and sitting as far away as the confines of the room allowed. Her mind was flooded with respect.

He said, "When you saw me making sounds, Novi, I was speaking at a long distance, scholar-fashion."

Novi said sadly, her eyes cast down, "I see, Master, that there be much to scowler-fashion I understand not and imagine not. It be difficult mountain-high art. I be ashamed to have come to you to be made scowler. How is it, Master, you did not be-laugh me?"

Gendibal said, "It is no shame to aspire to something even if it is beyond your reach. You are now too old to be made a scholar after my fashion, but you are never too old to learn more than you already know and to become able to do more than you already can. I will teach you something about this ship. By the time we reach our destination, you will know quite a bit about it."

He felt delighted. Why not? He was deliberately turning his back on the stereotype of the Hamish people. What right, in any case, had the heterogeneous group of the Second Foundation to set up such a stereotype? The young produced by them were only occasionally suited to become high-level Second Foundationers themselves. The children of Speakers almost never qualified to be Speakers. There were the three generations of Linguesters three centuries ago, but there was always the suspicion that the middle Speaker of that series did not really belong. And if that were true, who were the people of the University to place themselves on so high a pedestal?

He watched Novi's eyes glisten and was pleased that they did.

She said, "I try hard to learn all you teach me, Master."

"I'm sure you will," he said—and then hesitated. It occurred to him that, in his conversation with Compor, he had in no way indicated at any time that he was not alone. There was no hint of a companion.

A woman could be taken for granted, perhaps; at least,

Compor would no doubt not be surprised. —But a Hamish-woman?

For a moment, despite anything Gendibal could do, the stereotype reigned supreme and he found himself glad that Compor had never been on Trantor and would not recognize Novi as a Hamishwoman.

He shook it off. It didn't matter if Compor knew or knew not—or if anyone did. Gendibal was a Speaker of the Second Foundation and he could do as he pleased within the constraints of the Seldon Plan—and no one could interfere.

Novi said "Master, once we reach our destination, will we part?"

He looked at her and said, with perhaps more force than he intended, "We will not be separated, Novi."

And the Hamishwoman smiled shyly and looked for all the Galaxy as though she might have been—*any* woman.

13. UNIVERSITY

1.

Pelorat wrinkled his nose when he and Trevize re-entered the *Far Star*.

Trevize shrugged. "The human body is a powerful dispenser of odors. Recycling never works instantaneously and artificial scents merely overlay—they do not replace."

"And I suppose no two ships smell quite alike, once they've been occupied for a period of time by different people."

"That's right, but did you smell Sayshell Planet after the first hour?"

"No," admitted Pelorat.

"Well, you won't smell this after a while, either. In fact, if you live in the ship long enough, you'll welcome the odor that greets you on your return as signifying home. And by the way, if you become a Galactic rover after this, Janov, you'll have to learn that it is impolite to comment on the odor of any ship or, for that matter, any world to those who live on that ship or world. Between us, of course, it is all right."

"As a matter of fact, Golan, the funny thing is I *do* consider the *Far Star* home. At least it's Foundation-made." Pelorat smiled. "You know, I never considered myself a patriot. I like to think I recognize only humanity as my nation, but I must say that being away from the Foundation fills my heart with love for it."

Trevize was making his bed. "You're not very far from the Foundation, you know. The Sayshell Union is almost surrounded by Federation territory. We have an ambassador and an enormous presence here, from consuls on down. The

242

Sayshellians like to oppose us in words, but they are usually very cautious about doing anything that gives us displeasure. —Janov, do turn in. We got nowhere today and we have to do better tomorrow."

Still, there was no difficulty in hearing between the two rooms, however, and when the ship was dark, Pelorat, tossing restlessly, finally said in a not very loud voice, "Golan?"

"Yes."

"You're not sleeping?"

"Not while you're talking."

"We *did* get somewhere today. Your friend, Compor—"

"Ex-friend," growled Trevize.

"Whatever his status, he talked about Earth and told us something I hadn't come across in my researches before. Radioactivity!"

Trevize lifted himself to one elbow. "Look, Golan, if Earth is really dead, that doesn't mean we return home. I *still* want to find Gaia."

Pelorat made a puffing noise with his mouth as though he were blowing away feathers. "My dear chap, of course. So do I. Nor do I think Earth is dead. Compor may have been telling what he felt was the truth, but there's scarcely a sector in the Galaxy that doesn't have some tale or other that would place the origin of humanity on some local world. And they almost invariably call it Earth or some closely equivalent name.

"We call it 'globocentrism' in anthropology. People have a tendency to take it for granted that they are better than their neighbors; that their culture is older and superior to that of other worlds; that what is good in other worlds has been borrowed from them, while what is bad is distorted or perverted in the borrowing or invented elsewhere. And the tendency is to equate superiority in quality with superiority in duration. If they cannot reasonably maintain their own planet to be Earth or its equivalent—and the beginnings of the human species—they almost always do the best they can by placing Earth in their own sector, even when they cannot locate it exactly."

Trevize said, "And you're telling me that Compor was just following the common habit when he said Earth existed in the Sirius Sector. —Still, the Sirius Sector *does* have a long history, so every world in it should be well known and it should be easy to check the matter, even without going there."

Pelorat chuckled. "Even if you were to show that no world in the Sirius Sector could possibly be Earth, that wouldn't help. You underestimate the depths to which mysticism can bury rationality, Golan. There are at least half a dozen sectors in the Galaxy where respectable scholars repeat, with every appearance of solemnity and with no trace of a smile, local tales that Earth—or whatever they choose to call it—is located in hyperspace and cannot be reached, except by accident."

"And do they say anyone *has* ever reached it by accident?"

"There are always tales and there is always a patriotic refusal to disbelieve, even though the tales are never in the least credible and are never believed by anyone not of the world that produces them."

"Then, Janov, let's not believe them ourselves. Let's enter our own private hyperspace of sleep."

"But, Golan, it's this business of Earth's radioactivity that interests me. To me, that seems to bear the mark of truth—or a kind of truth."

"What do you mean, a *kind* of truth?"

"Well, a world that is radioactive would be a world in which hard radiation would be present in higher concentration than is usual. The rate of mutation would be higher on such a world and evolution would proceed more quickly— and more diversely. I told you, if you remember, that among the points on which almost all the tales agree is that life on Earth was incredibly diverse: millions of species of all kinds of life. It is this diversity of life—this *explosive* development—that might have brought intelligence to the Earth, and then the surge outward into the Galaxy. If Earth were for some reason radioactive—that is, more radioactive than other planets—that might account for everything else about Earth that is—or was—unique."

Trevize was silent for a moment. Then, "In the first place, we have no reason to believe Compor was telling the truth. He may well have been lying freely in order to induce us to leave this place and go chasing madly off to Sirius. I believe that's exactly what he was doing. And even if he were telling the truth, what he said was that there was so much radioactivity that life became impossible."

Pelorat made the blowing gesture again. "There wasn't too much radioactivity to allow life to develop on Earth and it is easier for life to maintain itself—once established— than to develop in the first place. Granted, then, that life was established and maintained on Earth. Therefore the level of radioactivity could not have been incompatible with life to begin with and it could only have fallen off with time. There is nothing that can *raise* the level."

"Nuclear explosions?" suggested Trevize.

"What would that have to do with it?"

"I mean, suppose nuclear explosions took place on Earth?"

"On Earth's surface? Impossible. There's no record in the history of the Galaxy of any society being so foolish as to use nuclear explosions as a weapon of war. We would never have survived. During the Trigellian insurrections, when both sides were reduced to starvation and desperation and when Jendippurus Khoratt suggested the initiation of a fusion reaction in—"

"He was hanged by the sailors of his own fleet. I know Galactic history. I was thinking of accident."

"There's no record of accidents of that sort that are capable of significantly raising the intensity of radioactivity of a planet, generally." He sighed. "I suppose that when we get around to it, we'll have to go to the Sirius Sector and do a little prospecting there."

"Someday, perhaps, we will. But for now—"

"Yes, yes, I'll stop talking."

He did and Trevize lay in the dark for nearly an hour considering whether he had attracted too much attention already and whether it might not be wise to go to the Sirius Sector and then return to Gaia when attention—everyone's attention—was elsewhere.

He had arrived at no clear decision by the time he fell asleep. His dreams were troubled.

2.

They did not arrive back in the city till midmorning. The tourist center was quite crowded this time, but they managed to obtain the necessary directions to a reference library, where in turn they received instruction in the use of the local models of data-gathering computers.

They went carefully through the museums and universities, beginning with those that were nearest, and checked out whatever information was available on anthropologists, archaeologists, and ancient historians.

Pelorat said, "Ah!"

"Ah?" said Trevize with some asperity. "Ah, what?"

"This name, Quintesetz. It seems familiar."

"You know him?"

"No, of course not, but I may have read papers of his. Back at the ship, where I have my reference collection—"

"We're not going back, Janov. If the name is familiar, that's a starting point. If he can't help us, he will undoubtedly be able to direct us further." He rose to his feet. "Let's find a way of getting to Sayshell University. And since there will be nobody there at lunchtime, let's eat first."

It was not till late afternoon that they had made their way out to the university, worked their way through its maze, and found themselves in an anteroom, waiting for a young woman who had gone off in search of information and who might—or might not—lead them to Quintesetz.

"I wonder," said Pelorat uneasily, "how much longer we'll have to wait. It must be getting toward the close of the schoolday."

And, as though that were a cue, the young lady whom

they had last seen half an hour before, walked rapidly toward them, her shoes glinting red and violet and striking the ground with a sharp musical tone as she walked. The pitch varied with the speed and force of her steps.

Pelorat winced. He supposed that each world had its own ways of assaulting the senses, just as each had its own smell. He wondered if, now that he no longer noticed the smell, he might also learn not to notice the cacophony of fashionable young women when they walked.

She came to Pelorat and stopped. "May I have your full name, Professor?"

"It's Janov Pelorat, miss."

"Your home planet?"

Trevize began to lift one hand as though to enjoin silence, but Pelorat, either not seeing or not regarding, said, "Terminus."

The young woman smiled broadly, and looked pleased. "When I told Professor Quintesetz that a Professor Pelorat was inquiring for him, he said he would see you if you were Janov Pelorat of Terminus, but not otherwise."

Pelorat blinked rapidly. "You—you mean, he's heard of me?"

"It certainly seems so."

And, almost creakily, Pelorat managed a smile as he turned to Trevize. "He's heard of me. I honestly didn't think— I mean, I've written very few papers and I didn't think that anyone—" He shook his head. "They weren't really important."

"Well then," said Trevize, smiling himself, "stop hugging yourself in an ecstasy of self-underestimation and let's go." He turned to the woman. "I presume, miss, there's some sort of transportation to take us to him?"

"It's within walking distance. We won't even have to leave the building complex and I'll be glad to take you there. —Are both of you from Terminus?" And off she went.

The two men followed and Trevize said, with a trace of annoyance, "Yes, we are. Does that make a difference?"

"Oh no, of course not. There are people on Sayshell that don't like Foundationers, you know, but here at the university, we're more cosmopolitan than that. Live and let live is what I always say. I mean, Foundationers are people, too. You know what I mean?"

"Yes, I know what you mean. Lots of us say that Sayshellians are people."

"That's just the way it should be. I've never seen Terminus. It must be a big city."

"Actually it isn't," said Trevize matter-of-factly. "I suspect it's smaller than Sayshell City."

"You're tweaking my finger," she said. "It's the capital of the Foundation Federation, isn't it? I mean, there isn't another Terminus, is there?"

"No, there's only one Terminus, as far as I know, and that's where we're from—the capital of the Foundation Federation."

"Well then, it must be an enormous city. —And you're coming all the way here to see the professor. We're very proud of him, you know. He's considered the biggest authority in the whole Galaxy."

"Really?" said Trevize. "On what?"

Her eyes opened wide again, "You *are* a teaser. He knows more about ancient history than—than I know about my own family." And she continued to walk on ahead on her musical feet.

One can only be called a teaser and a finger-tweaker so often without developing an actual impulse in that direction. Trevize smiled and said, "The professor knows all about Earth, I suppose?"

"Earth?" She stopped at an office door and looked at them blankly.

"You know. The world where humanity got its start."

"Oh, you mean the planet-that-was-first. I guess so. I guess he *should* know all about it. After all, it's located in the Sayshell Sector. Everyone knows *that*! —This is his office. Let me signal him."

"No, don't," said Trevize. "Not for just a minute. Tell me about Earth."

"Actually I never heard anyone call it Earth. I suppose that's a Foundation word. We call it Gaia, here."

Trevize cast a swift look at Pelorat. "Oh? And where is it located?"

"Nowhere. It's in hyperspace and there's no way anyone can get to it. When I was a little girl, my grandmother said that Gaia was once in real space, but it was so disgusted at the—"

"Crimes and stupidities of human beings," muttered Pelorat, "that, out of shame, it left space and refused to have anything more to do with the human beings it had sent out into the Galaxy."

"You know the story, then. See? —A girlfriend of mine says it's superstition. Well, I'll tell *her*. If it's good enough for professors from the Foundation—"

A glittering section of lettering on the smoky glass of the door read: SOTAYN QUINTESETZ ABT in the hard-to-read Sayshellian calligraphy—and under it was printed, in the same fashion: DEPARTMENT OF ANCIENT HISTORY.

The woman placed her finger on a smooth metal circle. There was no sound, but the smokiness of the glass turned a milky white for a moment and a soft voice said, in an abstracted sort of way, "Identify yourself, please."

"Janov Pelorat of Terminus," said Pelorat, "with Golan Trevize of the same world." The door swung open at once.

3.

The man who stood up, walked around his desk, and advanced to meet them was tall and well into middle age. He was light brown in skin color and his hair, which was set in crisp curls over his head, was iron-gray. He held out his hand in greeting and his voice was soft and low. "I am S.Q. I am delighted to meet you, Professor."

Trevize said, "I don't own an academic title. I merely

accompany Professor Pelorat. You may call me simply Trevize. I am pleased to meet you, Professor Abt."

Quintesetz held up one hand in clear embarrassment. "No no. Abt is merely a foolish title of some sort that has no significance outside of Sayshell. Ignore it, please, and call me S.Q. We tend to use initials in ordinary social intercourse on Sayshell. I'm so pleased to meet two of you when I had been expecting but one."

He seemed to hesitate a moment, then extended his right hand after wiping it unobtrusively on his trousers.

Trevize took it, wondering what the proper Sayshellian manner of greeting was.

Quintesetz said, "Please sit down. I'm afraid you'll find these chairs to be lifeless ones, but I, for one, don't want my chairs to hug me. It's all the fashion for chairs to hug you nowadays, but I prefer a hug to mean something, hey?"

Trevize smiled and said, "Who would not? Your name, S.Q., seems to be of the Rim Worlds and not Sayshellian. I apologize if the remark is impertinent."

"I don't mind. My family traces back, in part, to Askone. Five generations back, my great-great-grandparents left Askone when Foundation domination grew too heavy."

Pelorat said, "And we are Foundationers. Our apologies."

Quintesetz waved his hand genially, "I don't hold a grudge across a stretch of five generations. Not that such things haven't been done, more's the pity. Would you like to have something to eat? To drink? Would you like music in the background?"

"If you don't mind," said Pelorat, "I'd be willing to get right to business, if Sayshellian ways would permit."

"Sayshellian ways are not a barrier to that, I assure you. —You have no idea how remarkable this is, Dr. Pelorat. It was only about two weeks ago that I came across your article on origin myths in the *Archaeological Review* and it struck me as a remarkable synthesis—all too brief."

Pelorat flushed with pleasure. "How delighted I am that you have read it. I had to condense it, of course, since the

Review would not print a full study. I have been planning to do a treatise on the subject."

"I wish you would. In any case, as soon as I had read it, I had this desire to see you. I even had the notion of visiting Terminus in order to do so, though that would have been hard to arrange—"

"Why so?" asked Trevize.

Quintesetz looked embarrassed. "I'm sorry to say that Sayshell is not eager to join the Foundation Federation and rather discourages any social communication with the Foundation. We've a tradition of neutralism, you see. Even the Mule didn't bother us, except to extort from us a specific statement of neutrality. For that reason, any application for permission to visit Foundation territory generally—and particularly Terminus—is viewed with suspicion, although a scholar such as myself, intent on academic business, would probably obtain his passport in the end. —But none of that was necessary; you have come to me. I can scarcely believe it. I ask myself: Why? Have you heard of me, as I have heard of you?"

Pelorat said, "I know your work, S.Q., and in my records I have abstracts of your papers. It is why I have come to you. I am exploring both the matter of Earth, which is the reputed planet of origin of the human species, and the early period of the exploration and settlement of the Galaxy. In particular, I have come here to inquire as to the founding of Sayshell."

"From your paper," said Quintesetz, "I presume you are interested in myths and legends."

"Even more in history—actual facts—if such exist. Myths and legends, otherwise."

Quintesetz rose and walked rapidly back and forth the length of his office, paused to stare at Pelorat, then walked again.

Trevize said impatiently, "Well, sir."

Quintesetz said, "Odd! Really odd! It was only yesterday—"

Pelorat said, "What was only yesterday?"

Quintesetz said, "I told you, Dr. Pelorat—may I call you J.P., by the way? I find using a full-length name rather unnatural."

"Please do."

"I told you, J.P., that I had admired your paper and that I had wanted to see you. The reason I wanted to see you was that you clearly had an extensive collection of legends concerning the beginnings of the worlds and yet didn't have ours. In other words, I wanted to see you in order to tell you precisely what you have come to see me to find out."

"What has this to do with yesterday, S.Q.?" asked Trevize.

"We have legends. A legend. An important one to our society, for it has become our central mystery—"

"Mystery?" said Trevize.

"I don't mean a puzzle or anything of that sort. That, I believe, would be the usual meaning of the word in Galactic Standard. There's a specialized meaning here. It means 'something secret'; something only certain adepts know the full meaning of; something not to be spoken of to outsiders. —And yesterday was the day."

"The day of what, S.Q.?" asked Trevize, slightly exaggerating his air of patience.

"Yesterday was the Day of Flight."

"Ah," said Trevize, "a day of meditation and quiet, when everyone is supposed to remain at home."

"Something like that, in theory, except that in the larger cities, the more sophisticated regions, there is little observance in the older fashion. —But you know about it, I see."

Pelorat, who had grown uneasy at Trevize's annoyed tone, put in hastily, "We heard a little of it, having arrived yesterday."

"Of all days," said Trevize sarcastically. "See here, S.Q. As I said, I'm not an academic, but I have a question. You said you were speaking of a central mystery, meaning it was not to be spoken of to outsiders. Why, then, are you speaking of it to us? We are outsiders."

"So you are. But I'm not an observer of the day and the

depth of my superstition in this matter is slight at best. J.P.'s paper, however, reinforced a feeling I have had for a long time. A myth or legend is simply not made up out of a vacuum. Nothing is—or can be. Somehow there is a kernel of truth behind it, however distorted that might be, and I would like the truth behind our legend of the Day of Flight."

Trevize said, "Is it safe to talk about it?"

Quintesetz shrugged. "Not entirely, I suppose. The conservative elements among our population would be horrified. However, they don't control the government and haven't for a century. The secularists are strong and would be stronger still, if the conservatives didn't take advantage of our—if you'll excuse me—anti-Foundation bias. Then, too, since I am discussing the matter out of my scholarly interest in ancient history, the League of Academicians will support me strongly, in case of need."

"In that case," said Pelorat, "would you tell us about your central mystery, S.Q.?"

"Yes, but let me make sure we won't be interrupted or, for that matter, overheard. Even if one must stare the bull in the face, one needn't slap its muzzle, as the saying goes."

He flicked a pattern on the work-face of an instrument on his desk and said, "We're incommunicado now."

"Are you sure you're not bugged?" asked Trevize.

"Bugged?"

"Tapped! Eavesdropped! —Subjected to a device that will have you under observation—visual or auditory or both."

Quintesetz looked shocked. "Not here on Sayshell!"

Trevize shrugged. "If you say so."

"Please go on, S.Q.," said Pelorat.

Quintesetz pursed his lips, leaned back in his chair (which gave slightly under the pressure) and put the tips of his fingers together. He seemed to be speculating as to just how to begin.

He said, "Do you know what a robot is?"

"A robot?" said Pelorat. "No."

Quintesetz looked in the direction of Trevize, who shook his head slowly.

"You know what a computer is, however?"

"Of course," said Trevize impatiently.

"Well then, a mobile computerized tool—"

"Is a mobile computerized tool." Trevize was still impatient. "There are endless varieties and I don't know of any generalized term for it except mobile computerized tool."

"—that looks exactly like a human being is a robot." S.Q. completed his definition with equanimity. "The distinction of a robot is that it is humaniform."

"Why humaniform?" asked Pelorat in honest amazement.

"I'm not sure. It's a remarkably inefficient form for a tool, I grant you, but I'm just repeating the legend. 'Robot' is an old word from no recognizable language, though our scholars say it bears the connotation of 'work.'"

"I can't think of any word," said Trevize skeptically, "that sounds even vaguely like 'robot' and that has any connection with 'work.'"

"Nothing in Galactic, certainly," said Quintesetz, "but that's what they say."

Pelorat said, "It may have been reverse etymology. These objects were used for work, and so the word was said to mean 'work.' —In any case, why do you tell us this?"

"Because it is a firmly fixed tradition here on Sayshell that when Earth was a single world and the Galaxy lay all uninhabited before it, robots were invented and devised. There were then two sorts of human beings: natural and invented, flesh and metal, biological and mechanical, complex and simple—"

Quintesetz came to a halt and said with a rueful laugh, "I'm sorry. It is impossible to talk about robots without quoting from the *Book of Flight*. The people of Earth devised robots—and I need say no more. That's plain enough."

"And why did they devise robots?" asked Trevize.

Quintesetz shrugged. "Who can tell at this distance in time? Perhaps they were few in numbers and needed help, particularly in the great task of exploring and populating the Galaxy."

Trevize said, "That's a reasonable suggestion. Once the Galaxy was colonized, the robots would no longer be needed. Certainly there are no humanoid mobile computerized tools in the Galaxy today."

"In any case," said Quintesetz, "the story is as follows— if I may vastly simplify and leave out many poetic ornamentations which, frankly, I don't accept, though the general population does or pretends to. Around Earth, there grew up colony worlds circling neighboring stars and these colony worlds were far richer in robots than was Earth itself. There was more use for robots on raw, new worlds. Earth, in fact, retreated, wished no more robots, and rebelled against them."

"What happened?" asked Pelorat.

"The Outer Worlds were the stronger. With the help of their robots, the children defeated and controlled Earth— the Mother. Pardon me, but I can't help slipping into quotation. But there were those from Earth who fled their world—with better ships and stronger modes of hyperspatial travel. They fled to far distant stars and worlds, far beyond the closer worlds earlier colonized. New colonies were founded—without robots—in which human beings could live freely. Those were the Times of Flight, so-called, and the day upon which the first Earthmen reached the Sayshell Sector—this very planet, in fact—is *the* Day of Flight, celebrated annually for many thousands of years."

Pelorat said, "My dear chap, what you are saying, then, is that Sayshell was founded directly from Earth."

Quintesetz thought and hesitated for a moment. Then he said, "That is the official belief."

"Obviously," said Trevize, "you don't accept it."

"It seems to me—" Quintesetz began and then burst out, "Oh, Great Stars and Small Planets, I don't! It is entirely too unlikely, but it's official dogma and however secularized the government has become, lip service to that, at least, is essential. —Still, to the point. In your article, J.P., there is no indication that you're aware of this story—of robots and of two waves of colonization, a lesser one with robots and a greater one without."

"I certainly was not," said Pelorat. "I hear it now for the first time and, my dear S.Q., I am eternally grateful to you for making this known to me. I am astonished that no hint of this has appeared in any of the writings—"

"It shows," said Quintesetz, "how effective our social system is. It's our Sayshellian secret—our great mystery."

"Perhaps," said Trevize dryly. "Yet the second wave of colonization—the robotless wave—must have moved out in all directions. Why is it only on Sayshell that this great secret exists?"

Quintesetz said, "It may exist elsewhere and be just as secret. Our own conservatives believe that *only* Sayshell was settled from Earth and that all the rest of the Galaxy was settled from Sayshell. That, of course, is probably nonsense."

Pelorat said, "These subsidiary puzzles can be worked out in time. Now that I have the starting point, I can seek out similar information on other worlds. What counts is that I have discovered the question to ask and a good question is, of course, the key by which infinite answers can be educed. How fortunate that I—"

Trevize said, "Yes, Janov, but the good S.Q. has not told us the whole story, surely. What happened to the older colonies and their robots? Do your traditions say?"

"Not in detail, but in essence. Human and humanoid cannot live together, apparently. The worlds with robots died. They were not viable."

"And Earth?"

"Humans left it and settled here and presumably (though the conservatives would disagree) on other planets as well."

"Surely not every human being left Earth. The planet was not deserted."

"Presumably not. I don't know."

Trevize said abruptly, "Was it left radioactive?"

Quintesetz looked astonished. "Radioactive?"

"That's what I'm asking."

"Not to my knowledge. I never heard of such a thing."

Trevize put a knuckle to his teeth and considered. Finally he said, "S.Q., it's getting late and we have trespassed sufficiently on your time, perhaps." (Pelorat made a motion as though he were about to protest, but Trevize's hand was on the other's knee and his grip tightened—so Pelorat, looking disturbed, subsided.)

Quintesetz said, "I was delighted to be of use."

"You have been and if there's anything we can do in exchange, name it."

Quintesetz laughed gently. "If the good J.P. will be so kind as to refrain from mentioning my name in connection with any writing he does on our mystery, that will be sufficient repayment."

Pelorat said eagerly, "You would be able to get the credit you deserve—and perhaps be more appreciated—if you were allowed to visit Terminus and even, perhaps, remain there as a visiting scholar at our university for an extended period. We might arrange that. Sayshell might not like the Federation, but they might not like refusing a direct request that you be allowed to come to Terminus to attend, let us say, a colloquium on some aspect of ancient history."

The Sayshellian half-rose. "Are you saying you can pull strings to arrange *that*?"

Trevize said, "Why, I hadn't thought of it, but J.P. is perfectly right. That would be feasible—if we tried. And, of course, the more grateful you make us, the harder we will try."

Quintesetz paused, then frowned. "What do you mean, sir?"

"All you have to do is tell us about Gaia, S.Q.," said Trevize.

And all the light in Quintesetz's face died.

4.

Quintesetz looked down at his desk. His hand stroked absent-mindedly at his short, tightly curled hair. Then he looked at Trevize and pursed his lips tightly. It was as though he were determined not to speak.

Trevize lifted his eyebrows and waited and finally Quintesetz said in a strangled sort of way, "It is getting indeed late—quite glemmering."

Until then he had spoken in good Galactic, but now his words took on a strange shape as though the Sayshellian mode of speech were pushing past his classical education.

"Glemmering, S.Q.?"

"It is nearly full night."

Trevize nodded. "I am thoughtless. And I am hungry, too. Could you please join us for an evening meal, S.Q., at our expense? We could then, perhaps, continue our discussion—about Gaia."

Quintesetz rose heavily to his feet. He was taller than either of the two men from Terminus, but he was older and pudgier and his height did not lend him the appearance of strength. He seemed more weary than when they had arrived.

He blinked at them and said, "I forget my hospitality. You are Outworlders and it would not be fitting that you entertain me. Come to my home. It is on campus and not far and, if you wish to carry on a conversation, I can do so in a more relaxed manner there than here. My only regret" (he seemed a little uneasy) "is that I can offer you only a limited meal. My wife and I are vegetarians and if you are meat-eating, I can only express my apologies and regrets."

Trevize said, "J.P. and I will be quite content to forego our carnivorous natures for one meal. Your conversation will more than make up for it—I hope."

"I can promise you an interesting meal, whatever the conversation," said Quintesetz, "if your taste should run to our Sayshellian spices. My wife and I have made a rare study of such things."

"I look forward to any exoticism you choose to supply, S.Q.," said Trevize coolly, though Pelorat looked a little nervous at the prospect.

Quintesetz led the way. The three left the room and walked down an apparently endless corridor, with the Sayshellian greeting students and colleagues now and then, but making no attempt to introduce his companions. Trevize was uneasily aware that others stared curiously at his sash, which happened to be one of his gray ones. A subdued color was not something that was *de rigueur* in campus clothing, apparently.

Finally they stepped through the door and out into the open. It was indeed dark and a little cool, with trees bulking in the distance and a rather rank stand of grass on either side of the walkway.

Pelorat came to a halt—with his back to the glimmer of lights that came from the building they had just left and from the glows that lined the walks of the campus. He looked straight upward.

"Beautiful!" he said. "There is a famous phrase in a verse by one of our better poets that speaks of 'the speckle-shine of Sayshell's soaring sky.'"

Trevize gazed appreciatively and said in a low voice, "We are from Terminus, S.Q., and my friend, at least, has seen no other skies. On Terminus, we see only the smooth dim fog of the Galaxy and a few barely visible stars. You would appreciate your own sky even more, had you lived with ours."

Quintesetz said gravely, "We appreciate it to the full, I assure you. It's not so much that we are in an uncrowded area of the Galaxy, but that the distribution of stars is remarkably even. I don't think that you will find, anywhere in the Galaxy, first-magnitude stars so generally distributed. —And yet not too many, either. I have seen the skies of worlds that are inside the outer reaches of a globular cluster and there you will see too many bright stars. It spoils the darkness of the night sky and reduces the splendor considerably."

"I quite agree with that," said Trevize.

"Now I wonder," said Quintesetz, "if you see that almost regular pentagon of almost equally bright stars. The Five Sisters, we call them. It's in that direction, just above the line of trees. Do you see it?"

"I see it," said Trevize. "Very attractive."

"Yes," said Quintesetz. "It's supposed to symbolize success in love—and there's no love letter that doesn't end in a pentagon of dots to indicate a desire to make love. Each of the five stars stands for a different stage in the process and there are famous poems which have vied with each other in making each stage as explicitly erotic as possible. In my younger days, I attempted versifying on the subject myself and I wouldn't have thought that the time would come when I would grow so indifferent to the Five Sisters, though I suppose it's the common fate. —Do you see the dim star just about in the center of the Five Sisters."

"Yes."

"That," said Quintesetz, "is supposed to represent unrequited love. There is a legend that the star was once as bright as the rest, but faded with grief." And he walked on rapidly.

5.

The dinner, Trevize had been forced to admit to himself, was delightful. There was endless variety and the spicing and dressing were subtle but effective.

Trevize said, "All these vegetables—which have been a pleasure to eat, by the way—are part of the Galactic dietary, are they not, S.Q.?"

"Yes, of course."

"I presume, though, that there are indigenous forms of life, too."

"Of course. Sayshell Planet was an oxygen world when the first settlers arrived, so it had to be life-bearing. And we have preserved some of the indigenous life, you may be sure. We have quite extensive natural parks in which both the flora and the fauna of Old Sayshell survive."

Pelorat said sadly, "There you are in advance of us, S.Q. There was little land life on Terminus when human beings arrived and I'm afraid that for a long time no concerted effort was made to preserve the sea life, which had produced the oxygen that made Terminus habitable. Terminus has an ecology now that is purely Galactic in nature."

"Sayshell," said Quintesetz, with a smile of modest pride, "has a long and steady record of life-valuing."

And Trevize chose that moment to say, "When we left your office, S.Q., I believe it was your intention to feed us dinner and then tell us about Gaia."

Quintesetz's wife, a friendly woman—plump and quite dark, who had said little during the meal—looked up in astonishment, rose, and left the room without a word.

"My wife," said Quintesetz uneasily, "is quite a conservative, I'm afraid, and is a bit uneasy at the mention of—the world. Please excuse her. But why do you ask about it?"

"Because it is important for J.P.'s work, I'm afraid."

"But why do you ask it of *me*? We were discussing Earth, robots, the founding of Sayshell. What has all this to do with—what you ask?"

"Perhaps nothing, and yet there are so many oddnesses about the matter. Why is your wife uneasy at the mention of Gaia? Why are *you* uneasy? Some talk of it easily enough. We have been told only today that Gaia is Earth itself and that it has disappeared into hyperspace because of the evil done by human beings."

A look of pain crossed Quintesetz's face. "Who told you that gibberish?"

"Someone I met here at the university."

"That's just superstition."

"Then it's not part of the central dogma of your legends concerning the Flight?"

"No, of course not. It's just a fable that arose among the ordinary, uneducated people."

"Are you sure?" asked Trevize coldly.

Quintesetz sat back in his chair and stared at the remnant of the meal before him. "Come into the living room," he said. "My wife will not allow this room to be cleared and set to rights while we are here and discussing—this."

"Are you sure it is just a fable?" repeated Trevize, once they had seated themselves in another room, before a window that bellied upward and inward to give a clear view of Sayshell's remnant night sky. The lights within the room glimmered down to avoid competition and Quintesetz's dark countenance melted into the shadow.

Quintesetz said, "Aren't *you* sure? Do you think that any world can dissolve into hyperspace? You must understand that the average person has only the vaguest notion of what hyperspace is."

"The truth is," said Trevize, "that I myself have only the vaguest notion of what hyperspace is and I've been through it hundreds of times."

"Let me speak realities, then. I assure you that Earth—wherever it is—is not located within the borders of the Sayshell Union and that the world you mentioned is not Earth."

"But even if you don't know where Earth is, S.Q., you ought to know where the world I mentioned is. *It* is certainly within the borders of the Sayshell Union. We know that much, eh, Pelorat?"

Pelorat, who had been listening stolidly, started at being suddenly addressed and said, "If it comes to that, Golan, I know where it is."

Trevize turned to look at him. "Since when, Janov?"

"Since earlier this evening, my dear Golan. You showed us the Five Sisters, S.Q., on our way from your office to your house. You pointed out a dim star at the center of the pentagon. I'm positive that's Gaia."

Quintesetz hesitated—his face, hidden in the dimness, was beyond any chance of interpretation. Finally he said, "Well, that's what our astronomers tell us—privately. It is a planet that circles that star."

Trevize gazed contemplatively at Pelorat, but the expression on the professor's face was unreadable. Trevize turned to Quintesetz, "Then tell us about that star. Do you have its co-ordinates?"

"I? No." He was almost violent in his denial. "I have no stellar co-ordinates here. You can get it from our astronomy department, though I imagine not without trouble. No travel to that star is permitted."

"Why not? It's within your territory, isn't it?"

"Spaciographically, yes. Politically, no."

Trevize waited for something more to be said. When that didn't come, he rose. "Professor Quintesetz," he said formally, "I am not a policeman, soldier, diplomat, or thug. I am not here to force information out of you. Instead, I shall, against my will, go to our ambassador. Surely, you must understand that it is not I, for my own personal interest, that request this information. This is Foundation business and I don't want to make an interstellar incident out of this. I don't think the Sayshell Union would want to, either."

Quintesetz said uncertainly, "What is this Foundation business?"

"That's not something I can discuss with you. If Gaia is not something you can discuss with me, then we will transfer it all to the government level and, under the circumstances, it may be the worse for Sayshell. Sayshell has kept its independence of the Federation and I have no objection to that. I have no reason to wish Sayshell ill and I do not wish to approach our ambassador. In fact, I will harm my own career in doing so, for I am under strict instruction to get this information *without* making a government matter of it. Please tell me, then, if there is some firm reason why you cannot discuss Gaia. Will you be arrested or otherwise punished, if you speak? Will you tell me plainly that I have no choice but to go to the ambassadorial height?"

"No, no," said Quintesetz, who sounded utterly confused. "I know nothing about government matters. We simply don't speak of that world."

"Superstition?"

"Well, yes! Superstition! —Skies of Sayshell, in what way am I better than that foolish person who told you that Gaia was in hyperspace—or than my wife who won't even stay in a room where Gaia is mentioned and who may even have left the house for fear it will be smashed by—"

"Lightning?"

"By *some* stroke from afar. And I, even I, hesitate to pronounce the name. Gaia! Gaia! The syllables do not hurt! I am unharmed! Yet I hesitate. —But please believe me when I say that I honestly don't know the co-ordinates for Gaia's star. I can try to help you get it, if that will help, but let me tell you that we don't discuss the world here in the Union. We keep hands and minds off it. I can tell you what little is known—really known, rather than supposed— and I doubt that you can learn anything more anywhere in these worlds of the Union.

"We know Gaia is an ancient world and there are some who think it is the oldest world in this sector of the Galaxy, but we are not certain. Patriotism tells us Sayshell Planet is the oldest; fear tells us Gaia Planet is. The only way of combining the two is to suppose that Gaia is Earth, since it is known that Sayshell was settled by Earthpeople.

"Most historians think—among themselves—that Gaia Planet was founded independently. They think it is not a colony of any world of our Union and that the Union was not colonized by Gaia. There is no consensus on comparative age, whether Gaia was settled before or after Sayshell was."

Trevize said, "So far, what you know is nothing, since every possible alternative is believed by someone or other."

Quintesetz nodded ruefully. "It would seem so. It was comparatively late in our history that we became conscious of the existence of Gaia. We had been preoccupied at first in forming the Union, then in fighting off the Galactic Empire, then in trying to find our proper role as an Imperial province and in limiting the power of the Viceroys.

"It wasn't till the days of Imperial weakness were far advanced that one of the later Viceroys, who was under very weak central control by then, came to realize that Gaia existed and seemed to maintain its independence from the Sayshellian province and even from the Empire itself. It simply kept to itself in isolation and secrecy, so that virtually nothing was known about it, anymore than is now known. The Viceroy decided to take it over. We have no details what happened, but his expedition was broken and few ships returned. In those days, of course, the ships were neither very good nor very well led.

"Sayshell itself rejoiced at the defeat of the Viceroy, who was considered an Imperial oppressor, and the debacle led almost directly to the re-establishment of our independence. The Sayshell Union snapped its ties with the Empire and we still celebrate the anniversary of that event as Union Day. Almost out of gratitude we left Gaia alone for nearly a century, but the time came when we were strong enough to begin to think of a little imperialistic expansion of our own. Why not take over Gaia? Why not at least establish a Customs Union? We sent out a fleet and it was broken, too.

"Thereafter, we confined ourselves to an occasional attempt at trade—attempts that were invariably unsuccessful. Gaia remained in firm isolation and never—to anyone's knowledge—made the slightest attempt to trade or communicate with any other world. It certainly never made the slightest hostile move against anyone in any direction. And then—"

Quintesetz turned up the light by touching a control in the arm of his chair. In the light, Quintesetz's face took on a clearly sardonic expression. He went on, "Since you are citizens of the Foundation, you perhaps remember the Mule."

Trevize flushed. In five centuries of existence, the Foundation had been conquered only once. The conquest had been only temporary and had not seriously interfered with its climb toward Second Empire, but surely no one who resented the Foundation and wished to puncture its self-satisfaction would fail to mention the Mule, its one conqueror. And it was likely (thought Trevize) that Quintesetz had raised the level of light in order that he might *see* Foundational self-satisfaction punctured.

He said, "Yes, we of the Foundation remember the Mule."

"The Mule," said Quintesetz, "ruled an Empire for a while, one that was as large as the Federation now controlled by the Foundation. He did not, however, rule *us*. He left us in peace. He passed through Sayshell at one time, however. We signed a declaration of neutrality and a statement of friendship. He asked nothing more. We were the only ones of whom he asked nothing more in the days before illness called a halt to his expansion and forced him to wait for death. He was not an unreasonable man, you know. He did not use unreasonable force, he was not bloody, and he ruled humanely."

"It was just that he was a conqueror," said Trevize sarcastically.

"Like the Foundation," said Quintesetz.

Trevize, with no ready answer, said irritably, "Do you have more to say about Gaia?"

"Just a statement that the Mule made. According to the account of the historic meeting between the Mule and President Kallo of the Union, the Mule is described as having put his signature to the document with a flourish and to have said, "You are neutral even toward Gaia by this document, which is fortunate for you. Even I will not approach Gaia.""

Trevize shook his head. "Why should he? Sayshell was eager to pledge neutrality and Gaia had no record of ever troubling anyone. The Mule was planning the conquest of the entire Galaxy at the time, so why delay for trifles? Time enough to turn on Sayshell *and* Gaia, when that was done."

"Perhaps, perhaps," said Quintesetz, "but according to one witness at the time, a person we tend to believe, the Mule put down his pen as he said, 'Even I will not approach Gaia.' His voice then dropped and, in a whisper not meant to be heard, he added 'again.'"

"Not meant to be heard, you say. Then how was it he was heard?"

"Because his pen rolled off the table when he put it down and a Sayshellian automatically approached and bent to pick it up. His ear was close to the Mule's mouth when the word 'again' was spoken and he heard it. He said nothing until after the Mule's death."

"How can you prove it was not an invention."

"The man's life is not the kind that makes it probable he would invent something of this kind. His report is accepted."

"And if it is?"

"The Mule was never in—or anywhere near—the Sayshell Union except on this one occasion, at least after he appeared on the Galactic scene. If he had ever been on Gaia, it had to be before he appeared on the Galactic scene."

"Well?"

"Well, where was the Mule born?"

"I don't think anyone knows," said Trevize.

"In the Sayshell Union, there is a strong feeling he was born on Gaia."

"Because of that one word?"

"Only partly. The Mule could not be defeated because he had strange mental powers. Gaia cannot be defeated either."

"Gaia has not been defeated as yet. That does not necessarily prove it cannot be."

"Even the Mule would not approach. Search the records of his Overlordship. See if any region other than the Sayshell Union was so gingerly treated. And do you know that no one who has ever gone to Gaia for the purpose of peaceful trade has ever returned? Why do you suppose we know so little about it?"

Trevize said, "Your attitude seems much like superstition."

"Call it what you will. Since the time of the Mule, we have wiped Gaia out of our thinking. We don't want it to think of us. We only feel safe if we pretend it isn't there. It may be that the government has itself secretly initiated and encouraged the legend that Gaia has disappeared into hyperspace in the hope that people will forget that there is a real star of that name."

"You think that Gaia is a world of Mules, then?"

"It may be. I advise you, for *your* good, not to go there. If you do, you will never return. If the Foundation interferes with Gaia, it will show less intelligence than the Mule did. You might tell your ambassador *that*."

Trevize said, "Get me the co-ordinates and I will be off your world at once. I will reach Gaia and I will return."

Quintesetz said, "I will get you the co-ordinates. The astronomy department works nights, of course, and I will get it for you *now*, if I can. —But let me suggest once more that you make no attempt to reach Gaia."

Trevize said, "I intend to make that attempt."

And Quintesetz said heavily, "Then you intend suicide."

14. FORWARD!

I.

Janov Pelorat looked out at the dim landscape in the graying dawn with an odd mixture of regret and uncertainty.

"We aren't staying long enough, Golan. It seems a pleasant and interesting world. I would like to learn more about it."

Trevize looked up from the computer with a wry smile. "You don't think I would like to? We had three proper meals on the planet—totally different and each excellent. I'd like more. And the only women we saw, we saw briefly—and some of them looked quite enticing, for—well, for what I've got in mind."

Pelorat wrinkled his nose slightly. "Oh, my dear chap. Those cowbells they call shoes, and all wrapped around in clashing colors, and whatever do they do to their eyelashes. Did you notice their eyelashes?"

"You might just as well believe I noticed everything, Janov. What you object to is superficial. They can easily be persuaded to wash their faces and, at the proper time, off come the shoes and the colors."

Pelorat said, "I'll take your word for that, Janov. However, I was thinking more of investigating the matter of Earth further. What we've been told about Earth, thus far, is so unsatisfactory, so contradictory—radiation according to one person, robots according to another."

"Death in either case."

"True," said Pelorat reluctantly, "but it may be that one is true and not the other, or that both are true to some extent, or that neither is true. Surely, Janov, when you hear tales that simply shroud matters in thickening mists of doubt, *surely* you must feel the itch to explore, to find out."

"I do," said Golan. "By every dwarf star in the Galaxy, I do. The problem at hand, however, is Gaia. Once that is straightened out, we can go to Earth, or come back here to Sayshell for a more extended stay. But first, Gaia."

Pelorat nodded. "The problem at hand! If we accept what Quintesetz told us, death is waiting for us on Gaia. Ought we to be going?"

Trevize said, "I ask myself that. Are you afraid?"

Pelorat hesitated as though he were probing his own feelings. Then he said in a quite simple and matter-of-fact manner, "Yes. Terribly!"

Trevize sat back in his chair and swiveled to face the other. He said, just as quietly and matter-of-factly, "Janov, there's no reason for you to chance this. Say the word and I'll let you off on Sayshell with your personal belongings and with half our credits. I'll pick you up when I return and it will be on to Sirius Sector, if you wish, and Earth, if that's where it is. If I don't return, the Foundation people on Sayshell will see to it that you get back to Terminus. No hard feelings if you stay behind, old friend."

Pelorat's eyes blinked rapidly and his lips pressed together for a few moments. Then he said, rather huskily, "Old friend? We've known each other what? A week or so? Isn't it strange that I'm going to refuse to leave the ship? I *am* afraid, but I want to remain with you."

Trevize moved his hands in a gesture of uncertainty. "But why? I honestly don't ask it of you."

"I'm not sure why, but I ask it of myself. It's—it's— Golan, I have faith in you. It seems to me you always know what you're doing. I wanted to go to Trantor, where probably—as I now see—nothing would have happened. *You* insisted on Gaia and Gaia must somehow be a raw nerve in the Galaxy. Things seem to *happen* in connection with it. And if that's not enough, Golan, I watched you force Quintesetz to give you the information about Gaia. That was *such* a skillful bluff. I was lost in admiration."

"You have faith in me, then."

Pelorat said, "Yes, I do."

Trevize put his hand on the other's upper arm and seemed, for a moment, to be searching for words. Finally he said, "Janov, will you forgive me in advance if my judgment is wrong, and if you in one way or another meet with—whatever unpleasant may be awaiting us?"

Pelorat said, "Oh, my dear fellow, why do you ask? I make the decision freely for *my* reasons, not yours. And, please—let us leave quickly. I don't trust my cowardice not to seize me by the throat and shame me for the rest of my life."

"As you say, Janov," said Trevize. "We'll leave at the earliest moment the computer will permit. This time, we'll be moving gravitically—straight up—as soon as we can be assured the atmosphere above is clear of other ships. And as the surrounding atmosphere grows less and less dense, we'll put on more and more speed. Well within the hour, we'll be in open space."

"Good," Pelorat said and pinched the tip off a plastic coffee container. The opened orifice almost at once began steaming. Pelorat put the nipple to his mouth and sipped, allowing just enough air to enter his mouth to cool the coffee to a bearable temperature.

Trevize grinned. "You've learned how to use those things beautifully. You're a space veteran, Janov."

Pelorat stared at the plastic container for a moment and said, "Now that we have ships that can adjust a gravitational field at will, surely we can use ordinary containers, can't we?"

"Of course, but you're not going to get space people to give up their space-centered apparatus. How is a space rat going to put distance between himself and surface worms if he uses an open-mouthed cup? See those rings on the walls and ceilings? Those have been traditional in spacecraft for twenty thousand years and more, but they're absolutely useless in a gravitic ship. Yet they're there and I'll bet the entire ship to a cup of coffee that your space rat will pretend he's being squashed into asphyxiation on takeoff and will then sway back and forth from those rings as though he's under zero-grav when its gee-one—normal-grav, that is—on both occasions."

"You're joking."

"Well, maybe a little, but there's always social inertia to everything—even technological advance. Those useless wall rings are there and the cups they supply us have nipples."

Pelorat nodded thoughtfully and continued to sip at his coffee. Finally he said, "And when do we take off?"

Trevize laughed heartily and said, "Got you. I began talking about wall rings and you never noticed that we were taking off right at that time. We're a mile high right now."

"You don't mean it."

"Look out."

Pelorat did and then said, "But I never felt a thing."

"You're not supposed to."

"Aren't we breaking the regulations? Surely we ought to have followed a radio beacon in an upward spiral, as we did in a downward spiral on landing?"

"No reason to, Janov. No one will stop us. No one at all."

"Coming down, you said—"

"That was different. They weren't anxious to see us arrive, but they're ecstatic to see us go."

"Why do you say that, Golan? The only person who talked to us about Gaia was Quintesetz and he begged us not to go."

"Don't you believe it, Janov. That was for form. He made sure we'd go to Gaia. —Janov, you admired the way I bluffed the information out of Quintesetz. I'm sorry, but I don't deserve the admiration. If I had done nothing at all, he would have offered the information. If I had tried to plug my ears, he would have shouted it at me."

"Why do you say that, Golan? That's crazy."

"Paranoid? Yes, I know." Trevize turned to the computer and extended his sense intently. He said, "We're not being stopped. No ships in interfering distance, no warning messages of any kind."

Again he swiveled in the direction of Pelorat. He said, "Tell me, Janov, how did you find out about Gaia? You knew about Gaia while we were still on Terminus. You knew it was in the Sayshell Sector. You knew the name was, somehow, a form of Earth. Where did you hear all this?"

Pelorat seemed to stiffen. He said, "If I were back in my office on Terminus, I might consult my files. I have not brought *everything* with me—certainly not the dates on which I first encountered this piece of data or that."

"Well, think about it," said Trevize grimly. "Consider that the Sayshellians themselves are close-mouthed about the matter. They are so reluctant to talk about Gaia as it really is that they actually encourage a superstition that has the common people of the sector believing that no such planet exists in ordinary space. In fact, I can tell you something else. Watch this!"

Trevize swung to the computer, his fingers sweeping across the direction hand-rests with the ease and grace of long practice. When he placed his hands on the manuals, he welcomed their warm touch and enclosure. He felt, as always, a bit of his will oozing outward.

He said, "This is the computer's Galactic map, as it existed within its memory banks before we landed on Sayshell. I am going to show you that portion of the map that represents the night sky of Sayshell as we saw it this past night."

The room darkened and a representation of a night sky sprang out onto the screen.

Pelorat said in a low voice, "As beautiful as we saw it on Sayshell."

"More beautiful," said Trevize, impatiently. "There is no atmospheric interference of any kind, no clouds, no absorption at the horizon. But wait, let me make an adjustment."

The view shifted steadily, giving the two the uncomfortable impression that it was they who were moving. Pelorat instinctively took hold of the arms of his chair to steady himself.

"There!" said Trevize. "Do you recognize that?"

"Of course. Those are the Five Sisters—the pentagon of stars that Quintesetz pointed out. It is unmistakable."

"Yes indeed. But where is Gaia?"

Pelorat blinked. There was no dim star at the center.

"It's not there," he said.

"That's right. It's not there. And that's because its location is not included in the data banks of the computer. Since it passes the bounds of likelihood that those data banks were deliberately made incomplete in this respect for our benefit, I conclude that to the Foundation galactographers who designed those data banks—and who had tremendous quantities of information at their disposal—Gaia was unknown."

"Do you suppose if we had gone to Trantor—" began Pelorat.

"I suspect we would have found no data on Gaia there, either. Its existence is kept a secret by the Sayshellians— and even more so, I suspect, by the Gaians themselves. You yourself said a few days ago it was not entirely uncommon that some worlds deliberately stayed out of sight to avoid taxation or outside interference."

"Usually," said Pelorat, "when mapmakers and statisticians come across such a world, they are found to exist in thinly populated sections of the Galaxy. It's isolation that makes it possible for them to hide. Gaia is not isolated."

"That's right. That's another of the things that makes it unusual. So let's leave this map on the screen so that you and I might continue to ponder the ignorance of our galactographers—and let me ask you again— In view of this ignorance on the part of the most knowledgeable of people, how did *you* come to hear of Gaia?"

"I have been gathering data on Earth myths, Earth legends, and Earth histories for over thirty years, my good

Golan. Without my complete records, how could I possibly—"

"We can begin somewhere, Janov. Did you learn about it in, say, the first fifteen years of your research or in the last fifteen?"

"Oh? Well, if we're going to be that broad, it was later on."

"You can do better than that. Suppose I suggest that you learned of Gaia only in the last couple of years."

Trevize peered in Pelorat's direction, felt the absence of any ability to read an unseen expression in the dimness, and raised the light level of the room a bit. The glory of the representation of the night sky on the screen dimmed in proportion. Pelorat's expression was stony and revealed nothing.

"Well?" said Trevize.

"I'm thinking," said Pelorat mildly. "You may be right. I wouldn't swear to it. When I wrote Jimbor of Ledbet University, I didn't mention Gaia, though in that case it would have been appropriate to do so, and that was in—let's see—in '95 and that was three years ago. I think you're right, Golan."

"And how did you come upon it?" asked Trevize. "In a communication? A book? A scientific paper? Some ancient song? How? —Come on!"

Pelorat sat back and crossed his arms. He fell into deep thought and didn't move. Trevize said nothing and waited.

Finally Pelorat said, "In a private communication. —But it's no use asking me from whom, my dear chap. I don't remember."

Trevize moved his hands over his sash. They felt clammy as he continued his efforts to elicit information without too clearly forcing words into the other's mouth. He said, "From a historian? From an expert in mythology? From a galactographer?"

"No use. I cannot match a name to the communication."

"Because, perhaps, there was none."

"Oh no. That scarcely seems possible."

"Why? Would you have rejected an anonymous communication?"

"I suppose not."

"Did you ever receive any?"

"Once in a long while. In recent years, I had become well known in certain academic circles as a collector of particular types of myths and legends and some of my correspondents were occasionally kind enough to forward material they had picked up from nonacademic sources. Sometimes these might not be attributed to anyone in particular."

Trevize said, "Yes, but did you ever receive anonymous information directly, and not by way of some academic correspondent?"

"That sometimes happened—but very rarely."

"And can you be certain that this was not so in the case of Gaia?"

"Such anonymous communications took place so rarely that I should think I *would* remember if it had happened in this case. Still, I can't say certainly that the information was not of anonymous origin. Mind, though, that's not to say that I *did* receive the information from an anonymous source."

"I realize that. But it remains a possibility, doesn't it?"

Pelorat said, very reluctantly, "I suppose it does. But what's all this about?"

"I'm not finished," said Trevize peremptorily. "Where did you get the information from—anonymous or not? What world?"

Pelorat shrugged. "Come now, I haven't the slightest idea."

"Could it possibly have been from Sayshell?"

"I told you. I don't know."

"I'm suggesting you *did* get it from Sayshell."

"You can suggest all you wish, but that does not necessarily make it so."

"No? When Quintesetz pointed out the dim star at the center of the Five Sisters, you knew at once it was Gaia.

You said so later on to Quintesetz, identifying it before he did. Do you remember?"

"Yes, of course."

"How was that possible? How did you recognize at once that the dim star was Gaia?"

"Because in the material I had on Gaia, it was rarely referred to by that name. Euphemisms were common, many different ones. One of the euphemisms, several times repeated, was 'the little Brother of the Five Sisters.' Another was 'the Pentagon's Center' and sometimes it was called 'o Pentagon.' When Quintesetz pointed out the Five Sisters and the central star, the allusions came irresistibly to mind."

"You never mentioned those allusions to me earlier."

"I didn't know what they meant and I didn't think it would have been important to discuss the matter with you, who were a—" Pelorat hesitated.

"A nonspecialist?"

"Yes."

"You realize, I hope, that the pentagon of the Five Sisters is an entirely relative form."

"What do you mean?"

Trevize laughed affectionately. "You surface worm. Do you think the sky has an objective shape of its own? That the stars are nailed in place? The pentagon has the shape it has from the surface of the worlds of the planetary system to which Sayshell Planet belongs—and from there *only*. From a planet circling any other star, the appearance of the Five Sisters is different. They are seen from a different angle, for one thing. For another, the five stars of the pentagon are at different distances from Sayshell and, seen from other angles, there could be no visible relationship among them at all. One or two stars might be in one half of the sky, the others in the other half. See here—"

Trevize darkened the room again and leaned over the computer. "There are eighty-six populated planetary systems making up the Sayshell Union. Let us keep Gaia—or the spot where Gaia ought to be—in place" (as he said that, a small red circle appeared in the center of the pentagon of the Five Sisters) "and shift to the skies as seen from any of the other eighty-six worlds taken at random."

The sky shifted and Pelorat blinked. The small red circle remained at the center of the screen, but the Five Sisters had disappeared. There were bright stars in the neighborhood but no tight pentagon. Again the sky shifted, and again, and again. It went on shifting. The red circle remained in place always, but at no time did a small pentagon of equally bright stars appear. Sometimes what might be a distorted pentagon of stars—unequally bright—appeared, but nothing like the beautiful asterism Quintesetz had pointed out.

"Had enough?" said Trevize. "I assure you, the Five Sisters can never be seen exactly as we have seen it from any populated world but the worlds of the Sayshell planetary system."

Pelorat said, "The Sayshellian view might have been exported to other planets. There were many proverbs in Imperial times—some of which linger into our own, in fact—that are Trantor-centered."

"With Sayshell as secretive about Gaia as we know it to be? And why should worlds outside the Sayshell Union be interested? Why would they care about a 'little Brother of the Five Sisters' if there were nothing in the skies at which to point?"

"Maybe you're right."

"Then don't you see that your original information must have come from Sayshell itself? Not just from somewhere in the Union, but precisely from the planetary system to which the capital world of the Union belongs."

Pelorat shook his head. "You make it sound as though it must, but it's not something I remember. I simply don't."

"Nevertheless, you *do* see the force of my argument, don't you?"

"Yes, I do."

"Next— When do you suppose the legend could have originated?"

"Anytime. I should suppose it developed far back in the Imperial Era. It has the feel of an ancient—"

"You are wrong, Janov. The Five Sisters are moderately close to Sayshell Planet, which is why they're so bright. Four of them have high proper motions in consequence and no two are part of a family, so that they move in different directions. Watch what happens as I shift the map backward in time slowly."

Again the red circle that marked the site of Gaia remained in place, but the pentagon slowly fell apart, as four of the stars drifted in different directions and the fifth shifted slightly.

"Look at that, Janov," said Trevize. "Would you say that was a regular pentagon?"

"Clearly lopsided," said Pelorat.

"And is Gaia at the center?"

"No, it's well to the side."

"Very well. That is how the asterism looked one hundred and fifty years ago. One and a half centuries, that's all. —The material you received concerning 'the Pentagon's Center' and so on made no real sense till this century *anywhere*, not even in Sayshell. The material you received had to originate in Sayshell and sometime in this century, perhaps in the last decade. And you got it, even though Sayshell is so close-mouthed about Gaia."

Trevize put the lights on, turned the star map off, and sat there staring sternly at Pelorat.

Pelorat said, "I'm confused. What's this about?"

"You tell me. Consider! Somehow I got the idea into my head that the Second Foundation still existed. I was giving a talk during my election campaign. I started a bit of emotional byplay designed to squeeze votes out of the undecided with a dramatic 'If the Second Foundation still existed—' and later that day I thought to myself: What if it *did* still exist? I began reading history books and within a week, I was convinced. There was no real evidence, but I have always felt that I had the knack of snatching the right conclusion out of a welter of speculation. This time, though—"

Trevize brooded a bit, then went on. "And look at what has happened since. Of all people, I chose Compor as my confidant and he betrayed me. Whereupon Mayor Branno had me arrested and sent into exile. Why into exile, rather than just having me imprisoned, or trying to threaten me into silence? And why in a very late-model ship which gives me extraordinary powers of Jumping through the Galaxy? And why, of all things, does she insist I take you and suggest that I help you search for Earth?

"And why was I so certain that we should not go to Trantor? I was convinced you had a better target for our investigations and at once you come up with the mystery world of Gaia, concerning which, as it now turns out, you gained information under very puzzling circumstances.

"We go to Sayshell—the first natural stop—and at once we encounter Compor, who gives us a circumstantial story about Earth and its death. He then assures us its location is in the Sirius Sector and urges us to go there."

Pelorat said, "There you are. You seem to be implying that all circumstances are forcing us toward Gaia, but, as you say, Compor tried to persuade us to go elsewhere."

"And in response, I was determined to continue on our original line of investigation out of my sheer distrust for the man. Don't you suppose that that was what he might have been counting on? He may have deliberately told us to go elsewhere just to keep us from doing so."

"That's mere romance," muttered Pelorat.

"Is it? Let's go on. We get in touch with Quintesetz simply because he was handy—"

"Not at all," said Pelorat. "I recognized his name."

"It seemed familiar to you. You had never read anything he had written—that you could recall. Why was it familiar to you? —In any case, it turned out he had read a paper of yours and was overwhelmed by it—and how likely was *that*? You yourself admit your work is not widely known.

"What's more, the young lady leading us to him quite gratuitously mentions Gaia and goes on to tell us it is in hyperspace, as though to be sure we keep it in mind. When we ask Quintesetz about it, he behaves as though he doesn't want to talk about it, but he doesn't throw us out—even though I am rather rude to him. He takes us to his home instead and, on the way there, goes to the trouble of pointing out the Five Sisters. He even makes sure we note the dim star at the center. Why? Is not all this an extraordinary concatenation of coincidence?"

Pelorat said, "If you list it like that—"

"List it any way you please," said Trevize. "I don't believe in extraordinary concatenations of coincidence."

"What does all this mean, then? That we are being maneuvered to Gaia?"

"Yes."

"By whom?"

Trevize said, "Surely there can be no question about that. Who is capable of adjusting minds, of giving gentle nudges to this one or that, of managing to divert progress in this direction or that?"

"You're going to tell me it's the Second Foundation."

"Well, what have we been told about Gaia? It is untouchable. Fleets that move against it are destroyed. People who reach it do not return. Even the Mule didn't dare move against it—and the Mule, in fact, was probably born there. Surely it seems that Gaia *is* the Second Foundation—and finding that, after all, is my ultimate goal."

Pelorat shook his head. "But according to some historians, the Second Foundation stopped the Mule. How could he have been one of them?"

"A renegade, I suppose."

"But why should we be so relentlessly maneuvered toward the Second Foundation by the Second Foundation?"

Trevize's eyes were unfocused, his brow furrowed. He said, "Let's reason it out. It has always seemed important to the Second Foundation that as little information as possible about it should be available to the Galaxy. Ideally it wants its very existence to remain unknown. We know that much about them. For a hundred twenty years, the Second Foundation *was* thought to be extinct and that must have suited them right down to the Galactic core. Yet when I began to suspect that they *did* exist, they did nothing. Compor knew. They might have used him to shut me up one way or another—had me killed, even. Yet they did nothing."

Pelorat said, "They had you arrested, if you want to blame that on the Second Foundation. According to what you told me, that resulted in the people of Terminus not knowing about your views. The people of the Second Foundation accomplished that much without violence and they may be devotees of Salvor Hardin's remark that 'Violence is the last refuge of the incompetent.'"

"But keeping it from the people of Terminus accomplishes nothing. Mayor Branno knows my view and—at the very least—must wonder if I am correct. So now, you see, it is too late for them to harm us. If they had gotten rid of me to begin with, they would be in the clear. If they had left me alone altogether, they might have still remained in the clear, for they might have maneuvered Terminus into believing I was an eccentric, perhaps a madman. The prospective ruin of my political career might even have forced me into silence as soon as I saw what the announcement of my beliefs would mean.

"And now it is too late for them to do anything. Mayor Branno was suspicious enough of the situation to send Compor after me and—having no faith in him either, being wiser than I was—she placed a hyper-relay on Compor's ship. In consequence, she knows we are on Sayshell. And last night, while you were sleeping, I had our computer place a message directly into the computer of the Foundation ambassador here on Sayshell, explaining that we were on our way to Gaia. I took the trouble of giving its co-ordinates, too. If the Second Foundation does anything to us now, I am certain that Branno will have the matter investigated—and the concentrated attention of the Foundation must surely be what they don't want."

"Would they care about attracting the Foundation's attention, if they are so powerful?"

"Yes," said Trevize forcefully. "They lie hidden because, in some ways, they must be weak and because the Foundation is technologically advanced perhaps beyond even what Seldon himself might have foreseen. The very quiet, even stealthy, way in which they've been maneuvering us to their world would seem to show their eager desire to do nothing that will attract attention. And if so, then they have already lost, at least in part—for they've attracted attention and I doubt they can do anything to reverse the situation."

Pelorat said, "But why do they go through all this? Why do they ruin themselves—if your analysis is correct—by angling for us across the Galaxy? What is it they want of us?"

Trevize stared at Pelorat and flushed. "Janov," he said, "I have a feeling about this. I have this gift of coming to a correct conclusion on the basis of almost nothing. There's a kind of *sureness* about me that tells me when I'm right— and I'm sure now. There's something I have that they want— and want enough to risk their very existence for. I don't know what it can be, but I've got to find out, because if I've got it and if it's that powerful, then I want to be able to use it for what I feel is right." He shrugged slightly. "Do you still want to come along with me, old friend, now that you see how much a madman I am?"

Pelorat said, "I told you I had faith in you. I still do."

And Trevize laughed with enormous relief. "Marvelous! Because another feeling I have is that you are, for some reason, also essential to this whole thing. In that case, Janov, we move on to Gaia, full speed. Forward!"

2.

Mayor Harla Branno looked distinctly older than her sixty-two years. She did not always look older, but she did now. She had been sufficiently wrapped up in thought to forget to avoid the mirror and had seen her image on her way into the map room. So she was aware of the haggardness of her appearance.

She sighed. It drained the life out of one. Five years a Mayor and for twelve years before that the real power behind two figureheads. All of it had been quiet, all of it successful, all of it—draining. How would it have been, she wondered, if there had been strain—failure—disaster.

Not so bad for her personally, she suddenly decided. Action would have been invigorating. It was the horrible knowledge that nothing but drift was possible that had worn her out.

It was the Seldon Plan that was successful and it was the Second Foundation that made sure it would continue to be. She, as the strong hand at the helm of the Foundation (actually the *First* Foundation, but no one on Terminus ever thought of adding the adjective) merely rode the crest.

History would say little or nothing about her. She merely sat at the controls of a spaceship, while the spaceship was maneuvered from without.

Even Indbur III, who had presided over the Foundation's catastrophic fall to the Mule, had done *something*. He had, at least, collapsed.

For Mayor Branno there would be nothing!

Unless this Golan Trevize, this thoughtless Councilman, this lightning rod, made it possible—

She looked at the map thoughtfully. It was not the kind of structure produced by a modern computer. It was, rather, a three-dimensional cluster of lights that pictured the Galaxy holographically in midair. Though it could not be made to move, to turn, to expand, or to contract, one could move about it and see it from any angle.

A large section of the Galaxy, perhaps a third of the whole (excluding the core, which was a "no-life's land") turned red when she touched a contact. That was the Foundation Federation, the more than seven million inhabited worlds ruled by the Council and by herself—the seven million inhabited worlds who voted for and were represented in the House of Worlds, which debated matters of minor importance, and then voted on them, and never, by any chance, dealt with anything of major importance.

Another contact and a faint pink jutted outward from the edges of the Federation, here and there. Spheres of influence! This was not Foundation territory, but the regions, though nominally independent, would never dream of resistance to any Foundation move.

There was no question in her mind that no power in the Galaxy could oppose the Foundation (not even the Second Foundation, if one but knew where it was), that the Foundation could, at will, reach out its fleet of modern ships and simply set up the Second Empire.

But only five centuries had passed since the beginning of the Plan. The Plan called for ten centuries before the Second Empire could be set up and the Second Foundation would make sure the Plan would hold. The Mayor shook her sad, gray head. If the Foundation acted now, it would somehow fail. Though its ships were irresistible, action now would fail.

Unless Trevize, the lightning rod, drew the lightning of the Second Foundation—and the lightning could be traced back to its source.

She looked about. Where was Kodell? This was no time for him to be late.

It was as though her thought had called him, for he came striding in, smiling cheerfully, looking more grandfatherly than ever with his gray-white mustache and tanned complexion. Grandfatherly, but not old. To be sure, he was eight years younger than she was.

How was it he showed no marks of strain? Did not fifteen years as Director of Security leave its scar?

3.

Kodell nodded slowly in the formal greeting that was necessary in initiating a discussion with the Mayor. It was a tradition that had existed since the bad days of the Indburs. Almost everything had changed, but etiquette least of all.

He said, "Sorry I'm late, Mayor, but your arrest of Councilman Trevize is finally beginning to make its way through the anesthetized skin of the Council."

"Oh?" said the Mayor phlegmatically. "Are we in for a palace revolution?"

"Not the least chance. We're in control. But there'll be noise."

"Let them make noise. It will make them feel better, and I—I shall stay out of the way. I can count, I suppose, on general public opinion?"

"I think you can. Especially away from Terminus. No one outside Terminus cares what happens to a stray Councilman."

"I do."

"Ah? More news?"

"Liono," said the Mayor, "I want to know about Sayshell."

"I'm not a two-legged history book," said Liono Kodell, smiling.

"I don't want history. I want the truth. Why is Sayshell independent? —Look at it." She pointed to the red of the Foundation on the holographic map and there, well into the inner spirals, was an in-pocketing of white.

Branno said, "We've got it almost encapsulated—almost sucked in—yet it's white. Our map doesn't even show it as a loyal-ally-in-pink."

Kodell shrugged. "It's not officially a loyal ally, but it never bothers us. It is neutral."

"All right. See this, then." Another touch at the controls. The red sprang out distinctly further. It covered nearly half the Galaxy. "That," said Mayor Branno, "was the Mule's realm at the time of his death. If you'll peer in among the red, you'll find the Sayshell Union, completely surrounded this time, but still white. It is the only enclave left free by the Mule."

"It was neutral then, too."

"The Mule had no great respect for neutrality."

"He seems to have had, in this case."

"*Seems* to have had. What has Sayshell got?"

Kodell said, "Nothing! Believe me, Mayor, she is ours any time we want her."

"Is she? Yet somehow she isn't ours."

"There's no need to want her."

Branno sat back in her chair and, with a sweep of her arm over the controls, turned the Galaxy dark. "I think we now want her."

"Pardon, Mayor?"

"Liono, I sent that foolish Councilman into space as a lightning rod. I felt that the Second Foundation would see him as a greater danger than he was and see the Foundation itself as the lesser danger. The lightning would strike him and reveal its origin to us."

"Yes, Mayor!"

"My intention was that he go to the decayed ruins of Trantor to fumble through what—if anything—was left of its Library and search for the Earth. That's the world, you remember, that these wearisome mystics tell us was the site of origin of humanity, as though that matters, even in the unlikely case it is true. The Second Foundation couldn't possibly have believed that was really what he was after and they would have moved to find out what he was really looking for."

"But he didn't go to Trantor."

"No. Quite unexpectedly, he has gone to Sayshell. Why?"

"I don't know. But please forgive an old bloodhound whose duty it is to suspect everything and tell me how you know he and this Pelorat have gone to Sayshell. I know that Compor reports it, but how far can we trust Compor?"

"The hyper-relay tells us that Compor's ship has indeed landed on Sayshell Planet."

"Undoubtedly, but how do you know that Trevize and Pelorat have? Compor may have gone to Sayshell for his own reasons and may not know—or care—where the others are."

"The fact is, that our ambassador on Sayshell has informed us of the arrival of the ship on which we placed

Trevize and Pelorat. I am not ready to believe the ship arrived at Sayshell without them. What is more, Compor reports having talked to them and, if he cannot be trusted, we have other reports placing them at Sayshell University, where they consulted with a historian of no particular note."

"None of this," said Kodell mildly, "has reached me."

Branno sniffed. "Do not feel stepped on. I am dealing with this personally and the information has now reached you—with not much in the way of delay, either. The latest news—just received—is from the ambassador. Our lightning rod is moving on. He stayed on Sayshell Planet two days, then left. He is heading for another planet system, he says, some ten parsecs away. He gave the name and the Galactic co-ordinates of his destination to the ambassador, who passed them on to us."

"Is there anything corroborative from Compor?"

"Compor's message that Trevize and Pelorat have left Sayshell came even before the ambassador's message. Compor has not yet determined where Trevize is going. Presumably he will follow."

Kodell said, "We are missing the why's of the situation." He popped a pastille into his mouth and sucked at it meditatively. "Why did Trevize go to Sayshell? Why did he leave?"

"The question that intrigues me most is: Where? Where is Trevize going?"

"You did say, Mayor, did you not, that he gave the name and co-ordinates of his destination to the ambassador. Are you implying that he lied to the ambassador? Or that the ambassador is lying to us?"

"Even assuming everyone told the truth all round and that no one made any errors, there is a name that interests me. Trevize told the ambassador he was going to Gaia. That's G-A-I-A. Trevize was careful to spell it."

Kodell said, "Gaia? I never heard of it."

"Indeed? That's not strange." Branno pointed to the spot in the air where the map had been. "Upon the map in this room, I can set up, at a moment's notice, every star—

supposedly—around which there circles an inhabited world and many prominent stars with uninhabited systems. Over thirty million stars can be marked out—if I handle the controls properly—in single units, in pairs, in clusters. I can mark them out in any of five different colors, one at a time, or all together. What I cannot do is locate Gaia on the map. As far as the map is concerned, Gaia does not exist."

Kodell said, "For every star the map shows, there are ten thousand it doesn't show."

"Granted, but the stars it doesn't show lack inhabited planets and why would Trevize want to go to an uninhabited planet?"

"Have you tried the Central Computer? It has all three hundred billion Galactic stars listed."

"I've been told it has, but does it? We know very well, you and I, that there are thousands of inhabited planets that have escaped listing on any of our maps—not only on the one in this room, but even on the Central Computer. Gaia is apparently one of them."

Kodell's voice remained calm, even coaxing. "Mayor, there may well be nothing at all to be concerned about. Trevize may be off on a wild goose chase or he may be lying to us and there is no star called Gaia—and no star at all at the co-ordinates he gave us. He is trying to throw us off his scent, now that he has met Compor and perhaps guesses he is being traced."

"How will this throw us off the scent? Compor will still follow. No, Liono, I have another possibility in mind, one with far greater potentiality for trouble. Listen to me—"

She paused and said, "This room is shielded, Liono. Understand that. We cannot be overheard by anyone, so please feel free to speak. And I will speak freely, as well.

"This Gaia is located, if we accept the information, ten parsecs from Sayshell Planet and is therefore part of the Sayshell Union. The Sayshell Union is a well-explored portion of the Galaxy. All its star systems—inhabited or not inhabited—are recorded and the inhabited ones are known in detail. Gaia is the one exception. Inhabited or not, none have heard of it; it is present in no map. Add to this that the Sayshell Union maintains a peculiar state of independence with respect to the Foundation Federation, and did so even with respect to the Mule's former realm. It has been independent since the fall of the Galactic Empire."

"What of all this?" asked Kodell cautiously.

"Surely the two points I have made must be connected. Sayshell incorporates a planetary system that is totally unknown and Sayshell is untouchable. The two cannot be independent. Whatever Gaia is, it protects itself. It sees to it that there is no knowledge of its existence outside its immediate surroundings and it protects those surroundings so that outsiders cannot take over."

"You are telling me, Mayor, that Gaia is the seat of the Second Foundation?"

"I am telling you that Gaia deserves inspection."

"May I mention an odd point that might be difficult to explain by this theory?"

"Please do."

"If Gaia is the Second Foundation and if, for centuries, it has protected itself physically against intruders, protecting all of the Sayshell Union as a broad, deep shield for itself, and if it has even prevented knowledge of itself leaking into the Galaxy—then why has all that protection suddenly vanished? Trevize and Pelorat leave Terminus and, even though you had advised them to go to Trantor, they go immediately and without hesitation to Sayshell and now to Gaia. What is more, you can think of Gaia and speculate on it. Why are you not somehow prevented from doing so?"

Mayor Branno did not answer for a long time. Her head was bent and her gray hair gleamed dully in the light. Then she said, "Because I think Councilman Trevize has somehow upset things. He has done something—or is doing something—that is in some way endangering the Seldon Plan."

"That surely is impossible, Mayor."

"I suppose everything and everyone has its flaws. Even

Hari Seldon was not perfect, surely. Somewhere the Plan has a flaw and Trevize has stumbled upon it, perhaps without even knowing that he has. We must know what is happening and we must be on the spot."

Finally Kodell looked grave. "Don't make decisions on your own, Mayor. We don't want to move without adequate consideration."

"Don't take me for an idiot, Liono. I'm not going to make war. I'm not going to land an expeditionary force on Gaia. I just want to be on the spot—or near it, if you prefer. Liono, find out for me—I hate talking to a war office that is as ridiculously hidebound as one is sure to be after one hundred and twenty years of peace, but you don't seem to mind—just how many warships are stationed close to Sayshell. Can we make their movements seem routine and not like a mobilization?"

"In these piping times of peace, there are not many ships in the vicinity, I am sure. But I will find out."

"Even two or three will be sufficient, especially if one is of the Supernova class."

"What do you want to do with them?"

"I want them to nudge as close to Sayshell as they can—without creating an incident—and I want them sufficiently close to each other to offer mutual support."

"What's all this intended for?"

"Flexibility. I want to be able to strike if I have to."

"Against the Second Foundation? If Gaia can keep itself isolated and untouchable against the Mule, it can surely withstand a few ships now."

Branno said, with the gleam of battle in her eyes, "My friend, I told you that nothing and no one is perfect, not even Hari Seldon. In setting up his Plan, he could not help being a person of his times. He was a mathematician of the days of the dying Empire, when technology was moribund. It followed that he could not have made sufficient allowance in his Plan for technological advance. Gravitics, for instance, is a whole new direction of advance he could not possibly have guessed at. And there are other advances, too.

"Gaia might also have advanced."

"In isolation? Come. There are ten quadrillion human beings within the Foundation Federation, from among whom contributors to technological advance can step forward. A single isolated world can do nothing in comparison. Our ships will advance and I will be with them."

"Pardon me, Mayor. What was that?"

"I will be going myself to the ships that will gather at the borders of Sayshell. I wish to see the situation for myself."

Kodell's mouth fell open for a moment. He swallowed and made a distinct noise as he did so. "Mayor, that is— not wise." If ever a man clearly intended a stronger remark, Kodell did.

"Wise or not," said Branno violently, "I will do it. I am tired of Terminus and of its endless political battles, its infighting, its alliances and counteralliances, its betrayals and renewals. I've had seventeen years at the center of it and I want to do something else—*anything* else. Out there," she waved her hand in a direction taken at random, "the whole history of the Galaxy may be changing and I want to take part in the process."

"You know nothing about such things, Mayor."

"Who does, Liono?" She rose stiffly to her feet. "As soon as you bring me the information I need on the ships and as soon as I can make arrangements for carrying on with the foolish business at home, I will go. —And, Liono, don't try to maneuver me out of this decision in any way or I'll wipe out our long friendship in a stroke and break you. I can still do *that*."

Kodell nodded. "I know you can, Mayor, but before you decide, may I ask you to reconsider the power of Seldon's Plan? What you intend may be suicide."

"I have no fears on that score, Liono. It was wrong with respect to the Mule, whom it could not anticipate—and a failure to anticipate at one time implies the possibility of failure at another."

Kodell sighed. "Well then, if you are really determined, I will support you to the best of my ability and with complete loyalty."

"Good. I warn you once again that you had better mean that remark with all your heart. And with that in mind, Liono, let us move on to Gaia. Forward!"

15. GAIA-S

1.

Sura Novi stepped into the control room of the small and rather old-fashioned ship that was carrying Stor Gendibal and herself across the parsecs in deliberate Jumps.

She had clearly been in the compact cleaning room, where oils, warm air, and a minimum of water freshed her body. She had a robe wrapped about her and was holding it tightly to herself in an agony of modesty. Her hair was dry but tangled.

She said in a low voice, "Master?"

Gendibal looked up from his charts and from his computer. "Yes, Novi?"

"I be sorrow-laden—" She paused and then said slowly, "I am very sorry to bother you, Master" (then she slipped again) "but I be loss-ridden for my clothing."

"Your clothing?" Gendibal stared at her blankly for a moment and then rose to his feet in an access of contrition. "Novi, I forgot. They needed cleaning and they're in the detergent-hamper. They're cleaned, dried, folded, all set. I should have taken them out and placed them in clear sight. I forgot."

"I did not like to—to—" (she looked down at herself) "offend."

"You don't offend," said Gendibal cheerily. "Look, I promise you that when this is over I shall see to it that you have a great deal of clothing—new and in the latest fashion. We left in a hurry and it never occurred to me to bring a supply, but really, Novi, there are only the two of us and we'll be together for some time in very close quarters and it's needless to be—to be—so concerned—about—" He gestured vaguely, became aware of the horrified look in her eyes, and thought: Well, she's only a country girl after all and has her standards; probably wouldn't object to improprieties of all kinds—but with her clothes on.

Then he felt ashamed of himself and was glad that she was no "scholar" who could sense *his* thoughts. He said, "Shall I get your clothes for you?"

"Oh no, Master. It be not for you— I know where they are."

He next saw her properly dressed and with her hair combed. There was a distinct shyness about her. "I am ashamed, Master, to have behaved so improper—*ly*. I should have found them for myself."

"No matter," said Gendibal. "You are doing very well with your Galactic, Novi. You are picking up the language of scholars very quickly."

Novi smiled suddenly. Her teeth were somewhat uneven, but that scarcely detracted from the manner in which her face brightened and grew almost sweet under praise, thought Gendibal. He told himself that it was for that reason that he rather liked to praise her.

"The Hamish will think little of me when I am back home," she said. "They will say I be—*am* a word-chopper. That is what they call someone who speaks—odd. They do not like such."

"I doubt that you will be going back to the Hamish, Novi," said Gendibal. "I am sure there will continue to be a place for you in the complex—with the scholars, that is—when this is over."

"I would like that, Master."

"I don't suppose you would care to call me 'Speaker Gendibal' or just— No, I see you wouldn't," he said, responding to her look of scandalized objection. "Oh well."

"It would not be fitting, Master. —But may I ask when this will be over?"

Gendibal shook his head. "I scarcely know. Right now, I must merely get to a particular place as quickly as I can. This ship, which is a very good ship for its kind, is slow and 'as quickly as I can' is not very quick. You see" (he gestured at the computer and the charts) "I must work out ways to get across large stretches of space, but the computer is limited in its abilities and I am not very skillful."

"Must you be there quickly because there is danger, Master?"

"What makes you think there is danger, Novi?"

"Because I watch you sometimes when I don't think you see me and your face looks—I do not know the word. Not afeared—I mean, frightened—and not bad-expecting, either."

"Apprehensive," muttered Gendibal.

"You look—concerned. Is that the word?"

"It depends. What do you mean by concerned, Novi?"

"I means you look as though you are saying to yourself, 'What am I going to do next in this great trouble?'"

Gendibal looked astonished. "That is 'concerned,' but do you see *that* in my face, Novi? Back in the Place of Scholars, I am extremely careful that no one should see anything in my face, but I did think that, alone in space— except for you—I could relax and let it sit around in its underwear, so to speak. —I'm sorry. That has embarrassed you. What I'm trying to say is that if you're so perceptive, I shall have to be more careful. Every once in a while I have to relearn the lesson that even nonmentalics can make shrewd guesses."

Novi looked blank. "I don't understand, Master."

"I'm talking to myself, Novi. Don't be concerned. —See, there's that word again."

"But is there danger?"

"There's a problem, Novi. I do not know what I shall find when I reach Sayshell—that is the place to which we are going. I may find myself in a situation of great difficulty.

"Does that mean danger?"

"No, because I will be able to handle it."

"How can you tell this?"

"Because I am a—scholar. And I am the best of them. There is nothing in the Galaxy I cannot handle."

"Master," and something very like agony twisted Novi's face, "I do not wish to offensify—I mean, give offense—and make you angry. I have seen you with that oafish Rufirant and you were in danger then—and he was only a Hamish farmer. Now I do not know what awaits you—and you do not, either."

Gendibal felt chagrined, "Are you afraid, Novi?"

"Not for myself, Master. I fear—I am afraid—for you."

"You can say, 'I fear,'" muttered Gendibal. "That is good Galactic, too."

For a moment he was engaged in thought. Then he looked up, took Sura Novi's rather coarse hands in his, and said, "Novi, I don't want you to fear anything. Let me explain. You know how you could tell there was—or rather might be—danger from the look on my face—almost as though you could read my thoughts?"

"Yes?"

"I can read thoughts better than you can. That is what scholars learn to do and I am a very good scholar."

Novi's eyes widened and her hand pulled loose from his. She seemed to be holding her breath. "You can read my thoughts?"

Gendibal held up a finger hurriedly. "I don't, Novi. I *don't* read your thoughts, except when I must. I do *not* read *your* thoughts."

(He knew that, in a practical sense, he was lying. It was impossible to be with Sura Novi and not understand the general tenor of some of her thoughts. One scarcely needed to be a Second Foundation for that. Gendibal felt himself to be on the edge of blushing. But even from a Hamish-woman, such an attitude was flattering. —And yet she had to be reassured—out of common humanity—)

He said, "I can also change the way people think. I can make people feel hurt. I can—"

But Novi was shaking her head. "How can you do all that, Master? Rufirant—"

"Forget Rufirant," said Gendibal testily. "I could have stopped him in a moment. I could have made him fall to the ground. I could have made *all* the Hamish—" He stopped suddenly and felt uneasily that he was boasting, that he was trying to impress this provincial woman. And she was shaking her head still.

"Master," she said, "you are trying to make me not afraid, but I am not afraid except for you, so there is no need. I know you are a great scholar and can make this ship fly through space where it seems to me that no person can do aught but—I mean, anything but—be lost. And you use machines I cannot understand—and that no Hamish person could understand. But you need not tell me of these powers of mind, which surely cannot be so, since all the things you say you could have done to Rufirant, you did *not* do, though you were in danger."

Gendibal pressed his lips together. Leave it at that, he thought. If the woman insists she is not afraid for herself, let it go at that. Yet he did not want her to think of him as a weakling and braggart. He simply did *not*.

He said, "If I did nothing to Rufirant, it was because I did not wish to. We scholars must never do anything to the Hamish. We are guests on your world. Do you understand that?"

"You are our masters. That is what *we* always say."

For a moment Gendibal was diverted. "How is it, then, that this Rufirant attacked me?"

"I do not know," she said simply. "I don't think he knew. He must have been mind-wandering—uh, out of his mind."

Gendibal grunted. "In any case, we do not harm the Hamish. If I had been forced to stop him by—hurting him, I might have been poorly thought of by the other scholars and might perhaps have lost my position. But to save myself being badly hurt, I might have had to handle him just a small bit—the smallest possible."

Novi drooped. "Then I need not have come rushing in like a great fool myself."

"You did exactly right," said Gendibal. "I have just said I would have done ill to have hurt him. You made it un-

necessary to do so. *You* stopped him and that was well done.
I am grateful."

She smiled again—blissfully. "I see, then, why you have
been so kind to me."

"I was grateful, of course," said Gendibal, a little flus-
tered, "but the important thing is that you must understand
there is no danger. I can handle an army of ordinary people.
Any scholar can—especially the important ones—and I
told you I am the best of all of them. There is no one in
the Galaxy who can stand against me."

"If you say so, Master, I am sure of it."

"I do say so. Now, are you afraid for me?"

"No, Master, except— Master, is it only *our* scholars
who can read minds and— Are there other scholars, other
places, who can oppose you?"

For a moment Gendibal was staggered. The woman had
an astonishing gift of penetration.

It was necessary to lie. He said, "There are none."

"But there are many stars in the sky. I once tried to count
them and couldn't. If there are as many worlds of people
as there are stars, wouldn't some of them be scholars? Besides the scholars on our own world, I mean?"

"No."

"What if there are?"

"They would not be as strong as I am."

"What if they leap upon you suddenly before you are
aware?"

"They cannot do that. If any strange scholar were to
approach, I would know at once. I would know it long
before he could harm me."

"Could you run?"

"I would not have to run. —But" (anticipating her objection) "if I had to, I could be in a new ship soon—better
than any in the Galaxy. They would not catch me."

"Might they not change your thoughts and make you
stay?"

"No."

"There might be many of them. You are but one."

"As soon as they are there, long before they can imagine it would be possible, I would know they were there and I would leave. Our whole world of scholars would then turn against them and they would not stand. And they would know that, so they would not dare do anything against me. In fact, they would not want me to know of them at all—and yet I will."

"Because you are so much better than they?" said Novi, her face shining with a doubtful pride.

Gendibal could not resist. Her native intelligence, her quick understanding was such that it was simple joy to be with her. That soft-voiced monster, Speaker Delora Delarmi, had done him an incredible favor when she had forced this Hamish farmwoman upon him.

He said, "No, Novi, not because I am better than they, although I am. It is because I have *you* with me."

"I?"

"Exactly, Novi. Had you guessed that?"

"No, Master," she said, wondering. "What is it I could do?"

"It is your mind." He held up his hand at once. "I am not reading your thoughts. I see merely the outline of your mind and it is a smooth outline, an unusually smooth outline."

She put her hand to her forehead. "Because I am unlearned, Master? Because I am so foolish?"

"No, dear." He did not notice the manner of address. "It is because you are honest and possess no guile; because you are truthful and speak your mind; because you are warm of heart and—and other things. If other scholars send out anything to touch our minds—yours and mine—the touch will be instantly visible on the smoothness of your mind. I will be aware of that even before I would be aware of a touch of my own mind—and I will then have time for counteractive strategy; that is, to fight it off."

There was a silence for long moments after that. Gendibal realized that it was not just happiness in Novi's eyes, but exultation and pride, too. She said softly, "And you took me with you for that reason?"

Gendibal nodded. "That was an important reason. Yes."

Her voice sank to a whisper. "How can I help as much as possible, Master?"

He said, "Remain calm. Don't be afraid. And just—just stay as you are."

She said, "I will stay as I am. And I will stand between you and danger, as I did in the case of Rufirant."

She left the room and Gendibal looked after her.

It was strange how much there was to her. How could so simple a creature hold such complexity? The smoothness of her mind structure had, beneath it, enormous intelligence, understanding, and courage. What more could he ask—of anyone?

Somehow, he caught an image of Sura Novi—who was not a Speaker, not even a Second Foundationer, not even educated—grimly at his side, playing a vital auxiliary role in the drama that was coming.

Yet he could not see the details clearly. —He could not yet see precisely what it was that awaited them.

2.

"A single Jump," muttered Trevize, "and there it is."

"Gaia?" asked Pelorat, looking over Trevize's shoulder at the screen.

"Gaia's sun," said Trevize. "Call it Gaia-S, if you like, to avoid confusion. Galactographers do that sometimes."

"And where is Gaia itself, then? Or do we call it Gaia-P —for planet?"

"Gaia would be suffecient for the planet. We can't see Gaia yet, however. Planets aren't as easy to see as stars are and we're still a hundred microparsecs away from Gaia-S. Notice that it's only a star, even though a bright one. We're not close enough for it to show as a disc. —And don't stare at it directly, Janov. It's still bright enough to damage the retina. I'll throw in a filter, once I'm through with my observations. Then you can stare."

"How much is a hundred microparsecs in units which a mythologist can understand, Golan?"

"Three billion kilometers; about twenty times the distance of Terminus from our own sun. Does that help?"

"Enormously. —But shouldn't we get closer?"

"No!" Trevize looked up in surprise. "Not right away. After what we've heard about Gaia, why should we rush? It's one thing to have guts; it's another to be crazy. Let's take a look first."

"At what, Golan? You said we can't see Gaia yet?"

"Not at a glance, no. But we have telescopic viewers and we have an excellent computer for rapid analysis. We can certainly study Gaia-S, to begin with, and we can perhaps make a few other observations. —Relax, Janov." He reached out and slapped the other's shoulder with an avuncular flourish.

After a pause Trevize said, "Gaia-S is a single star or, if it has a companion, that companion is much farther away from it than we are at the present moment and it is, at best, a red dwarf, which means we need not be concerned with it. Gaia-S is a G4 star, which means it is perfectly capable of having a habitable planet, and that's good. If it were an A or an M, we would have to turn around and leave right now."

Pelorat said, "I may be only a mythologist, but couldn't we have determined the spectral class of Gaia-S from Sayshell?"

"We could and we did, Janov, but it never hurts to check at closer quarters. —Gaia-S has a planetary system, which is no surprise. There are two gas giants in view and one of them is nice and large—if the computer's distance estimate is accurate. There could easily be another on the other side of the star and therefore not easily detectable, since we happen—by chance—to be somewhat close to the planetary plane. I can't make out anything in the inner regions, which is also no surprise."

"Is that bad?"

"Not really. It's expected. The habitable planets would be of rock and metal and would be much smaller than the gas giants and much closer to the star, if they're to be warm enough—and on both counts they would be much harder to see from out here. It means we'll have to get in considerably closer in order to probe the area within four microparsecs of Gaia-S."

"I'm ready."

"I'm not. We'll make the Jump tomorrow."

"Why tomorrow?"

"Why not? Let's give them a day to come out and get us—and for us to get away, perhaps, if we spot them coming and don't like what we see."

3.

It was a slow and cautious process. During the day that passed, Trevize grimly directed the calculation of several different approaches and tried to choose between them. Lacking hard data, he could depend only on intuition, which unfortunately told him nothing. He lacked that "sureness" he sometimes experienced.

Eventually he punched in directions for a Jump that moved them far out of the planetary plane.

"That will give us a better view of the region as a whole," he said, "since we will see the planets in every part of their orbit as maximum apparent distance from the sun. And *they*—whoever they may be—might not be quite as watchful over regions outside the plane. —I hope."

They were now as close to Gaia-S as the nearest and largest of the gas giants was and they were nearly half a billion kilometers from it. Trevize placed it under full magnification on the screen for Pelorat's benefit. It was an impressive sight, even if the three sparse and narrow rings of debris were left out of account.

"It has the usual train of satellites," said Trevize, "but

at this distance from Gaia-S, we know that none of them are habitable. Nor are any of them settled by human beings who survive, let us say, under a glass dome or under other strictly artificial conditions."

"How can you tell?"

"There's no radio noise with characteristics that point them out as of intelligent origin. Of course," he added, qualifying his statement at once, "it is conceivable that a scientific outpost might go to great pains to shield its radio signals and the gas giant produces radio noise that could mask what I was looking for. Still, our radio reception is delicate and our computer is an extraordinarily good one. I'd say the chance of human occupation of those satellites is extremely small."

"Does that mean there's no Gaia?"

"No. But it does mean that if there *is* a Gaia, it hasn't bothered to settle those satellites. Perhaps it lacks the capacity to do so—or the interest."

"Well, *is* there a Gaia?"

"Patience, Janov. Patience."

Trevize considered the sky with a seemingly endless supply of patience. He stopped at one point to say, "Frankly, the fact that they haven't come out to pounce on us is disheartening, in a way. Surely, if they had the capacities they were described as having, they would have reacted to us by now."

"It's conceivable, I suppose," said Pelorat glumly, "that the whole thing is a fantasy."

"Call it a myth, Janov," said Trevize with a wry smile, "and it will be right up your alley. Still, there's a planet moving through the ecosphere, which means it might be habitable. I'll want to observe it for at least a day."

"Why?"

"To make sure it's habitable, for one thing."

"You just said it was in the ecosphere, Golan."

"Yes, at the moment it is. But its orbit could be very eccentric, and could eventually carry it within a microparsec of the star, or out to fifteen microparsecs, or both. We'll have to determine and compare the planet's distance from Gaia-S with its orbital speed—and it would help to note the direction of its motion."

4.

Another day.

"The orbit is nearly circular," Trevize said finally, "which means that habitability becomes a much safer bet. Yet no one's coming out to get us even now. We'll have to try a closer look."

Pelorat said, "Why does it take so long to arrange a Jump? You're just taking little ones."

"Listen to the man. Little Jumps are harder to control than big ones. Is it easier to pick up a rock or a fine grain of sand? Besides, Gaia-S is nearby and space is sharply curved. That complicates the calculations even for the computer. Even a mythologist should see that."

Pelorat grunted.

Trevize said, "You can see the planet with the unaided eye now. Right there. See it? The period of rotation is about twenty-two Galactic Hours and the axial inclination is twelve degrees. It is practically a textbook example of a habitable planet and it *is* life-bearing."

"How can you tell?"

"There are substantial quantities of free oxygen in the atmosphere. You can't have that without well-established vegetation."

"What about intelligent life?"

"That depends on the analysis of radio-wave radiation. Of course, there could be intelligent life that has abandoned technology, I suppose, but that seems very unlikely."

"There have been cases of that," said Pelorat.

"I'll take your word for it. That's your department. However, it's not likely that there would be nothing but pastoral survivors on a planet that frightened off the Mule."

Pelorat said, "Does it have a satellite?"

"Yes, it does," said Trevize casually.

"How big?" Pelorat said in a voice that was suddenly choking.

"Can't tell for sure. Perhaps a hundred kilometers across."

"Dear me," said Pelorat wistfully. "I wish I had some worthier set of expletives on instant call, my dear chap, but there was just that one little chance—"

"You mean, if it had a giant satellite, it might be Earth itself?"

"Yes, but it clearly isn't."

"Well, if Compor is right, Earth wouldn't be in this Galactic region, anyway. It would be over Sirius way. —Really, Janov, I'm sorry."

"Oh well."

"Look, we'll wait, and risk one more small Jump. If we find no signs of intelligent life, then it should be safe to land—except that there will then be no reason to land, will there?"

5.

After the next jump, Trevize said in an astonished voice, "That does it, Janov. It's Gaia, all right. At least, it possesses a technological civilization."

"Can you tell that from the radio waves?"

"Better than that. There's a space station circling the planet. Do you see that?"

There was an object on display on the viewscreen. To Pelorat's unaccustomed eye, it didn't seem very remarkable, but Trevize said, "Artificial, metallic, and a radio-source."

"What do we do now?"

"Nothing, for a while. At this stage of technology, they cannot fail to detect us. If, after a while, they do nothing, I will beam a radio message at them. If they still do nothing, I will approach cautiously."

"What if they *do* do something?"

"It will depend on the 'something.' If I don't like it, then

I'll have to take advantage of the fact that it is very unlikely that they have anything that can match the facility with which this ship can make a Jump."

"You mean we'll leave?"

"Like a hyperspatial missile."

"But we'll leave no wiser than we came."

"Not at all. At the very least we'll know that Gaia exists, that it has a working technology, and that it's done something to scare us."

"But, Golan, let's not be too easily scared."

"Now, Janov, I know that you want nothing more in the Galaxy than to learn about Earth at any cost, but please remember that I don't share your monomania. We are in an unarmed ship and those people down there have been isolated for centuries. Suppose they have never heard of the Foundation and don't know enough to be respectful of it. Or suppose this *is* the Second Foundation and once we're in their grip—if they're annoyed with us—we may never be the same again. Do you want them to wipe your mind clear and find you are no longer a mythologist and know nothing about any legends whatever?"

Pelorat looked grim. "If you put it that way— But what do we do once we leave?"

"Simple. We get back to Terminus with the news. —Or as near to Terminus as the old woman will allow. Then we might return to Gaia once again—more quickly and without all this inching along—and we return with an armed ship or an armed fleet. Things may well be different then."

6.

They waited. It had grown to be a routine. They had spent far more time waiting in the approaches to Gaia than they had spent in all the flight from Terminus to Sayshell.

Trevize set the computer to automatic alarm and was even nonchalant enough to doze in his padded chair.

This meant he woke with a start when the alarm chimed.

Pelorat came into Trevize's room, just as startled. He had been interrupted while shaving.

"Have we received a message?" asked Pelorat.

"No," said Trevize energetically. "We're *moving*."

"Moving? Where?"

"Toward the space station."

"Why is that?"

"I don't know. The motors are on and the computer doesn't respond to me — but we're moving. — Janov, we've been seized. We've come a little too close to Gaia."

16. CONVERGENCE

I.

When Stor Gendibal finally made out Compor's ship on his viewscreen, it seemed like the end of an incredibly long journey. Yet, of course, it was not the end, but merely the beginning. The journey from Trantor to Sayshell had been nothing but prologue.

Novi looked awed. "Is that another ship of space, Master?"

"Spaceship, Novi. It is. It's the one we have been striving to reach. It is a larger ship than this one—and a better one. It can move through space so quickly that if it fled from us, this ship could not possibly catch it—or even follow it."

"Faster than a ship of the masters?" Sura Novi seemed appalled by the thought.

Gendibal shrugged. "I may be, as you say, a master, but I am not a master in all things. We scholars do not have ships like these, nor do we have many of the material devices that the owners of those ships have."

"But how can scholars lack such things, Master?"

"Because we are masters in what is important. The material advances that these others have are trifles."

Novi's brows bent together in thought. "It seems to me that to go so quickly that a master cannot follow is no trifle. Who are these people who are wonder-having—who have such things?"

Gendibal was amused. "They call themselves the Foundation. Have you ever heard of the Foundation?"

(He caught himself wondering what the Hamish knew or did not know of the Galaxy and why it never occurred to the Speakers to wonder about such things. —Or was it only

309

he who had never wondered about such things—only he who assumed that the Hamish cared for nothing more than grubbing in the soil.)

Novi shook her head thoughtfully. "I have never heard of it, Master. When the schoolmaster taught me letter-lore—how to read, I mean—he told me there were many other worlds and told me the names of some. He said our Hamish world had the proper name of Trantor and that it once ruled all the worlds. He said Trantor was covered with gleaming iron and had an Emperor who was an all-master."

Her eyes looked up at Gendibal with a shy merriment. "I unbelieve most of it, though. There are many stories the word-spinners tell in the meeting-halls in the time of longer nights. When I was a small girl, I believed them all, but as I grew older, I found that many of them were not true. I believe very few now; perhaps none. Even schoolmasters tell unbelievables."

"Just the same, Novi, that particular story of the schoolmaster is true—but it was long ago. Trantor was indeed covered by metal and had indeed an Emperor who ruled all the Galaxy. Now, however, it is the people of the Foundation who will someday rule all the worlds. They grow stronger all the time."

"They will rule *all*, Master?"

"Not immediately. In five hundred years."

"And they will master the masters as well?"

"No, no. They will rule the worlds. We will rule *them*—for their safety and the safety of all the worlds."

Novi was frowning again. She said, "Master, do these people of the Foundation have many of these remarkable ships?"

"I imagine so, Novi."

"And other things that are very—astonishing?"

"They have powerful weapons of all kinds."

"Then, Master, can they not take all the worlds now?"

"No, they cannot. It is not yet time."

"But why can they not? Would the masters stop them?"

"We wouldn't have to, Novi. Even if we did nothing, they could not take all the worlds."

"But what would stop them?"

"You see," began Gendibal, "there is a plan that a wise man once devised—"

He stopped, smiled slightly, and shook his head. "It is hard to explain, Novi. Another time, perhaps. In fact, when you see what will happen before we ever see Trantor again, you may even understand without my explaining."

"What will happen, Master?"

"I am not sure, Novi. But all will happen well."

He turned away and prepared to make contact with Compor. And, as he did so, he could not quite keep an inner thought from saying: At least I hope so.

He was instantly angry with himself, for he knew the source of that foolish and weakening drift of thought. It was the picture of the elaborate and enormous Foundation might in the shape of Compor's ship and it was his chagrin at Novi's open admiration of it.

Stupid! How could he let himself compare the possession of mere strength and power with the possession of the ability to guide events? It was what generations of Speakers had called "the fallacy of the hand at the throat."

To think that he was not yet immune to its allures.

2.

Munn Li Compor was not in the least sure as to how he ought to comport himself. For most of his life, he had had the vision of all-powerful Speakers existing just beyond his circle of experience—Speakers, with whom he was occasionally in contact and who had, in their mysterious grip, the whole of humanity.

Of them all, it had been Stor Gendibal to whom, in recent years, he had turned for direction. It was not even a voice he had encountered most times, but a mere presence in his mind—hyperspeech without a hyper-relay.

In this respect, the Second Foundation had gone far beyond the Foundation. Without material device, but just by the educated and advanced power of the mind alone, they could reach across the parsecs in a manner that could not be tapped, could not be infringed upon. It was an invisible, indetectable network that held all the worlds fast through the mediation of a relatively few dedicated individuals.

Compor had, more than once, experienced a kind of uplifting at the thought of his role. How small the band of which he was one; how enormous an influence they exerted. —And how secret it all was. Even his wife knew nothing of his hidden life.

And it was the Speakers who held the strings—and this one Speaker, this Gendibal, who might (Compor thought) be the next First Speaker, the more-than-Emperor of a more-than-Empire.

Now Gendibal was here, in a ship of Trantor, and Compor fought to stifle his disappointment at not having such a meeting take place on Trantor itself.

Could *that* be a ship of Trantor? Any of the early Traders who had carried the Foundation's wares through a hostile Galaxy would have had a better ship than that. No wonder it had taken the Speaker so long to cover the distance from Trantor to Sayshell.

It was not even equipped with a unidock mechanism that would have welded the two ships into one when the cross-transfer of personnel was desired. Even the contemptible Sayshellian fleet was equipped with it. Instead, the Speaker had to match velocities and then cast a tether across the gap and swing along it, as in Imperial days.

That was it, thought Compor gloomily, unable to repress the feeling. The ship was no more than an old-fashioned Imperial vessel—and a small one at that.

Two figures were moving across the tether—one of them so clumsily that it was clear it had never attempted to maneuver through space before.

Finally they were on board and removed their space suits. Speaker Stor Gendibal was of moderate height and of unimpressive appearance; he was not large and powerful, nor did he exude an air of learning. His dark, deep-set eyes were the only indication of his wisdom. But now the Speaker looked about with a clear indication of being in awe *himself*.

The other was a woman as tall as Gendibal, plain in appearance. Her mouth was open in astonishment as she looked about.

3.

Moving across the tether had not been an entirely unpleasant experience for Gendibal. He was not a spaceman—no Second Foundationer was—but neither was he a complete surface worm, for no Second Foundationer was allowed to be that. The possible need for space flight was, after all, always looming above them, though every Second Foundationer hoped the need would arise only infrequently. (Preem Palver—the extent of whose space travels was legendary—had once said, ruefully, that the measure of the success of a Speaker was the fewness of the times he was compelled to move through space in order to assure the success of the Plan.)

Gendibal had had to use a tether three times before. This was his fourth use and even if he had felt tension over the matter, it would have disappeared in his concern for Sura Novi. He needed no mentalics to see that stepping into nothingness had totally upset her.

"I be afeared, Master," she said when he explained what would have to be done. "It be naughtness into which I will make footstep." If nothing else, her sudden descent into thick Hamish dialect showed the extent of her disturbance.

Gendibal said gently, "I cannot leave you on board this ship, Novi, for I will be going into the other and I must have you with me. There is no danger, for your space suit will protect you from all harm and there is no place for you to fall to. Even if you lose your grip on the tether, you will remain nearly where you are and I will be within arm's reach so that I can gather you in. Come, Novi, show me that you are brave enough—as well as bright enough—to become a scholar."

She made no further objection and Gendibal, unwilling to do anything that might disturb the smoothness of her mind-set, nevertheless managed to inject a soothing touch upon the surface of her mind.

"You can still speak to me," he said, after they were each enclosed in a space suit. "I can hear you if you think hard. Think the words hard and clearly, one by one. You can hear me now, can't you?"

"Yes, Master," she said.

He could see her lips move through the transparent face-plate and he said, "Say it without moving your lips, Novi. There is no radio in the kind of suits that scholars have. It is all done with the mind."

Her lips did not move and her look grew more anxious: Can you hear me, Master?

Perfectly well, thought Gendibal—and his lips did not move either: Do you hear me?

I do, Master.

Then come with me and do as I do.

They moved across. Gendibal knew the theory of it, even if he could handle the practice only moderately well. The trick was to keep one's legs extended and together and to swing them from the hips alone. That kept the center of gravity moving in a straight line as the arms swung forward in steady alternation. He had explained this to Sura Novi and, without turning to look at her, he studied the stance of her body from the set of the motor areas of her brain.

For a first-timer, she did very well, almost as well as Gendibal was managing to do. She repressed her own tensions and she followed directions. Gendibal found himself, once again, very pleased with her.

She was, however, clearly glad to be on board ship again—and so was Gendibal. He looked about as he removed his space suit and was rather dumbfounded at the luxury and style of the equipment. He recognized almost nothing and his heart sank at the thought that he might have very little time to learn how to handle it all. He might have to transfer expertise directly from the man already on board, something that was never quite as satisfactory as true learning.

Then he concentrated on Compor. Compor was tall and lean, a few years older than himself, rather handsome in a slightly weak way, with tightly waved hair of a startling buttery yellow.

And it was clear to Gendibal that this person was disappointed in, and even contemptuous of, the Speaker he was now meeting for the first time. What was more, he was entirely unsuccessful in hiding the fact.

Gendibal did not mind such things, on the whole. Compor was not a Trantorian—nor a full Second Foundationer—and he clearly had his illusions. Even the most superficial scan of his mind showed that. Among these was the illusion that true power was necessarily related to the appearance of power. He might, of course, keep his illusions as long as they did not interfere with what Gendibal needed, but at the present moment, this particular illusion *did* so interfere.

What Gendibal did was the mentalic equivalent of a snap of the fingers. Compor staggered slightly under the impress of a sharp but fleeting pain. There was an impress of enforced concentration that puckered the skin of his thought and left the man with the awareness of a casual but awesome power that could be utilized if the Speaker chose.

Compor was left with a vast respect for Gendibal.

Gendibal said pleasantly, "I am merely attracting your attention, Compor, my friend. Please let me know the present whereabouts of your friend, Golan Trevize, and his friend, Janov Pelorat."

Compor said hesitantly, "Shall I speak in the presence of the woman, Speaker?"

"The woman, Compor, is an extension of myself. There is no reason, therefore, why you should not speak openly."

"As you say, Speaker. Trevize and Pelorat are now approaching a planet known as Gaia."

"So you said in your last communication the other day. Surely they have already landed on Gaia and perhaps left again. They did not stay long on Sayshell Planet."

"They had not yet landed during the time I followed them, Speaker. They are approaching the planet with great caution, pausing substantial periods between micro-Jumps. It is clear to me they have no information about the planet they are approaching and therefore hesitate."

"Do *you* have information, Compor?"

"I have none, Speaker," said Compor, "or at least my ship's computer has none."

"This computer?" Gendibal's eyes fell upon the control panel and he asked in sudden hope, "Can it aid usefully in running the ship?"

"It can run the ship completely, Speaker. One need merely think into it."

Gendibal felt suddenly uneasy. "The Foundation has gone that far?"

"Yes, but clumsily. The computer does not work well. I must repeat my thoughts several times and even then I get but minimal information."

Gendibal said, "It may be able to do better than that."

"I am sure of it, Speaker," said Compor respectfully.

"But never mind that for the moment. Why does it have no information on Gaia?"

"I do not know, Speaker. It claims to have—as far as a computer may be said to be able to *claim*—records on every human-inhabited planet in the Galaxy."

"It cannot have more information than has been fed into it and if those who did the feeding thought they had records of all such planets when, in actual fact, they did not, then the computer would labor under the same misapprehension. Correct?"

"Certainly, Speaker."

"Did you inquire at Sayshell?"

"Speaker," said Compor uneasily, "there are people who

speak of Gaia on Sayshell, but what they say is valueless.
Clearly superstition. The tale they tell is that Gaia is a
powerful world that held off even the Mule."

"Is that what they say, indeed?" said Gendibal, sup-
pressing excitement. "Were you so sure that this was superstition that you asked for no details?"

"No, Speaker. I asked a great deal, but what I have just
told you is all that anyone can say. They can speak on the
subject at great length, but when they have done so, all that
it boils down to is what I have just said."

"Apparently," said Gendibal, "that is what Trevize had
heard, too, and he goes to Gaia for some reason connected
with that—to tap this great power, perhaps. And he does
so cautiously, for perhaps he also fears this great power."

"That is certainly possible, Speaker."

"And yet you did not follow?"

"I did follow, Speaker, long enough to make sure he was
indeed making for Gaia. I then returned here to the outskirts
of the Gaian system."

"Why?"

"Three reasons, Speaker. First, you were about to arrive
and I wanted to meet you at least partway and bring you
aboard at the earliest moment, as you had directed. Since
my ship has a hyper-relay on board, I could not move too
far away from Trevize and Pelorat without rousing suspicion
on Terminus, but I judged I could risk moving this far.
Second, when it was clear that Trevize was approaching
Gaia Planet very slowly, I judged there would be time enough
for me to move toward you and hasten our meeting without
being overtaken by events, especially since you would be
more competent than I to follow him to the planet itself and
to handle any emergency that might arise."

"Quite true. And the third reason?"

"Since our last communication, Speaker, something has
happened that I did not expect and do not understand. I felt
that—for that reason, too—I had better hasten our meeting
as soon as I dared."

"And this event that you did not expect and do not understand?"

"Ships of the Foundation fleet are approaching the Sayshellian frontier. My computer has picked up this information from Sayshellian news broadcasts. At least five advanced ships are in the flotilla and these have enough power to overwhelm Sayshell."

Gendibal did not answer at once, for it would not do to show that he had not expected such a move—or that he didn't understand it. So, after a moment, he said negligently, "Do you suppose that this has something to do with Trevize's movement toward Gaia?"

"It certainly came immediately afterward—and if B follows A, then there is at least a possibility that A caused B," said Compor.

"Well, then, it seems we all converge upon Gaia—Trevize, and I, and the First Foundation. —Come, you acted well, Compor," said Gendibal, "and here is what we will now do. First, you will show me how this computer works and, through that, how the ship may be handled. I am sure that will not take long.

"After that, you will get into my ship, since by then I will have impressed on your mind how to handle it. You will have no trouble maneuvering it, although I must tell you (as you have no doubt guessed from its appearance) that you will find it primitive indeed. Once you are in control of the ship, you will keep it here and wait for me."

"How long, Speaker?"

"Until I come for you. I do not expect to be gone long enough for you to be in danger of running out of supplies, but if I am unduly delayed, you may find your way to some inhabited planet of the Sayshell Union and wait there. Wherever you are, I will find you."

"As you say, Speaker."

"And do not be alarmed. I can handle this mysterious Gaia and, if need be, the five ships of the Foundation as well."

4.

Littoral Thoobing had been the Foundation's Ambassador to Sayshell for seven years. He rather liked the position.

Tall and rather stout, he wore a thick brown mustache at a time when the predominant fashion, both in the Foundation and in Sayshell, was smooth-shaven. He had a strongly lined countenance, though he was only fifty-four—and was much given to a schooled indifference. His attitude toward his work was not easily seen.

Still, he rather liked the position. It kept him away from the hurly-burly of politics on Terminus—something he appreciated—and it gave him the chance to live the life of a Sayshellian sybarite and to support his wife and daughter in the style to which they had become addicted. He didn't want his life disturbed.

On the other hand, he rather disliked Liono Kodell, perhaps because Kodell also sported a mustache, though one which was smaller, shorter, and grayish-white. In the old days, they had been the only two people in prominent public life who had worn one and there had been rather a competition between them over the matter. Now (thought Thoobing) there was none; Kodell's was contemptible.

Kodell had been Director of Security when Thoobing was still on Terminus, dreaming of opposing Harla Branno in the race for Mayor, until he had been bought off with the ambassadorship. Branno had done it for her own sake, of course, but he had ended up owing her goodwill for that.

But not to Kodell, somehow. Perhaps it was because of Kodell's determined cheerfulness—the manner in which he was always such a *friendly* person—even after he had decided on just exactly the manner in which your throat was to be cut.

Now he sat there in hyperspatial image, cheerful as ever, brimming over with bonhomie. His actual body was, of course, back on Terminus, which spared Thoobing the necessity of offering him any physical sign of hospitality.

"Kodell," he said. "I want those ships withdrawn."

Kodell smiled sunnily. "Why, so do I, but the old lady has made up her mind."

"You've been known to persuade her out of this or that."

"On occasion. Perhaps. When she wanted to be persuaded. This time she doesn't want to be. —Thoobing, do your job. Keep Sayshell calm."

"I'm not thinking about Sayshell, Kodell. I'm thinking about the Foundation."

"So are we all."

"Kodell, don't fence. I want you to listen to me."

"Gladly, but these are hectic times on Terminus and I will not listen to you forever."

"I will be as brief as I can be—when discussing the possibility of the Foundation's destruction. If this hyperspatial line is not being tapped, I will speak openly."

"It is not being tapped."

"Then let me go on. I have received a message some days ago from one Golan Trevize. I recall a Trevize in my own political days, a Commissioner of Transportation."

"The young man's uncle," Kodell said.

"Ah, then you know the Trevize who sent the message to me. According to the information I have since gathered, he was a Councilman who, after the recent successful resolution of a Seldon Crisis, was arrested and sent into exile."

"Exactly."

"I don't believe it."

"What is it that you don't believe?"

"That he was sent into exile."

"Why not?"

"When in history has any citizen of the Foundation been sent into exile?" demanded Thoobing. "He is arrested or not arrested. If he is arrested, he is tried or not tried. If he is tried, he is convicted or not convicted. If he is convicted, he is fined, demoted, disgraced, imprisoned, or executed. No one is sent into exile."

"There is always a first time."

"Nonsense. In an advanced naval vessel? What fool can

fail to see that he is on a special mission for your old woman? Whom can she possibly expect to deceive?"

"What would the mission be?"

"Supposedly to find the planet Gaia."

Some of the cheerfulness left Kodell's face. An unaccustomed hardness entered his eyes. He said, "I know that you feel no overwhelming impulse to believe my statements, Mr. Ambassador, but I make a special plea that you believe me in this one case. Neither the Mayor nor I had ever heard of Gaia at the time that Trevize was sent into exile. We have heard of Gaia, for the first time, just the other day. If you believe that, this conversation may continue."

"I will suspend my tendency toward skepticism long enough to accept that, Director, though it is difficult to do so."

"It is quite true, Mr. Ambassador, and if I have suddenly adopted a formal note to my statements it is because when this is done, you will find that you have questions to answer and that you will not find the occasion joyful. You speak as though Gaia is a world familiar to you. How is it that you know something we did not know? Is it not your duty to see to it that we know everything that you know about the political unit to which you are assigned?"

Thoobing said softly, "Gaia is not part of the Sayshell Union. It, in fact, probably does not exist. Am I to transmit to Terminus all the fairy tales that the superstitious lower orders of Sayshell tell of Gaia? Some of them say that Gaia is located in hyperspace. According to others, it is a world that supernaturally protects Sayshell. According to still others, it sent forth the Mule to prey on the Galaxy. If you are planning to tell the Sayshellian government that Trevize has been sent out to find Gaia and that five advanced ships of the Foundation Navy have been sent out to back him in this search, they will never believe you. The people may believe fairy tales about Gaia, but the government does not—and they will not be convinced that the Foundation does. They will feel that you intend to force Sayshell into the Foundation Federation."

"And what if we do plan that?"

"It would be fatal. Come, Kodell, in the five-century history of the Foundation, when have we fought a war of conquest? We have fought wars to prevent our own conquest—and failed once—but no war has ended with an extension of our territory. Accessions to the Federation have been through peaceful agreements. We have been joined by those who saw benefits in joining."

"Isn't it possible that Sayshell may see benefits in joining?"

"They will never do so while our ships remain on their borders. Withdraw them."

"It can't be done."

"Kodell, Sayshell is a marvelous advertisement for the benevolence of the Foundation Federation. It is nearly enclosed by our territory, it is in an utterly vulnerable position, and yet until now it has been safe, has gone its own way, has even been able to maintain an anti-Foundation foreign policy freely. How better can we show the Galaxy that we force no one, that we come in friendship to all? —If we take over Sayshell, we take that which, in essence, we already have. After all, we dominate it economically—if quietly. But if we take it over by military force, we advertise to all the Galaxy that we have become expansionist."

"And if I tell you that we are really interested only in Gaia?"

"Then I will believe it no more than the Sayshell Union will. This man, Trevize, sends me a message that he is on his way to Gaia and asks me to transmit it to Terminus. Against my better judgment, I do so because I must and, almost before the hyperspatial line is cool, the Foundation Navy is in motion. How will you get to Gaia, without penetrating Sayshellian space?"

"My *dear* Thoobing, surely you are not listening to yourself. Did you not tell me just a few minutes ago that Gaia, if it exists at all, is not part of the Sayshell Union? And I presume you know that hyperspace is free to all and is part of no world's territory. How then can Sayshell complain if we move from Foundation territory (where our ships stand right now), through hyperspace, into Gaian territory, and never in the process occupy a single cubic centimeter of Sayshellian territory?"

"Sayshell will not interpret events like that, Kodell. Gaia, if it exists at all, is totally enclosed by the Sayshell Union, even if it is not a political part of it, and there are precedents that make such enclaves virtual parts of the enclosing territory, as far as enemy warships are concerned."

"Ours are not enemy warships. We are at peace with Sayshell."

"I tell you that Sayshell may declare war. They won't expect to win such a war through military superiority, but the fact is, war will set off a wave of anti-Foundation activity throughout the Galaxy. The new expansionist policies of the Foundation will encourage the growth of alliances against us. Some of the members of the Federation will begin to rethink their ties to us. We may well lose the war through internal disarray and we will then certainly reverse the process of growth that has served the Foundation so well for five hundred years."

"Come, come, Thoobing," said Kodell indifferently, "You speak as though five hundred years is nothing, as though we are still the Foundation of Salvor Hardin's time, fighting the pocket-kingdom of Anacreon. We are far stronger now than the Galactic Empire ever was at its very height. A squadron of our ships could defeat the entire Galactic Navy, occupy any Galactic sector, and never know it had been in a fight."

"We are not fighting the Galactic Empire. We fight planets and sectors of our own time."

"Who have not advanced as we have. We could gather in all the Galaxy now."

"According to the Seldon Plan, we can't do that for another five hundred years."

"The Seldon Plan underestimates the speed of technological advance. We can do it now! —Understand me, I don't say we *will* do it now or even *should* do it now. I merely say we *can* do it now."

"Kodell, you have lived all your life on Terminus. You don't know the Galaxy. Our Navy and our technology can beat down the Armed Forces of other worlds, but we cannot yet govern the entire rebellious, hate-ridden Galaxy—and that is what it will be if we take it by force. Withdraw the ships!"

"It can't be done, Thoobing. Consider— What if Gaia is not a myth?"

Thoobing paused, scanning the other's face as though anxious to read his mind. "A world in hyperspace not a myth?"

"A world in hyperspace is superstition, but even superstitions may be built around kernels of truth. This man, Trevize, who was exiled, speaks of it as though it were a real world in real space. What if he is right?"

"Nonsense. I don't believe it."

"No? Believe it for just a moment. A real world that has lent Sayshell safety against the Mule and against the Foundation!"

"But you refute yourself. How is Gaia keeping the Sayshellians safe from the Foundation? Are we not sending ships against it?"

"Not against it, but against Gaia, which is so mysteriously unknown—which is so careful to avoid notice that while it is in real space it somehow convinces its neighbor worlds that it is in hyperspace—and which even manages to remain outside the computerized data of the best and most unabridged of Galactic maps."

"It must be a most unusual world, then, for it must be able to manipulate minds."

"And did you not say a moment ago that one Sayshellian tale is that Gaia sent forth the Mule to prey upon the Galaxy? And could not the Mule manipulate minds?"

"And Gaia is a world of Mules, then?"

"Are you sure it might not be?"

"Why not a world of a reborn Second Foundation, in that case?"

"Why not indeed? Should it not be investigated?"

Thoobing grew sober. He had been smiling scornfully during the last exchanges, but now he lowered his head and stared up from under his eyebrows. "If you are serious, is such an investigation not dangerous?"

"Is it?"

"You answer my questions with other questions because you have no reasonable answers. Of what use will ships be against Mules or Second Foundationers? Is it not likely, in fact, that if they exist they are luring you into destruction? See here, you tell me that the Foundation can establish its Empire now, even though the Seldon Plan has reached only its midway point, and I have warned you that you would be racing too far ahead and that the intricacies of the Plan would slow you down by force. Perhaps, if Gaia exists and is what you say it is, all this is a device to bring about that slowdown. Do voluntarily now what you may soon be constrained to do. Do peacefully and without bloodshed now what you may be forced to do by woeful disaster. Withdraw the ships."

"It can't be done. In fact, Thoobing, Mayor Branno herself plans to join the ships, and scoutships have already flitted through hyperspace to what is supposedly Gaian territory."

Thoobing's eyes bulged. "There will surely be war, I tell you."

"You are our ambassador. Prevent that. Give the Sayshellians whatever assurances they need. Deny any ill will on our part. Tell them, if you have to, that it will pay them to sit quietly and wait for Gaia to destroy us. Say anything you want to, but keep them quiet."

He paused, searching Thoobing's stunned expression, and said, "Really, that's all. As far as I know, no Foundation ship will land on any world of the Sayshell Union or penetrate any point in real space that is part of that Union. However, any Sayshellian ship that attempts to challenge us outside Union territory—and therefore inside Foundation territory—will promptly be reduced to dust. Make that perfectly clear, too, and keep the Sayshellians quiet. You will be held to strict account if you fail. You have had an easy job so far, Thoobing, but hard times are upon you and the next few weeks decide all. Fail us and no place in the Galaxy will be safe for you."

There was neither merriment nor friendliness in Kodell's face as contact was broken and as his image disappeared.

Thoobing stared open-mouthed at the place where he had been.

5.

Golan Trevize clutched at his hair as though he were trying, by feel, to judge the condition of his thinking. He said to Pelorat abruptly, "What is your state of mind?"

"State of mind?" said Pelorat blankly.

"Yes. Here we are, trapped — with our ship under outside control and being drawn inexorably to a world we know nothing about. Do you feel panic?"

Pelorat's long face registered a certain melancholia. "No," he said. "I don't feel joyful. I do feel a little apprehensive, but I'm not panicky."

"Neither am I. Isn't that odd? Why aren't we more upset than we are?"

"This is something we expected, Golan. *Something* like this."

Trevize turned to the screen. It remained firmly focused on the space station. It was larger now, which meant they were closer.

It seemed to him that it was not an impressive space station in design. There was nothing to it that bespoke superscience. In fact, it seemed a bit primitive. —Yet it had the ship in its grip.

He said, "I'm being very analytical, Janov. Cool! —I like to think that I am not a coward and that I can behave well under pressure, and I tend to flatter myself. Everyone does. I should be jumping up and down right now and sweating a little. We may have expected *something*, but that doesn't change the fact that we are helpless and that we may be killed."

Pelorat said, "I don't think so, Golan. If the Gaians could take over the ship at a distance, couldn't they kill us at a distance? If we're still alive—"

"But we're not altogether untouched. We're too calm, I tell you. I think they've tranquilized us."

"Why?"

"To keep us in good shape mentally, I think. It's possible they wish to question us. After all, they may kill us."

"If they are rational enough to want to question us, they may be rational enough not to kill us for no good reason."

Trevize leaned back in his chair (it bent back at least— they hadn't deprived the chair of its functioning) and placed his feet on the desk where ordinarily his hands made contact with the computer. He said, "They may be quite ingenious enough to work up what they consider a good reason. —Still, if they've touched our minds, it hasn't been by much. If it were the Mule, for instance, he would have made us *eager* to go—exalted, exultant, every fiber of ourselves crying out for arrival there." He pointed to the space station. "Do you feel that way, Janov?"

"Certainly not."

"You see that I'm still in a state where I can indulge in cool, analytical reasoning. Very odd! Or can I tell? Am I in a panic, incoherent, mad—and merely under the illusion that I am indulging in cool, analytical reasoning?"

Pelorat shrugged. "You seem sane to me. Perhaps I am as insane as you and am under the same illusion, but that sort of argument gets us nowhere. All humanity could share a common insanity and be immersed in a common illusion while living in a common chaos. That can't be disproved, but we have no choice but to follow our senses." And then, abruptly, he said, "In fact, I've been doing some reasoning myself."

"Yes?"

"Well, we talk about Gaia as a world of Mules, possibly, or as the Second Foundation reborn. Has it occurred to you that a third alternative exists, one that is more reasonable than either of the first two."

"What third alternative?"

Pelorat's eyes seemed concentrating inward. He did not look at Trevize and his voice was low and thoughtful. "We have a world—Gaia—that has done its best, over an indefinite period of time, to maintain a strict isolation. It has in no way attempted to establish contact with any other world—not even the nearby worlds of the Sayshell Union. It has an advanced science, in some ways, if the stories of their destruction of fleets is true and certainly their ability to control us right now bespeaks it—and yet they have made no attempt to expand their power. They ask only to be left alone."

Trevize narrowed his eyes. "So?"

"It's all very inhuman. The more than twenty thousand years of human history in space has been an uninterrupted tale of expansion and attempted expansion. Just about every known world that can be inhabited *is* inhabited. Nearly every world has been quarreled over in the process and nearly every world has jostled each of its neighbors at one time or another. If Gaia is so inhuman as to be so different in this respect, it may be because it really is—inhuman."

Trevize shook his head. "Impossible."

"Why impossible?" said Pelorat warmly. "I've told you what a puzzle it is that the human race is the only evolved intelligence in the Galaxy. What if it isn't? Might there not be one more—on one planet—that lacked the human expansionist drive? In fact," Pelorat grew more excited, "what if there are a million intelligences in the Galaxy, but only *one* that is expansionist—ourselves? The others would all remain at home, unobtrusive, hidden—"

"Ridiculous!" said Trevize. "We'd come across them. We'd land on their worlds. They would come in all types and stages of technology and most of them would be unable to stop us. But we've never come across any of them. Space! We've never even come across the ruins or relics of a nonhuman civilization, have we? You're the historian, so you tell me. Have we?"

Pelorat shook his head. "We haven't. —But Golan, there could be one! This one!"

"I don't believe it. You say the name is Gaia, which is some ancient dialectical version of the name 'Earth.' How can that be nonhuman?"

"The name 'Gaia' is given the planet by human beings—and who knows why? The resemblance to an ancient word might be coincidental. —Come to think of it, the very fact that we've been lured to Gaia—as you explained in great detail some time ago—and are now being drawn in against our will is an argument in favor of the nonhumanity of the Gaians."

"Why? What has that to do with nonhumanity?"

"They're *curious* about us—about humans."

Trevize said, "Janov, you're mad. They've been living in a Galaxy surrounded by humans for thousands of years. Why should they be curious right now? Why not long before? And if right now, why *us*? If they want to study human beings and human culture, why not the Sayshell worlds? Why would they reach all the way to Terminus for us?"

"They may be interested in the Foundation."

"Nonsense," said Trevize violently. "Janov, you *want* a nonhuman intelligence and you *will* have one. Right now, I think that if you thought you were going to encounter nonhumans, you wouldn't worry about having been captured, about being helpless, about being killed even—if they but gave you a little time to sate your curiosity."

Pelorat began to stutter an indignant negative, then stopped, drew a deep breath, and said, "Well, you may be right, Golan, but I'll hold to my belief for a while just the same. I don't think we'll have to wait very long to see who's right. —Look!"

He pointed to the screen. Trevize—who had, in his excitement, ceased watching—now looked back. "What is it?" he said.

"Isn't that a ship taking off from the station?"

"It's *something*," admitted Trevize reluctantly. "I can't make out the details yet and I can't magnify the view any further. It's a maximum magnification." After awhile he said, "It seems to be approaching us and I suppose it's a ship. Shall we make a bet?"

"What sort of bet?"

Trevize said sardonically, "If we ever get back to Terminus, let's have a big dinner for ourselves and any guests we each care to invite, up to, say, four—and it will be on me if that ship approaching us carries nonhumans and on you if it carries humans."

"I'm willing," said Pelorat.

"Done, then," and Trevize peered at the screen, trying to make out details and wondering if any details could reasonably be expected to give away, beyond question, the nonhumanity (or humanity) of the beings on board.

6.

Branno's iron-gray hair lay immaculately in place and she might have been in the Mayoral Palace, considering her equanimity. She showed no sign that she was deep in space for only the second time in her life. (And the first time— when she accompanied her parents on a holiday tour to Kalgan—could scarcely count. She had been only three at the time.)

She said to Kodell with a certain weary heaviness, "It is Thoobing's job, after all, to express his opinion and to warn me. Very well, he has warned me. I don't hold it against him."

Kodell, who had boarded the Mayor's ship in order to speak to her without the psychological difficulty of imaging, said, "He's been at his post too long. He's beginning to think like a Sayshellian."

"That's the occupational hazard of an ambassadorship, Liono. Let us wait till this is over and we'll give him a long sabbatical and then send him on to another assignment elsewhere. He's a capable man. —After all, he did have the wit to forward Trevize's message without delay."

Kodell smiled briefly. "Yes, he told me he did it against his better judgment. 'I do so because I must' he said. You see, Madam Mayor, he had to, even against his better judgment, because as soon as Trevize entered the space of the Sayshell Union, I informed Ambassador Thoobing to forward, at once, any and all information concerning him."

"Oh?" Mayor Branno turned in her seat to see his face more clearly. "And what made you do that?"

"Elementary considerations, actually. Trevize was using a late-model Foundation naval vessel and the Sayshellians would be bound to notice *that*. He's an undiplomatic young jackass and they would be bound to notice *that*. Therefore, he might get into trouble—and if there's one thing a Foundationer knows, it is that if he gets into trouble anywhere in the Galaxy, he can cry out for the nearest Foundation representative. Personally I wouldn't mind seeing Trevize in trouble—it might help him grow up and that would do him a great deal of good—but you've sent him out as your lightning rod and I wanted you to be able to estimate the nature of any lightning that might strike, so I made sure that the nearest Foundation representative would keep watch over him, that's all."

"I see! Well, I understand now why Thoobing reacted so strenuously. I had sent him a similar warning. Since he heard from us both independently, one can scarcely blame him for thinking that the approach of a few Foundation vessels might mean a great deal more than it actually does. —How is it, Liono, you did not consult me on the matter before sending the warning?"

Kodell said coolly, "If I involved you in everything I do, you would have no time to be Mayor. How is it that you did not inform me of your intention?"

Branno said sourly, "If I informed you of all my intentions, Liono, you would know far too much. —But it is a small matter, and so is Thoobing's alarm, and, for that matter, so is any fit that the Sayshellians throw. I am more interested in Trevize."

"Our scouts have located Compor. He is following Trevize and both are moving very cautiously toward Gaia."

"I have the full reports of those scouts, Liono. Apparently both Trevize and Compor are taking Gaia seriously."

"Everyone sneers at the superstitions concerning Gaia, Madam Mayor, but everyone thinks, 'Yet what if—' Even Ambassador Thoobing manages to be a little uneasy about it. It could be a very shrewd policy on the part of the Sayshellians. A kind of protective coloration. If one spreads stories of a mysterious and invincible world, people will shy away not only from the world, but from any other worlds closeby—such as the Sayshell Union."

"You think that is why the Mule turned away from Sayshell?"

"Possibly."

"Surely you don't think the Foundation has held its hand from Sayshell because of Gaia, when there is no record that we have ever heard of the world?"

"I admit there's no mention of Gaia in our archives, but neither is there any other reasonable explanation for our moderation with respect to the Sayshell Union."

"Let us hope, then, that the Sayshellian government, despite Thoobing's opinion to the contrary, has convinced itself—even just a little bit—of Gaia's might and of its deadly nature."

"Why so?"

"Because then the Sayshell Union will raise no objections to our moving toward Gaia. The more they resent that movement, the more they will persuade themselves that it should be permitted so that Gaia will swallow us. The lesson, they will imagine, will be a salutary one and will not be lost on future invaders."

"Yet what if they should be right in such a belief, Mayor? What if Gaia *is* deadly?"

Branno smiled. "You raise the 'Yet what if—' yourself, do you, Liono?"

"I must raise all possibilities, Mayor. It is my job."

"If Gaia is deadly, Trevize will be taken by them. That is *his* job as my lightning rod. And so may Compor, I hope."

"You hope. Why?"

"Because it will make them overconfident, which should be useful to us. They will underestimate our power and be the easier to handle."

"But what if it is *we* who are overconfident?"

"We are not," said Branno flatly.

"These Gaians—whatever they are—may be something we have no concept of and cannot properly estimate the danger of. I merely suggest that, Mayor, because even that possibility should be weighed."

"Indeed? Why does such a notion fall into your head, Liono?"

"Because I think you feel that, at the worst, Gaia is the Second Foundation. I suspect you think they *are* the Second Foundation. However, Sayshell has an interesting history, even under the Empire. Sayshell alone had a measure of self-rule. Sayshell alone was spared some of the worst taxations under the so-called 'Bad Emperors.' In short, Sayshell seems to have had the protection of Gaia, even in Imperial times."

"Well then?"

"But the Second Foundation was brought into existence by Hari Seldon at the same time our Foundation was. The Second Foundation did not exist in Imperial times—and Gaia did. Gaia, therefore, is *not* the Second Foundation. It is something else—and, just possibly, something worse."

"I don't propose to be terrified by the unknown, Liono. There are only two possible sources of danger—physical weapons and mental weapons—and we are fully prepared for both. —You get back to your ship and keep the units on the Sayshellian outskirts. This ship will move toward Gaia alone, but will stay in contact with you at all times and will expect you to come to us in one Jump, if necessary. —Go, Liono, and get that perturbed look off your face."

"One last question? Are you *sure* you know what you're doing?"

"I do," she said grimly. "I, too, have studied the history of Sayshell and have seen that Gaia cannot be the Second Foundation, but, as I told you, I have the full report of the scouts and from that—"

"Yes?"

"Well, I know where the Second Foundation is located and we will take care of both, Liono. We will take care of Gaia first and then Trantor."

17. GAIA

1.

It took hours for the ship from the space station to reach the vicinity of the *Far Star*—very long hours for Trevize to endure.

Had the situation been normal, Trevize would have tried to signal and would have expected a response. If there had been no response, he would have taken evasive action.

Since he was unarmed and there had been no response, there was nothing to do but wait. The computer would not respond to any direction he could give it that involved anything outside the ship.

Internally, at least, everything worked well. The life-support systems were in perfect order, so that he and Pelorat were physically comfortable. Somehow, that didn't help. Life dragged on and the uncertainty of what was to come was wearing him down. He noticed with irritation that Pelorat seemed calm. As though to make it worse, while Trevize felt no sense of hunger at all, Pelorat opened a small container of chicken-bits, which on opening had rapidly and automatically warmed itself. Now he was eating it methodically.

Trevize said irritably, "Space, Janov! That stinks!"

Pelorat looked startled and sniffed at the container. "It smells all right to me, Golan."

Trevize shook his head. "Don't mind me. I'm just upset. But do use a fork. Your fingers will smell of chicken all day."

Pelorat looked at his fingers with surprise. "Sorry! I didn't notice. I was thinking of something else."

Trevize said sarcastically, "Would you care to guess at

what type of nonhumans the creatures on the approaching ship must be?" He was ashamed that he was less calm than Pelorat was. He was a Navy veteran (though he had never seen battle, of course) and Pelorat was a historian. Yet his companion sat there quietly.

Pelorat said, "It would be impossible to imagine what direction evolution would take under conditions differing from those of Earth. The possibilities may not be infinite, but they would be so vast that they might as well be. However, I can predict that they are not senselessly violent and they will treat us in a civilized fashion. If that wasn't true, we would be dead by now."

"At least you can still reason, Janov, my friend—you can still be tranquil. My nerves seem to be forcing their way through whatever tranquilization they have put us under. I have an extraordinary desire to stand up and pace. Why doesn't that blasted ship arrive?"

Pelorat said, "I am a man of passivity, Golan. I have spent my life doubled over records while waiting for other records to arrive. I do nothing but wait. You are a man of action and you are in deep pain when action is impossible."

Trevize felt some of his tension leave. He muttered, "I underestimate your good sense, Janov."

"No, you don't," said Pelorat placidly, "but even a naïve academic can sometimes make sense out of life."

"And even the cleverest politician can sometimes fail to do so."

"I didn't say that, Golan."

"No, but I did. —So let me become active. I can still observe. The approaching ship is close enough to seem distinctly primitive."

"Seem?"

Trevize said, "If it's the product of nonhuman minds and hands, what may seem primitive may, in actual fact, be merely nonhuman."

"Do you think it might be a nonhuman artifact?" asked Pelorat, his face reddening slightly.

"I can't tell. I suspect that artifacts, however much they

may vary from culture to culture, are never quite as plastic as products of genetic differences might be."

"That's just a guess on your part. All we know are different cultures. We don't know different intelligent species and therefore have no way of judging how different artifacts might be."

"Fish, dolphins, penguins, squids, even the ambiflexes, which are not of Earthly origin—assuming the others are—all solve the problem of motion through a viscous medium by streamlining, so that their appearances are not as different as their genetic makeup might lead one to believe. It might be so with artifacts."

"The squid's tentacles and the ambiflex's helical vibrators," responded Pelorat, "are enormously different from each other, and from the fins, flippers, and limbs of vertebrates. It might be so with artifacts."

"In any case," said Trevize, "I feel better. Talking nonsense with you, Janov, quiets my nerves. And I suspect we'll know what we're getting into soon, too. The ship is not going to be able to dock with ours and whatever is on it will come across on an old-fashioned tether—or we will somehow be urged to cross to it on one—since the unilock will be useless. —Unless some nonhuman will use some other system altogether."

"How big is the ship?"

"Without being able to use the ship's computer to calculate the distance of the ship by radar, we can't possibly know the size."

A tether snaked out toward the *Far Star*.

Trevize said, "Either there's a human aboard or nonhumans use the same device. Perhaps nothing but a tether can possibly work."

"They might use a tube," said Pelorat, "or a horizontal ladder."

"Those are inflexible things. It would be far too complicated to try to make contact with those. You need something that combines strength and flexibility."

The tether made a dull clang on the *Far Star* as the solid

hull (and consequently the air within) was set to vibrating. There was the usual slithering as the other ship made the fine adjustments of speed required to bring the two into a common velocity. The tether was motionless relative to both.

A black dot appeared on the hull of the other ship and expanded like the pupil of an eye.

Trevize grunted. "An expanding diaphragm, instead of a sliding panel."

"Nonhuman?"

"Not necessarily, I suppose. But interesting."

A figure emerged.

Pelorat's lips tightened for a moment and then he said in a disappointed voice, "Too bad. Human."

"Not necessarily," said Trevize calmly. "All we can make out is that there seem to be five projections. That could be a head, two arms, and two legs—but it might not be. —Wait!"

"What?"

"It moves more rapidly and smoothly than I expected. —Ah!"

"What?"

"There's some sort of propulsion. It's not rocketry, as nearly as I can tell, but neither is it hand over hand. Still, not necessarily human."

There seemed an incredibly long wait despite the quick approach of the figure along the tether, but there was finally the noise of contact.

Trevize said, "It's coming in, whatever it is. My impulse is to tackle it the minute it appears." He balled a fist.

"I think we had better relax," said Pelorat. "It may be stronger than we. It can control our minds. There are surely others on the ship. We had better wait till we know more about what we are facing."

"You grow more and more sensible by the minute, Janov," said Trevize, "and I, less and less."

They could hear the airlock moving into action and finally the figure appeared inside the ship.

"About normal size," muttered Pelorat. "The space suit could fit a human being."

"I never saw or heard of such a design, but it doesn't fall outside the limits of human manufacture, it seems to me. —It doesn't say anything."

The space-suited figure stood before them and a forelimb rose to the rounded helmet, which—if it were made of glass—possessed one-way transparency only. Nothing could be seen inside.

The limb touched something with a quick motion that Trevize did not clearly make out and the helmet was at once detached from the rest of the suit. It lifted off.

What was exposed was the face of a young and undeniably pretty woman.

2.

Pelorat's expressionless face did what it could to look stupefied. He said hesitantly, "Are you human?"

The woman's eyebrows shot up and her lips pouted. There was no way of telling from the action whether she was faced with a strange language and did not understand or whether she understood and wondered at the question.

Her hand moved quickly to the left side of her suit, which opened in one piece as though it were on a set of hinges. She stepped out and the suit remained standing without content for a moment. Then, with a soft sigh that seemed almost human, it collapsed.

She looked even younger, now that she had stepped out. Her clothing was loose and translucent, with the skimpy items beneath visible as shadows. The outer robe reached to her knees.

She was small-breasted and narrow-waisted, with hips rounded and full. Her thighs, which were seen in shadow, were generous, but her legs narrowed to graceful ankles.

Her hair was dark and shoulder-length, her eyes brown and large, her lips full and slightly asymmetric.

She looked down at herself and then solved the problem of her understanding of the language by saying, "Don't I *look* human?"

She spoke Galactic Standard with just a trifle of hesitation, as though she were straining a bit to get the pronunciation quite right.

Pelorat nodded and said with a small smile, "I can't deny it. Quite human. Delightfully human."

The young woman spread her arms as though inviting closer examination. "I should hope so, gentlemen. Men have died for this body."

"I would rather live for it," said Pelorat, finding a vein of gallantry which faintly surprised him.

"Good choice," said the woman solemnly. "Once this body is attained, all sighs become sighs of ecstasy."

She laughed and Pelorat laughed with her.

Trevize, whose forehead had puckered into a frown through this exchange, rapped out, "How old are you?"

The woman seemed to shrink a little. "Twenty-three— gentleman."

"Why have you come? What is your purpose here?"

"I have come to escort you to Gaia." Her command of Galactic Standard was slipping slightly and her vowels tended to round into diphthongs. She made "come" sound like "comb" and "Gaia" like "Gay-uh."

"A *girl* to escort us."

The woman drew herself up and suddenly she had the bearing of one in charge. "I," she said, "am Gaia, as well as another. It was my stint on the station."

"*Your* stint? Were you the only one on board?"

Proudly. "I was all that was needed."

"And is it empty now?"

"I am no longer on it, gentleman, but it is not empty. *It* is there."

"It? To what do you refer?"

"To the station. It is Gaia. It doesn't need me. It holds your ship."

"Then what are you doing on the station?"

"It is my stint."

Pelorat had taken Trevize by the sleeve and had been shaken off. He tried again. "Golan," he said in an urgent half-whisper. "Don't shout at her. She's only a girl. Let me deal with this."

Trevize shook his head angrily, but Pelorat said, "Young woman, what is your name?"

The woman smiled with sudden sunniness, as though responding to the softer tone. She said, "Bliss."

"Bliss?" said Pelorat. "A very nice name. Surely that's not all there is."

"Of course not. A fine thing it would be to have one syllable. It would be duplicated on every section and we wouldn't tell one from another, so that the men would be dying for the wrong body. Blissenobiarella is my name in full."

"Now *that's* a mouthful."

"What? Seven syllables? That's not much. I have friends with fifteen syllables in their names and they never get done trying combinations for the friend-name. I've stuck with Bliss now ever since I turned fifteen. My mother called me 'Nobby,' if you can imagine such a thing."

"In Galactic Standard, 'bliss' means 'ecstasy' or 'extreme happiness,'" said Pelorat.

"In Gaian language, too. It's not *very* different from Standard, and 'ecstasy' is the impression I intend to convey."

"My name is Janov Pelorat."

"I know that. And this other gentleman—the shouter— is Golan Trevize. We received word from Sayshell."

Trevize said at once, his eyes narrow, "How did you receive word?"

Bliss turned to look at him and said calmly, "I didn't. Gaia did."

Pelorat said, "Miss Bliss, may my partner and myself speak privately for a moment?"

"Yes, certainly, but we have to get on with it, you know."

"I won't take long." He pulled hard at Trevize's elbow and was reluctantly followed into the other room.

Trevize said in a whisper, "What's all this? I'm sure she can hear us in here. She can probably read our minds, blast the creature."

"Whether she can or can't, we need a bit of psychological isolation for just a moment. Look, old chap, leave her alone. There's nothing we can do, and there's no use taking that out on her. There's probably nothing she can do either. She's just a messenger girl. Actually, as long as she's on board, we're probably safe; they wouldn't have put her on board if they intended to destroy the ship. Keep bullying and perhaps they will destroy it—and us—after they take her off."

"I don't like being helpless," said Trevize grumpily.

"Who does? But acting like a bully doesn't make you less helpless. It just makes you a helpless bully. Oh, my dear chap, I don't mean to be bullying you like this and you must forgive me if I'm excessively critical of you, but the girl is not to be blamed."

"Janov, she's young enough to be your youngest daughter."

Pelorat straightened. "All the more reason to treat her gently. Nor do I know what you imply by the statement."

Trevize thought a moment, then his face cleared. "Very well. You're right. I'm wrong. It is irritating, though, to have them send a girl. They might have sent a military officer, for instance, and given us a sense of some *value*, so to speak. Just a girl? And she keeps placing responsibility on Gaia?"

"She's probably referring to a ruler who takes the name of the planet as an honorific—or else she's referring to the planetary council. We'll find out, but probably not by direct questioning."

"Men have died for her body!" said Trevize. "Huh!" —She's bottom-heavy!"

"No one is asking you to die for it, Golan," said Pelorat gently. "Come! Allow her a sense of self-mockery. I consider it amusing and good-natured, myself."

They found Bliss at the computer, bending down and staring at its component parts with her hands behind her back as though she feared touching it.

She looked up as they entered, ducking their heads under the low lintel. "This is an amazing ship," she said. "I don't understand half of what I see, but if you're going to give me a greeting-present, this is it. It's beautiful. It makes my ship look awful."

Her face took on a look of ardent curiosity. "Are you really from the Foundation?"

"How do you know about the Foundation?" asked Pelorat.

"We learn about it in school. Mostly because of the Mule."

"Why because of the Mule, Bliss?"

"He's one of us, gentle— What syllable of your name may I use, gentleman?"

Pelorat said, "Either Jan or Pel. Which do you prefer?"

"He's one of us, Pel," said Bliss with a comradely smile. "He was born on Gaia, but no one seems to know where exactly."

Trevize said, "I imagine he's a Gaian hero, Bliss, eh?" He had become determinedly, almost aggressively, friendly and cast a placating glance in Pelorat's direction. "Call me Trev," he added.

"Oh no," she said at once. "He's a criminal. He left Gaia without permission, and no one should do that. No one knows *how* he did it. But he left, and I guess that's why he came to a bad end. The Foundation beat him in the end."

"The *Second* Foundation?" said Trevize.

"Is there more than one? I suppose if I thought about it I would know, but I'm not interested in history, really. The way I look at it is, I'm interested in what Gaia thinks best.

If history just goes past me, it's because there are enough historians or that I'm not well adapted to it. I'm probably being trained as a space technician myself. I keep being assigned to stints like this and I seem to like it and it stands to reason I wouldn't like it if—"

She was speaking rapidly, almost breathlessly, and Trevize had to make an effort to insert a sentence. "Who's Gaia?"

Bliss looked puzzled at that. "Just Gaia. —Please, Pel and Trev, let's get on with it. We've got to surface."

"We're going there, aren't we?"

"Yes, but slowly. Gaia feels you can move much more rapidly if you use the potential of your ship. Would you do that?"

"We could," said Trevize grimly. "But if I get the control of the ship back, wouldn't I be more likely to zoom off in the opposite direction?"

Bliss laughed. "You're funny. Of course you can't go in any direction Gaia doesn't want you to go. But you can go faster in the direction Gaia *does* want you to go. See?"

"We see," said Trevize, "and I'll try to control my sense of humor. *Where* do I land on the surface?"

"It doesn't matter. You just head downward and you'll land at the right place. Gaia will see to that."

Pelorat said, "And will you stay with us, Bliss, and see that we are treated well?"

"I suppose I can do that. Let's see now, the usual fee for my services—I mean *that* kind of services—can be entered on my balance-card."

"And the other kind of services?"

Bliss giggled. "You're a nice old man."

Pelorat winced.

3.

Bliss reacted to the swoop down to Gaia with a naïve excitement. She said, "There's no feeling of acceleration."

"It's a gravitic drive," said Pelorat. "Everything accelerates together, ourselves included, so we don't feel anything."

"But how does it work, Pel?"

Pelorat shrugged. "I think Trev knows," he said, "but I don't think he's really in a mood to talk about it."

Trevize had dropped down Gaia's gravity-well almost recklessly. The ship responded to his direction, as Bliss had warned him, in a partial manner. An attempt to cross the lines of gravitic force obliquely was accepted—but only with a certain hesitation. An attempt to rise upward was utterly ignored.

The ship was still not his.

Pelorat said mildly, "Aren't you going downward rather rapidly, Golan?"

Trevize, with a kind of flatness to his voice, attempting to avoid anger (more for Pelorat's sake, than anything else) said, "The young lady says that Gaia will take care of us."

Bliss said, "Surely, Pel. Gaia wouldn't let this ship do anything that wasn't safe. Is there anything to eat on board?"

"Yes indeed," said Pelorat. "What would you like?"

"No meat, Pel," said Bliss in a businesslike way, "but I'll take fish or eggs, along with any vegetables you might have."

"Some of the food we have is Sayshellian, Bliss," said Pelorat. "I'm not sure I know what's in it, but you might like it."

"Well, I'll taste some," said Bliss dubiously.

"Are the people on Gaia vegetarian?" asked Pelorat.

"A lot are." Bliss nodded her head vigorously. "It depends on what nutrients the body needs in particular cases. Lately I haven't been hungry for meat, so I suppose I don't need any. And I haven't been aching for anything sweet. Cheese tastes good, and shrimp. I think I probably need to lose weight." She slapped her right buttock with a resounding noise. "I need to lose five or six pounds right here."

"I don't see why," said Pelorat. "It gives you something comfortable to sit on."

Bliss twisted to look down at her rear as best she might.

"Oh well, it doesn't matter. Weight goes up or down as it ought. I shouldn't concern myself."

Trevize was silent because he was struggling with the *Far Star*. He had hesitated a bit too long for orbit and the lower limits of the planetary exosphere were now screaming past the ship. Little by little, the ship was escaping from his control altogether. It was as though something else had learned to handle the gravitic engines. The *Far Star*, acting apparently by itself, curved upward into thinner air and slowed rapidly. It then took a path on its own that brought it into a gentle downward curve.

Bliss had ignored the edgy sound of air resistance and sniffed delicately at the steam rising from the container. She said, "It must be all right, Pel, because if it weren't, it wouldn't smell right and I wouldn't want to eat it." She put a slim finger into it and then licked at the finger. "You guessed correctly, Pel. It's shrimp or something like it. Good!"

With a gesture of dissatisfaction, Trevize abandoned the computer.

"Young woman," he said, as though seeing her for the first time.

"My name is Bliss," said Bliss firmly.

"Bliss, then! You knew our names."

"Yes, Trev."

"How did you know them?"

"It was important that I know them, in order for me to do my job. So I knew them."

"Do you know who Munn Li Compor is?"

"I would—if it were important for me to know who he is. Since I do not know who he is, Mr. Compor is not coming here. For that matter," she paused a moment, "no one is coming here but you two."

"We'll see."

He was looking down. It was a cloudy planet. There wasn't a solid layer of cloud, but it was a broken layer that was remarkably evenly scattered and offered no clear view of any part of the planetary surface.

He switched to microwave and the radarscope glittered. The surface was almost an image of the sky. It seemed a world of islands—rather like Terminus, but more so. None of the islands was very large and none was very isolated. It was something of an approach to a planetary archipelago. The ship's orbit was well inclined to the equatorial plane, but he saw no sign of ice caps.

Neither were there the unmistakable marks of uneven population distribution, as would be expected, for instance, in the illumination of the night side.

"Will I be coming down near the capital city, Bliss?" asked Trevize.

Bliss said indifferently, "Gaia will put you down somewhere convenient."

"I'd prefer a big city."

"Do you mean a large people-grouping?"

"Yes."

"It's up to Gaia."

The ship continued its downward path and Trevize tried to find amusement in guessing on which island it would land.

Whichever it might be, it appeared they would be landing within the hour.

4.

The ship landed in a quiet, almost feathery manner, without a moment of jarring, without one anomalous gravitational effect. They stepped out, one by one: first Bliss, then Pelorat, and finally Trevize.

The weather was comparable to early summer at Terminus City. There was a mild breeze and with what seemed to be a late-morning sun shining brightly down from a mottled sky. The ground was green underfoot and in one direction there were the serried rows of trees that bespoke an orchard, while in the other there was the distant line of seashore.

There was the low hum of what might have been insect life, a flash of bird—or *some* small flying creature—above and to one side, and the *clack-clack* of what might have been some farm instrument.

Pelorat was the first to speak and he mentioned nothing he either saw or heard. Instead, he drew in his breath raspingly and said, "Ah, it smells *good*, like fresh-made applesauce."

Trevize said, "That's probably an apple orchard we're looking at and, for all we know, they're making applesauce."

"On your ship, on the other hand," said Bliss, "it smelled like— Well, it smelled terrible."

"You didn't complain when you were on it," growled Trevize.

"I had to be polite. I was a guest on your ship."

"What's wrong with staying polite?"

"I'm on my own world now. *You're* the guest. *You* be polite."

Pelorat said, "She's probably right about the smell, Golan. Is there any way of airing out the ship?"

"Yes," said Trevize with a snap. "It can be done—if this little creature can assure us that the ship will not be disturbed. She has already shown us she can exert unusual power over the ship."

Bliss drew herself up to her full height. "I'm not exactly little and if leaving your ship alone is what it takes to get it cleaned up, I assure you leaving it alone will be a pleasure."

"And then can we be taken to whoever it is that you speak of as Gaia?" said Trevize.

Bliss looked amused. "I don't know if you're going to believe this, Trev. *I'm* Gaia."

Trevize stared. He had often heard the phrase, "collect one's thoughts" used metaphorically. For the first time in his life, he felt as though he were engaged in the process literally. Finally he said, *"You?"*

"Yes. And the ground. And those trees. And that rabbit

over there in the grass. And the man you can see through the trees. The whole planet and everything on it is Gaia. We're all individuals—we're all separate organisms—but we all share an overall consciousness. The inanimate planet does so least of all, the various forms of life to a varying degree, and human beings most of all—but we all share."

Pelorat said, "I think, Trevize, that she means Gaia is some sort of group consciousness."

Trevize nodded. "I gathered that. —In that case, Bliss, who runs this world?"

Bliss said, "It runs itself. Those trees grow in rank and file of their own accord. They multiply only to the extent that is needed to replace those that for any reason die. Human beings harvest the apples that are needed; other animals, including insects, eat their share—and only their share."

"The insects know what their share is, do they?" said Trevize.

"Yes, they do—in a way. It rains when it is necessary and occasionally it rains rather hard when *that* is necessary—and occasionally there's a siege of dry weather when *that* is necessary."

"And the rain knows what to do, does it?"

"Yes, it does," said Bliss very seriously. "In your own body, don't all the different cells know what to do? When to grow and when to stop growing? When to form certain substances and when not to—and when they form them, just how much to form, neither more nor less? Each cell is, to a certain extent, an independent chemical factory, but all draw from a common fund of raw materials brought to it by a common transportation system, all deliver wastes into common channels, and all contribute to an overall group consciousness."

Pelorat said with a certain enthusiasm, "But that's remarkable. You are saying that the planet is a superorganism and that you are a cell of that superorganism."

"I'm making an analogy, not an identity. We are the

analog of cells, but we are not identical with cells—do you understand?"

"In what way," said Trevize, "are you not cells?"

"We are ourselves made up of cells and have a group consciousness, as far as cells are concerned. This group consciousness, this consciousness of an individual organism—a human being, in my case—"

"With a body men die for."

"Exactly. My consciousness is far advanced beyond that of any individual cell—incredibly far advanced. The fact that we, in turn, are part of a still greater group consciousness on a higher level does not reduce us to the level of cells. I remain a human being—but above us is a group consciousness as far beyond my grasp as my consciousness is beyond that of one of the muscle cells of my biceps."

Trevize said, "Surely someone ordered our ship to be taken."

"No, not someone! Gaia ordered it. All of us ordered it."

"The trees and the ground, too, Bliss?"

"They contributed very little, but they contributed. Look, if a musician writes a symphony, do you ask which particular cell in his body ordered the symphony written and supervised its construction?"

Pelorat said, "And, I take it, the group mind, so to speak, of the group consciousness is much stronger than an individual mind, just as a muscle is much stronger than an individual muscle cell. Consequently Gaia can capture our ship at a distance by controlling our computer, even though no individual mind on the planet could have done so."

"You understand perfectly, Pel," said Bliss.

"And I understand it, too," said Trevize. "It is not that hard to understand. But what do you want of us? We have not come to attack you. We have come seeking information. Why have you seized us?"

"To talk to you."

"You might have talked to us on the ship."

Bliss shook her head gravely, "I am not the one to do it."

"Aren't you part of the group mind?"

"Yes, but I cannot fly like a bird, buzz like an insect, or grow as tall as a tree. I do what it is best for me to do and it is not best that I give you the information—though the knowledge could easily be assigned to me."

"Who decided *not* to assign it to you?"

"We all did."

"Who will give us the information?"

"Dom."

"And who is Dom?"

"Well," said Bliss. "His full name is Endomandioviza-marondeyaso—and so on. Different people call him different syllables at different times, but I know him as Dom and I think you two will use that syllable as well. He probably has a larger share of Gaia than anyone on the planet and he lives on this island. He asked to see you and it was allowed."

"Who allowed it?" asked Trevize—and answered himself at once, "Yes, I know; you all did."

Bliss nodded.

Pelorat said, "When will we be seeing Dom, Bliss?"

"Right away. If you follow me, I'll take you to him now, Pel. And you, too, of course, Trev."

"And will you leave, then?" asked Pelorat.

"You don't want me to, Pel?"

"Actually, no."

"There you are," said Bliss as they followed her along a smoothly paved road that skirted the orchard. "Men grow addicted to me on short order. Even dignified elderly men are overcome with boyish ardor."

Pelorat laughed. "I wouldn't count on much boyish ardor, Bliss, but if I had it I could do no worse than have it on your account, I think."

Bliss said, "Oh, don't discount your boyish ardor. I work wonders."

Trevize said impatiently, "Once we get to where we're going, how long will we have to wait for this Dom?"

"*He* will be waiting for *you*. After all, Dom-through-Gaia has worked for years to bring you here."

Trevize stopped in midstep and looked quickly at Pelorat, who quietly mouthed: You were right.

Bliss, who was looking straight ahead, said calmly, "I know, Trev, that you have suspected that I/we/Gaia was interested in you."

"'I/we/Gaia'?" said Pelorat softly.

She turned to smile at him. "We have a whole complex of different pronouns to express the shades of individuality that exist on Gaia. I could explain them to you, but till then 'I/we/Gaia' gets across what I mean in a groping sort of way. —Please move on, Trev. Dom is waiting and I don't wish to force your legs to move against your will. It is an uncomfortable feeling if you're not used to it."

Trevize moved on. His glance at Bliss was compounded of the deepest suspicion.

5.

Dom was an elderly man. He recited the two hundred and fifty-three syllables of his name in a musical flowing of tone and emphasis.

"In a way," he said, "it is a brief biography of myself. It tells the hearer—or reader, or senser—who I am, what part I have played in the whole, what I have accomplished. For fifty years and more, however, I have been satisfied to be referred to as Dom. When there are other Doms at issue, I can be called Domandio—and in my various professional relationships other variants are used. Once a Gaian year—on my birthday—my full name is recited-in-mind, as I have just recited it for you in voice. It is very effective, but it is personally embarrassing."

He was tall and thin—almost to the point of emaciation. His deep-set eyes sparkled with anomalous youth, though he moved rather slowly. His jutting nose was thin and long and flared at the nostrils. His hands, prominently veined though they were, showed no signs of arthritic disability. He wore a long robe that was as gray as his hair. It descended to his ankles and his sandals left his toes bare.

Trevize said, "How old are you, sir?"

"Please address me as Dom, Trev. To use other modes of address induces formality and inhibits the free exchange of ideas between you and me. In Galactic Standard Years, I am just past ninety-three, but the real celebration will come not very many months from now, when I reach the ninetieth anniversary of my birth in Gaian years."

"I would have not have guessed you at more than seventy-five, s—Dom," said Trevize.

"By Gaian standards I am not remarkable, either in years or in appearance of years, Trev. —But come, have we eaten?"

Pelorat looked down at his plate, on which perceptible remnants of a most unremarkable and indifferently prepared meal remained, and said in a diffident manner, "Dom, may I attempt to ask an embarrassing question? Of course, if it's offensive, you will please say so, and I will withdraw it."

"Go ahead," said Dom, smiling. "I am anxious to explain to you anything about Gaia which arouses your curiosity."

"Why?" said Trevize at once.

"Because you are honored guests— May I have Pel's question?"

Pelorat said, "Since all things on Gaia share in the group consciousness, how is it that you—one element of the group—can eat this, which was clearly another element?"

"True! But all things recycle. We must eat and everything we can eat, plant as well as animal—even the inanimate seasonings—are part of Gaia. But, then, you see, nothing is killed for pleasure or sport, nothing is killed with unnecessary pain. And I'm afraid we make no attempt to glorify our meal preparations, for no Gaian would eat except that one must. You did not enjoy this meal, Pel? Trev? Well, meals are not to enjoy.

"Then, too, what is eaten remains, after all, part of the planetary consciousness. Insofar as portions of it are incorporated into my body, it will participate in a larger share of the total consciousness. When I die, I, too, will be eaten—even if only by decay bacteria—and I will then participate in a far smaller share of the total. But someday, parts of me will be parts of other human beings, parts of many."

Pelorat said, "A sort of transmigration of souls."

"Of what, Pel?"

"I speak of an old myth that is current on some worlds."

"Ah, I don't know of it. You must tell me on some occasion."

Trevize said, "But your individual consciousness—whatever it is about you that is Dom—will never fully reassemble."

"No, of course not. But does that matter? I will be part of Gaia and that is what counts. There are mystics among us who wonder if we should take measures to develop group memories of past existences, but the sense-of-Gaia is that this cannot be done in any practical way and would serve no useful purpose. It would merely blur present consciousness. —Of course, as conditions change, the sense-of-Gaia may change, too, but I find no chance of that in the foreseeable future."

"Why must you die, Dom?" asked Trevize. "Look at you in your nineties. Could not the group consciousness—"

For the first time, Dom frowned. "Never," he said. "I can contribute only so much. Each new individual is a reshuffling of molecules and genes into something new. New talents, new abilities, new contributions to Gaia. We must have them—and the only way we can is to make room. I have done more than most, but even I have my limit and it is approaching. There is no more desire to live past one's time than to die before it."

And then, as if realizing he had lent a suddenly somber note to the evening, he rose and stretched his arms out to the two. "Come, Trev—Pel—let us move into my studio where I can show you some of my personal art objects. You won't blame an old man for his little vanities, I hope."

He led the way into another room where, on a small circular table, there was a group of smoky lenses connected in pairs.

"These," said Dom, "are Participations I have designed. I am not one of the masters, but I specialize in inanimates, which few of the masters bother with."

Pelorat said, "May I pick one up? Are they fragile?"

"No no. Bounce them on the floor if you like. —Or perhaps you had better not. Concussion could dull the sharpness of the vision."

"How are they used, Dom?"

"You put them over your eyes. They'll cling. They do not transmit light. Quite the contrary. They obscure light that might otherwise distract you—though the sensations do reach your brain by way of the optic nerve. Essentially your consciousness is sharpened and is allowed to participate in other facets of Gaia. In other words, if you look at that wall, you will experience that wall as it appears to itself."

"Fascinating," muttered Pelorat. "May I try that?"

"Certainly, Pel. You may take one at random. Each is a different construct that shows the wall—or any other inanimate object you look at—in a different aspect of the object's consciousness."

Pelorat placed one pair over his eyes and they clung there at once. He started at the touch and then remained motionless for a long time.

Dom said, "When you are through, place your hands on either side of the Participation and press them toward each other. It will come right off."

Pelorat did so, blinked his eyes rapidly, then rubbed them.

Dom said, "What did you experience?"

Pelorat said, "It's hard to describe. The wall seemed to twinkle and glisten and, at times, it seemed to turn fluid. It seemed to have ribs and changing symmetries. I—I'm sorry, Dom, but I did not find it attractive."

Dom sighed. "You do not participate in Gaia, so you would not see what we see. I had rather feared that. Too bad! I assure you that although these Participations are enjoyed primarily for their aesthetic value, they have their practical uses, too. A happy wall is a long-lived wall, a practical wall, a useful wall."

"A *happy* wall?" said Trevize, smiling slightly.

Dom said, "There is a dim sensation that a wall experiences that is analogous to what 'happy' means to us. A wall is happy when it is well designed, when it rests firmly on its foundation, when its symmetry balances its parts and produces no unpleasant stresses. Good design can be worked out on the mathematical principles of mechanics, but the use of a proper Participation can fine tune it down to virtually atomic dimensions. No sculptor can possibly produce a first-class work of art here on Gaia without a well-crafted Participation and the ones I produce of this particular type are considered excellent—if I do say so myself."

"Animate Participations, which are not my field," and Dom was going on with the kind of excitement one expects in someone riding his hobby, "give us, by analogy, a direct experience of ecological balance. The ecological balance on Gaia is rather simple, as it is on all worlds, but here, at least, we have the hope of making it more complex and thus enriching the total consciousness enormously."

Trevize held up his hand in order to forestall Pelorat and wave him into silence. He said, "How do you know that a planet can bear a more complex ecological balance if they all have simple ones?"

"Ah," said Dom, his eyes twinkling shrewdly, "you are testing the old man. You know as well as I do that the original home of humanity, Earth, had an enormously complex ecological balance. It is only the secondary worlds—the derived worlds—that are simple."

Pelorat would not be kept silent. "But that is the problem I have set myself in life. Why was it only Earth that bore a complex ecology? What distinguished it from other worlds? Why did millions upon millions of other worlds in the Galaxy—worlds that were capable of bearing life—develop only an undistinguished vegetation, together with small and unintelligent animal life-forms?"

Dom said, "We have a tale about that—a fable, perhaps. I cannot vouch for its authenticity. In fact, on the face of it, it sounds like fiction."

It was at this point that Bliss—who had not participated in the meal—entered, smiling at Pelorat. She was wearing a silvery blouse, very sheer.

Pelorat rose at once. "I thought you had left us."

"Not at all. I had reports to make out, work to do. May I join you now, Dom?"

Dom had also risen (though Trevize remained seated). "You are entirely welcome and you ravish these aged eyes."

"It is for your ravishment that I put on this blouse. Pel is above such things and Trev dislikes them."

Pelorat said, "If you think I am above such things, Bliss, I may surprise you someday."

"What a delightful surprise that would be," Bliss said, and sat down. The two men did as well. "Please don't let me interrupt you."

Dom said, "I was about to tell our guests the story of Eternity. —To understand it, you must first understand that there are many different Universes that can exist—virtually an infinite number. Every single event that takes place can take place or not take place, or can take place in this fashion or in that fashion, and each of an enormous number of alternatives will result in a future course of events that are distinct to at least some degree.

"Bliss might not have come in just now; or she might have been with us a little earlier; or much earlier; or having come in now, she might have worn a different blouse; or even in this blouse, she might not have smiled roguishly at elderly men as is her kindhearted custom. In each of these alternatives—or in each of a very large number of other alternatives of this one event—the Universe would have taken a different track thereafter, and so on for every other variation of every other event, however minor."

Trevize stirred restlessly. "I believe this is a common speculation in quantum mechanics—a very ancient one, in fact."

"Ah, you've heard of it. But let us go on. Imagine it is possible for human beings to freeze all the infinite number of Universes, to step from one to another at will, and to choose which one should be made 'real'—whatever that word means in this connection."

Trevize said, "I hear your words and can even imagine the concept you describe, but I cannot make myself believe that anything like this could ever happen."

"Nor I, on the whole," said Dom, "which is why I say that it would all seem to be a fable. Nevertheless, the fable states that there *were* those who could step out of time and examine the endless strands of potential reality. These people were called the Eternals and when they were out of time they were said to be in Eternity.

"It was their task to choose a Reality that would be most suitable to humanity. They modified endlessly—and the story goes into great detail, for I must tell you that it has been written in the form of an epic of inordinate length. Eventually they found (or it is said) a Universe in which Earth was the only planet in the entire Galaxy on which could be found a complex ecological system, together with the development of an intelligent species capable of working out a high technology.

"That, they decided, was the situation in which humanity could be most secure. They froze that strand of events as Reality and then ceased operations. Now we live in a Galaxy that has been settled by human beings only, and, to a large extent, by the plants, animals, and microscopic life that they carry with them—voluntarily or inadvertently—from planet to planet and which usually overwhelm the indigenous life.

"Somewhere in the dim mists of probability there are other Realities in which the Galaxy is host to many intelligences, but they are unreachable. We in our Reality are alone. From every action and every event in our Reality, there are new branches that set off, with only one in each separate case being a continuation of Reality, so that there are vast numbers of potential Universes—perhaps an infinite number—stemming from ours, but all of them are presumably alike in containing the one-intelligence Galaxy in which we live. —Or perhaps I should say that all but a vanishingly small percentage are alike in this way, for it is dangerous to rule out anything where the possibilities approach the infinite."

He stopped, shrugged slightly, and added, "At least, that's the story. It dates back to before the founding of Gaia. I don't vouch for its truth."

The three others had listened intently. Bliss nodded her head, as though it were something she had heard before and she were checking the accuracy of Dom's account.

Pelorat reacted with a silent solemnity for the better part of a minute and then balled his fist and brought it down upon the arm of his chair.

"No," he said in a strangled voice, "that affects nothing. There's no way of demonstrating the truth of the story by observation or by reason, so it can't ever be anything but a piece of speculation, but aside from that— Suppose it's true! The Universe we live in is still one in which only Earth has developed a rich life and an intelligent species, so that in *this* Universe—whether it is the all-in-all or only one out of an infinite number of possibilities—there must be something unique in the nature of the planet Earth. We should still want to know what that uniqueness is."

In the silence that followed, it was Trevize who finally stirred and shook his head.

"No, Janov," he said, "that's not the way it works. Let us say that the chances are one in a billion trillion—one in 10^{21}—that out of the billion of habitable planets in the Galaxy only Earth—through the workings of sheer chance—would happen to develop a rich ecology and, eventually, intelligence. If that is so, then one in 10^{21} of the various strands of potential Realities would represent such a Galaxy and the Eternals picked it. We live, therefore, in a Universe in which Earth is the only planet to develop a complex ecology, an intelligent species, a high technology—not because there is something special about Earth, but because simply by chance it developed on Earth and nowhere else.

"I suppose, in fact," Trevize went on thoughtfully, "that there are strands of Reality in which only Gaia has developed an intelligent species, or only Sayshell, or only Terminus, or only some plane which in *this* Reality happens to bear no life at all. And all of these very special cases are a vanishingly small percentage of the total number of Realities in which there is more than one intelligent species in the Galaxy. —I suppose that if the Eternals had looked long enough they would have found a potential strand of Reality in which every single habitable planet had developed an intelligent species."

Pelorat said, "Might you not also argue that a Reality had been found in which Earth was for some reason not as it was in other strands, but specially suited in some way for the development of intelligence? In fact, you can go further and say that a Reality had been found in which the whole Galaxy was not as it was in other strands, but was somehow in such a state of development that only Earth could produce intelligence."

Trevize said, "You might argue so, but I would suppose that my version makes more sense."

"That's a purely subjective decision, of course—" began Pelorat with some heat, but Dom interrupted, saying, "This is logic-chopping. Come, let us not spoil what is proving, at least for me, a pleasant and leisurely evening."

Pelorat endeavored to relax and to allow his heat to drain away. He smiled finally and said, "As you say, Dom."

Trevize, who had been casting glances at Bliss, who sat with mocking demurity, hands in her lap, now said, "And how did *this* world come to be, Dom? Gaia, with its group consciousness?"

Dom's old head leaned back and he laughed in a high-pitched manner. His face crinkled as he said, "Fables again! I think about that sometimes, when I read what records we

have on human history. No matter how carefully records
are kept and filed and computerized, they grow fuzzy with
time. Stories grow by accretion. Tales accumulate—like
dust. The longer the time lapse, the dustier the history—
until it degenerates into fables."

Pelorat said, "We historians are familiar with the process,
Dom. There is a certain preference for the fable. 'The falsely
dramatic drives out the truly dull,' said Liebel Gennerat
about fifteen centuries ago. It's called Gennerat's Law now."

"Is it?" said Dom. "And I thought the notion was a
cynical invention of my own. Well, Gennerat's Law fills
our past history with glamour and uncertainty. —Do you
know what a robot is?"

"We found out on Sayshell," said Trevize dryly.

"You saw one?"

"No. We were asked the question and, when we answered
in the negative, it was explained to us."

"I understand. —Humanity once lived with robots, you
know, but it didn't work well."

"So we were told."

"The robots were deeply indoctrinated with what are
called the Three Laws of Robotics, which date back into
prehistory. There are several versions of what those Three
Laws might have been. The orthodox view has the following
reading: '1) A robot may not harm a human being or, through
inaction, allow a human being to come to harm; 2) A robot
must obey the orders given it by human beings, except where
such orders would conflict with the First Law; 3) A robot
must protect its own existence, as long as such protection
does not conflict with the First or Second Law.'

"As robots grew more intelligent and versatile, they interpreted these Laws, especially the all-overriding First,
more and more generously and assumed, to a greater and
greater degree, the role of protector of humanity. The protection stifled people and grew unbearable.

"The robots were entirely kind. Their labors were clearly
humane and were meant entirely for the benefit of all—
which somehow made them all the more unbearable.

"Every robotic advance made the situation worse. Robots were developed with telepathic capacity, but that meant that even human thought could be monitored, so that human behavior became still more dependent on robotic oversight.

"Again robots grew steadily more like human beings in appearance, but they were unmistakably robots in behavior and being humanoid made them more repulsive. So, of course, it had to come to an end."

"Why 'of course'?" asked Pelorat, who had been listening intently.

Dom said, "It's a matter of following the logic to the bitter end. Eventually, the robots grew advanced enough to become just sufficiently human to appreciate why human beings should resent being deprived of everything human in the name of their own good. In the long run, the robots were forced to decide that humanity might be better off caring for themselves, however carelessly and ineffectively.

"Therefore, it is said, it was the robots who established Eternity somehow and became the Eternals. They located a Reality in which they felt that human beings could be as secure as possible—alone in the Galaxy. Then, having done what they could to guard us and in order to fulfill the First Law in the truest sense, the robots of their own accord ceased to function and ever since we have been human beings— advancing, however we can, alone."

Dom paused. He looked from Trevize to Pelorat, and then said, "Well, do you believe all that?"

Trevize shook his head slowly. "No. There is nothing like this in any historical record I have ever heard of. How about you, Janov?"

Pelorat said, "There are myths that are similiar in some ways."

"Come, Janov, there are myths that would match anything that any of us can make up, given sufficiently ingenious interpretation. I'm talking about history—reliable records."

"Oh well. Nothing there, as far as I know."

Dom said, "I'm not surprised. Before the robots withdrew, many parties of human beings left to colonize robotless worlds in deeper space, in order to take their own measures of freedom. They came particularly from overcrowded Earth, with its long history of resistance to robots. The new worlds were founded fresh and they did not even want to remember their bitter humiliation as children under robot nursemaids. They kept no records of it and they forgot."

Trevize said, "This is unlikely."

Pelorat turned to him. "No, Golan. It's not at all unlikely. Societies create their own history and tend to wipe out lowly beginnings, either by forgetting them or inventing totally fictitious heroic rescues. The Imperial government made attempts to suppress knowledge of the pre-Imperial past in order to strengthen the mystic aura of eternal rule. Then, too, there are almost no records of the days before hyperspatial travel—and you know that the very existence of Earth is unknown to most people today."

Trevize said, "You can't have it both ways, Janov. If the Galaxy has forgotten the robots, how is it that Gaia remembers?"

Bliss intervened with a sudden lilt of soprano laughter. "We're different."

"Yes?" said Trevize. "In what way?"

Dom said, "Now, Bliss, leave this to me. We *are* different, men of Terminus. Of all the refugee groups fleeing from robotic domination, we who eventually reached Gaia (following in the track of others who reached Sayshell) were the only ones who had learned the craft of telepathy from the robots.

"It *is* a craft, you know. It is inherent in the human mind, but it must be developed in a very subtle and difficult manner. It takes many generations to reach its full potential, but once well begun, it feeds on itself. We have been at it for over twenty thousand years and the sense-of-Gaia is that full potential has even now not been reached. It was long ago that our development of telepathy made us aware of group consciousness—first only of human beings; then animals; then plants; and finally, not many centuries ago, the inanimate structure of the planet itself."

"Because we traced this back to the robots, we did not forget them. We considered them not our nursemaids but our teachers. We felt they had opened our mind to something we would never for one moment want them closed to. We remember them with gratitude."

Trevize said, "But just as once you were children to the robots, now you are children to the group consciousness. Have you not lost humanity now, as you had then?"

"It is different, Trev. What we do now is our own choice— our own choice. That is what counts. It is not forced on us from outside, but is developed from the inside. It is something we never forget. And we are different in another way, too. We are unique in the Galaxy. There is no world like Gaia."

"How can you be sure?"

"We would know, Trev. We would detect a world consciousness such as ours even at the other end of the Galaxy. We can detect the beginnings of such a consciousness in your Second Foundation, for instance, though not until two centuries ago."

"At the time of the Mule?"

"Yes. One of ours." Dom looked grim. "He was an aberrant and he left us. We were naïve enough to think that was not possible, so we did not act in time to stop him. Then, when we turned our attention to the Outside Worlds, we became aware of what you call the Second Foundation and we left it to them."

Trevize stared blankly for several moments, then muttered, "There go our history books!" He shook his head and said in a louder tone of voice, "That was rather cowardly of Gaia, wasn't it, to do so?" said Trevize. "He was your responsibility."

"You are right. But once we finally turned our eyes upon the Galaxy, we saw what until then we had been blind to, so that the tragedy of the Mule proved a life-saving matter to us. It was then that we recognized that eventually a dangerous crisis would come upon us. And it has—but not before we were able to take measures, thanks to the incident of the Mule."

"What sort of crisis?"

"One that threatens us with destruction."

"I can't believe that. You held off the Empire, the Mule, and Sayshell. You have a group consciousness that can pluck a ship out of space at a distance of millions of kilometers. What can you have to fear? —Look at Bliss. She doesn't look the least bit perturbed. *She* doesn't think there's a crisis."

Bliss had placed one shapely leg over the arm of the chair and wriggled her toes at him. "Of course I'm not worried, Trev. You'll handle it."

Trev said forcefully, *"Me?"*

Dom said, "Gaia has brought you here by means of a hundred gentle manipulations. It is you who must face our crisis."

Trev stared at him and slowly his face turned from stupefaction into gathering rage. *"Me?* Why, in all of space, *me?"* I have nothing to do with this."

"Nevertheless, Trev," said Dom with an almost hypnotic calmness, *"you.* Only you. In all of space, only you."

18. COLLISION

I.

Stor Gendibal was edging toward Gaia almost as cautiously as Trevize had—and now that its star was a perceptible disc and could be viewed only through strong filters, he paused to consider.

Sura Novi sat to one side, looking up at him now and then in a timorous manner.

She said softly, "Master?"

"What is it, Novi?" he asked abstractedly.

"Are you unhappy?"

He looked up at her quickly. "No. Concerned. Remember that word? I am trying to decide whether to move in quickly or to wait longer. Shall I be very brave, Novi?"

"I think you are very brave all times, Master."

"To be brave is sometimes to be foolish."

Novi smiled. "How can a master scholar be foolish? —That is a sun, is it not, Master?" She pointed to the screen.

Gendibal nodded.

Novi said, after an irresolute pause, "Is it the sun that shines on Trantor? Is it the Hamish sun?"

Gendibal said, "No, Novi. It is a far different sun. There are many suns, billions of them."

"Ah! I have known this with my head. I could not make myself believe, however. How is it, Master, that one can know with the head—and yet not believe?"

Gendibal smiled faintly, "In your head, Novi—" he began and, automatically, as he said that, he found himself in her head. He stroked it gently, as he always did, when he found himself there—just a soothing touch of mental tendrils to keep her calm and untroubled—and he would then have left again, as he always did, had not something drawn him back.

What he sensed was indescribable in any but mentalic terms, but metaphorically, Novi's brain glowed. It was the faintest possible glow.

It would not be there except for the existence of a mentalic field imposed from without—a mentalic field of an intensity so small that the finest receiving function of Gendibal's own well-trained mind could just barely detect it, even against the utter smoothness of Novi's mentalic structure.

He said sharply, "Novi, how do you feel?"

Her eyes opened wide. "I feel well, Master."

"Are you dizzy, confused? Close your eyes and sit absolutely still until I say, 'Now.'"

Obediently she closed her eyes. Carefully Gendibal brushed away all extraneous sensations from her mind, quieted her thoughts, soothed her emotions, stroked—stroked— He left nothing but the glow and it was so faint that he could almost persuade himself it was not there.

"Now," he said and Novi opened her eyes.

"How do you feel, Novi?"

"Very calm, Master. Rested."

It was clearly too feeble for it to have any noticeable effect on her.

He turned to the computer and wrestled with it. He had to admit to himself that he and the computer did not mesh very well together. Perhaps it was because he was too used to using his mind directly to be able to work through an intermediary. But he was looking for a ship, not a mind, and the initial search could be done more efficiently with the help of the computer.

And he found the sort of ship he suspected might be present. It was half a million kilometers away and it was much like his own in design, but it was much larger and more elaborate.

Once it was located with the computer's help, Gendibal could allow his mind to take over directly. He sent it outward—tight-beamed—and with it felt (or the mentalic equivalent of "felt") the ship, inside and out.

He then sent his mind toward the planet Gaia, approaching it more closely by several millions of kilometers of space—and withdrew. Neither process was sufficient in itself to tell him, unmistakably, which—if either—was the source of the field.

He said, "Novi, I would like you to sit next to me for what is to follow."

"Master, is there danger?"

"You are not to be in any way concerned, Novi. I will see to it that you are safe and secure."

"Master, I am not concerned that I be safe and secure. If there is danger, I want to be able to help you."

Gendibal softened. He said, "Novi, you have already helped. Because of you, I became aware of a very small thing it was important to be aware of. Without you, I might have blundered rather deeply into a bog and might have had to pull out only through a great deal of trouble."

"Have I done this with my mind, Master, as you once explained?" asked Novi, astonished.

"Quite so, Novi. No instrument could have been more sensitive. My own mind is not; it is too full of complexity."

Delight filled Novi's face. "I am so grateful I can help."

Gendibal smiled and nodded—and then subsided into the somber knowledge that he would need other help as well. Something childish within him objected. The job was his—his alone.

Yet it could not be his alone. The odds were climbing—

2.

On Trantor, Quindor Shandess felt the responsibility of First Speakerhood resting upon him with a suffocating weight. Since Gendibal's ship had vanished into the darkness beyond the atmosphere, he had called no meetings of the Table. He had been lost in his own thoughts.

Had it been wise to allow Gendibal to go off on his own? Gendibal was brilliant, but not so brilliant that it left no room for overconfidence. Gendibal's great fault was arrogance, as Shandess's own great fault (he thought bitterly) was the weariness of age.

Over and over again, it occurred to him that the precedent of Preem Palver, flitting over the Galaxy to set things right, was a dangerous one. Could anyone else be a Preem Palver? Even Gendibal? And Palver had had his wife with him.

To be sure, Gendibal had this Hamishwoman, but she was of no consequence. Palver's wife had been a Speaker in her own right.

Shandess felt himself aging from day to day as he waited for word from Gendibal—and with each day that word did not come, he felt an increasing tension.

It should have been a fleet of ships, a flotilla—

No. The Table would not have allowed it.

And yet—

When the call finally came, he was asleep—an exhausted sleep that was bringing him no relief. The night had been windy and he had had trouble falling asleep to begin with. Like a child, he had imagined voices in the wind.

His last thoughts before falling into an exhausted slumber had been a wistful building of the fancy of resignation, a wish he could do so together with the knowledge he could not, for at this moment Delarmi would succeed him.

And then the call came and he sat up in bed, instantly awake.

"You are well?" he said.

"Perfectly well, First Speaker," said Gendibal. "Should we have visual connection for more condensed communication?"

"Later, perhaps," said Shandess. "First, what is the situation?"

Gendibal spoke carefully, for he sensed the other's recent arousal and he perceived a deep weariness. He said, "I am in the neighborhood of an inhabited planet called Gaia, whose existence is not hinted at in any of the Galactic records, as far as I know."

"The world of those who have been working to perfect the Plan? The Anti-Mules?"

"Possibly, First Speaker. There is the reason to think so. First, the ship bearing Trevize and Pelorat has moved far in toward Gaia and has probably landed there. Second, there is, in space, about half a million kilometers from me, a First Foundation warship."

"There cannot be this much interest for no reason.."

"First Speaker, this may not be independent interest. I am here only because I am following Trevize—and the warship may be here for the same reason. It remains only to be asked why Trevize is here."

"Do you plan to follow him in toward the planet, Speaker?"

"I had considered that a possibility, but something has come up. I am now a hundred million kilometers from Gaia and I sense in the space about me a mentalic field—a homogeneous one that is excessively faint. I would not have been aware of it at all, but for the focusing effect of the mind of the Hamishwoman. It is an unusual mind; I agreed to take her with me for that very purpose."

"You were right, then, in supposing it would be so— Did Speaker Delarmi know this, do you think?"

"When she urged me to take the woman? I scarcely think so—but I gladly took advantage of it, First Speaker."

"I am pleased that you did. Is it your opinion, Speaker Gendibal, that the planet is the focus of the field?"

"To ascertain that, I would have to take measurements at widely spaced points in order to see if there is a general spherical symmetry to the field. My unidirectional mental probe made this seem likely but not certain. Yet it would not be wise to investigate further in the presence of the First Foundation warship."

"Surely it is no threat."

"It may be. I cannot as yet be sure that it is not itself the focus of the field, First Speaker."

"But they—"

"First Speaker, with respect, allow me to interrupt. We do not know what technological advances the First Foundation has made. They are acting with a strange self-confidence and may have unpleasant surprises for us. It must be decided whether they have learned to handle mentalics by means of some of their devices. In short, First Speaker, I am facing either a warship of mentalics or a planet of them.

"If it is the warship, then the mentalics may be far too weak to immobilize me, but they might be enough to slow me—and the purely physical weapons on the warship may then suffice to destroy me. On the other hand, if it is the planet that is the focus, then to have the field detectable at such a distance could mean enormous intensity at the surface—more than even I can handle.

"In either case, it will be necessary to set up a network— a total network—in which, at need, the full resources of Trantor can be placed at my disposal."

The First Speaker hesitated. "A *total* network. This has never been used, never even suggested—except in the time of the Mule."

"This crisis may well be even greater than that of the Mule, First Speaker."

"I do not know that the Table would agree."

"I do not think you should ask them to agree, First Speaker. You should invoke a state of emergency."

"What excuse can I give?"

"Tell them what I have told you, First Speaker."

"Speaker Delarmi will say that you are an incompetent coward, driven to madness by your own fears."

Gendibal paused before answering. Then he said, "I imagine she will say something like that, First Speaker, but let her say whatever she likes and I will survive it. What is at stake now is not my pride or self-love but the actual existence of the Second Foundation."

3.

Harla Branno smiled grimly, her lined face setting more deeply into its fleshy crags. She said, "I think we can push on with it. I'm ready for them."

Kodell said, "Do you still feel sure you know what you're doing?"

"If I were as mad as you pretend you think I am, Liono, would you have insisted on remaining on this ship with me?"

Kodell shrugged and said, "Probably. I would then be here on the off chance, Madam Mayor, that I might stop you, divert you, at least slow you, before you went too far. And, of course, if you're not mad—"

"Yes?"

"Why, then I wouldn't want to have the histories of the future give you all the mention. Let them state that I was here with you and wonder, perhaps, to whom the credit really belongs, eh, Mayor?"

"Clever, Liono, clever—but quite futile. I was the power behind the throne through too many Mayoralties for anyone to believe I would permit such a phenomenon in my own administration."

"We shall see."

"No, we won't, for such historical judgments will come after we are dead. However, I have no fears. Not about my place in history and not about *that*," and she pointed to the screen.

"Compor's ship," said Kodell.

"Compor's ship, true," said Branno, "but without Compor aboard. One of our scoutships observed the changeover. Compor's ship was stopped by another. Two people from the other ship boarded that one and Compor later moved off and entered the other."

Branno rubbed her hands. "Trevize fulfilled his role perfectly. I cast him out into space in order that he might serve as lightning rod and so he did. He drew lightning. The ship that stopped Compor was Second Foundation."

"How can you be sure of that, I wonder?" said Kodell, taking out his pipe and slowly beginning to pack it with tobacco.

"Because I always wondered if Compor might not be under Second Foundation control. His life was too smooth. Things always broke right for him—and he was such an expert at hyperspatial tracking. His betrayal of Trevize might easily have been the simple politics of an ambitious man— but he did it with such unnecessary thoroughness, as though there were more than personal ambition to it."

"All guesswork, Mayor!"

"The guesswork stopped when he followed Trevize through multiple Jumps as easily as if there had been but one."

"He had the computer to help, Mayor."

But Branno leaned her head back and laughed. "My dear Liono, you are so busy devising intricate plots that you forget the efficacy of simple procedures. I sent Compor to follow Trevize, not because I needed to have Trevize followed. What need was there for that? Trevize, however much he might want to keep his movements secret, could not help but call attention to himself in any non-Foundation world he visited. His advanced Foundation vessel—his strong Terminus accent—his Foundation credits—would automatically surround him with a glow of notoriety. And in case of any emergency, he would automatically turn to Foundation officials for help, as he did on Sayshell, where we knew all that he did as soon as he did it—and quite independently of Compor.

"No," she went on thoughtfully, "Compor was sent out to test *Compor*. And that succeeded, for we gave him a defective computer quite deliberately; not one that was defective enough to make the ship unmaneuverable, but certainly one that was insufficiently agile to aid him in following a multiple Jump. Yet Compor managed that without trouble."

"I see there's a great deal you don't tell me, Mayor, until you decide you ought to."

"I only keep those matters from you, Liono, that it will

not hurt you not to know. I admire you and I use you, but there are sharp limits to my trust, as there is in yours for me—and please don't bother to deny it."

"I won't," said Kodell dryly, "and someday, Mayor, I will take the liberty of reminding you of that. —Meanwhile, is there anything else that I ought to know now? What is the nature of the ship that stopped them? Surely, if Compor is Second Foundation, so was that ship."

"It is always a pleasure to speak to you, Liono. You see things quickly. The Second Foundation, you see, doesn't bother to hide its tracks. It has defenses that it relies on to make those tracks invisible, even when they are not. It would never occur to a Second Foundationer to use a ship of alien manufacture, even if they knew how neatly we could identify the origin of a ship from the pattern of its energy use. They could always remove that knowledge from any mind that had gained it, so why bother taking the trouble to hide? Well, our scout ship was able to determine the origin of the ship that approached Compor within minutes of sighting it."

"And now the Second Foundation will wipe that knowledge from our minds, I suppose."

"If they can," said Branno, "but they may find that things have changed."

Kodell said, "Earlier you said you knew where the Second Foundation was. You would take care of Gaia first, then Trantor. I deduce from this that the other ship was of Trantorian origin."

"You suppose correctly. Are you surprised?"

Kodell shook his head slowly. "Not in hindsight. Ebling Mis, Toran Darell and Bayta Darell were all on Trantor during the period when the Mule was stopped. Arkady Darell, Bayta's granddaughter, was born on Trantor and was on Trantor again when the Second Foundation was itself supposedly stopped. In her account of events, there is a Preem Palver who played a key role, appearing at convenient times, and he was a Trantorian trader. I should think it was obvious that the Second Foundation was on Trantor, where, incidentally, Hari Seldon himself lived at the time he founded both Foundations."

"Quite obvious, except that no one ever suggested the possibility. The Second Foundation saw to that. It is what I meant when I said they didn't have to cover their tracks, when they could so easily arrange to have no one look in the direction of those tracks—or wipe out the memory of those tracks after they had been seen."

Kodell said, "In that case, let us not look too quickly in the direction in which they may simply be wanting us to look. How is it, do you suppose, that Trevize was able to decide the Second Foundation existed? Why didn't the Second Foundation stop him?"

Branno held up her gnarled fingers and counted on them. "First, Trevize is a very unusual man who, for all his obstreperous inability to use caution, has *something* about him that I have not been able to penetrate. He may be a special case. Second, the Second Foundation was not entirely ignorant. Compor was on Trevize's tail at once and reported him to me. I was relied on to stop Trevize without the Second Foundation having to risk open involvement. Third, when I didn't quite react as expected—no execution, no imprisonment, no memory erasure, no Psychic Probe of his brain— when I merely sent him out into space, the Second Foundation went further. They made the direct move of sending one of their own ships after him."

And she added with tight-lipped pleasure, "Oh, excellent lightning rod."

Kodell said, "And our next move?"

"We are going to challenge that Second Foundationer we now face. In fact, we're moving toward him rather sedately right now."

4.

Gendibal and Novi sat together, side by side, watching the screen.

Novi was frightened. To Gendibal, that was quite ap-

parent, as was the fact that she was desperately trying to
fight off that fright. Nor could Gendibal do anything to help
her in her struggle, for he did not think it wise to touch her
mind at this moment, lest he obscure the response she displayed to the feeble mentalic field that surrounded them.

The Foundation warship was approaching slowly—but
deliberately. It was a large warship, with a crew of perhaps
as many as six, judging from past experience with Foundation ships. Her weapons, Gendibal was certain, would be
sufficient in themselves to hold off and, if necessary, wipe
out a fleet made up of every ship available to the Second
Foundation—if those ships had to rely on physical force
alone.

As it was, the advance of the warship, even against a
single ship manned by a Second Foundationer, allowed certain conclusions to be drawn. Even if the ship possessed
mentalic ability, it would not be likely to advance into the
teeth of the Second Foundation in this manner. More likely,
it was advancing out of ignorance—and this might exist in
any of several degrees.

It could mean that the captain of the warship was not
aware that Compor had been replaced, or—if aware—did
not know the replacement was a Second Foundationer, or
perhaps was not even aware what a Second Foundationer
might be.

Or (and Gendibal intended to consider everything) what
if the ship did possess mentalic force and, nevertheless,
advanced in this self-confident manner? That could only
mean it was under the control of a megalomaniac *or* that it
possessed powers far beyond any that Gendibal could bring
himself to consider possible.

But what he considered possible was not the final judgment—

Carefully he sensed Novi's mind. Novi could not sense
mentalic fields consciously, whereas Gendibal, of course,
could—yet Gendibal's mind could not do so as delicately
or detect as feeble a mental field as could Novi's. This was
a paradox that would have to be studied in future and might

produce fruit that would in the long run prove of far greater importance than the immediate problem of an approaching spaceship.

Gendibal had grasped the possibility of this, intuitively, when he first became aware of the unusual smoothness and symmetry of Novi's mind—and he felt a somber pride in this intuitive ability he possessed. Speakers had always been proud of their intuitive powers, but how much was this the product of their inability to measure fields by straightforward physical methods and their failure, therefore, to understand what it was that they really did? It was easy to cover up ignorance by the mystical word "intuition." And how much of this ignorance of theirs might arise from their underestimation of the importance of physics as compared to mentalics?

And how much of *that* was blind pride? When he became First Speaker, Gendibal thought, this would change. There would have to be some narrowing of the physical gap between the Foundations. The Second Foundation could not face forever the possibility of destruction any time the mentalic monopoly slipped even slightly.

—Indeed, the monopoly might be slipping now. Perhaps the First Foundation had advanced or there was an alliance between the First Foundation and the Anti-Mules. (That thought occurred to him now for the first time and he shivered.)

His thoughts of the subject slipped through his mind with a rapidity common to a Speaker—and while he was thinking, he also remained sensitively aware of the glow in Novi's mind, the response to the gently pervasive mentalic field about them. It was *not* growing stronger as the Foundation warship drew nearer.

This was not, in itself, an absolute indication that the warship was not equipped with mentalics. It was well known that the mentalic field did not obey the inverse-square law. It did not grow stronger precisely as the square of the extent to which distance between emitter and receiver lessened. It differed in this way from the electromagnetic and the grav-

itational fields. Still, although mentalic fields varied less
with distance than the various physical fields did, it was not
altogether insensitive to distance, either. The response of
Novi's mind should show a detectable increase as the warship approached—*some* increase.

(How was it that no Second Foundationer in five centuries—from Hari Seldon on—had ever thought of working
out a mathematical relationship between mentalic intensity
and distance? This shrugging off of physics must and would
stop, Gendibal silently vowed.)

If the warship possessed mentalics and if it felt quite
certain it was approaching a Second Foundationer, would
it not increase the intensity of its field to maximum before
advancing? And in that case, would not Novi's mind *surely*
register an increased response of some kind?

—Yet it did not!

Confidently Gendibal eliminated the possibility that the
warship possessed mentalics. It was advancing out of ignorance and, as a menace, it could be downgraded.

The mentalic field, of course, still existed, but it had to
originate on Gaia. This was disturbing enough, but the immediate problem was the ship. Let that be eliminated and
he could then turn his attention to the world of the Anti-
Mules.

He waited. The warship would make some move or it
would come close enough to him to feel confident that he
could pass over to an effective offense.

The warship still approached—quite rapidly now—and
still did nothing. Finally Gendibal calculated that the strength
of his push would be sufficient. There would be no pain,
scarcely any discomfort—all those on board would merely
find that the large muscles of their backs and limbs would
respond but sluggishly to their desires.

Gendibal narrowed the mentalic field controlled by his
mind. It intensified and leaped across the gap between the
ships at the speed of light. (The two ships were close enough
to make hyperspatial contact—with its inevitable loss of
precision—unnecessary.)

And Gendibal then fell back in numbed surprise.

The Foundation warship was possessed of an efficient mentalic shield that gained in density in proportion as his own field gained in intensity. —The warship was not approaching out of ignorance after all—and it had an unexpected if passive weapon.

5.

"Ah," said Branno. "He has attempted an attack, Liono. See!"

The needle on the psychometer moved and trembled in its irregular rise.

The development of the mentalic shield had occupied Foundation scientists for a hundred and twenty years in the most secret of all scientific projects, except perhaps for Hari Seldon's lone development of psychohistorical analysis. Five generations of human beings had labored in the gradual improvement of a device backed by no satisfactory theory.

But no advance would have been possible without the invention of the psychometer that could act as a guide, indicating the direction and amount of advance at every stage. No one could explain how it worked, yet all indications were that it measured the immeasurable and gave numbers to the indescribable. Branno had the feeling (shared by some of the scientists themselves) that if ever the Foundation could explain the workings of the psychometer, they would be the equal of the Second Foundation in mind control.

But that was for the future. At present, the shield would have to be enough, backed as it was by an overwhelming preponderance in physical weapons.

Branno sent out the message, delivered in a male voice from which all overtones of emotion had been removed, till it was flat and deadly.

"Calling the ship *Bright Star* and its occupants. You have forcibly taken a ship of the Navy of the Foundation Fed-

eration in an act of piracy. You are directed to surrender
the ship and yourselves at once or face attack."

The answer came in natural voice: "Mayor Branno of
Terminus, I know you are on the ship. The *Bright Star* was
not taken by piratical action. I was freely invited on board
by its legal captain, Munn Li Compor of Terminus. I ask
a period of truce that we may discuss matters of importance
to each of us alike."

Kodell whispered to Branno, "Let me do the speaking,
Mayor."

She raised her arm contemptuously, "The responsibility
is mine, Liono."

Adjusting the transmitter, she spoke in tones scarcely
less forceful and unemotional than the artificial voice that
had spoken before:

"Man of the Second Foundation, understand your position. If you do not surrender forthwith, we can blow your
ship out of space in the time it takes light to travel from
our ship to yours—and we are ready to do that. Nor will
we lose by doing this, for you have no knowledge for which
we need keep you alive. We know you are from Trantor
and, once we have dealt with you, we will be ready to deal
with Trantor. We are willing to allow you a period in which
to have your say, but since you cannot have much of worth
to tell us, we are not prepared to listen long."

"In that case," said Gendibal, "let me speak quickly and
to the point. Your shield is not perfect and cannot be. You
have overestimated it and underestimated me. I can handle
your mind and control it. Not as easily, perhaps, as if there
were no shield, but easily enough. The instant you attempt
to use any weapon, I will strike you—and there is this for
you to understand: Without a shield, I can handle your mind
smoothly and do it no harm. With the shield, however, I
must smash through, which I can do, and I will be unable
then to handle you either smoothly or deftly. Your mind
will be smashed as the shield and the effect will be irreversible. In other words, you cannot stop me and I, on the
other hand, *can* stop you by being forced to do worse than

killing you. I will leave you a mindless hulk. Do you wish to risk that?"

Branno said, "You know you cannot do as you say."

"Do you, then, wish to risk the consequences I have described?" asked Gendibal with an air of cool indifference.

Kodell leaned over and whispered, "For Seldon's sake, Mayor—"

Gendibal said (not exactly at once, for it took light— and everything at light-speed—a little over one second to travel from one vessel to the other), "I follow your thoughts, Kodell. No need to whisper. I also follow the Mayor's thoughts. She is irresolute, so you have no need to panic just yet. And the mere fact that I know this is ample evidence that your shield leaks."

"It can be strengthened," said the Mayor defiantly.

"So can my mentalic force," said Gendibal.

"But I sit here at my ease, consuming merely physical strength to maintain the shield, and I have enough to maintain that shield for very long periods of time. You must use mentalic energy to penetrate the shield and you will tire."

"I am not tired," said Gendibal. "At the present moment, neither of you is capable of giving any order to any member of the crew of your ship or to any crewman on any other ship. I can manage so much without any harm to you, but do not make any unusual effort to escape this control, for if I match that by increasing my own force, as I will have to do, you will be damaged as I have said."

"I will wait," said Branno, placing her hands in her lap with every sign of solid patience. "You will tire and when you do, the orders that will go out will not be to destroy you, for you will then be harmless. The orders will be to send the main Foundation Fleet against Trantor. If you wish to save your world—surrender. A second orgy of destruction will not leave your organization untouched, as the first one did at the time of the Great Sack."

"Don't you see that if I feel myself tiring, Mayor, which I won't, I can save my world very simply by destroying you before my strength to do so is gone?"

"You won't do that. Your main task is to maintain the Seldon Plan. To destroy the Mayor of Terminus and thus to strike a blow at the prestige and confidence of the First Foundation, producing a staggering setback to its power and encouraging its enemies everywhere, will produce such a disruption to the Plan that it will be almost as bad for you as the destruction of Trantor. You might as well surrender."

"Are you willing to gamble on my reluctance to destroy you?"

Branno's chest heaved as she took a deep breath and let it out slowly. She then said firmly, "Yes!"

Kodell, sitting at her side, paled.

6.

Gendibal stared at the figure of Branno, superimposed upon the volume of room just in front of the wall. It was a little flickery and hazy thanks to the interference of the shield. The man next to her was almost featureless with haze, for Gendibal had no energy to waste on him. He had to concentrate on the Mayor.

To be sure, she had no image of him in return. She had no way of knowing that he too had a companion, for instance. She could make no judgment from his expressions, from his body language. In this respect, she was at a disadvantage.

Everything he had said was true. He *could* smash her at the cost of an enormous expenditure of mentalic force—and in so doing, he could scarcely avoid disrupting her mind irreparably.

Yet everything she had said was true as well. Destroying her would damage the Plan as much as the Mule himself had damaged it. Indeed, the new damage might be more serious, since it was now later in the game and there would be less time to retrieve the misstep.

Worse still, there was Gaia, which was still an unknown

quantity—with its mentalic field remaining at the faint and tantalizing edge of detection.

For a moment, he touched Novi's mind to make sure that the flow was still there. It was, and it was unchanged.

She could not have sensed that touch in any way, but she turned to him and in an awed whisper said, "Master, there is a faint mist there. Is it to that you talk?"

She must have sensed the mist through the small connection between their two minds. Gendibal put a finger to his lips. "Have no fear, Novi. Close your eyes and rest."

He raised his voice. "Mayor Branno, your gamble is a good one in this respect. I do not wish to destroy you at once, since I think that if I explain something to you, you will listen to reason and there will then be no need to destroy in either direction.

"Suppose, Mayor, that you win out and that I surrender. What follows? In an orgy of self-confidence and in undue reliance on your mentalic shield, you and your successors will attempt to spread your power over the Galaxy with undue haste. In doing so, you will actually postpone the establishment of the Second Empire, because you will also destroy the Seldon Plan."

Branno said, "I am not suprised that you do not wish to destroy me at once and I think that, as you sit there, you will be forced to realize that you do not dare to destroy me at all."

Gendibal said, "Do not deceive yourself with self-congratulatory folly. *Listen* to me. The majority of the Galaxy is still non-Foundation and, to a great extent, anti-Foundation. There are even portions of the Foundation Federation itself that have not forgotten their days of independence. If the Foundation moves too quickly in the wake of my surrender, it will deprive the rest of the Galaxy of its greatest weakness—its disunity and indecision. You will force them to unite by fear and you will feed the tendency toward rebellion within."

"You are threatening with clubs of straw," said Branno. "We have the power to win easily against all enemies, even if every world in the non-Foundation Galaxy combined against us, and even if these were helped by a rebellion in half the worlds of the Federation itself. There would be no problem."

"No *immediate* problem, Mayor. Do not make the mistake of seeing only the results that appear at once. You can establish a Second Empire merely by proclaiming it, but you will not be able to maintain it. You will have to reconquer it every ten years."

"Then we will do so until the worlds tire, as you are tiring."

"They will not tire, any more than I will. Nor will the process continue for a very long time, for there is a second and greater danger to the Pseudo-Empire you would proclaim. Since it can be temporarily maintained only by an ever-stronger military force which will be ever-exercised, the generals of the Foundation will, for the first time, become more important and more powerful than the civilian authorities. The Pseudo-Empire will break up into military regions within which individual commanders will be supreme. There will be anarchy—and a slide back into a barbarism that may last longer than the thirty thousand years forecast by Seldon before the Seldon Plan was implemented."

"Childish threats. Even if the mathematics of the Seldon Plan predicted all this, it predicts only probabilities—not inevitabilities."

"Mayor Branno," said Gendibal earnestly. "Forget the Seldon Plan. You do not understand its mathematics and you cannot visualize its pattern. But you do not have to, perhaps. You are a tested politician; and a successful one, to judge from the post you hold; even more so, a courageous one, to judge from the gamble you are now taking. Therefore, use your political acumen. Consider the political and military history of humanity and consider it in the light of what you know of human nature—of the manner in which people, politicians, and military officers act, react, and interact—and see if I'm not right."

Branno said, "Even if you were right, Second Foundationer, it is a risk we must take. With proper leadership and with continuing technological advance—in mentalics, as well as in physics—we can overcome. Hari Seldon never calculated such advances properly. He couldn't. Where in the Plan does it allow for the development of a mentalic shield by the First Foundation? Why should we want the Plan, in any case? We will risk founding a new Empire without it. Failure without it would, after all, be better than success with it. We do not want an Empire in which we play puppets to the hidden manipulators of the Second Foundation."

"You say that only because you do not understand what failure will be like for the people of the Galaxy."

"Perhaps!" said Branno stonily. "Are you beginning to weary, Second Foundationer?"

"Not at all. —Let me propose an alternative action that you have not considered—one in which I need not surrender to you, nor you to me. —We are in the vicinity of a planet called Gaia."

"I am aware of that."

"Are you aware that it is probably the birthplace of the Mule?"

"I would want more evidence than resides in your mere statement to that effect."

"The planet is surrounded by a mentalic field. It is the home of many Mules. If you accomplish your dream of destroying the Second Foundation, you will make yourselves the slaves of this planet of Mules. What harm have Second Foundationers ever done you—specific, rather than imagined or theorized harm? Now ask yourself what harm a single Mule has done you."

"I still have nothing more than your statements."

"As long as we remain here, I can give you nothing more. —I propose a truce, therefore. Keep your shield up, if you don't trust me, but be prepared to co-operate with me. Let us, together, approach this planet—and when you are convinced that it is dangerous, then I will nullify its mentalic field and you will order your ships to take possession of it."

"And then?"

"And then, at least, it will be the First Foundation against the Second Foundation, with no outside forces to be considered. The fight will then be clear whereas now, you see, we dare not fight, for both Foundations are at bay."

"Why did you not say this before?"

"I thought I might convince you that we were not enemies, so that we might co-operate. Since I have apparently failed at that, I suggest co-operation in any case."

Branno paused, her head bent in thought. Then she said, "You are trying to put me to sleep with lullabies. How will you, by yourself, nullify the mentalic field of a whole planet of Mules? The thought is so ludicrous that I cannot trust in the truth of your proposition."

"I am not alone," said Gendibal. "Behind me is the full force of the Second Foundation—and that force, channeled through me, will take care of Gaia. What's more, it can, at any time, brush aside your shield as though it were thin fog."

"If so, why do you need my help?"

"First, because nullifying the field is not enough. The Second Foundation cannot devote itself, now and forever, to the eternal task of nullifying, any more than I can spend the rest of my life dancing this conversational minuet with you. We need the physical action your ships can supply. —And besides, if I cannot convince you by reason that the two Foundations should look upon each other as allies, perhaps a co-operative venture of the greatest importance can be convincing. Deeds may do the job where words fail."

A second silence and then Branno said, "I am willing to approach Gaia more closely, if we can approach co-operatively. I make no promises beyond that."

"That will be enough," said Gendibal, leaning toward his computer.

Novi said, "No, Master, up to this point, it didn't matter, but please make no further move. We must wait for Councilman Trevize of Terminus."

19. DECISION

1.

Janov Pelorat said, with a small trace of petulance in his voice, "Really, Golan, no one seems to care for the fact that this is the first time in a moderately long life—not *too* long, I assure you, Bliss—in which I have been traveling through the Galaxy. Yet each time I come to a world, I am off it again and back in space before I can really have a chance to study it. It has happened twice now."

"Yes," said Bliss, "but if you had not left the other one so quickly, you would not have met me until who knows when. Surely that justifies the first time."

"It does. Honestly, my—my dear, it does."

"And this time, Pel, you may be off the planet, but you have me—and *I* am Gaia, as much as any particle of it, as much as all of it."

"You *are*, and surely I want no other particle of it."

Trevize, who had been listening to the exchange with a frown, said, "This is disgusting. Why didn't Dom come with us? —Space, I'll never get used to this monosyllabization. Two hundred fifty syllables to a name and we use just one of them. —Why didn't *he* come, together with all two hundred fifty syllables? If all this is so important—if the very existence of Gaia depends on it—why didn't he come with us to direct us?"

"*I* am here, Trev," said Bliss, "and I am as much Gaia as he is." Then, with a quick sideways and upward look from her dark eyes, "Does it annoy you, then, to have me call you 'Trev'?"

"Yes, it does. I have as much right to my ways as you to yours. My name is Trevize. Two syllables. Tre-vize."

"Gladly. I do not wish to anger you, Trevize."

"I am not angry. I am annoyed." Her rose suddenly, walked from one end of the room to the other, stepping over the outstretched legs of Pelorat (who drew them in quickly), and then back again. He stopped, turned, and faced Bliss.

He pointed a finger at her. "Look! I am not my own master! I have been maneuvered from Terminus to Gaia—and even when I began to suspect that this was so, there seemed no way to break the grip. And then, when I get to Gaia, I am told the whole purpose for my arrival was to save Gaia. Why? How? What is Gaia to me—or I to Gaia—that I should save it? Is there no other of the quintillion human beings in the Galaxy who could do the job?"

"Please, Trevize," said Bliss—and there was a sudden downcast air about her, all of the gamine affectation disappearing. "Do not be angry. You see, I use your name properly and I will be very serious. Dom asked you to be patient."

"By every planet in the Galaxy, habitable or not, I don't want to be patient. If I am so important, do I not deserve an explanation? To begin with, I ask again why Dom did not come with us? Is it not sufficiently important for him to be here on the *Far Star* with us?"

"He *is* here, Trevize," said Bliss. "While I am here, he is here, and everyone on Gaia is here, and every living thing, and every speck of the planet."

"*You* are satisfied that that is so, but it's not my way of thinking. I'm not Gaian. We can't squeeze the whole planet on to my ship, we can only squeeze one person on to it. We have you, and Dom is part of you. Very well. Why couldn't we have taken Dom, and let you be part of him?"

"For one thing," said Bliss, "Pel—I mean, Pel-o-rat—asked that I be on the ship with you. I, not Dom."

"He was being gallant. Who would take that seriously?"

"Oh, now, my dear fellow," said Pelorat, rising to his feet with his face reddening, "I was quite serious. I don't want to be dismissed like that. I accept the fact that it doesn't matter which component of the Gaian whole is on board, and it is more pleasant for me to have Bliss here than Dom, and it should be for you as well. Come, Golan, you are behaving childishly."

"Am I? Am I?" said Trevize, frowning darkly. "All right, then, I am. Just the same," again he pointed at Bliss, "whatever it is I am expected to do, I assure you that I won't do it if I am not treated like a human being. Two questions to begin with— What am I supposed to do? And why me?"

Bliss was wide-eyed and backing away. She said, "Please, I can't tell you that now. All of Gaia can't tell you. You *must* come to the place without knowing anything to begin with. You *must* learn it all there. You must then do what you must do—but you must do it calmly and unemotionally. If you remain as you are, nothing will be of use and, one way or another, Gaia will come to an end. You must change this feeling of yours and I do not know how to change it."

"Would Dom know if *he* were here?" said Trevize remorselessly.

"Dom *is* here," said Bliss. "He/I/we do not know how to change you or calm you. We do not understand a human being who cannot sense his place in the scheme of things, who does not feel like part of a greater whole."

Trevize said, "That is not so. You could seize my ship at a distance of a million kilometers and more—and keep us calm while we were helpless. Well, calm me now. Don't pretend you are not capable of doing it."

"But we *mustn't*. Not now. If we changed you or adjusted you in any way now, then you would be no more valuable to us than any other person in the Galaxy and we could not use you. We can only use you because you are *you*—and you must remain you. If we touch you at this moment in any way, we are lost. Please. You must be calm of your own accord."

"Not a chance, miss, unless you tell me some of what I want to know."

Pelorat said, "Bliss, let me try. Please go into the other room."

Bliss left, backing slowly out. Pelorat closed the door behind her.

Trevize said, "She can hear and see—sense everything. What difference does this make?"

Pelorat said, "It makes a difference to me. I want to be alone with you, even if isolation is an illusion. —Golan, you're afraid."

"Don't be a fool."

"Of course you are. You don't know where you're going, what you'll be facing, what you'll be expected to do. You have a right to be afraid."

"But I'm not."

"Yes, you are. Perhaps you're not afraid of physical danger in the way that I am. I've been afraid of venturing out into space, afraid of each new world I see, afraid of every new thing I encounter. After all, I've lived half a century of a constricted, withdrawn and limited life, while you have been in the Navy and in politics, in the thick and hurly-burly at home and in space. Yet I've tried not to be afraid and you've helped me. In this time that we've been together, you've been patient with me, you've been kind to me and understanding, and because of you, I've managed to master my fears and behave well. Let me, then, return the favor and help you."

"I'm not afraid, I tell you."

"Of course you are. If nothing else, you're afraid of the responsibility you'll be facing. Apparently there's a whole world depending on you—and you will therefore have to live with the destruction of a whole world if you fail. Why should you have to face that possibility for a world that means nothing to you? What right have they to place this load upon you? You're not only afraid of failure, as any person would be in your place, but you're furious that they should put you in the position where you have to be afraid."

"You're all wrong."

"I don't think so. Consequently let me take your place. I'll do it. Whatever it is they expect you to do, I volunteer as substitute. I assume that it's not something that requires great physical strength or vitality, since a simple mechanical device would outdo you in that respect. I assume it's not something that requires mentalics, for they have enough of that themselves. It's something that—well, I don't know, but if it requires neither brawn nor brain, then I have everything else as well as you—and I am ready to take the responsibility."

Trevize said sharply, "Why are you so willing to bear the load?"

Pelorat looked down at the floor, as though fearing to meet the other's eyes. He said, "I have had a wife, Golan. I have known women. Yet they have never been very important to me. Interesting. Pleasant. Never very important. Yet, this one—"

"Who? Bliss?"

"She's different, somehow—to me."

"By Terminus, Janov, she knows every word you're saying."

"That makes no difference. She knows anyhow. —I want to please her. I will undertake this task, whatever it is; run any risk, take any responsibility, on the smallest chance that it will make her—think well of me."

"Janov, she's a child."

"She's not a child—and what you think of her makes no difference to me."

"Don't you understand what you must seem to her?"

"An old man? What's the difference? She's part of a greater whole and I am not—and that alone builds an insuperable wall between us. Don't you think I know that? But I don't ask anything of her but that she—"

"Think well of you?"

"Yes. Or whatever else she can make herself feel for me."

"And for that you will do my job? —But Janov, haven't you been listening. They don't want you; they want *me* for some space-ridden reason I can't understand."

"If they can't have you and if they must have someone, I will be better than nothing, surely."

Trevize shook his head. "I can't believe that this is happening. Old age is overtaking you and you have discovered youth. Janov, you're trying to be a hero, so that you can die for that body."

"Don't say that, Golan. This is not a fit subject for humor."

Trevize tried to laugh, but his eyes met Pelorat's grave face and he cleared his throat instead. He said, "You're right. I apologize. Call her in, Janov. Call her in."

Bliss entered, shrinking a little. She said in a small voice, "I'm sorry, Pel. You cannot substitute. It must be Trevize or no one."

Trevize said, "Very well. I'll be calm. Whatever it is, I'll try to do it. Anything to keep Janov from trying to play the romantic hero at his age."

"I know my age," muttered Pelorat.

Bliss approached him slowly, placed her hand on his shoulder. "Pel, I—I think well of you."

Pelorat looked away. "It's all right, Bliss. You needn't be kind."

"I'm not being kind, Pel. I think — very well of you."

2.

Dimly, then more strongly, Sura Novi knew that she was Surano-viremblastiran and that when she was a child, she had been known as Su to her parents and Vi to her friends.

She had never really forgotten, of course, but the facts were, on occasion, buried deep within her. Never had it been buried as deeply or for so long as in this last month, for never had she been so close for so long to a mind so powerful.

But now it was time. She did not will it herself. She had no need to. The vast remainder of her was pushing her portion of itself to the surface, for the sake of the global need.

Accompanying that was a vague discomfort, a kind of

itch that was rapidly overwhelmed by the comfort of selfness
unmasked. Not in years had she been so close to the globe
of Gaia.

She remembered one of the life-forms she had loved on
Gaia as a child. Having understood its feelings then as a
dim part of her own, she recognized her own sharper ones
now. She was a butterfly emerging from a cocoon.

3.

Stor Gendibal stared sharply and penetratingly at Novi—
and with such surprise that he came within a hair of loos-
ening his grip upon Mayor Branno. That he did not do so
was, perhaps, the result of a sudden support from without
that steadied him and that, for the moment, he ignored.

He said, "What do you know of Councilman Trevize,
Novi?" And then, in cold disturbance at the sudden and
growing complexity of her mind, he cried out, "What are
you?"

He attempted to seize hold of her mind and found it
impenetrable. At that moment, he recognized that his hold
on Branno was supported by a grip stronger than his own.
He repeated, "What are you?"

There was a hint of the tragic on Novi's face. "Master,"
she said, "Speaker Gendibal. My true name is Suranoviremblastiran and I am Gaia."

It was all she said in words, but Gendibal, in sudden
fury, had intensified his own mental aura and with great
skill, now that his blood was up, evaded the strengthening
bar and held Branno on his own and more strongly than
before, while he gripped Novi's mind in a tight and silent
struggle.

She held him off with equal skill, but she could not keep
her mind closed to him—or perhaps she did not wish to.

He spoke to her as he would to another Speaker. "You
have played a part, deceived me, lured me here, and you
are one of the species from which the Mule was derived."

"The Mule was an aberration, Speaker. I/we are not Mules. I/we are Gaia."

The whole essence of Gaia was described in what she complexly communicated, far more than it could have been in any number of words.

"A whole planet alive," said Gendibal.

"And with a mentalic field greater as a whole than is yours as an individual. Please do not resist with such force. I fear the danger of harming you, something I do not wish to do."

"Even as a living planet, you are not stronger than the sum of my colleagues on Trantor. We, too, are, in a way, a planet alive."

"Only some thousands of people in mentalic co-operation, Speaker, and you cannot draw upon their support, for I have blocked it off. Test that and you will see."

"What is it you plan to do, Gaia?"

"I would hope, Speaker, that you would call me Novi. What I do now I do as Gaia, but I am Novi also—and with reference to you, I am only Novi."

"What is it you plan to do, Gaia?"

There was the trembling mentalic equivalent of a sigh and Novi said, "We will remain in triple stalemate. You will hold Mayor Branno through her shield, and I will help you do so, and we will not tire. You, I suppose, will maintain your grip on me, and I will maintain mine on you, and neither one of us will tire there either. And so it will stay."

"To what end?"

"As I have told you— We are waiting for Councilman Trevize of Terminus. It is he who will break the stalemate— as he chooses."

4.

The computer on board the *Far Star* located the two ships and Golan Trevize displayed them together on the split screen.

They were both Foundation vessels. One was precisely like the *Far Star* and was undoubtedly Compor's ship. The other was larger and far more powerful.

He turned toward Bliss and said, "Well, do you know what's going on? Is there anything you can tell me?"

"Yes! Do not be alarmed! They will not harm you."

"Why is everyone convinced I'm sitting here all a-tremble with panic?" Trevize demanded petulantly.

Pelorat said hastily, "Let her talk, Golan. Don't snap at her."

Trevize raised his arms in a gesture of impatient surrender. "I will not snap. Speak, lady."

Bliss said, "On the large ship is the ruler of your Foundation. With her—"

Trevize said in astonishment, "The ruler? You mean Old Lady Branno?"

"Surely that is not her title," said Bliss, her lips twitching a little in amusement. "But she is a woman, yes." She paused a little, as though listening intently to the general organism of which she was part. "Her name is Harlabranno. It seems odd to have only four syllables when one is so important on her world, but I suppose non-Gaians have their own ways."

"I suppose," said Trevize dryly. "You would call her Brann, I think. But what is she doing here? Why isn't she back on— I see. Gaia has maneuvered her here, too. Why?"

Bliss did not answer that question. She said, "With her is Lionokodell, five syllables, though her underling. It seems a lack of respect. He is an important official of your world. With them are four others who control the ship's weapons. Do you want their names?"

"No. I take it that on the other ship there is one man, Munn Li Compor, and that he represents the Second Foundation. You've brought both Foundations together, obviously. Why?"

"Not exactly, Trev—I mean, Trevize—"

"Oh, go ahead and say Trev. I don't give a puff of comet gas."

"Not exactly, Trev. Compor has left that ship and has been replaced by two people. One is Storgendibal, an important official of the Second Foundation. He is called a Speaker."

"An important official? He's got mentalic power, I imagine."

"Oh yes. A great deal."

"Will you be able to handle that?"

"Certainly. The second person, on the ship with him, is Gaia."

"One of *your* people?"

"Yes. Her name is Suranoviremblastiran. It should be much longer, but she has been away from me/us/rest so long."

"Is she capable of holding a high official of the Second Foundation?"

"It is not she, it is Gaia who holds him. She/I/we/all are capable of crushing him."

"Is that what she's going to do? She's going to crush him and Branno? What is this? Is Gaia going to destroy the Foundations and set up a Galactic Empire of its own? The Mule back again? A greater Mule—"

"No no, Trev. Do not become agitated. You must not. All three are in a stalemate. They are waiting."

"For what?"

"For your decision."

"Here we go again. *What* decision? Why *me*?"

"Please, Trev," said Bliss. "It will soon be explained. I/we/she have said as much as I/we/she can for now."

5.

Branno said wearily, "It is clear I have made a mistake, Liono, perhaps a fatal one."

"Is this something that ought to be admitted?" muttered Kodell through motionless lips.

"They know what I think. It will do no further harm to

say so. Nor do they know less about what you think if you do not move your lips. —I should have waited until the shield was further strengthened."

Kodell said, "How could you have known, Mayor? If we waited until assurance was doubly and triply and quadruply and endlessly sure, we would have waited forever. —To be sure, I wish we had not gone ourselves. It would have been well to have experimented with someone else— with your lightning rod, Trevize, perhaps."

Branno sighed. "I wanted to give them no warning, Liono. Still, there you put the finger on the nub of my mistake. I might have waited until the shield was reasonably impenetrable. Not ultimately impenetrable but reasonably so. I knew there was perceptible leakage now, but I could not bear to wait longer. To wipe out the leakage would have meant waiting past my term of office and I wanted it done in *my* time—and *I* wanted to be on the spot. So like a fool, I forced myself to believe the shield was adequate. I would listen to no caution—to your doubts, for instance."

"We may still win out if we are patient."

"Can you give the order to fire on the other ship?"

"No, I cannot, Mayor. The thought is, somehow, not something I can endure."

"Nor I. And if you or I managed to give the order, I am certain that the men on board would not follow it, that they would not be able to."

"Not under present circumstances, Mayor, but circumstances might change. As a matter of fact, a new actor appears on the scene."

He pointed to the screen. The ship's computer had automatically split the screen as a new ship came within its ken. The second ship appeared on the right-hand side.

"Can you magnify the image, Liono?"

"No trouble. The Second Foundationer is skillful. We are free to do anything he is not troubled by."

"Well," said Branno, studying the screen, "that's the *Far Star*, I'm sure. And I imagine Trevize and Pelorat are on board. Then, bitterly, "Unless they too have been replaced by Second Foundationers. My lightning rod has been very efficient indeed. —If only my shield had been stronger."

"Patience!" said Kodell.

A voice rang out in the confines of the ship's control room and Branno could somehow tell it did not consist of sound waves. She heard it in her mind directly and a glance at Kodell was sufficient to tell her that he had heard it, too.

It said, "Can you hear me, Mayor Branno? If you can, don't bother saying so. It will be enough if you think so."

Branno said calmly, "What are you?"

"I am Gaia."

6.

The three ships were each essentially at rest, relative to the other two. All three were turning very slowly about the planet Gaia, as a distant three-part satellite of the planet. All three were accompanying Gaia on its endless journey about its sun.

Trevize sat, watching the screen, tired of guessing what his role might be—what he had been dragged across a thousand parsecs to do.

The sound in his mind did not startle him. It was as though he had been waiting for it.

It said, "Can you hear me, Golan Trevize? If you can, don't bother saying so. It will be enough if you think it."

Trevize looked about. Pelorat, clearly startled, was looking in various directions, as though trying to find the source. Bliss sat quietly, her hands held loosely in her lap. Trevize had no doubt, for a moment, that she was aware of the sound.

He ignored the order to use thoughts and spoke with deliberate clarity of enunciation. "If I don't find out what this is about, I will do nothing I am asked to do."

And the voice said, "You are about to find out."

7.

Novi said, "You will all hear me in your mind. You are all free to respond in thought. I will arrange it so that all of you can hear each other. And, as you are all aware, we are all close enough so that at the normal light-speed of the spatial mentalic field, there will be no inconvenient delays. To begin with, we are all here by arrangement."

"In what manner?" came Branno's voice.

"Not by mental tampering," said Novi. "Gaia has interfered with no one's mind. It is not our way. We merely took advantage of ambition. Mayor Branno wanted to establish a Second Empire at once; Speaker Gendibal wanted to be Frist Speaker. It was enough to encourage these desires and to ride the wind, selectively, and with judgment."

"I know how I was brought here," said Gendibal stiffly. And indeed he did. He knew why he had been so anxious to move out into space, so anxious to pursue Trevize, so sure he could handle it all. —It was all Novi. —Oh, Novi!

"You were a particular case, Speaker Gendibal. Your ambition was powerful, but there were softnesses about you that offered a shortcut. You were a person who would be kind to someone whom you had been trained to think of as beneath you in every respect. I took advantage of this in you and turned it against you. I/we am/are deeply ashamed. The excuse is that the future of the Galaxy is in hazard."

Novi paused and her voice (though she was not speaking by way of vocal cords) grew more somber, her face more drawn.

"This was the time. Gaia could wait no longer. For over a century, the people of Terminus had been developing a mentalic shield. Left to themselves another generation, it would have been impervious even to Gaia and they would have been free to use their physical weapons at will. The Galaxy would not have been able to resist them and a Second Galactic Empire, after the fashion of Terminus, would have been established at once, despite the Seldon Plan, despite the people of Trantor, and despite Gaia. Mayor Branno had to be somehow maneuvered into making her move while the shield was still imperfect.

"Then there is Trantor. The Seldon Plan was working perfectly, for Gaia itself labored to keep it on track with precision. And for over a century, there had been quietist First Speakers, so that Trantor vegetated. Now, however, Stor Gendibal was rising quickly. He would certainly become First Speaker and under him Trantor would take on an activist role. It would surely concentrate on physical power and would recognize the danger of Terminus and take action against it. If he could act against Terminus before its shield was perfected, then the Seldon Plan would be worked out to its conclusion in a Second Galactic Empire—after the fashion of Trantor—despite the people of Terminus and despite Gaia. Consequently Gendibal had to be somehow maneuvered into making his move before he became First Speaker.

"Fortunately, because Gaia has been working carefully for decades, we have brought both Foundations to the proper place at the proper time. I repeat all this primarily so that Councilman Golan Trevize of Terminus may understand."

Trevize cut in at once and again ignored the effort to converse by thought. He spoke words firmly, "I do *not* understand. What is wrong with either version of the Second Galactic Empire?"

Novi said, "The Second Galactic Empire—worked out after the fashion of Terminus—will be a military Empire, established by strife, maintained by strife, and eventually destroyed by strife. It will be nothing but the First Galactic Empire reborn. That is the view of Gaia.

"The Second Galactic Empire—worked out after the fashion of Trantor—will be a paternalistic Empire, established by calculation, maintained by calculation, and in perpetual living death by calculation. It will be a dead end. That is the view of Gaia."

Trevize said, "And what does Gaia have to offer as an alternative?"

"Greater Gaia! Galaxia! Every inhabited planet as alive

as Gaia. Every living planet combined into a still greater hyperspatial life. Every uninhabited planet participating. Every star. Every scrap of interstellar gas. Perhaps even the great central black hole. A living galaxy and one that can be made favorable for all life in ways that we yet cannot foresee. A way of life fundamentally different from all that has gone before and repeating none of the old mistakes."

"Originating new ones," muttered Gendibal sarcastically.

"We have had thousands of years of Gaia to work those out."

"But not on a Galactic scale."

Trevize, ignoring the short exchange and driving to his point, said, "And what is my role in all this?"

The voice of Gaia—channeled through Novi's mind—thundered, *"Choose!* Which alternative is it to be?"

There was a vast silence that followed and finally, in that silence, Trevize's voice—mental at last, for he was too taken aback to speak—sounded small and still defiant. "Why me?"

Novi said, "Though we recognized the moment had come when either Terminus or Trantor would become too powerful to stop—or worse yet, when both might become so powerful that a deadly stalemate would develop that would devastate the Galaxy—we still could not move. For our purposes, we needed someone—a particular someone—with the talent for rightness. We found you, Councilman. —No, we cannot take the credit. The people of Trantor found you through the man named Compor, though even they did not know what they had. The act of finding you attracted our attention to you. Golan Trevize, you have the gift of knowing the right thing to do."

"I deny it," said Trevize.

"You are, every once in a while, *sure.* And we want you to be sure this time on behalf of the Galaxy. You do not wish the responsibility, perhaps. You may do your best not to have to choose. Nevertheless, you will realize that it is right to do so. You will be *sure!* And you will then choose. Once we found you, we knew the search was over and for years we have labored to encourage a course of action that would, without direct mentalic interference, so influence events that all three of you—Mayor Branno, Speaker Gendibal, and Councilman Trevize—would be in the neighborhood of Gaia at the same time. We have done it."

Trevize said, "At this point in space, under present circumstances, is it not true, Gaia—if that is what you want me to call you—that you can overpower both the Mayor and the Speaker? Is it not true that you can establish this living Galaxy you speak of without my doing anything? Why, then, do you not?"

Novi said, "I do not know if I can explain this to your satisfaction. Gaia was formed thousands of years ago with the help of robots that once, for a brief time, served the human species and now serve them no more. They made it quite clear to us that we could survive only by a strict application of the Three Laws of Robotics as applied to life generally. The First Law, in those terms, is: 'Gaia may not harm life or, through inaction, allow life to come to harm.' We have followed this rule through all of our history and we can do no other.

"The result is that we are now helpless. We cannot force our vision of the living Galaxy upon a quintillion human beings and countless other forms of life and perhaps do harm to vast numbers. Nor can we do nothing and watch the Galaxy half-destroy itself in a struggle that we might have prevented. We do not know whether action or inaction will cost the Galaxy less; nor, if we choose action, do we know whether supporting Terminus or Trantor will cost the Galaxy less. Let Councilman Trevize decide then—and whatever that decision is, Gaia will follow it."

Trevize said, "How do you expect me to make a decision? What do I do?"

Novi said, "You have your computer. The people of Terminus did not know that when they made it, they made it better than they knew. The computer on board your ship incorporates some of Gaia. Place your hands on the terminals and think. You may think Mayor Branno's shield impervious, for instance. If you do, it is possible that she will at once use her weapons to disable or destroy the other two ships, establish physical rule over Gaia and, later on, Trantor."

"And you will do nothing to stop that?" said Trevize with astonishment.

"Not a thing. If you are sure that domination by Terminus will do the Galaxy less harm than any other alternative, we will gladly help that domination along—even at the cost of our own destruction.

"On the other hand, you may find Speaker Gendibal's mentalic field and you may then join your computer-magnified push to his. He will, in that case, surely break free of me and push me back. He may then adjust the Mayor's mind and, in combination with her ships, establish physical domination over Gaia and assure the continued supremacy of the Seldon Plan. Gaia will not move to stop that.

"Or you may find *my* mentalic field and join that—and then the living Galaxy will be set in motion to reach its fulfillment, not in this generation or the next, but after centuries of labor during which the Seldon Plan will continue. The choice is yours."

Mayor Branno said, "Wait! Do not make a decision just yet. May I speak?"

Novi said, "You may speak freely. So may Speaker Gendibal."

Branno said, "Councilman Trevize. The last time we met on Terminus, you said, 'The time may come, Madam Mayor, when you will ask me for an effort, and I will then do as I choose, and I will remember the past two days.' I don't know whether you foresaw this, or intuitively felt it would happen, or simply had what this woman who speaks of a living Galaxy calls a talent for rightness. In any case, you were right. I am asking you for an effort on behalf of the Federation.

"You may, I suppose, feel that you would like to even the score with me for having arrested and exiled you. I ask you to remember that I did it for what I considered the good

of the Foundation Federation. Even if I were wrong or even
if I acted out of callous self-interest, remember that it was
I who did it—and not the Federation. Do not destroy the
entire Federation out of a desire to balance what I alone
have done to you. Remember that you are a Foundationer
and a human being, that you do not want to be a cipher in
the plans of the bloodless mathematicians of Trantor or less
than a cipher in a Galactic mish-mash of life and nonlife.
You want yourself, your descendants, your fellow-people
to be independent organisms, possessing free will. Nothing
else matters.

"These others may tell you that our Empire will lead to
bloodshed and misery—but it need not. It is our free-will
choice whether this should be so or not. We may choose
otherwise. And, in any case, it is better to go to defeat with
free will than to live in meaningless security as a cog in a
machine. Observe that you are now being asked to make a
decision as a free-will human being. These things of Gaia
are unable to make a decision because their machinery will
not allow them to, so that they depend on you. And they
will destroy themselves if you bid them to. Is that what you
want for all the Galaxy?"

Trevize said, "I do not know that I have free will, Mayor.
My mind may have been subtly dealt with, so that I will
give the answer that is desired."

Novi said, "Your mind is totally untouched. If we could
bring ourselves to adjust you to suit our purposes, this whole
meeting would be unnecessary. Were we that unprincipled,
we could have proceeded with what we would find most
pleasing to ourselves with no concern for the greater needs
and good of humanity as a whole."

Gendibal said, "I believe it is my turn to speak. Councilman Trevize, do not be guided by narrow parochialism.
The fact that you are Terminus-born should not lead you to
believe that Terminus comes before the Galaxy. For five
centuries now, the Galaxy has been operating in accordance
with the Seldon Plan. In and out of the Foundation Federation, that operation has been proceeding.

"You are, and have been, part of the Seldon Plan above and beyond your lesser role as Foundationer. Do not do anything to disrupt the Plan, either on behalf of a narrow concept of patriotism or out of a romantic longing for the new and untried. The Second Foundationers will in no way hamper the free will of humanity. We are guides, not despots.

"And we offer a Second Galactic Empire fundamentally different from the First. Throughout human history, no decade in all the tens of thousands of years during which hyperspatial travel has existed has been completely free of bloodshed and violent death throughout the Galaxy, even in those periods when the Foundation itself was at peace. Choose Mayor Branno and that will continue endlessly into the future. The same dreary, deadly round. The Seldon Plan offers release from that at last—and *not* at the price of becoming one more atom in a Galaxy of atoms, being reduced to equality with grass, bacteria, and dust."

Novi said, "What Speaker Gendibal says of the First Foundation's Second Empire, I agree with. What he says of his own, I do not. The Speakers of Trantor are, after all, independent free-will human beings and are the same as they have always been. Are they free of destructive competition, of politics, of clawing upward at all costs? Are there no quarrels and even hatreds at the Speaker's Table— and will they always be guides you dare follow? Put Speaker Gendibal on his honor and ask him this."

"No need to put me on my honor," said Gendibal. "I freely admit we have our hatreds, competitions, and betrayals at the Table. But once a decision is reached, it is obeyed by all. There has never been an exception to this."

Trevize said, "What if I will not make a choice?"

"You must," said Novi. "You will know that it is right to do so and you will therefore make a choice."

"What if I try to make a choice and cannot?"

"You must."

Trevize said, "How much time do I have?"

Novi said, "Until you are *sure*, however much time that takes."

Trevize sat silently.

Though the others were silent too, it seemed to Trevize that he could hear the pulsing of his bloodstream.

He could hear Mayor Branno's voice say firmly, "Free will!"

Speaker Gendibal's voice said peremptorily, "Guidance and peace!"

Novi's voice said wistfully, "Life."

Trevize turned and found Pelorat looking at him intently. He said, "Janov. Have you heard all this?"

"Yes, I have, Golan."

"What do you think?"

"The decision is not mine."

"I know that. But what do you think?"

"I don't know. I am frightened by all three alternatives. And yet a peculiar thought comes to me—"

"Yes?"

"When we first went into space, you showed me the Galaxy. Do you remember?"

"Of course."

"You speeded time and the Galaxy rotated visibly. And I said, as though anticipating this very time, 'The Galaxy looks like a living thing, crawling through space.' Do you think that, in a way, it is alive already?"

And Trevize, remembering that moment, was suddenly *sure*. He remembered suddenly his feeling that Pelorat, too, would have a vital role to play. He turned in haste, anxious not to have time to think, to doubt, to grow uncertain.

He placed his hands on the terminals and thought with an intensity he had never known before.

He had made his decision—the decision on which the fate of the Galaxy hung.

20. CONCLUSION

1.

Mayor Harla Branno had every reason for satisfaction. The state visit had not lasted long, but it had been thoroughly productive.

She said, as though in deliberate attempt to avoid *hubris*, "We can't, of course, trust them completely."

She was watching the screen. The ships of the Fleet were, one by one, entering hyperspace and returning to their normal stations.

There was no question but that Sayshell had been impressed by their presence, but they could not have failed to notice two things: one, that the ships had remained in Foundation space at all times; two, that once Branno had indicated they would leave, they were indeed leaving with celerity.

On the other hand, Sayshell would not forget either that those ships could be recalled to the border at a day's notice—or less. It was a maneuver that had combined both a demonstration of power and a demonstration of goodwill.

Kodell said, "Quite right, we can't trust them completely, but then no one in the Galaxy can be trusted completely and it is in the self-interest of Sayshell to observe the terms of the agreement. We have been generous."

Branno said, "A lot will depend on working out the details and I predict that will take months. The general brushstrokes can be accepted in a moment, but then come the shadings: just how we arrange for quarantine of imports and exports, how we weigh the value of their grain and cattle compared to ours, and so on."

"I know, but it will be done eventually and the credit

will be yours, Mayor. It was a bold stroke and one, I admit, whose wisdom I doubted."

"Come, Liono. It was just a matter of the Foundation recognizing Sayshellian pride. They've retained a certain independence since early Imperial times. It's to be admired, actually."

"Yes, now that it will no longer inconvenience us."

"Exactly, so it was only necessary to bend our own pride to the point of making some sort of gesture to theirs. I admit it took an effort to decide that I, as Mayor of a Galaxy-straddling Federation, should condescend to visit a provincial star-grouping, but once the decision was made it didn't hurt too much. And it pleased them. We had to gamble that they would agree to the visit once we moved our ships to the border, but it meant being humble and smiling very broadly."

Kodell nodded. "We abandoned the appearance of power to preserve the essence of it."

"Exactly. —Who first said that?"

"I believe it was in one of Eriden's plays, but I'm not sure. We can ask one of our literary lights back home."

"If I remember. We must speed the return visit of Sayshellians to Terminus and see to it that they are given the full treatment as equals. And I'm afraid, Liono, you will have to organize tight security for them. There is bound to be some indignation among our hotheads and it would not be wise to subject them to even slight and transient humiliation through protest demonstrations."

"Absolutely," said Kodell. "It was a clever stroke, by the way, sending out Trevize."

"My lightning rod? He worked better than I thought he would, to be honest. He blundered his way into Sayshell and drew their lightning in the form of protests with a speed I could not have believed. Space! What an excellent excuse that made for my visit—concern lest a Foundation national be in any way disturbed and then gratitude for their forbearance."

"Shrewd! —You don't think it would have been better, though, to have brought Trevize back with us?"

"No. On the whole, I prefer him anywhere but at home. He would be a disturbing factor on Terminus. His nonsense about the Second Foundation served as the perfect excuse for sending him out and, of course, we counted on Pelorat to lead him to Sayshell, but I don't want him back, continuing to spread the nonsense. We can never tell what that might lead to."

Kodell chuckled. "I doubt that we can ever find anyone more gullible than an intellectual academic. I wonder how much Pelorat would have swallowed if we had encouraged him."

"Belief in the literal existence of the mythical Sayshellian Gaia was quite enough—but forget it. We will have to face the Council when we return and we will need their votes for the Sayshellian treaty. Fortunately we have Trevize's statement—voiceprint and all—to the effect that he left Terminus voluntarily. I will offer official regrets as to Trevize's brief arrest and that will satisfy the Council."

"I can rely on you for the soft soap, Mayor," said Kodell dryly. "Have you considered, though, that Trevize may continue to search for the Second Foundation?"

"Let him," said Branno, shrugging, "as long as he doesn't do it on Terminus. It will keep him busy and get him nowhere. The Second Foundation's continued existence is our myth of the century, as Gaia is Sayshell's myth."

She leaned back and looked positively genial. "And now we have Sayshell in our grip—and by the time they see that, it will be too late for them to break the grip. So the Foundation's growth continues and will continue, smoothly and regularly."

"And the credit will be entirely yours, Mayor."

"That has not escaped my notice," said Branno, and their ship slipped into hyperspace and reappeared in the neighborhood space of Terminus.

2.

Speaker Stor Gendibal, on his own ship again, had every reason for satisfaction. The encounter with the First Foundation had not lasted long, but it had been thoroughly productive.

He had sent back his message of carefully muted triumph. It was only necessary—for the moment—to let the First Speaker know that all had gone well (as, indeed, he might guess from the fact that the general force of the Second Foundation had never had to be used after all). The details could come later on.

He would describe how a careful—and very minor—adjustment to Mayor Branno's mind had turned her thoughts from imperialistic grandiosity to the practicality of commercial treaty; how a careful—and rather long-distance—adjustment of the leader of the Sayshell Union had led to an invitation to the Mayor of a parley and how, thereafter, a rapprochement had been reached with no further adjustments at all with Compor returning to Terminus on his own ship, to see that the agreement would be kept. It had been, Gendibal thought complacently, almost a storybook example of large results brought about by minutely crafted mentalics.

It would, he was sure, squash Speaker Delarmi flat and bring about his own elevation to First Speaker very soon after the presentation of the details at a formal meeting of the Table.

And he did not deny to himself the importance of Sura Novi's presence, though that would not need to be stressed to the Speakers generally. Not only had she been essential to his victory, but she gave him the excuse he now needed for indulging his childish (and very human, for even Speakers are very human) need to exult before what he knew to be a guaranteed admiration.

She did not understand anything that had happened, he knew, but she was aware that he had arranged matters to his liking and she was bursting with pride over that. He caressed the smoothness of her mind and felt the warmth of that pride.

He said, "I could not have done it without you, Novi. It was because of you I could tell that the First Foundation—the people on the large ship—"

"Yes, Master, I know whom you mean."

"I could tell, because of you, that they had a shield, together with weak powers of the mind. From the effect on *your* mind, I could tell, exactly, the characteristics of both. I could tell how most efficiently to penetrate the one and deflect the other."

Novi said tentatively, "I do not understand exactly what it is you say, Master, but I would have done much more to help, if I could."

"I know that, Novi. But what you did was enough. It is amazing how dangerous they might have been. But caught now, before either their shield or their field had been developed more strongly, they could be stopped. The Mayor goes back now, the shield and the field forgotten, satisfied over the fact that she has obtained a commercial treaty with Sayshell that will make it a working part of the Federation. I don't deny that there is much more to do to dismantle the work they have done on shield and field—it is something concerning which we have been remiss—but it will be done."

He brooded about the matter and went on in a lower voice, "We took far too much for granted with the First Foundation. We must place them under closer supervision. We must knit the Galaxy closer together somehow. We must make use of mentalics to build a closer co-operation of consciousness. That would fit the Plan. I'm convinced of that and I'll see to it."

Novi said anxiously, "Master?"

Gendibal smiled suddenly. "I'm sorry. I'm talking to myself. —Novi, do you remember Rufirant?"

"That bone-skulled farmer who attacked you? I should say I do."

"I'm convinced that First Foundation agents, armed with

personal shields, arranged that, together will all the other anomalies that have plagued us. Imagine being blind to a thing like that. But then, I was bemused into overlooking the First Foundation altogether by this myth of a mysterious world, this Sayshellian superstition concerning Gaia. There, too, your mind came in handy. It helped me determine that the source of that mentalic field was the warship and nothing else."

He rubbed his hands.

Novi said timidly, "Master?"

"Yes, Novi?"

"Will you not be rewarded for what you have done?"

"Indeed I will. Shandess will retire and I will be First Speaker. Then will come my chance to make us an active factor in revolutionizing the Galaxy."

"First Speaker?"

"Yes, Novi. I will be the most important and the most powerful scholar of them all."

"The most important?" She looked woebegone.

"Why do you make a face, Novi? Don't you want me to be rewarded?"

"Yes, Master, I do. —But if you are the most important scholar of them all, you will not want a Hamishwoman near you. It would not be fitting."

"Won't I, though? Who will stop me?" He felt a gush of affection for her. "Novi, will you stay with me wherever I go and whatever I am. Do you think I would risk dealing with some of the wolves we occasionally have at the Table without your mind always there to tell me, even before they know themselves, what their emotions might be—your own innocent, absolutely smooth mind. Besides—" He seemed startled by a sudden revelation, "Even aside from that, I— I like having you with me and I intend having you with me. —That is, if you are willing."

"Oh, Master," whispered Novi and, as his arm moved around her waist, her head sank to his shoulder.

Deep within, where the enveloping mind of Novi could scarcely be aware of it, the essence of Gaia remained and guided events, but it was that impenetrable mask that made the continuance of the great task possible.

And that mask—the one that belonged to a Hamish-woman—was completely happy. It was so happy that Novi was almost reconciled for the distance she was from herself/them/all, and she was content to be, for the indefinite future, what she seemed to be.

3.

Pelorat rubbed his hands and said, with carefully controlled enthusiasm, "How glad I am to be back on Gaia."

"Umm," said Trevize abstractedly.

"You know what Bliss has told me? The Mayor is going back to Terminus with a commercial treaty with Sayshell. The Speaker from the Second Foundation is going back to Trantor convinced that he has arranged it—and that woman, Novi, is going back with him to see to it that the changes that will bring about Galaxia are initiated. And neither Foundation is in the least aware that Gaia exists. It's absolutely amazing."

"I know," said Trevize. "I was told all this, too. But we know that Gaia exists and we can talk."

"Bliss doesn't think so. She says no one would believe us, and we would know that. Besides, I, for one, have no intention of ever leaving Gaia."

Trevize was pulled out of his inner musing. He looked up and said, "What?"

"I'm going to stay here. —You know, I can't believe it. Just weeks ago, I was living a lonely life on Terminus, the same life I had lived for decades, immersed in my records and my thoughts and never dreaming anything but that I would go to my death, whenever it might be, still immersed in my records and my thoughts and still living my lonely life—contentedly vegetating. Then, suddenly and unexpectedly, I became a Galactic traveler; I was involved with

a Galactic crisis; and—do not laugh, Golan—I have found
Bliss."

"I'm not laughing, Janov," said Trevize, "but are you
sure you know what you're doing?"

"Oh yes. This matter of Earth is no longer important to
me. The fact that it was the only world with a diverse
ecology and with intelligent life has been adequately explained. The Eternals, you know."

"Yes, I know. And you're going to stay on Gaia?"

"Absolutely. Earth is the past and I'm tired of the past.
Gaia is the future."

"You're not part of Gaia, Janov. Or do you think you
can become part of it?"

"Bliss says that I can become somewhat a part of it—
intellectually if not biologically. She'll help, of course."

"But since she *is* part of it, how can you two find a
common life, a common point of view, a common interest—"

They were in the open and Trevize looked gravely at the
quiet, fruitful island, and beyond it the sea, and on the
horizon, purpled by distance, another island—all of it
peaceful, civilized, alive, and a unit.

He said, "Janov, she is a world; you are a tiny individual.
What if she gets tired of you? She is young—"

"Golan, I've thought of that. I've thought of nothing but
that for days. I expect her to grow tired of me; I'm no
romantic idiot. But whatever she gives me till then will be
enough. She has already given me enough. I have received
more from her than I dreamed existed in life. If I saw her
no more from this moment on, I have ended the winner."

"I don't believe it," said Trevize gently. "I think you *are*
a romantic idiot and, mind you, I wouldn't want you any
other way. Janov, we haven't known each other for long,
but we've been together every moment for weeks and—
I'm sorry if it sounds silly—I like you a great deal."

"And I, you, Golan," said Pelorat.

"And I don't want you hurt. I must talk to Bliss."

"No no. Please don't. You'll lecture her."

"I won't lecture her. It's not entirely to do with you—
and I want to talk to her privately. Please, Janov, I don't
want to do it behind your back, so grant me your willingness
to have me talk to her and get a few things straight. If I am
satisfied, I will give you my heartiest congratulations and
goodwill—and I will forever hold my peace, whatever happens."

Pelorat shook his head. "You'll ruin things."

"I promise I won't. I *beg* you—"

"Well— But do be careful, my dear fellow, won't you?"

"You have my solemn word."

4.

Bliss said, "Pel says you want to see me."

Trevize said, "Yes."

They were indoors, in the small apartment allotted to
him.

She sat down gracefully, crossed her legs, and looked at
him shrewdly, her beautiful brown eyes luminous and her
long, dark hair glistening.

She said, "You disapprove of me, don't you? You have
disapproved of me from the start."

Trevize remained standing. He said, "You are aware of
minds and of their contents. You know what I think of you
and why."

Slowly Bliss shook her head. "Your mind is out of bounds
to Gaia. You know that. Your decision was needed and it
had to be the decision of a clear and untouched mind. When
your ship was first taken, I placed you and Pel within a
soothing field, but that was essential. You would have been
damaged—and perhaps rendered useless for a crucial time—
by panic or rage. And that was all. I could never go beyond
that and I haven't—so I don't know what you're thinking."

Trevize said, "The decision I had to make has been made.
I decided in favor of Gaia and Galaxia. Why, then, all this

talk of a clear and untouched mind? You have what you want and you can do with me now as you wish."

"Not at all, Trev. There are other decisions that may be needed in the future. You remain what you are and, while you are alive, you are a rare natural resource of the Galaxy. Undoubtedly, there are others like you in the Galaxy and others like you will appear in the future, but for now we know of you—and only you. We still cannot touch you."

Trevize considered. "You are Gaia and I don't want to talk to Gaia. I want to talk to you as an individual, if that has any meaning at all."

"It has meaning. We are far from existing in a common melt. I can block off Gaia for a period of time."

"Yes," said Trevize. "I think you can. Have you now done so?"

"I have now done so."

"Then, first, let me tell you that you have played games. You did not enter my mind to influence my decision, perhaps, but you certainly entered Janov's mind to do so, didn't you?"

"Do you think I did?"

"I think you did. At the crucial moment, Pelorat reminded me of his own vision of the Galaxy as alive and the thought drove me on to make my decision at that moment. The thought may have been his, but yours was the mind that triggered it, was it not?"

Bliss said, "The thought was in his mind, but there were many thoughts there. I smoothed the path before that reminiscence of his about the living Galaxy—and not before any other thought of his. That particular thought, therefore, slipped easily out of his consciousness and into words. Mind you, I did not create the thought. It was there."

"Nevertheless, that amounted to an indirect tampering with the perfect independence of my decision, did it not?"

"Gaia felt it necessary."

"Did it? —Well, it may make you feel better—or nobler—to know that although Janov's remark persuaded me to make the decision at that moment, it was the decision I think I would have made even if he had said nothing or if he had tried to argue me into a decision of a different kind. I want you to know that."

"I am relieved," said Bliss coolly. "Is that what you wanted to tell me when you asked to see me?"

"No."

"What else is there?"

Now Trevize sat down in a chair he had drawn opposite her so that their knees nearly touched. He leaned toward her.

"When we approached Gaia, it was you on the space station. It was you who trapped us; you who came out to get us; you who have remained with us ever since—except for the meal with Dom, which you did not share with us. In particular, it was you on the *Far Star* with us, when the decision was made. Always you."

"I am Gaia."

"That does not explain it. A rabbit is Gaia. A pebble is Gaia. Everything on the planet is Gaia, but they are not all equally Gaia. Some are more equal than others. Why you?"

"Why do you think?"

Trevize made the plunge. He said, "Because I don't think you're Gaia. I think you're more than Gaia."

Bliss made a derisive sound with her lips.

Trevize kept to his course. "At the time I was making the decision, the woman with the Speaker—"

"He called her Novi."

"This Novi, then, said that Gaia was set on its course by the robots that no longer exist and that Gaia was taught to follow a version of the Three Laws of Robotics."

"That is quite true."

"And the robots no longer exist?"

"So Novi said."

"So Novi did *not* say. I remember her exact words. She said: 'Gaia was formed thousands of years ago with the help of robots that once, for a brief time, served the human species and now serve them no more.'"

"Well, Trev, doesn't that mean they exist no more?"

"No, it means they serve no more. Might they not rule instead?"

"Ridiculous!"

"Or supervise? Why were you there at the time of the decision? You did not seem to be essential. It was Novi who conducted matters and she was Gaia. What need of you? Unless—"

"Well? Unless?"

"Unless you are the supervisor whose role it is to make certain that Gaia does not forget the Three Laws. Unless you are a robot, so cleverly made that you cannot be told from a human being."

"If I cannot be told from a human being, how is it you think that you can tell?" asked Bliss with a trace of sarcasm.

Trevize sat back. "Do you not all assure me I have the faculty of being *sure*; of making decisions, seeing solutions, drawing correct conclusions. I don't claim this; it is what *you* say of me. Well, from the moment I saw you I felt uneasy. There was something wrong with you. I am certainly as susceptible to feminine allure as Pelorat is—more so, I should think—and you are an attractive woman in appearance. Yet not for one moment did I feel the slightest attraction."

"You devastate me."

Trevize ignored that. He said, "When you first appeared on our ship, Janov and I had been discussing the possibility of a nonhuman civilization on Gaia, and when Janov saw you, he asked, in his innocence, 'Are you human?' Perhaps a robot must answer the truth, but I suppose it can be evasive. You merely said, 'Don't I *look* human?' Yes, you look human, Bliss, but let me ask you again. Are you human?"

Bliss said nothing and Trevize continued. "I think that even at that first moment, I felt you were not a woman. You are a robot and I could somehow tell. And because of my feeling, all the events that followed had meaning for me—particularly your absence from the dinner."

Bliss said, "Do you think I cannot eat, Trev? Have you

forgotten I nibbled a shrimp dish on your ship? I assure you that I am able to eat and perform any of the other biological functions. —Including, before you ask, sex. And yet that in itself, I might as well tell you, does not prove that I am not a robot. Robots had reached the pitch of perfection, even thousands of years ago, where only by their brains were they distinguishable from human beings, and then only by those able to handle mentalic fields. Speaker Gendibal might have been able to tell whether I were robot or human, if he had bothered even once to consider me. Of course, he did not."

"Yet, though I am without mentalics, I am nevertheless convinced you are a robot."

Bliss said, "But what if I am? I admit nothing, but I am curious. What if I am?"

"You have no need to admit anything. I know you are a robot. If I needed a last bit of evidence, it was your calm assurance that you could block off Gaia and speak to me as an individual. I don't think you could do that if you were part of Gaia—but you are not. You are a robot supervisor and, therefore, outside of Gaia. I wonder, come to think of it, how many robot supervisors Gaia requires and possesses?"

"I repeat: I admit nothing, but I am curious. What if I am a robot?"

"In that case, what I want to know is: What do you want of Janov Pelorat? He is my friend and he is, in some ways, a child. He thinks he loves you; he thinks he wants only what you are willing to give and that you have already given him enough. He doesn't know—and cannot conceive—the pain of the loss of love or, for that matter, the peculiar pain of knowing that you are not human—"

"Do *you* know the pain of lost love?"

"I have had my moments. I have not led the sheltered life of Janov. I have not had my life consumed and anesthetized by an intellectual pursuit that swallowed up everything else, even wife and child. He has. Now suddenly, he gives it all up for you. I do not want him hurt. I will not

have him hurt. If I have served Gaia, I deserve a reward—
and my reward is your assurance that Janov Pelorat's well-
being will be preserved."

"Shall I pretend I am a robot and answer you?"

Trevize said, "Yes. And right now."

"Very well, then. Suppose I am a robot, Trev, and suppose I am in a position of supervision. Suppose there are a
few, a very few, who have a similar role to myself and
suppose we rarely meet. Suppose that our driving force is
the need to care for human beings and suppose there are no
true human beings on Gaia, because all are part of an overall
planetary being.

"Suppose that it fulfills us to care for Gaia—but not
entirely. Suppose there is something primitive in us that
longs for a human being in the sense that existed when
robots were first formed and designed. Don't mistake me;
I do not claim to be age-old (assuming I am a robot). I am
as old as I told you I was or, at least, (assuming I am a
robot) my fundamental design would be as it always was
and I would long to care for a true human being.

"Pel is a human being. He is not part of Gaia. He is too
old to ever become a true part of Gaia. He wants to stay
on Gaia with me, for he does not have the feelings about
me that you have. He does not think that I am a robot. Well, I want him, too. If you assume that I am a
robot, you see that I would. I am capable of all human
reactions and I would love him. If you were to insist I was
a robot, you might not consider me capable of love in some
mystic human sense, but you would not be able to distinguish my reactions from that which you would call love—
so what difference would it make?"

She stopped and looked at him—intransigently proud.

Trevize said, "You are telling me that you would not
abandon him?"

"If you assume that I am a robot, then you can see for
yourself that by First Law I could never abandon him, unless
he ordered me to do so and I were, in addition, convinced

that he meant it and that I would be hurting him more by staying than by leaving."

"Would not a younger man—"

"What younger man? You are a younger man, but I do not conceive you as needing me in the same sense that Pel does, and, in fact, you do not want me, so that the First Law would prevent me from attempting to cling to you."

"Not me. Another younger man—"

"There is no other. Who is there on Gaia other than Pel and yourself that would qualify as human beings in the non-Gaian sense?"

Trevize said, more softly, "And if you are *not* a robot?"

"Make up your mind," said Bliss.

"I say, *if* you are not a robot?"

"Then I say that, in that case, you have no right to say anything at all. It is for myself and for Pel to decide."

Trev said, "Then I return to my first point. I want my reward and that reward is that you will treat him well. I won't press the point of your identity. Simply assure me, as one intelligence to another, that you will treat him well."

And Bliss said softly, "I will treat him well—not as a reward to you, but because I wish to. It is my earnest desire. I will treat him well." She called "Pel!" And again, "Pel!"

Pelorat entered from outside, "Yes, Bliss."

Bliss held out her hand to him. "I think Trev wants to say something."

Pelorat took her hand and Trevize then took the doubled hand in his two. "Janov," he said, "I am happy for both of you."

Pelorat said, "Oh, my dear fellow."

Trevize said, "I will probably be leaving Gaia. I go now to speak to Dom about that. I don't know when or if we will meet again, Janov, but, in any case, we did well together."

"We did well," said Pelorat, smiling.

"Good-bye, Bliss, and, in advance, thank you."

"Good-bye, Trev."

And Trevize, with a wave of his hand, left the house.

5.

Dom said, "You did well, Trev. —But then, you did as I thought you would."

They were once more sitting over a meal, as unsatisfactory as the first had been, but Trevize did not mind. He might not be eating on Gaia again.

He said, "I did as I thought you would, but not, perhaps, for the reason you thought I would."

"Surely you were sure of the correctness of your decision."

"Yes, I was, but not because of any mystic grip I have on certainty. If I chose Galaxia, it was through ordinary reasoning—the sort of reasoning that anyone else might have used to come to a decision. Would you care to have me explain?"

"I most certainly would, Trev."

Trevize said, "There are three things I might have done. I might have joined the First Foundation, or joined the Second Foundation, or joined Gaia.

"If I had joined the First Foundation, Mayor Branno would have taken immediate action to establish domination over the Second Foundation and over Gaia. If I had joined the Second Foundation, Speaker Gendibal would have taken immediate action to establish domination over the First Foundation and over Gaia. In either case, what would have taken place would have been irreversible—and if either were the wrong solution, it would have been irreversibly catastrophic.

"If I joined with Gaia, however, then the First Foundation and the Second Foundation would each have been left with the conviction of having won a relatively minor victory. All would then have continued as before, since the building of Galaxia, I had already been told, would take generations, even centuries.

"Joining with Gaia was my way of temporizing, then, and of making sure that there would remain time to modify" matters—or even reverse them—if my decision were wrong."

Dom raised his eyebrows. His old, almost cadaverous face remained otherwise expressionless. He said in his piping voice, "And is it your opinion that your decision may turn out wrong?"

Trevize shrugged. "I don't think so, but there is one thing I must do in order that I might know. It is my intention to visit Earth, if I can find that world."

"We will certainly not stop you if you wish to leave us, Trev—"

"I do not fit on your world."

"No more than Pel does, yet you are as welcome to remain as he is. Still, we will not hold you. —But tell me, why do you wish to visit Earth?"

Trevize said, "I rather think you understand."

"I do not."

"There is a piece of information you withheld from me, Dom. Perhaps you had your reasons, but I wish you had not."

Dom said, "I do not follow you."

"Look, Dom, in order to make my decision, I used my computer and for a brief moment I found myself in touch with the minds of those about me—Mayor Branno, Speaker Gendibal, Novi. I caught glimpses of a number of matters that, in isolation, meant little to me, as, for example, the various effects Gaia, through Novi, had produced on Trantor—effects that were intended to maneuver the Speaker into going to Gaia."

"Yes?"

"And one of those things was the clearing from Trantor's library of all references to Earth."

"The clearing of references to Earth?"

"Exactly. So Earth must be important—and not only does it appear that the Second Foundation must know nothing about it, but that I must not, either. And if I am to take the responsibility for the direction of Galactic development, I do not willingly accept ignorance. Would you consider telling me why it was so important to keep knowledge of Earth hidden?"

Dom said solemnly, "Trev, Gaia knows nothing about such clearance. Nothing!"

"Are you telling me that Gaia is not responsible?"

"It is not responsible."

Trevize thought for a while, the tip of his tongue moving slowly and meditatively over his lips. "Who was responsible, then?"

"I don't know. I can see no purpose in it."

The two men stared at each other and then Dom said, "You are right. We had seemed to have reached a most satisfactory conclusion, but while this point remains unsettled, we dare not rest. —Stay a while with us and let us see what we can reason out. Then you can leave, with our full help."

"Thank you," said Trevize.

THE END
(for now)

AFTERWORD BY THE AUTHOR

This Book, while self-contained, is a continuation of *The Foundation Trilogy*, which is made up of three books: *Foundation*, *Foundation and Empire*, and *Second Foundation*.

In addition, there are other books I have written which, while not dealing with the Foundations directly, are set in what we might call "the Foundation universe."

Thus, the events in *The Stars, Like Dust* and *The Currents of Space* take place in the years when Trantor was expanding toward Empire, while the events in *Pebble in the Sky* take place when the First Galactic Empire was at the height of its power. In *Pebble*, Earth is central and some of the material in it is alluded to tangentially in this new book.

In none of the earlier books of the Foundation universe were robots mentioned. In this new book, however, there are references to robots. In this connection, you may wish to read my robot stories. The short stories are to be found in *The Complete Robot*, while the two novels, *The Caves of Steel* and *The Naked Sun*, describe the robotic period of the colonization of the Galaxy.

If you wish an account of the Eternals and the way in which they adjusted human history, you will find it (not entirely consistent with the references in this new book) in *The End of Eternity*.

All the books mentioned existed as Doubleday hardcovers, to begin with. *The Foundation Trilogy* and *The Complete Robot* are still in print in hardcover. Of the others, *Pebble in the Sky* and *The End of Eternity* are included in the omnibus volume *The Far Ends of Time and Earth*, while *The Stars, Like Dust* and *The Currents of Space* are in the omnibus volume *Prisoners of the Stars*. Both omnibus volumes are in print in hardcover. As for *The Caves of Steel* and *The Naked Sun*, they are included in the omnibus volume *The Robot Novels*, still available from the Science Fiction Book Club. And all are in print in softcover editions, of course.

ABOUT THE AUTHOR

Isaac Asimov was born in the Soviet Union to his great surprise. He moved quickly to correct the situation. When his parents emigrated to the United States, Isaac (three years old at the time) stowed away in their baggage. He has been an American citizen since the age of eight.

Brought up in Brooklyn, and educated in its public schools, he eventually found his way to Columbia University and, over the protests of the school administration, managed to annex a series of degrees in chemistry, up to and including a Ph.D. He then infiltrated Boston University and climbed the academic ladder, ignoring all cries of outrage, until he found himself Professor of Biochemistry.

Meanwhile, at the age of nine, he found the love of his life (in the inanimate sense) when he discovered his first science-fiction magazine. By the time he was eleven, he began to write stories, and at eighteen, he actually worked up the nerve to submit one. It was rejected. After four long months of tribulation and suffering, he sold his first story and, thereafter, he never looked back.

In 1941, when he was twenty-one years old, he wrote the classic short story "Nightfall" and his future was assured. Shortly before that he had begun writing his robot stories, and shortly after that he had begun his Foundation series.

What was left except quantity? At the present time, he has published over 260 books, distributed through every major division of the Dewey system of library classification, and shows no signs of slowing up. He remains as youthful, as lively, and as lovable as ever, and grows more handsome with each year. You can be sure that this is so since he has written this little essay himself and his devotion to absolute objectivity is notorious.

He is married to Janet Jeppson, psychiatrist and writer, has two children by a previous marriage, and lives in New York City.